D0238528

PRINCE OF
FOOLS

Mark Lawrence is married with four children, one of whom is severely disabled. His day job is as a research scientist focused on various rather intractable problems in the field of artificial intelligence. He has held secret level clearance with both US and UK governments. At one point he was qualified to say 'this isn't rocket science ... oh wait, it actually is'.

Between work and caring for his disabled child, Mark spends his time writing, playing computer games, tending an allotment, brewing beer, and avoiding DIY.

http://www.facebook.com/MarkLawrenceBooks
Twitter: @mark__lawrence
(Please note: there are two underscores)

Also by Mark Lawrence

The Broken Empire
Prince of Thorns
King of Thorns
Emperor of Thorns

PRINCE OF FOOLS

Book One of The Red Queen's War

Mark Lawrence

HARPER
Voyager

HarperCollins*Publishers*
77–85 Fulham Palace Road,
Hammersmith, London W6 8JB

www.harpercollins.co.uk

Published by Harper*Voyager*
An imprint of HarperCollins*Publishers* 2014
1

Copyright © Mark Lawrence 2014

Mark Lawrence asserts the moral right to
be identified as the author of this work

A catalogue record for this book
is available from the British Library

ISBN: 978 0 00 753154 7

This novel is entirely a work of fiction.
The names, characters and incidents portrayed in it are
the work of the author's imagination. Any resemblance to
actual persons, living or dead, events or localities is
entirely coincidental.

Set in Plantin Light by Palimpsest Book Production Limited,
Falkirk, Stirlingshire

Printed and bound in Great Britain by
Clays Ltd, St Ives plc

Map © Andrew Ashton

All rights reserved. No part of this publication may be
reproduced, stored in a retrieval system, or transmitted,
in any form or by any means, electronic, mechanical,
photocopying, recording or otherwise, without the prior
permission of the publishers.

MIX
Paper from
responsible sources
FSC
www.fsc.org **FSC™ C007454**

FSC™ is a non-profit international organisation established to promote
the responsible management of the world's forests. Products carrying the
FSC label are independently certified to assure consumers that they come
from forests that are managed to meet the social, economic and
ecological needs of present and future generations,
and other controlled sources.

Find out more about HarperCollins and the environment at
www.harpercollins.co.uk/green

Acknowledgements

Many thanks to the good folk at Voyager who have made this all happen and put the book in your hands.

Special thanks to Jane Johnson for her continued support on all fronts and highly valued editing.

And another round of applause for my agent, Ian Drury, and the team at Sheil Land for all their sterling work.

Dedicated to my daughter, Heather.

200 miles

BITTER ICE

Black
Fort

JARLSON UPLANDS

Trond

MALVIK

NORSEHEIM COAST

TRONDHEIM

BERGEN

ALESUND

FINN

OSLAU

UNTERHEIM

DANELORE

RING SEA

KARLSWATER

Den Hagen

MALADON

EAST
THURTAN

OSHEIM

HAGENFAST

WEST
THURTAN

Gelleth

Castle Red

CHARLAND

OST
REICH

CONQUENCE

MAYAR

ATTAR

Vyene

ZAGRE

VYENE
TERRITORY

SUDREICH

SCORRON

SLOV

SERBAN

RED MARCH

FLORENCE

CORSAIR
ISLES

ROMA

Roma

1

I'm a liar and a cheat and a coward, but I will never, ever, let a friend down. Unless of course not letting them down requires honesty, fair play, or bravery.

I've always found hitting a man from behind to be the best way to go about things. This can sometimes be accomplished by dint of a simple ruse. Classics such as, 'What's that over there?' work surprisingly often, but for truly optimal results it's best if the person doesn't ever know you were there.

'Ow! Jesu! What the hell did you do that for?' Alain DeVeer turned, clamping his hand to the back of his head and bringing it away bloody.

When the person you hit doesn't have the grace to fall over it's generally best to have a back-up plan. I dropped what remained of the vase, turned and ran. In my mind he'd folded up with a pleasing 'oofff' and left me free to leave the mansion unobserved, stepping over his prone and senseless form on the way. Instead his senseless form was now chasing me down the hall bellowing for blood.

I crashed back through Lisa's door and slammed it behind me, bracing myself for the impact.

'What the hell?' Lisa sat in the bed, silken sheets flowing off her nakedness like water.

'Uh.' Alain hammered into the door, jolting the air from my lungs and scraping my heels over the tiles. The trick is to never rush for the bolt. You'll be fumbling for it and get a face full of opening door. Brace for the impact, when that's done slam the bolt home while the other party is picking himself off the floor. Alain proved worryingly fast in getting back on his feet and I nearly got the doorhandle for breakfast despite my precautions.

'Jal!' Lisa was out of bed now, wearing nothing but the light and shade through the shutters. Stripes suited her. Sweeter than her elder sister, sharper than her younger sister. Even then I wanted her, even with her murderous brother held back by just an inch of oak and with my chances for escape evaporating by the moment.

I ran to the largest window and tore the shutters open. 'Say sorry to your brother for me.' I swung a leg over the casement. 'Mistaken identity or something...' The door started to shudder as Alain pounded the far side.

'Alain?' Lisa managed to look both furious with me and terrified at the same time.

I didn't stop to reply but vaulted down into the bushes, which were thankfully the fragrant rather than thorny variety. Dropping into a thorn bush can lead to no end of grief.

Landing is always important. I do a lot of falling and it's not how you start that matters so much as how you finish. In this instance, I finished concertinaed, heels to arse, chin to knees, half an azalea bush up my nose and all the air driven from my lungs, but with no bones broken. I fought my way out and limped toward the garden wall, gasping for breath and hoping the staff were too busy with pre-dawn chores to be poised and ready to hunt me down.

I took off, across the formal lawns, through the herb garden, cutting a straight path through all the little diamonds of sage, and triangles of thyme and whatnot. Somewhere back at the house a hound bayed, and that put the fear in me. I'm a good runner any day of the week. Scared shitless I'm world class. Two years ago, in the 'border incident' with Scorron, I ran from a patrol of Teutons, five of them on big old destriers. The men I had charge of stayed put, lacking any orders. I find the important thing in running away is not how fast you run but simply that you run faster than the next man. Unfortunately my lads did a piss-poor job of slowing the Scorrons down and that left poor Jal running for his life with hardly twenty years under his belt and a great long list of things still to do – with

3

the DeVeer sisters near the top and dying on a Scorron lance not even making the first page. In any event, the borderlands aren't the place to stretch a warhorse's legs and I kept a gap between us by running through a boulderfield at breakneck speed. Without warning I found myself charging into the back of a pitched battle between a much larger force of Scorron irregulars and the band of Red March skirmishers I'd been scouting on behalf of in the first place. I rocketed into the midst of it all, flailed around with my sword in blind terror trying to escape, and when the dust settled and the blood stopped squirting, I discovered myself the hero of the day, breaking the enemy with a courageous attack that showed complete disregard for my own safety.

So here's the thing: bravery may be observed when a person tramples one fear whilst in secret flight from a greater terror. And those whose greatest terror is being thought a coward are always brave. I, on the other hand, am a coward. But with a little luck, a dashing smile, and the ability to lie from the hip, I've done a surprisingly good job of seeming a hero and of fooling most of the people most of the time.

The DeVeers's wall was a high and forbidding one but it and I were old friends: I knew its curves and foibles as well as any contour Lisa, Sharal, or Micha might possess. Escape routes have always been an obses-sion of mine.

Most barriers are there to keep the unwashed out, not the washed in. I vaulted a rain barrel, onto the roof of a gardener's outbuilding, and jumped for the wall. Teeth snapped at my heels as I hauled myself over. I clung by my fingers and dropped. A shiver of relief ran through me as the hound found its voice and scrabbled against the far side of the wall in frustration. The beast had run silent and almost caught me. The silent ones are apt to kill you. The more sound and fury there is, the less murderous the animal. True of men too. I'm nine parts bluster and one part greed and so far not an ounce of murder.

I landed in the street, less heavily this time, free and clear, and if not smelling of roses then at least of azalea and mixed herbs. Alain would be a problem for another day. He could take his place in the queue. It was a long one and at its head stood Maeres Allus clutching a dozen promissory notes, IOUs, and intents to pay drunkenly scrawled on whores' silken lingerie. I stood, stretched, and listened to the hound complain behind the wall. I'd need a taller wall than that to keep Maeres' bullies at bay.

Kings Way stretched before me, strewn with shadows. On Kings Way the townhouses of noble families vie with the ostentation of merchant-princes' mansions, new money trying to gleam brighter than the old. The city of Vermillion has few streets as fine.

'Take him to the gate! He's got the scent.' Voices back in the garden.

5

'Here, Pluto! Here!'

That didn't sound good. I set off sprinting in the direction of the palace, sending rats fleeing and scattering dungmen on their rounds, the dawn chasing after me, throwing red spears at my back.

2

The palace at Vermillion is a sprawling affair of walled compounds, exquisite gardens, satellite mansions for extended family, and finally the Inner Palace, the great stone confection that has for generations housed the kings of Red March. The whole thing is garnished with marble statuary teased into startlingly lifelike forms by the artistry of Milano masons, and a dedicated man could probably scrape enough gold leaf off the walls to make himself slightly richer than Croesus. My grandmother hates it with a passion. She'd be happier behind granite barricades a hundred feet thick and spiked with the heads of her enemies.

Even the most decadent of palaces can't be entered without some protocol, though. I slipped in via the Surgeons' Gate, flipping a silver crown to the guard.

'Got you out early again, Melchar.' I make a point of knowing the guards' names. They still think of me as the hero of Aral Pass and it's helpful to have the gate-keepers on side when your life dangles from as large a web of lies as mine does.

'Aye, Prince Jal. Them's as works best works hardest they do say.'

'So true.' I had no idea what he'd said but my fake laugh is even better than my real one, and nine-tenths of being popular is the ability to jolly the menials along. 'I'd get one of those lazy bastards to take a turn.' I nodded toward the lantern glow bleeding past the crack of the guardhouse door, and strolled on through the gates as Melchar drew them open.

Once inside, I made a straight line for the Roma Hall. As the queen's third son, Father got invested in the Roma Hall, a palatial Vatican edifice constructed by the pope's own craftsmen for Cardinal Paracheck way back whenever. Grandmother has little enough time for Jesu and his cross though she'll say the words at celebrations and look to mean them. She has far less time for Roma, and none at all for the pope that sits there now – the Holy Cow, she calls her.

As Father's third son I get bugger all. A chamber in Roma Hall, an unwanted commission in the Army of the North, one that didn't even swing me a cavalry rank since the northern borders are too damn hilly for horse. Scorron deploy cavalry on the borders but Grandmother declared their pigheadedness a failing the Red March should exploit rather than a foolishness we should continue to follow. Women and war don't mix. I've said it before. I should have been breaking hearts on a white charger, armoured for tourney. But no, that old witch had me crawling around the peaks trying not to get murdered by Scorron peasants.

I entered the Hall – really a collection of halls, state-rooms, a ballroom, kitchens, stables, and a second floor with endless bedchambers – by the west port, a service door meant for scullions and such. Fat Ned sat at guard, his halberd against the wall.

'Ned!'

'Master Jal!' He woke with a start and came perilously close to tipping the chair over backwards.

'As you were.' I gave him a wink and went by. Fat Ned kept a tight lip and my excursions were safe with him. He'd known me since I was a little monster bullying the smaller princes and princesses and toadying to the ones big enough to clout me. He'd been fat back in those days. The flesh hung off him now as the reaper closed in for the final swing, but the name stuck. There's power in a name. 'Prince' has served me very well – something to hide behind when trouble comes, and 'Jalan' carries echoes of King Jalan of the Red March, Fist of the Emperor back when we had one. A title and a name like Jalan carry an aura with them, enough to give me the benefit of the doubt – and there was never a doubt I needed that.

I nearly made it back to my room.

'Jalan Kendeth!'

I stopped two steps from the balcony that led to my chambers, toe poised for the next step, boots in my hand.

I said nothing. Sometimes the bishop would just bellow my name when he discovered random mischief. In fairness I was normally the root cause. This time however he was looking directly at me.

'I see you right there, Jalan Kendeth, footsteps black with sin as you creep back to your lair. Get down here!'

I turned with an apologetic grin. Churchmen like you to be sorry and often it doesn't matter what you're sorry about. In this case I was sorry for being caught.

'And the best of mornings to you, your excellency.' I put the boots behind my back and swaggered down toward him as if it had been my plan all along.

'His eminence directs me to present your brothers and yourself at the throne room by second bell.' Bishop James scowled at me, cheeks grey with stubble as if he too had been turfed out of bed at an unreasonable hour, though perhaps not by Lisa DeVeer's shapely foot.

'Father directed that?' He'd said nothing at table the previous night and the cardinal was not one to rise before noon whatever the good book had to say about sloth. They call it a deadly sin but in my experience lust will get you into more trouble and sloth's only a sin when you're being chased.

'The message came from the queen.' The bishop's scowl deepened. He liked to attribute all commands to Father as the church's highest, albeit least enthusiastic, representative in Red March. Grandmother once said she'd been tempted to set the cardinal's hat on the nearest donkey but Father had been closer and promised to be more easily led. 'Martus and Darin have already left.'

I shrugged. 'They arrived before me too.' I'd yet to forgive my elder brothers that slight. I stopped, out of arms' reach as the bishop loved nothing better than to slap the sin out of a wayward prince, and turned to go upstairs. 'I'll get dressed.'

'You'll go now! It's almost second bell and your preening never takes less than an hour.'

As much as I would have liked to dispute the old fool he happened to be right and I knew better than to be late for the Red Queen. I suppressed a sneer and hurried past him. I had on what I'd worn for my midnight escapades and whilst it was stylish enough, the slashed velvets hadn't fared too well during my escape. Still, it would have to serve. Grandmother would rather see her spawn battle armoured and dripping blood in any event, so a touch of mud here and there might earn me some approval.

3

I came late to the throne room with the second bell's echoes dying before I reached the bronze doors, huge out-of-place things stolen from some still-grander palace by one of my distant and bloody-handed relatives. The guards eyed me as if I might be bird crap that had sailed uninvited through a high window to splat before them.

'Prince Jalan.' I rolled my hands to chivvy them along. 'You may have heard of me? I *am* invited.'

Without commentary the largest of them, a giant in fire-bronze mail and crimson plumed helm, hauled the left door wide enough to admit me. My campaign to befriend every guard in the palace had never penetrated as far as Grandmother's picked men: they thought too much of themselves for that. Also they were too well paid to be impressed by my largesse, and perhaps fore-warned against me in any case.

I crept in unannounced and hurried across the echoing expanse of marble. I've never liked the throne room. Not for the arching grandness of it, or the history set in grim-faced stone and staring at us from every wall, but because the place has no escape routes. Guards, guards, and more guards, along with the scrutiny of that awful old woman who claims to be my grandmother.

I made my way toward my nine siblings and cousins. It seemed this was to be an audience exclusively for the royal grandchildren: the nine junior princes and singular princess of Red March. By rights I should have been tenth in line to the throne after my two uncles, their sons, my father and elder brothers, but the old witch who'd kept that particular seat warm these past forty years had different ideas about succession. Cousin Serah, still a month shy of her eighteenth birthday, and containing not an ounce of whatever it is that makes a princess, was the apple of the Red Queen's eye. I won't lie, Serah had more than several ounces of whatever it is that lets a woman steal the sense from a man and accordingly I would gladly have ignored the common views on what cousins should and shouldn't get up to. Indeed I'd tried to ignore them several times, but Serah had a vicious right hook and a knack for kicking the tenderest of spots that a man owns. She'd come today wearing some kind of riding suit in fawn and suede that looked better suited to the hunt than to court. But, damn, she looked good.

I brushed past her and elbowed my way in between my brothers near the front of the group. I'm a decent sized fellow, tall enough to give men pause, but I don't normally care to stand by Martus and Darin. They make me look small and, with nothing to set us apart, all with the same dark-gold hair and hazel eyes, I get referred to as 'the little one'. That I don't like. On this occasion, though, I was prepared to be overlooked. It wasn't just being in the throne room that made me nervous. Nor even because of Grandmother's pointed disapproval. It was the blind-eye woman. She scares the hell out of me.

I first saw her when they brought me before the throne on my fifth birthday, my name day, flanked by Martus and Darin in their church finest, Father in his cardinal's hat, sober despite the sun having passed its zenith, my mother in silks and pearls, a clutch of churchmen and court ladies forming the periphery. The Red Queen sat forward in her great chair booming out something about her grandfather's grandfather, Jalan, the Fist of the Emperor, but it passed me by – I'd seen *her*. An ancient woman, so old it turned my stomach to look at her. She crouched in the shadow of the throne, hunched up so she'd be hidden away if you looked from the other side. She had a face like paper that had been soaked then left to dry, her lips a greyish line, cheekbones sharp. Clad in rags and tatters, she had no place in that throne room, at odds with the finery, the fire-bronzed guards and the glittering retinue come to see my name set in place upon me. There was no motion in the crone: she could almost have been a trick of the light, a discarded cloak, an illusion of lines and shade.

'...Jalan?' The Red Queen stopped her litany with a question.

I had answered with silence, tearing my gaze from the creature at her side.

'Well?' Grandmother narrowed her regard to a sharp point that held me.

Still I had nothing. Martus had elbowed me hard enough to make my ribs creak. It hadn't helped. I wanted to look back at the old woman. Was she still there? Had she moved the moment my eyes left her? I imagined how she'd move. Quick like a spider. My stomach made a tight knot of itself.

'Do you accept the charge I have laid upon you, child?' Grandmother asked, attempting kindness.

My glance flickered back to the hag. Still there, exactly the same, her face half-turned from me, fixed on Grandmother. I hadn't noticed her eye at first, but now it drew me. One of the cats at the Hall had an eye like that. Milky. Pearly almost. Blind, my nurse called it. But to me it seemed to see more than the other eye.

'What's wrong with the boy? Is he simple?' Grandmother's displeasure had rippled through the court, silencing their murmurs.

I couldn't look away. I stood there sweating. Barely able to keep from wetting myself. Too scared to speak, too scared even to lie. Too scared to do anything but sweat and keep my eyes on that old woman.

When she moved, I nearly screamed and ran. Instead just a squeak escaped me. 'Don–don't you see her?'

She stole into motion. So slow at first you had to measure her against the background to be sure it wasn't imagination. Then speeding up, smooth and sure. She turned that awful face toward me, one eye dark, the other milk and pearl. It had felt hot, suddenly, as if all the great hearths had roared into life with one scorching voice, sparked into fury on a fine summer's day, the flames leaping from iron grates as if they wanted nothing more than to be amongst us.

She was tall. I saw that now, hunched but tall. And thin, like a bone.

'Don't you see her?' My words rising to a shriek, I pointed and she stepped toward me, a white hand reaching.

'Who?' Darin beside me, nine years under his belt and too old for such foolishness.

I had no voice to answer him. The blind-eye woman had laid her hand of paper and bones over mine. She smiled at me, an ugly twisting of her face, like worms writhing over each other. She smiled, and I fell.

I fell into a hot, blind place. They tell me I had a fit, convulsions. A 'lepsy', the chirurgeon said to Father the next day, a chronic condition, but I've never had it again, not in nearly twenty years. All I know is that I fell, and I don't think I've stopped falling since.

16

Grandmother had lost patience and set my name upon me as I jerked and twitched on the floor. 'Bring him back when his voice breaks,' she said.

And that was it for eight years. I came back to the throne room aged thirteen, to be presented to Grandmother before the Saturnalia feast in the hard winter of 89. On that occasion, and all others since, I've followed everyone else's example and pretended not to see the blind-eye woman. Perhaps they really don't see her because Martus and Darin are too dumb to act and poor liars at that, and yet their eyes never so much as flicker when they look her way. Maybe I'm the only one to see her when she taps her fingers on the Red Queen's shoulder. It's hard not to look when you know you shouldn't. Like a woman's cleavage, breasts squeezed together and lifted for inspection, and yet a prince is supposed not to notice, not to drop his gaze. I try harder with the blind-eye woman and for the most part I manage it – though Grandmother's given me an odd look from time to time.

In any event, on this particular morning, sweating in the clothes I wore the night before and with half the DeVeers' garden to decorate them, I didn't mind in the least being wedged between my hulking brothers and being 'the little one', easy to overlook. Frankly, the attention of either the Red Queen or her silent sister were things I could do without.

We stood for another ten minutes, unspeaking in the

17

main, some princes yawning, others shifting weight from one foot to the other, or casting sour glances my way. I do try to keep my misadventures from polluting the calm waters of the palace. It's ill advised to shit where you eat, and besides, it's hard to hide behind one's rank when the offended party is also a prince. Even so, over the course of the years, I'd given my cousins few reasons to love me.

At last the Red Queen came in, without fanfare but flanked by guards. The relief was momentary – the blind-eye woman followed in her wake, and although I turned away quicker than quick, she saw me looking. The queen settled herself into her royal seat and the guardsmen arrayed themselves around the walls. A single chamberlain – Mantal Drews, I think – stood ill at ease between the royal progeny and our sovereign, and once more the hall returned to silence.

I watched Grandmother and, with some effort, kept my gaze from sliding toward the white and shrivelled hand resting behind her head on the throne's shoulder. Over the years I'd heard many rumours about Grandmother's secret counsellor, an old and half-mad woman kept hidden away – the Silent Sister they called her. It seemed though that I stood alone in knowing that she waited at the Red Queen's side each day. Other people's eyes seemed to avoid her just as I always wished mine would.

The Red Queen cleared her throat. In taverns across

Vermillion they tell it that my grandmother was once a handsome woman, though monstrous tall with it. A heartbreaker who attracted suit from all corners of the Broken Empire and even beyond. To my eye she had a brutal face, raw-boned, her skin tight as if scorched, but still showing wrinkles as crumpled parchment will. She had to have seventy years on her but no one would have called her more than fifty. Her hair dark and without a hint of grey, still showing deepest red where the light caught it. Handsome or not, though, her eyes would turn any man's bowels to water. Flinty chips of dispassion. And no crown for the warrior queen, oh no. She sat near-swallowed by a robe of blacks and scarlets, just the thinnest circlet of gold to keep her locks in place, scraped back across her head.

'My children's children.' Grandmother's words came so thick with disappointment that you felt it reach out and try to throttle you. She shook her head, as if we were all of us an experiment in horse-breeding gone tragically astray. 'And some of you whelping new princes and princesses of your own I hear.' *L226,529*

'Yes w—'

'Idle, numerous, and breeding sedition in your numbers.' Grandmother rolled over Cousin Roland's announcement before he could puff himself up. His smile died in that stupid beard of his, the one he grew to allow people at least the suspicion that he might have a chin. 'Dark times are coming and this nation must be

a fortress. The time for being children has passed. My blood runs in each of you, thin though it's grown. And you will be soldiers in this coming war.'

Martus snorted at that, though quiet enough that it would be missed. Martus had been commissioned into the heavy horse, destined for knight-general, commander of Red March's elite. The Red Queen in a fit of madness five years earlier had all but eliminated the force. Centuries of tradition, honour, and excellence ploughed under at the whim of an old woman. Now we were all to be soldiers running to battle on foot, digging ditches, endlessly practising mechanical tactics that any peasant could master and which set a prince no higher than a pot boy.

'...greater foe. Time to put aside thoughts of empty conquest and draw in...'

I looked up from my disgust to find Grandmother still droning on about war. It's not that I care overmuch about honour. All that chivalry nonsense loads a man down and any sensible fellow will ditch it the moment he needs to run – but it's the look of the thing, the form of it. To be in one of the three horse corps, to earn your spurs and keep a trio of chargers at the city barracks ... it had been the birthright of young nobles since time immemorial. Damnit, I wanted my commission. I wanted in at the officers' mews, wanted to swap tall tales around the smoky tables at the Conarrf and ride along the Kings Way flying the colours of the Red Lance or Iron Hoof, with the long hair and bristling moustache of a cavalry man and a stallion between my legs. Tenth in line to a throne will get you into a not-insignificant number of bedchambers, but if a man dons the scarlet cloak of the Red March riders and wraps his legs around a destrier there are few ladies of quality who won't open theirs when he flashes a smile at them.

At the corner of my vision the blind-eye woman moved, spoiling my daydream and putting all thoughts of riding, of either kind, from my head.

'...burning all dead. Cremation is to be mandatory, for noble and commoner alike, and damn any dissent from Roma...'

That again. The old bird had been banging on about death rites for over a year now. As if men my age gave a fig for such things! She'd become obsessed with sailors' tales, ghost stories from the Drowned Isles, the ramblings of muddy drunkards from the Ken Marshes. Already men went chained into the ground – good iron wasted against superstition – and now chains weren't enough? Bodies must be burned? Well the church wouldn't like it. It would put a crimp in their plans for Judgment Day and us all rising from the grave for a big grimy hug. But who cared? Really? I watched the early light slide across the walls high above me and tried to picture Lisa as I'd left her that morning, clad in brightness and shadow and nothing more.

The crash of the chamberlain's staff on flagstones

jerked my head back up. In fairness I'd had very little sleep the night before and a trying morning. If I hadn't been caught a yard from my bedchamber door I would have been safely ensconced therein until well past noon, dreaming better versions of the daydream Grandmother kept interrupting.

'Bring in the witnesses!' The chamberlain had a voice that could make a death sentence boring.

Four guardsmen entered, flanking a Nuban warrior, scar-marked and tall, manacled wrist and ankle, the chains all threaded through an iron ring belted around his waist. That perked my interest. I misspent much of my youth gambling at the pit-fights in the Latin Quarter, and I intended to misspend much of what life remained to me there too. I've always enjoyed a good fight and a healthy dose of bloodshed, as long as it's not *me* being pummelled or *my* blood getting spilled. Gordo's pits, or the Blood Holes down by Mercants, got you close enough to wipe the occasional splatter from the toe of your boot, and offered endless opportunity for betting. Of late I'd even entered men on my own ticket. Likely lads bought off the slave boats out of Maroc. None had lasted more than two bouts yet, but even losing can pay if you know where to place your wagers. In any event, the Nuban looked like a solid bet. Perhaps he might even be the ticket that could get Maeres Allus off my back and silence his tiresome demands for payment for brandy already consumed and for whores already fucked.

A weedy half-caste with a decorative arrangement of missing teeth followed the Nuban to translate his mumbo jumbo. The chamberlain posed a question or two and the man answered with the usual nonsense about dead men rising from the Afrique sands, elaborating the tales this time to make it small legions of them. No doubt he hoped for freedom if his story proved sufficiently entertaining. He did a fine job of it, throwing in a djinn or two for good measure, though not the normal jolly fellows in satin pantaloons offering wishes. I felt tempted to applaud at the end, but Grandmother's face suggested that might not be a wise idea.

Two more reprobates followed, each similarly chained, each with a more outrageous fable than the last. The corsair, a swarthy fellow with torn ears where the gold had been ripped from him, spun a yarn about dead ships rising, crewed by drowned men. And the Slav spoke of bone men from the barrows out in the grass sea. Ancient dead clad in pale gold and grave goods from before the Builders' time. Neither man had much potential for the pits. The corsair looked wiry and was no doubt used to fighting in close quarters, but he'd lost fingers from both hands and age was against him. The Slav was a big fellow, but slow. Some men have a special kind of clumsiness that announces itself in every move they make. I started to dream about Lisa again. Then Lisa and Micha together. Then Lisa, Micha and Sharal. It got quite complicated. But when more guards marched

23

in with the fourth and last of these 'witnesses' Grandmother suddenly had all my attention. You only had to look at the man to tell the Blood Holes wouldn't know what had hit them. I'd found my new fighter!

The prisoner strode into the throne room with head held high. He dwarfed the four guards around him. I've seen taller men, though not often. I've seen men more heavily muscled, but seldom. I've even on rare occasions seen men larger in both dimensions, but this Norseman carried himself like a true warrior. I may not be much of a one for fighting, but I've a great eye for a fighter. He walked in like murder, and when they jerked him to a halt before the chamberlain he snarled. *Snarled.* I could almost count the gold crowns spilling into my hands when I got this one to the pits!

'Snorri ver Snagason, purchased off the slave-ship *Heddod.*' The chamberlain took a step back despite himself and kept his staff between them as he read from his notes. 'Sold in trade exchange off the Hardanger Fjord.' He traced a finger down the scroll, frowning. 'Describe the events you recounted to our agent.'

I had no idea where the place might be, but clearly they bred men tough up in Hardanger. The slavers had hacked off most of the man's hair, but the thick shock remaining was so black as to almost be blue. I'd thought Norsemen fair. The deep burn across his neck and shoulders showed he didn't take well to the sun, though. Innumerable lash marks intersected the sunburn – that had to sting a bit! Still, the fight-pits were always in shadow so he'd appreciate that part of my plans for him at least.

'Speak up, man.' Grandmother addressed the giant directly. He'd made an impression even on her.

Snorri turned his gaze on the Red Queen and gave her the type of look that's apt to lose men eyeballs. He had blue eyes, pale. That at least was in keeping with his heritage. That and the remnants of his furs and scalskins, and the Norse runes picked out in black ink and blue around his upper arms. Writing too, some sort of heathen script by the look of it but with the hammer and the axe in there as well.

Grandmother opened her mouth to speak again but the Norseman pre-empted her, stealing the tension for his own words.

'I left the North from Hardanger but it is not my home. Hardanger is quiet waters, green slopes, goats and cherry orchards. The people there are not the true folk of the North.'

He spoke with a deep voice and a shallow accent, sharpening the blunt edges of each word just enough so you knew he was raised in another tongue. He addressed the whole room, though he kept his eyes on the queen. He told his story with an orator's skill. I've heard tell that the winter in the North is a night that lasts three months. Such nights breed storytellers.

'My home was in Uuliskind, at the far reach of the Bitter Ice. I tell you my story because that place and

25

time are over and live only in memory. I would put these things into your minds, not to give them meaning or life, but to make them real to you, to let you walk among the Undoreth, the Children of the Hammer, and to have you hear of their last struggle.'

I don't know how he did it but when he wrapped his voice around the words Snorri wove a kind of magic. It set the hairs pricking on the backs of my arms, and damned if I didn't want to be a Viking too, swinging my axe on a longboat sailing up the Uulisk Fjord, with the spring ice crunching beneath its hull.

Every time he paused for breath the foolishness left me and I counted myself very lucky to be warm and safe in Red March, but while he spoke a Viking heart beat in every listener's chest, even mine.

'North of Uuliskind, past the Jarlson Uplands, the ice begins in earnest. The highest summer will drive it back a mile or three but before long you find yourself raised above the land on a blanket of ice that never melts, folded, fissured, and ancient. The Undoreth venture there only to trade with Inowen, the men who live in snow and hunt for seal on the sea-ice. The Inowen are not as other men, sewn into their sealskins and eating the fat of whales. They are … a different kind.

'Inowen offer walrus tusks, oils sweated from blubber, the teeth of great sharks, pelts of the white bear and skins. Also ivories carved into combs and picks and into the shapes of the true spirits of the ice.'

When my grandmother interjected into the story's flow she sounded like a screeching crow trying to overwrite a melody. Still, credit to her for finding the will to speak – I'd forgotten even that I stood in the throne room, sore-footed and yawning for my bed. Instead I was with Snorri trading shaped iron and salt for seals carved from the bones of whales.

'Speak of the dead, Snagason. Put some fear into these idle princes,' Grandmother told him.

I saw it then. The quickest flicker of his glance toward the blind-eye woman. I'd come to understand it was common knowledge that the Red Queen consulted with the Silent Sister. But like most such 'common knowledge' the recipients would be hard pressed to tell you how they came by their information, though willing to insist upon its veracity with considerable vigour. It was common knowledge, for example, that the Duke of Grast took young boys to his bed. I put that one about after he slapped me for making an improper suggestion to his sister – a buxom wench with plenty of improper suggestions of her own. The vicious slander stuck and I've taken great delight in defending his honour ever since against heated opposition who 'had it from a trusted source'! It was common knowledge that the Duke of Grast sodomized small boys in the privacy of his castle, common knowledge that the Red Queen practised forbidden sorceries in her highest tower, common knowledge that the Silent Sister, a parlous witch whose hand lay behind much of the empire's ills, was either in the Red Queen's palm or vice versa. But until this brutish Norseman glanced her way I'd never encountered any other person who truly saw the blind-eye woman at my grandmother's side.

Whether convinced by the Silent Sister's pearl-eyed stare or the Red Queen's command Snorri ver Snagason bowed his head and spoke of the dead.

'In the Jarlson Uplands the frozen dead wander. Corpse tribes, black with frost, stagger in columns, lost in the swirl of the frostral. They say mammoth walk with them, dead beasts freed from the ice cliffs that held them far to the north from times before Odin first gave men the curse of speech. Their numbers are unknown but they are many.

'When the gates of Niflheim open to release the winter, and the frost giants' breath rolls out across the North, the dead come with it, taking whoever they can find to join their ranks. Sometimes lone traders, or fishermen washed up on strange shores. Sometimes they cross a fjord by ice bridges and take whole villages.'

Grandmother rose from her throne and a score of gauntleted hands moved to cover sword hilts. She cast a sour glance toward her offspring. 'And how do you come to stand before me in chains, Snorri ver Snagason?'

'We thought the threat came from the north: from the Uplands and the Bitter Ice.' He shook his head. 'When ships came up the Uulisk in depths of night, black-sailed and silent, we slept, our sentries watching north for the frozen dead. Raiders had crossed the Quiet Sea and come against the Undoreth. Men of the Drowned Isles broke amongst us. Some living, others corpses preserved from rot, and other creatures still – half-men from the Brettan swamps, corpse-eaters, ghouls with venomed darts that steal a man's strength and leave him helpless as a newborn.

'Sven Broke-Oar guided their ships. Sven and others of the Hardassa. Without their treachery the Islanders would never have been able to navigate the Uulisk by night. Even by day they would have lost ships.' Snorri's hands closed into huge fists and muscle heaped across his shoulders, twitching for violence. 'The Broke-Oar took twenty warriors in chains as part of his payment. He sold us in Hardanger Fjord. The trader, a merchant of the Port Kingdoms, meant to have us sold again in Afrique after we'd rowed his cargo south. Your agent bought me in Kordoba, in the port of Albus.'

Grandmother must have been hunting far and wide for these tales – Red March had no tradition of slavery and I knew she didn't approve of the trade.

'And the rest?' Grandmother asked, stepping past him, beyond arms' reach, seemingly angled toward me. 'Those not taken by your countryman?'

Snorri stared into the empty throne, then directly at the blind-eye woman. He spoke past gritted teeth. 'Many were killed. I lay poisoned and saw ghouls swarm my wife. I saw Drowned men chase my children and couldn't turn my head to watch their flight. The Islanders returned to their ships with red swords. Prisoners were taken.' He paused, frowned, shook his head. 'Sven Broke-Oar told me ... tales. The truth would twist the Broke-Oar's tongue ... but he said the Islanders planned to take prisoners to excavate the Bitter Ice. Olaaf Rikeson's army is out there. The Broke-Oar told it that the Islanders had been sent to free them.'

'An army?' Grandmother stood almost close enough to touch now. A monster of a woman, taller than me – and I overtop six foot – and probably strong enough to break me across her knee. 'Who is this Rikeson?'

The Norseman raised an eyebrow at that, as if every monarch should know the tawdry history of his frozen wastes. 'Olaaf Rikeson marched north in the first summer of the reign of Emperor Orrin III. The sagas have it that he planned to drive the giants from Jotenheim and bore with him the key to their gates. More sober histories say perhaps his goal was just to bring the Inowen into the empire. Whatever the truth, the records agree he took a thousand and more with him, perhaps ten thousand.' Snorri shrugged and turned from the Silent Sister to face Grandmother. Braver than me – though that's not saying much – I'd not turn my back on that creature. 'Rikeson thought he marched with Odin's blessing but the giants' breath rolled down even so, and one summer's day every warrior in his army froze where he stood and the snows drowned them.

'The Broke-Oar has it that those taken from Uuliskind are excavating the dead. Freeing them from the ice.'

Grandmother paced along the front line of our number. Martus, little me, Darin, Cousin Roland with his stupid beard, Rotus, lean and sour, unmarried at thirty, duller than ditchwater, obsessed with reading – and histories at that! She paused by Rotus, another of her favourites and third in line by right – though still it seemed she would give her throne to Cousin Serah before him. 'And why, Snagason? Who has sent these forces on such an errand?' She met Rotus's gaze as if he of all of us would appreciate the answer.

The giant paused. It's hard for a Norseman to pale but I swear he did. 'The Dead King, lady.'

A guard made to strike him down, though whether for the improper address or for making mock with foolish tales I couldn't say. Grandmother stayed the man with a lifted finger. 'The Dead King.' She made a slow repetition of the words as if they somehow sealed her opinion. Perhaps she'd mentioned him before when I wasn't listening.

I'd heard tales of course. Children had started to tell them to scare each other on Hallows Night. The Dead King will come for you! Woo, woo, woo. It took a child to be scared. Anyone with a proper idea of how far away the Drowned Isles were and of how many kingdoms lay between us would have a hard time caring. Even if the stories held a core of truth I couldn't see any serious-minded gentleman getting overly excited about a bunch of heathen necromancers playing with old corpses on whatever wet hillocks remained to the Lords of the Isles. So what if they actually did raise a hundred dead men twitching from their coffins and dropping corpse-flesh with every step? Ten heavy horse would ride down any such in half an hour without loss and damn their rotting eyes.

I felt tired and out of sorts, grumpy that I'd had to stand half the morning and more listening to this parade of nonsense. If I'd been drunk too I might have given voice to my thoughts. It's probably a good job I wasn't, though – the Red Queen could scare me sober with a look.

Grandmother turned and pointed at the Norseman. 'Well told, Snorri ver Snagason. Let your axe guide you.' I blinked at that. Some sort of northern saying, I guessed. 'Take him away,' she said, and her guards led him off, chains clanking.

My fellow princes fell to muttering, and me to yawning. I watched the huge Norseman leave and hoped we'd be released soon. Despite the call of my bed I had important plans for Snorri ver Snagason and needed to get hold of him quickly.

Grandmother returned to her throne and held her peace until the doors had closed behind the last prisoner to exit.

'Did you know there is a door into death?' The Red Queen didn't raise her voice and yet it cut through the princes' chatter. 'An actual door. One you can set your hand against. And behind it, all the lands of death.' Her gaze swept across us. 'There's an important question you should ask me now.'

No one spoke – I hadn't a clue but was tempted to answer anyway just to hurry things along. I decided against it and the silence stretched until Rotus cleared his throat at last and asked, 'Where?'

'Wrong.' Grandmother cocked her head. 'The question was "why?" Why is there a door into death? The answer is as important as anything you've heard today.' Her stare fell upon me and I quickly turned my attention to the state of my fingernails. 'There is a door into death because we live in an age of myth. Our ancestors lived in a world of immutable laws. Times have changed. There is a door because there are tales of that door, because myths and legends have grown about it over centuries, because it is set in holy books, and because the stories of that door are told and retold. There is a door because in some way we wanted it, or expected it, or both. This is why. And this is why you must believe the tales that have been told today. The world is changing, moving beneath our feet. We are in a war, children of the Red March, though you may not see it yet, may not feel it. We are in a war against everything you can imagine and armed only with our desire to oppose it.'

Nonsense of course. Red March's only recent war was against Scorron and even that had fallen into an uneasy truce this past year... Grandmother must have sensed she was losing even the most gullible of her audience and switched tactics.

'Rotus asked "where", but I know where the door is. And I know that it cannot be opened.' She stood from her throne again. 'And what does a door demand?'

'A key?' Serah, ever eager to please.

'Yes. A key.' A smile for her protégée. 'Such a key would be sought by many. A dangerous thing, but better we should own it than our enemies. I will have tasks for you all soon, quests for some, questions for others, new lessons for others still. Be sure to commit yourselves to these labours as to nothing before. In this you will serve me, you will serve yourselves, and most importantly – you will serve the empire.'

Exchanged glances, muttering, 'Where was Red March in all that?' Martus perhaps.

'Enough!' Grandmother clapped her hands, releasing us. 'Go. Scurry back to your empty luxuries and enjoy them while you can. Or – if my blood runs hot in you – consider these words and act on them. These are the end days. All our lives draw in toward a single point and time, not too many miles or years from this room. A point in history when the emperor will either save us or damn us. All we can do is buy him the time he needs – and the price must be paid in blood.'

At last! I hurried out among the others, catching up with Serah. 'Well that settles it! The old bat's cracked. The emperor!' I laughed and flashed her my cavalry grin. 'Even Grandmother isn't old enough to have seen the last emperor?'

Serah fixed me with a look of disgust. 'Did you listen to *anything* she said?' And off she strode, leaving me standing there, jostled by Martus and Darin as they passed by.

4

From the throne room I sprinted down the grand corridor, turning left where all my family turned right. Armour, statuary, portraits, displays of fanned-out swords, all of them flashed past. My day boots pounded a hundred yards of staggeringly expensive woven rug, luxuriant silks patterned in the Indus style. I turned the corner at the far end, teetering on the edge of control, dodged two maids, and ran flat out along the central corridor of the guest range where scores of rooms were laid ready against the possibility of visiting nobility.

'Out the *fucking* way!' Some old retainer doddered from a doorway into my path. One of my father's – Robbin, a grey old cripple always limping about the place getting underfoot. I swerved past him, Lord knows why we keep such hangers-on, and accelerated down the hallway.

Twice guardsmen startled from their alcoves, one even calling a challenge before deciding I was more ass than assassin. Two doors short of the corridor's end I stopped and made an entrance to the Green Room, gambling that it would be unoccupied. The room, chambered in rustic style with a four-poster bed carved like spreading oaks, lay empty and shrouded in white linens. I passed the bed, wherein I'd once spent several pleasant nights in the company of a dusky contessa from the southernmost reaches of Roma, and threw back the shutters. Through the window, onto the balcony, vault the balustrade and drop to the peaked roof of the royal stables, an edifice that would put to shame any mansion on the Kings Way.

Now, I know how to fall, but the drop from the stables roof would kill a Chinee acrobat and so the speed with which I ran along the stone gutter was a careful balance between my desire not to fall to my death and my desire to not be stabbed to my death by Maeres Allus or one of his enforcers. The giant Norseman could bludgeon me a way out of debt altogether if I managed to secure his services and make the right wagers. Hell, if people saw what I saw in the man and wouldn't give me good odds then I could just slip him some bonewort and bet against him.

At the far end of the stables hall two Corinthian pillars supported ancient vines, or vice versa. Either way a good, or desperate, climber could make his way to ground there. I slid the last ten foot, bruised my heel, bit my tongue, and ran off toward the Battle Gate spitting blood.

I arrived there winded and had to bend double, palms on thighs, heaving in great lungfuls of air before I could assess the situation.

Two guards watched me with undisguised curiosity. An old soak commonly known as Double, and a youngster I didn't recognize.

'Double!' I straightened up and raised a hand in greeting. 'What dungeon are the queen's prisoners being taken to?' It would be the war cells up in the Marsail keep. They might be slaves but you wouldn't put the Norseman in with common stock. I asked anyway. It's always good to open with an easy question to put your man at ease.

'Ain't no cells for them lot.' Double made to spit then thought better of it and swallowed noisily.

'Wh—?' She couldn't be having them killed! It would be a criminal waste.

'They's going free. Tha's what I heard.' Double shook his head at the badness of the business, jowls wobbling. 'Contaph's coming up to process them.' He nodded out across the plaza and sure enough there was Contaph, layered in his official robes and beetling toward us with the sort of self-importance that only minor functionaries can muster. From the high latticed windows above the Battle Gate I could hear the distant clank of chains, drawing nearer.

'Damn it.' I glanced from door to sub-chamberlain and back again. 'Hold them here, Double,' I told him.

'Don't tell them anything. Not a thing. I'll see you right. Your friend too.' And with that I hurried off to intercept Ameral Contaph of House Mecer.

We met in the middle of the plaza where an ancient sundial spelled out the time with morning shadows. Already the flagstones were beginning to heat up and the day's promise simmered above the rooftops. 'Ameral!' I threw my hands wide as though he were an old friend.

'Prince Jalan.' He ducked his head as if seeking to take me from his sight. I could forgive him his suspicions, as a child I used to hide scorpions in his pockets.

'Those slaves that put on this morning's entertainment in the throne room … what's to become of them, Ameral?' I moved to intercept him while he tried to circumnavigate me, his order-scroll clutched tight in one pudgy fist.

'I'm to set them on a caravan for Port Ismuth with papers dissolving any indenture.' He stopped trying to get past me and sighed. 'What is it that you want, Prince Jalan?'

'Only the Norseman.' I gave him a smile and a wink. 'He's too dangerous to just set free. That should have been obvious to everyone. In any event Grandmother sent me to take charge of him.'

Contaph looked up at me, eyes narrow with distrust. 'I've had no such instructions.'

I have, I must confess, a very honest face. Bluff and courageous it's been called. I'm easy to mistake for a hero and with a little effort I can convince even the most cynical stranger of my sincerity. With people who know me that trick becomes more difficult. Much more difficult.

'Walk with me.' I set a hand to his shoulder and steered him toward the Battle Gate. It's good to steer a man in the direction they intended to go. It blurs the line between what he wants and what you want.

'In truth the Red Queen gave me a scroll with the order. A hasty scrawl on a scrap of parchment really. And to my shame I've let it drop in my rush to get here.' I took my hand from his shoulder and unfastened the gold chain from around my wrist, a thing of heavy links set with a small ruby on both clasps. 'It would be deeply embarrassing for me to have to return and admit the loss to my grandmother. A friend would understand such things.' I took to steering him again as if my only desire were for him to reach his destination safely. The chain I dangled before him. 'You *are* my friend aren't you, Ameral?' Rather than drop the chain into a pocket of his robe and risk reminding him of scorpions I pressed it into the midst of his sweaty palm and risked him realizing it was red glass and gold plated over lead, and thinly at that. Anything of true value I'd long since pawned against the interest on my debts.

'You'll retrace your steps and find this document?' Contaph asked, pausing to stare at the chain in his hand. 'And bring it for filing before sunset.'

'Assuredly.' I oozed sincerity. Any more and it would be dripping from me.

'He *is* dangerous, this Norseman.' Contaph nodded as if persuading himself. 'A heathen with false gods. I was surprised, I must admit, to see freedom set against his name.'

'An oversight.' I nodded. 'Now corrected.' Ahead of us Double appeared to be engaged in heated conversation through the view grille set into the Battle Gate's sub-door. 'You may allow the prisoners out,' I called to him. 'We're ready for them now!'

'You're looking uncommonly pleased with yourself.' Darin strolled into the High Hall, a dining gallery named for its elevation rather than the height of its ceiling. I like to eat there for the view it offers, both out across the palace compound and, via slit windows, into the great entrance hall of my father's house.

'Pheasant, pickled trout, hen's eggs.' I gestured at the silver plates set before me on the long trestle. 'What's not to be pleased about? Help yourself.' Darin is self-righteous and overly curious about my doings, but not the royal pain in the arse that Martus is, so by dint of not being Martus he carries the title of 'favourite brother'.

'The domo reports dishes keep going missing from the kitchens of late.' Darin took an egg and sat at the far end of the table with it.

'Curious.' That would be Jula, our sharp-eyed head cook, telling tales to the house domo, though how such whispers came to Darin's ear ... 'I'd have a few of the scullions beaten. Soon put a stop to it.'

'On what evidence?' He salted the egg and bit deep.

'Evidence be damned! Bloody up a few of the menials, put the fear into the lot of them. That'll put an end to it. That's what Grandmother would do. Light fingers get broken, she'd say.' I went for honest outrage, using my own discomfort to colour my reactions. No more selling off the family silver for Jal then ... that line of credit had come to an end. Still, I had the Norseman safely stowed away in the Marsail keep. I could see the keep from where I sat, a slouching edifice of stone more ancient than any part of the palace, scarred and disfigured but stubbornly resisting the plans of a dozen former kings to tear it down. A ring of tiny windows, heavily barred, ran around its girth like a belt. Snorri ver Snagason would be looking up at one of those from the floor of his cell. I'd told them to give him red meat, rare and bloody. Fighters thrive on blood.

For the longest time I stared out the window, watching the keep and the vast landscape of the heavens behind it, a sky of white and blue, all in motion so that the keep seemed to move and the clouds stay still, making a ship of all that stone, ploughing on through white waves.

'What did you think of all that rubbish this morning?'

I asked the question without expecting an answer, sure that Darin had taken his leave.

'I think if Grandmother is worried we should be too,' Darin said.

'A door into death? Corpses? Necromancy?' I sucked and the flesh came easily off a pheasant's bone. 'Am I to fear this?' I tapped the bone to the table, looked away from the window and grinned at him. 'Is it going to pursue me for vengeance?' I made it walk.

'You heard those men—'

'Have *you* ever seen a dead man walk? Forget distant deserts and ice wastes. Here in Red March has *anyone* ever seen such?'

Darin shrugged. 'Grandmother says at least one unborn has entered the city. That's something to be taken seriously.'

'A what?'

'Jesu! Did you really not listen to a word she said? She is the queen you know. You'd do well to pay attention from time to time.'

'An unborn?' The term rang no bells. It didn't even approach the belfry.

'Something born into death rather than life, remember?' Darin shook his head at my blank look. 'Forget it! Just listen now. Father expects you at this opera of his tonight. No showing up late, or drunk, or both. No pretending nobody told you.'

'Opera? Dear God why?' That was the last thing I

needed. A bunch of fat and painted idiots wailing at me from a stage for several hours.

'Just be there. A cardinal is expected to finance such projects from time to time. And when he does his family had better put in an appearance or the chattering classes will want to know why.'

I had opened my mouth to protest when it occurred to me that the DeVeer sisters would be among those chattering classes. Phenella Maitus too, the newly arrived and allegedly stunning daughter of Ortus Maitus whose pockets ran so deep it might even be worth a marriage contract to reach into them. And of course if I could have Snorri make his debut in the pits before the show started then I would likely find no end of aristocratic and mercantile purses opening in the opera intermissions to wager on this exciting new blood. If there's one good thing to be said about opera it's that it makes a man appreciate all other forms of entertainment so much more. I closed my mouth and nodded. Darin left, still munching his egg.

The appetite had left me. I pushed the plate away. Idle fingers discovered my old locket beneath the folds of my cloak and I fished it out, tapping it against the table. A cheap enough thing of plate and glass, it clicked open to reveal Mother's portrait. I snapped it shut again. She last saw me when I was seven: a flux took her. They call it a flux. It's just the shits really. You weaken, fever takes you, you die stinking. Not the way a princess is supposed to die, or a mother. I slipped the locket away unopened. Best she remember me as seven and not see me now.

Before leaving the palace I picked up my escort, the two elderly guardsmen allotted to the task of preserving my royal hide by my father's generosity. With the pair in tow I swung by the Red Hall and collected a handful of my usual cronies. Roust and Lon Greyjar, cousins of the Prince of Arrow, sent to 'further relations', which seemed to entail eating all our best vittles and chasing chamber maids. Also Omar, seventh son of the Caliph of Liba and a fine fellow for gambling. I'd met him during my brief and inglorious spell at the Mathema and he'd persuaded the caliph to send him to the continent to broaden his education! With Omar and the Greyjars I headed up to the guest range, that wing of the Inner Palace where more important dignitaries were housed and where Barras Jon's father, the Vyene ambassador to court, kept a suite of rooms. We had a servant fetch out Barras and he came sharp enough, with Rollas his companion-come-bodyguard trailing behind.

'What a perfect night to get drunk on!' Barras saluted me as he came down the steps. He always said it was a perfect night to get drunk.

'For that we'd need wine!' I spread my hands.

Barras stepped aside to reveal Rollas behind him carrying a large flask. 'Big goings-on in court today.'

'A meeting of the clan,' I said. Barras never stopped fishing for court news. I had a hunch half of his allowance depended on feeding gossip to his father.

'The Lady Blue playing her games again?' He flung an arm around my shoulders and steered me toward the Common Gate. With Barras everything was a plot of nation against nation or worse, a conspiracy to undermine what peace remained in the Broken Empire.

'Damned if I know.' Now he mentioned it there had been talk of the Lady Blue. Barras always insisted that my grandmother and this purported sorceress were fighting their own private war and had been for decades – if true then to my mind it was a piss-poor excuse for one as I'd seen precious little sign of it. Tales about the Lady Blue seemed as doubtful as those about the handful of so-called magicians who seemed to haunt the western courts. Kelem, Corion, half a dozen others: charlatans the lot of them. Only the existence of Grandmother's Silent Sister lent any credence at all to the rumours… 'Last I heard our friend in blue was flitting from one Teuton court to the next. Probably been hung for a witch by now.'

Barras grunted. 'Let's hope so. Let's hope she's not back in Scorron stirring up that little war again.'

I could agree with him there. Barras's father negotiated the peace and treated it like his second son. I'd rather a close relative came to harm than that particular peace deal. Nothing would induce me back into the mountains to fight the Scorrons.

We left the palace by the Victory Gate in fine spirits, passing our flask of Wennith red between us while I explained the virtues of wooing sisters.

As we entered Heroes' Plaza the wine turned to vinegar in my mouth. I half-choked and dropped the flask.

'There! Do you see her?' Coughing, wiping tears from my eyes, I forgot my own rule and pointed at the blind-eye woman. She stood at the base of a great statue, The Last Steward, sombre on his petty throne.

'Steady on!' Roust thumped me between the shoulders.

'See who?' Omar asked, staring where I pointed. Dressed in tatters, she might in another glance be nothing more than rags hanging on a dead bush. Perhaps that's what Omar saw.

'Nearly lost this!' Barras retrieved the flask, safe in its reed casing. 'Come to papa! I'll be looking after you from now on, little one!' And he cradled it like a baby.

None of them saw her. She watched a moment longer, the blind-eye burning across me, then turned and walked away through the crowds flowing toward Trent Market. Jostled into action by the others I walked on too, haunted by old fears.

We approached the Blood Holes in the early afternoon, me sweating and nervous, and not just because of the unseasonal heat or the fact that my financial future was about to ride on two very broad shoulders. The Silent Sister always unsettled me and I'd seen entirely too much of her today. I kept glancing about, half-expecting to spot her again along the crowded streets.

'Let's see this monster of yours!' Lon Greyjar slapped a hand to my shoulder, shaking me out of my rememberings and alerting me to the fact we'd arrived at the Blood Holes. I made a smile for him and promised myself I'd fleece the little fucker down to his last crown. He had an annoying way about him did Lon, too chummy, too keen to lay hands on you, and always snipping away at anything you said as if he doubted everything, even the boots you were standing in. Fair enough, I lie a lot, but that doesn't mean cousins of some minor princeling can take liberties.

I paused before approaching the doors and stepped back, casting my gaze along the outer walls. The place had been a slaughterhouse once, though a grand one, as if the king back in those days had wanted even his cattle murdered in buildings that would shame the homes of his copper-crown rivals.

On the only other occasion I'd seen the blind-eye woman outside the throne room she had been on the Street of Nails up close to one of the larger manses toward the western end. I'd come out of some ambassador's ballroom with an enticing young woman, got my face slapped for my efforts, and was cooling off, watching the street before going back in. I had been wiggling one of my teeth to check the damned girl hadn't knocked it loose when I saw the Silent Sister across the broadness of the street. She stood there, bolder than brass, a bucket in one white hand and a horsehair brush in the other, painting symbols on the walls of the manse. Not the garden walls facing the street but the walls of the building itself, seemingly unnoticed by guard or dog. I watched her, growing colder by the moment as if a crack had run through the night letting all the heat spill out of it. She showed no sign of hurry, painting one symbol, moving on to the next. In the moonlight it looked like blood she was painting with, broad dark strokes, each running with countless dribbles, and coming together to make sigils that seemed to twist the night around them. She was encircling the building, throwing a painted noose about it, patient, slow, relentless. I ran back in then, far more scared of that old woman and her bucket of blood than of the young Countess Loren, her over-quick hand, and whatever brothers she might set upon me to defend her honour. The joy of the night was gone though and I left for home quick enough.

A day later I heard report of a terrible fire on the Street of Nails. A house burned to ash with not a single survivor. Even today the site lies vacant, with nobody willing to build there again.

The walls of the Blood Holes were blessedly free of any decoration save perhaps the scratched names of temporary lovers here and there where a buttress provided shelter for such work. I cursed myself for a fool and led on through the doors.

The Terrif brothers who ran the Blood Holes had sent a wagon to collect Snorri from the Marsail keep earlier in the day. I'd been particular in the message I dispatched, warning them to take considerable care with the man and demanding assurances of a thousand in crown gold if they failed to ensure his attendance in the Crimson Pit for the first bout.

Flanked by my entourage I strode into the Blood Holes, enveloped immediately in the sweat and smoke and stink and din of the place. Damn but I loved it there. Silk-clad nobles strolled around the fight floor, each an island of colour and sophistication, close pressed by companions, then a ragged halo of hangers on, hawkers, beer-men, poppy-men and brazens, and at the periphery, urchins ready to scurry between one gentleman and the next bearing messages by mouth or hand. The bet-takers, each sanctioned and approved by the Terrifs, stood at their stalls around the edge of the hall, odds listed in chalk, boys ready to collect or deliver at the run.

The four main pits lay at the vertices of a great diamond, red-tiled into the floor. Scarlet, Umber, Ochre, and Crimson. All of a likeness, twenty-foot deep, twenty-foot across, but with Crimson first among equals. The nobility wound their way between these and the lesser pits, peering down, discussing the fighters on display, the odds on offer. A sturdy wooden rail surrounded each pit, set into a timber apron that overlapped the stonework, reaching a yard down into the depression. I led the way to Crimson and leaned over, the rail hard against my midriff. Snorri ver Snagason glowered up at me.

'Fresh meat here!' I raised my hand, still staring down at my meal ticket. 'Who'll take a cut!'

Two small olive hands slid out over the rail beside me. 'I believe *I* will. I feel you owe me a cut, or two, Prince Jalan.'

Aw hell. 'Maeres, how good to see you.' To my credit I kept the blind terror from my reply and didn't soil myself. Maeres Allus had the calm and reasonable voice that a scribe or tutor should have. The fact that he liked to watch when his collectors cut the lips off a man turned that reasonable tone from a comfort to a horror.

'He's a big fellow,' Maeres said.

'Yes.' I glanced around wildly for my friends. All of them, even the two old veterans picked specially by my father to guard me, had slunk off toward Umber without a word and let Maeres Allus slide up beside me unannounced. Only Omar had the grace to look guilty.

'How would he fare against Lord Gren's man, Norras, do you think?' Maeres asked.

Norras was a skilled pugilist but I thought Snorri

would pound the man flat. I could see Gren's fighter now, standing behind the barred gate opposite the one that Snorri had come through.

'Shouldn't we call the fight? Get the odds set?' I shot Barras Jon a look and called out to him, 'Norras against my fresh meat? What numbers there?'

Maeres set a soft hand to my arm. 'Time enough for wagering when the man's been tested, no?'

'B-but he might come to harm,' I flustered. 'I plan to make good coin here, Maeres, pay you back with interest.' My finger ached. The one Maeres had broken when I came up short two months back.

'Indulge me,' he said. 'That will be my interest. I'll cover any losses. A man like that … he might be worth three hundred crowns.'

I saw his game then. Three hundred was just half what I owed him. The bastard meant to see Snorri die and keep a royal prince on his leash. There didn't seem to be a way past it though. You don't argue with Maeres Allus, certainly not in his cousins' fight hall and owing him the best part of a thousand in gold. Maeres knew how far he could push me, minor princeling or not. He'd seen past my bluster to what lies beneath. You don't get to head an organization like Maeres's without being a good judge of men.

'Three hundred if he's not fit to fight wagered bouts tonight?' I could slip back after Father's ridiculous opera and buy into the serious fights. This afternoon's exercise had only ever been intended to whet appetites and stir up interest.

Maeres didn't answer, only clapped his soft hands and had the pit-guards raise the opposite gate. At the sound of iron grating on stone and chains ratcheting through their housings the crowds came to the rail, drawn by the pull of the pit.

'He's huge!'

'Handsome fella!'

'Norras will ugly him up.'

'Knows his stuff does Norras.'

The beefy Teuton came out of the archway, rolling his bald head on a thick neck.

'Fists only, Norseman,' Maeres called down. 'The only way out of that pit for you is to follow the rules.'

Norras raised both hands and balled them into fists as if to instruct the heathen. He closed the distance between them, swift on his feet, jerking his head in sharp stutters designed to fool the eye and tempt an ill-advised swing. He looked rather like a chicken to me, bobbing his head like that, fists at his face, elbows out like little wings. A big muscular hen.

Snorri clearly had the reach so Norras came in fast. He ducks his head, does Norras – takes punches on his skull. That's what I was going to say. I'd seen men hurt their hands on the Teuton's thick and bony head before. I didn't have time to get the words out. Norras jabbed and Snorri caught the man's fist in the flat of his palm, closing his fingers to trap it. He yanked Norras forward, punching with his other arm, brushing aside the wild swing of the Teuton's left with his elbow. The Norseman's huge fist hammered into Norras's face, knuckles impacting from chin to nose. The man flew back a yard or more, hitting the floor with a boneless thump, blood spattered his upturned face, mixed with teeth and muck from his flattened snout.

A moment of silence then a roar went up that hurt my ears. Half delight, half outrage. Betting parchments flew, coins changed hands, all informal wagers made in the moment.

'An impressive specimen,' Maeres said without passion. He watched while two pitmen dragged Norras away through the double-chambered exit valve. Snorri let them do their work. I could see he'd calculated his chances of escape and found them to be zero. The second iron gate could be raised only from the outside and then only when the first had been lowered.

'Send in Ootana.' Maeres never raised his voice but was always heard amid the din. He offered me a thin smile.

'No!' I strangled back the outrage, remembering that I had seen lipless men even in the palace. Maeres Allus had a long arm. 'Maeres, my friend, you can't be serious?' Ootana was a specialist with countless knife-bouts notched onto his belt. He'd sliced open half a dozen good knifemen this year already. 'At least let my fighter train with the hook-knife for a few weeks! He's from the ice. If it's not an axe they don't understand it.' I tried for humour but Ootana already waited behind the gate, a loose-limbed devil from the farthest shores of Afrique.

'Fight.' Maeres raised his hand.

'But—' Snorri hadn't even been given his weapon. It was murder, pure and simple. A public lesson to put a prince firmly in his place. The public didn't have to like it though! Boos rang out when Ootana stepped into the pit, his hooked blade held carelessly to the side. The nobles hooted as if we were watching mummers in the square. They might hoot again tonight with equal passion if Father's opera contained a suitably villainous party.

Snorri glanced up at us. I swear he was grinning. 'No rules now?'

Ootana began a slow advance, passing his knife from hand to hand. Snorri spread his arms, not fully but enough to make a wide man wider still in that confined space, and with a roar that drowned out the many voices above, he charged. Ootana jigged to one side, intending to slash and dodge clear, but the Norseman came too fast, swerved to compensate, and reached with arms every bit as long as the Afriqan's. At the last Ootana could do no more than attempt the killing blow, nothing else would save him from Snorri's grapple. The exchange was lost in the collision. Snorri pounded into his man, driving him back a yard and slamming him into the pit wall. He held there for a heartbeat, perhaps a word passed between them, then stepped away. Ootana slid to a crumpled heap at the base of the wall, white fragments of bone showing through dark skin at the back of his head.

Snorri turned to us, shot an unreadable glance my way, then looked down to inspect the hook-knife driven through his hand, hilt hard against his palm. The sacrifice he'd made to keep the blade from his throat.

'The bear.' Maeres said it more quietly than ever into the noise of the erupting crowd. I'd never seen him angry, few men had, but I could see it now in the thinness of his lips and the paling of his skin.

'Bear?' Why not just shoot him with crossbows from the rail and be done! I'd seen a Blood Holes' bear once before, a black beast from the western forests. They set it against a Conaught man with spear and net. It wasn't any bigger than him but the spear just made it angry and when it got in close it was all over. It doesn't matter how much muscle a man may carry, a bear's strength is a different thing and makes any warrior seem weak as a child.

It took them a while to produce the bear. This clearly hadn't been part of the plan that involved Norras and Ootana. Snorri simply stood where he was, holding his injured hand high above his head and gripping the wrist with his other hand. He left the hook-knife where it was, embedded in his palm.

The fury the crowd had shown at Ootana's entrance flared to new heights when the bear approached the gate, but Snorri's booming laugh silenced them.

'Call that a bear?' He lowered his arms and thumped his chest. 'I am of the Undoreth, The Children of the Hammer. The blood of Odin runs in our veins. Storm-born we!' He pointed up at Maeres with his transfixed hand, dripping crimson, knowing his tormentor. 'I am Snorri, Son of the Axe. I have fought trolls! You have a bigger bear. I saw it back in the cells. Send that one.'

'Bigger bear!' Roust Greyjar shouted out behind me, and his fool brother took up the chant. 'Bigger bear!' Within moments they were all baying it and the old slaughterhouse pulsed with the demand.

Maeres said nothing, only nodded.

'Bigger bear!' The crowd roared it time and again until at last the bigger bear arrived and awed them to silence.

Where Maeres had procured the beast I couldn't say but it must have cost him a fortune. The creature was simply the biggest thing I'd ever seen. Dwarfing the black bears of the Teuton forests, overtopping even the griz-zled bears from beyond the Slav lands. Even slouched behind the gate in its off-white pelt it stood nine foot and more, and heavy with muscle beneath fur and fat. The crowd drew breath and howled its delight and its horror, ecstatic at the prospect of death and gore, outraged at the unfairness of the killing to come.

As the gate lifted, and the bear snarled and went to all fours behind it, Snorri took hold of the hook-knife and pulled it free, making that curious turn of the blade at the last moment necessary to prevent the wound from becoming larger still. He bunched the injured hand into a scarlet fist and took the blade in an overhand grip in the other.

The bear, clearly some arctic breed, came in unhurriedly on all fours, swinging its head from side to side in great sweeps, drawing in the stink of men and blood. Snorri charged, stamping his great feet, arms wide, roaring that deafening challenge of his. He drew up short but it was enough to make the bear rear, returning the challenge with a snarl that nearly unloosed my waters even behind the safety of the rail. The bear stood ten foot, forelegs lifted, its black claws longer than fingers. Snorri's knife, crimson with his own blood, looked a sorry little thing. It would hardly penetrate the bear's fat. It would take a longsword to reach its vitals.

The Norseman shouted out some curse in his heathen tongue and flung out his wounded hand, holding it wide, splattering blood across the bear's chest, a pattern of red on white. 'Madness!' Even I knew not to let a wild thing see that you're wounded.

The bear, more curious than enraged, bent down, folding up to sniff and lick at its bloody fur. And at that instant Snorri charged. For a moment I wondered if he could actually kill the thing. If by some miracle of war he could drive his blade just so into its spine while its head was down. All of us drew a single breath. Snorri leapt. He set his injured hand flat to the top of the bear's head and like some court tumbler vaulted onto its shoulders, crouching. Roaring outrage, the bear snapped erect, reaching for the annoyance, powering up to its full height as if Snorri were a child and it the father carrying him aback. As the bear straightened Snorri straightened too, leaping upwards with their combined thrust and reaching high with his knife-hand. He drove the blade into the wooden skirts of the rail some twenty feet above the floor of the pit. He pulled, reached, swung, and in a broken second he was amongst us.

Snorri ver Snagason surged through the highborn crowd, trampling full-grown men underfoot. Somewhere in those first few steps he found a new knife. He left a trail of flattened and bleeding citizens, using his blade only three times when members of the Terrif pit team made more earnest efforts to stop him. Those he left gutted, one with his head nearly taken off. He was out into the street before half the crowd even knew what had happened.

I leaned over the rail. The hall was in chaos, everywhere men were finding their courage and starting to give chase now that their quarry was long gone. The bear had returned to sniffing the pit floor, licking blood from the flagstones, the red print of Snorri's hand stark across the back of its head.

Maeres had vanished. He had a way for coming and going, that one. I shrugged. The Norseman was clearly too dangerous to keep. He would have been the death of me, one way or another. At least this way I'd put a three hundred crown dent in my debt to Maeres Allus. It would keep him off my back for a good three months, maybe six. And a lot can happen in six months. Six months is an eternity.

5

Opera! There's nothing like it. Except wild boars rutting.

The only good thing about Father's interminable opera was the venue, a fine domed building in Vermillion's eastern quarter where a preponderance of Florentine bankers and Milano merchants gave the city a very different flavour. For the first hour I gazed up at the nymphs cavorting nude across the dome, somehow painted so that the curved surface presented them without distortion. As much as I admired the artist's eye for detail I found the scene frequently interrupted by flashes of imagery from the Blood Holes. Snorri felling Norras with what must have been a fatal punch. Ootana falling forward from the pit wall, the back of his head broken open. That leap. That spectacular, impossible, insane leap! On stage a soprano soared through an aria as I replayed the Norseman launching himself to freedom.

In the intermission I searched for familiar faces. I had come late to the showing and had shuffled my way noisily to a seat blocking everyone's view. In the dim light and separated from my more punctual companions I had to settle for sitting among strangers. Now under the lanterns of the intermisso hall and plucking glasses of wine from every passing tray, I found that despite my brother Darin's dire warnings the opening night was surprisingly poorly attended. It seemed that Father himself had failed to arrive. Taken to his bed, the gossip had it. He was never a music lover but the Vatican's coffers had financed this tripe of angels and devils wailing one against the other, fat men sweltering under wings of wax and feathers whilst belting out the chorus. The least their most senior local representative could do was attend and suffer with the rest of us. Damn it all, I couldn't even spot Martus, or fucking Darin.

I jostled past a man in a white enamel mask, as though he were attending a masquerade rather than an opera. Or at least I attempted to jostle past, failed, and bounced off him as if he were cast from iron. I turned, rubbing my shoulder. Something in the eyes watching from those slits swept away in a cold wash of fear any inclination I had to complain. I let the press of people separate us. Had it even been a man? The eyes haunted me. The irises white, the whites grey. My shoulder ached as though infection ate at the bone ... Unborn. Darin had said something about an unborn in the city...

'Prince Jalan!' Ameral Contaph hailed me with irritating familiarity, puffed up in ridiculous finery no doubt purchased for just this occasion. They must have been desperate to fill the seats if toadies of Contaph's water were invited to the premiere. 'Prince Jalan!' The flow of the crowd somehow pulled us further apart and I affected not to see him. The fellow was probably just pursuing me for the fictional paperwork regarding Snorri. Worse still, he might have already heard the Norseman was running amok in Vermillion's streets ... Or perhaps he'd scratched off the gold plate from my gift. Either way, none of the reasons he might want to talk to me seemed to be reasons I might want to talk to him! I turned sharply away and found myself face to face with Alain DeVeer, sporting an unbecoming bandage around his head and flanked by two large and ugly men in ill-fitting opera cloaks.

'Jalan!' Alain reached for me, finding only a handful of my own exquisitely tailored cape. I shrugged the garment off and let him keep it while I sprinted for the stairs, weaving a dangerous path around dowagers sporting diamonds in their hair and gruff old lords knocking back the wine with the grim determination of men wishing to dull their senses.

I have quick feet but it's probably my total disregard for other people's safety that allowed me to open a considerable lead so swiftly.

There are communal privies at the rear of the opera house. For the men, a dozen open seats above water flowing in channels that pour out into the alley behind.

The water runs from a large tank on the roof. A small band of urchins spend all day filling it with buckets – an activity I had occasion to note when using one of the cast changing rooms for an assignation with Duchess Sansera a season previously. I was banging away duti-fully as a chap does with a woman of declining years and increasing fortune when hoping to cadge a loan, but every time I seemed to be getting anywhere a small boy would wander past the door, heavy buckets sloshing. Quite put me off my stride. And the old cow didn't loan me so much as a silver penny.

That afternoon with Duchess Money-Buckets wasn't a complete waste though. After I'd let her usher me out of there with a wet kiss and a goosing of my buttocks, I chased down as many of those ratty little children as I could and kicked some arse. It's true that my foe outnumbered me but I am the hero of Aral Pass, after all, and sometimes when Prince Jalan Kendeth is roused to anger it's best to flee, whatever your number. If you're eight.

I had found three of the little bastards cowering in the tiny utility room where the buckets are stored along with assorted brooms and mops. And that was the pay-off – another hiding place to add to my list.

Racing along the same corridor now, with Alain and friends a corner or two behind me, I stopped dead, hauled the closet door open and dived in. The thing with closing doors behind you is to do it quickly but quietly. That proved a challenge whilst trying to disentangle myself from various broom handles in the dark without the teetering bucket towers crashing down around me. Seconds later when Alain and his heavies clattered down the corridor, the hero of Aral Pass was crouched among the mops, hands clamped to mouth to stifle a sneeze.

I managed to hold the sneeze back almost long enough, but no man can be in complete control of his body, and there's no stopping such things sometimes – as I told the Duchess Sansera when she expressed her disappointment.

'Achoo!'

The footsteps, fading at the edge of hearing, stopped.

'What was that?' Alain's voice, distant but not distant enough.

Cowards divide into two broad groups. Those paralysed by their fear, and those galvanized by it. Fortunately I belong to the latter group and burst out of that closet like a … well, like a lecherous prince hoping to escape a beating.

I've always made a close study of windows, and the most accessible windows in the opera house were in the aforementioned communal privies, which needed them for obvious reasons. I pounded down the corridor, swerved, banked, and crashed through into the fetid gloom of the men's privy. One old gent had settled himself there with a flagon of wine, clearly feeling that breathing in the sewer stink was preferable to a seat closer to the stage. I ran straight past, climbed onto the rear throne and tried to jam my head between the shutters. Normally they were propped ajar to offer sufficient ventilation to prevent the place exploding if one more over-fed lordling passed wind. Today, like everything else since I got up, they seemed to be against me and stood firmly closed. I shook them hard. They weren't latched and it made no sense that they wouldn't give. Fear lent strength to my arm and when the damn things wouldn't open I ripped out the slats before thrusting my head through.

For a half second I just stood with that cool, slightly less fetid, air on my face. Salvation! There's something almost orgasmic about getting out from under a heap of trouble, winning free and thumbing your nose at it. Tomorrow maybe that same trouble will be waiting around a corner for you, but today, right now, it's beaten, left in the dust. Cowards, over burdened with imagination as we are, spend most of our attention on the future, worrying what's coming next, so when that rare opportunity to live in the moment arrives I seize it with as many hands as I've got spare.

In the next half second I realized that we were on the second floor and the drop to the street below seemed likely to injure me more grievously than Alain and his friends would dare to. I should perhaps puff myself up, brazen it out, and remind Alain whose damned father's opera this was and whose grandmother happened to be warming the throne. No part of me wanted to bank on Alain's commonsense outweighing his anger, but an ankle-breaking drop into the alley where they flushed the shit … that didn't appeal either.

And then I saw her. A tattered figure in the alley, bent over some burden. A bucket? For one ridiculous moment I thought it was another of those little boys lugging water for the tank. A pale hand lifted a brush, moonlight glimmered on what dripped from it.

'Jalan Kendeth, hiding in the privies. How appropriate.' Alain DeVeer banging open the door behind me. I didn't turn my head even a fraction. If I hadn't taken care of business at the start of the intermission I would have rapidly filled the privy I was standing on by way of both trouser legs. The figure in the alley looked up and one eye caught the moonbeams, glowing pearly in the darkness. My shoulder ached with a sudden memory of the masked figure I'd barged into. Conviction seized me by the throat. That had not been a man. There had been nothing human in that stare. Outside the blind-eye woman painted her fatal runes, and inside, among the lords and ladies, hell walked with us.

I would have run head first into a dozen Alain DeVeers to get away from the Silent Sister. Hell, I'd have flattened Maeres Allus to put some space between me and that old witch. I'd have put my foot in his groin and told him to add it to the debt. I would have charged right at Alain and his two friends but for the memory of a fire on The Street of Nails. *The walls themselves had burned.* There had been nothing left but fine ash. Nobody got out. Not one person. And there had been four other fires like that across the city. Four in five years.

'Oh, Jalan!' Alain drew the 'a' out, making it a sing-song taunt, 'Jaaaalaan.' He really hadn't taken having that vase broken over his head very well.

I jammed myself further through the broken shutter, wedging both shoulders into the gap and splintering more slats. Some kind of webbing stretched across my face. *Because right now I needed a big spider on my head?* Once more the gods of fate were crapping on me from a height. I looked to the left. Black symbols covered the wall, each like some horrifying and twisted insect caught in its death throes. To the right, more of them, reaching up from where the blind-eye woman had returned to her work. They seemed to have grown along the sides of the building, like vines … or crawled up. There was no way she could reach so high. She planted her hideous seeds as she circled the building, painting a noose of symbols, and from each one more grew, and more, rising until the noose became a net.

'Hey!' Alain, his gloating turning to irritation at being ignored.

'We've got to get out of here.' I pulled free and glanced back at the three of them in the doorway, the old man clutching his wine looking on bemused. 'There's no time—'

'Get him down from there.' Alain shook his head in disgust.

The drop to the street had been knocked off the top of the list of today's most terrifying things, where it had nestled just above Alain and friends. The writing on the wall immediately outside swept all that other stuff right off the list and into the privies. I stuck both arms through the hole I'd made and launched myself out. I made it a couple of feet, and came to a splintering halt with my chest wedged into the shutter frame. Something dark and very cold stretched across my face again, feeling for all the world like a web spun by the world's toughest spider. The strands of it closed my left eye for me and resisted any further advance.

'Quick!'

'Grab him!'

Pounding feet as Alain led the charge. When it comes to wriggling out of things I'm pretty good, but my current situation offered little purchase. I seized the windowsill with both hands and tried to propel myself forward, managing an advance of a few inches, jacket ripping. The black stuff over my face pulled even harder, pressing my head back and threatening to throw me back into the room if I lessened my grip even a little.

Now, nature may have gifted me a pretty decent physique but I do try to avoid any strenuous activity, at least whilst clothed, and I'll lay no claims to any great strength. Raw terror does, however, have a startling effect on me and I've been known to toss extraordinarily heavy items aside if they stood between me and a swift escape.

Anticipating the arrival of Alain DeVeer's hand on my flailing shin occasioned just the right level of terror. It wasn't the thought of being dragged back in and given a good kicking that worried me – although it normally would … a lot. It was the idea that whilst they were kicking me, and whilst poor old Jalan was rolling about manfully taking his lumps and screaming for mercy, the Silent Sister would complete her noose, the fire would ignite, and we'd each and every one of us burn.

Whatever had stretched across my face had stopped stretching and was instead keeping me from getting any further forward, all its elasticity used up. It felt more like a length of wire now, cutting across my forehead and face. With my feet finding nothing to push against, I hung, one-third out, two-thirds in, thrashing helplessly and roaring all manner of threats and promises. I rather suspect Alain and his friends might have paused to have a laugh at my expense because it took longer than I expected before someone laid a hand on me.

They should have taken the matter more seriously. Flailing legs are a dangerous proposition. Fuelled by desperation I struck out and made a solid connection, booted heel to something that crunched like a nose. Someone made a noise very similar to the one Alain had made that morning when I broke the vase over his head.

The added thrust proved sufficient. The wire-like

obstruction bit deeper, like a cold knife carving through me, then something gave. It felt more as though it were me that gave rather than the obstruction, as if I cracked and it ran through me, but either way I won free and tumbled out in one piece rather than two.

As victories go it proved fairly Pyrrhic, my prize being the liberty to pitch out face-first with a two-storey drop between me and the flagstones. When you run out of screaming during a fall you know that you've dropped way too far. Too far and too fast in general for there to be any reasonable prospect of you ever getting up again. Something tugged at me though, slowing my descent a fraction, an awful ripping sound over-riding my scream as I fell. Even so, I hammered into the ground with more than enough force to kill me but for the large mound of semi-solid dung accumulated beneath the privy outlet. I hit with a splat.

I staggered up, spitting out mouthfuls of filth, roared an oath, slipped and plunged immediately back in. Derisive laughter from on high confirmed I had an audience. My second attempt left me on my back, scraping dung from my eyes. Looking up I saw the whole side of the opera house clothed in interlocking symbols, with one exception. The window from which I tumbled lay bare, a man's face peering from the hole I'd left. Elsewhere the black limbs of the Silent Sister's calligraphy bound the shutters closed, but across the broken privy shutter, not even a trace. And leading down from it, a crack, running deep into the masonry, following the path of my descent. A peculiar golden light bled from the crack, flickering with shadows all along its length, illuminating both alley and building.

With more speed and less haste I found my feet and cast around for the Silent Sister. She'd rounded the corner, quite possibly before I fell. How far she had to go until completing her noose I couldn't see. I backed to the middle of the alley, out of the dung heap, wiping the muck from my clothes to little avail. Something snagged at my fingers and I found myself holding what looked like black ribbon but felt more like the writhing leg of some nightmare insect. With a cry I tore it from me, and found the whole of one of the witch's symbols hanging from my hand, nearly reaching to the ground and twisting in a breeze that just wasn't there – as if it were somehow trying to wrap itself back around me. I flung it down in revulsion, sensing it was more filthy than anything else that coated me.

A sharp retort returned my gaze to the building. As I watched, the crack spread, darting down another five yards, almost reaching the ground. The shriek that burst from me was more girlish than I would have hoped for. Without hesitation, I turned and fled. More laughter from above. I paused at the alley's end, hoping for something clever to shout back at Alain. But any witticism which might have materialized vanished as all along the wall beside me the symbols started to light up. Each cracked open, glowing, as if they had become fissures into some world of fire waiting for us all just beneath the surface of the stone. I realized in that instant that the Silent Sister had completed her work and that Alain, his friends, the old man with his wine, and every other person inside was about to burn. I swear, in that moment I even felt sorry for the opera singers.

'Jump, you idiots!' I shouted it over my shoulder, already running.

I rounded the corner at speed and slipped, shoes still slick with muck. Sprawling across cobbles, I saw back along the alleyway, now lit in blinding incandescence shot through with pulsing shadow. Each symbol blazed. At the far end, one particular shadow stayed constant: the Silent Sister, ragged and immobile, still little more than a stain on the eye despite the glare from the wall beside her.

I gained my feet to the sound of awful screaming. The old hall rang to notes that had never before issued from any mouth within it down the long years of its history. I ran then, feet sliding and skittering beneath me – and out of the brilliance of that alleyway something gave chase. A bright and jagged line zigzagged along my trail as if the broken pattern sought to reclaim me, to catch me and light me up so that I too might share the fate I'd fought so hard to escape.

You would think it best to save your breath for running, but I often find screaming helps. The street I had turned into from the alley ran past the back of the opera house and was well-trodden even at this hour of the night, though nowhere near as crowded as Paint Street that runs past the grand entrance and delivers patrons to the doors. My ... manly bellowing ... served to clear my path somewhat, and where town-folk proved too slow to move I variously sidestepped or, if they were sufficiently small or frail, flattened them. The crack emerged into the street behind me, advancing in rapid stuttering steps, each accompanied by a sound like something expensive shattering.

Turning sideways to slot between two town-laws on patrol, I managed a glance back and saw the crack jag left, veering down the street, away from the opera house and in the direction I'd taken. The people in the road hardly noticed, transfixed as they were by the glow of the building beyond, its walls now wreathed in pale violet flame. The crack itself seemed more than it first appeared, being in truth two cracks running close together, crossing and re-crossing, one bleeding a hot golden light and the other revealing a consuming darkness that seemed to swallow what illumination fell its way. At each point where they crossed golden sparks boiled in darkness and the flagstones shattered.

I barged between the town-laws, the impact spinning me round, hopping on one foot to keep my balance. The crack ran under an old fellow I'd felled in my escape. More than that, it ran through him, and where the dark crossed the light something broke. Smaller fissures spread from each crossing point, encompassing the man for a heartbeat before he literally exploded. Red chunks of him were thrown skyward, burning as they flew, consumed with such ferocity that few made it to the ground.

Whatever anyone may say about running, the main thing is to pick your feet up as quickly as possible – as if the ground has developed a great desire to hurt you. Which it kind of had. I took off at a pace that would have left my dog-fleeing self of only that morning stopping to check if his legs were still moving. More people exploded in my wake as the crack ran through them. I vaulted a cart, which immediately detonated behind me, pieces of burning wood peppering the wall as I dived through an open window.

I rolled to my feet inside what looked to be, and certainly smelled like, a brothel of such low class I hadn't even been aware of its existence. Shapes writhed in the gloom to one side as I pelted across the chamber, knocking over a lamp, a wicker table, a dresser, and a small man with a toupee, before pulverizing the shutters on the rear window on my way out.

The room lit behind me. I crashed across the alleyway into which I'd spilled, let the opposite wall arrest my momentum, and charged off. The window I came through cracked, sill and lintel, the whole building splitting. The twin fissures, light and dark, wove their path after me, picking up still more speed. I jumped a poppy-head

75

slumped in the alley and raced on. From the sound of it the fissure cured his addiction permanently a heartbeat later.

Eyes forward is the second rule of running, right after the one about picking up your feet. Sometimes though you can't follow all the rules. Something about the crack demanded my attention, and I shot another glance back at it.

Slam! At first I thought I'd run into a wall. Drawing breath for more screaming and more running I pulled away, only to discover the wall was holding me. Two huge fists, one bandaged and bloody, bunched in the jacket over my chest. I looked up, then up some more, and found myself staring into Snorri Snagason's pale eyes.

'What—' He hadn't time for more words. The crack ran through us. I saw a black fracture race through the Norseman, jagged lines across his face, bleeding darkness. In the same moment something hot and unbearably brilliant cut through me, filling me with light and stealing the world away.

My vision cleared just in time to see Snorri's forehead descending. I heard a crack of an entirely different kind. My nose breaking. And the world went away again.

6

First check where my money pouch is, and pat for my locket. It's a habit I've developed. When you wake up in the kinds of places I wake up in, and in the company I often pay to keep ... well, it pays to keep your coin close. The bed was harder and more bumpy than I tend to like. As hard and bumpy as cobbles, in fact. And it smelled like shit. The glorious safe moment between being asleep and being awake was over. I rolled onto my side, clutching my nose. Either I'd not been unconscious very long, or the stink had kept even the beggars off. That and the excitement down the road, the trail of exploded citizens, the burning opera house, the blazing crack. The crack! I staggered to my feet at that, expecting to see the jagged path leading down the alley and pointing straight at me. Nothing. At least nothing to see by starlight and a quarter moon.

'Shit.' My nose hurt more than seemed reasonable. I remembered fierce eyes beneath heavy brows ... and then those heavy brows smacking into my face. 'Snorri...'

The Norseman was long gone. Why small charred chunks of us both weren't decorating the walls I couldn't say. I remembered the way those two fissures had run side by side, crossing and re-crossing, and at every junction, a detonation. The dark fracture-line had run through Snorri – I had seen it across his face. The light—

I patted myself down, sudden frantic hands searching for injury. The light one had run through me. Pulling up my trouser legs revealed grubby shins with no sign of golden light shining from any cracks. But the street showed no sign of the fissure either. Nothing remained but the damage it had wrought.

I shook thoughts of that blinding golden light from my mind. I'd survived! The screams from the opera house returned to me. How many had died? How many of my friends? My relatives? Had Alain's sisters been there? Pray God Maeres Allus had been. Let it be one of those nights he pretended to be a merchant and used his money to buy him into social circles far above his station. For now though I needed to put more distance between me and the site of the fire. But where to go? The Silent Sister's magic had pursued me. Would she be waiting at the palace to finish the job?

When in doubt, run.

I took off again, along dark streets, lost but knowing in time that I would hit the river and gain my bearings anew. Running blind is apt to get you a broken nose, and since I had one of those already and wasn't keen to find out what came next I kept my pace on the sensible side of break-neck. I normally find that showing trouble my heels and putting a few miles behind me makes things a whole lot better. As I ran though, breathing through my mouth and catching my side where a muscle kept cramping, I felt worse and worse. A general unease grew minute by minute and hardened into a general crippling anxiety. I wondered whether this was what conscience felt like. Not that any of it had been my fault. I couldn't have saved anyone even if I'd tried.

I paused and leaned against a wall, catching my breath and trying to shake off whatever it was that plagued me. My heart kept fluttering behind my ribs as if I'd started to sprint rather than come to a halt. Each part of me seemed, fragile, somehow brittle. My hands looked wrong, too white, too light. I started to run again, accelerating, any fatigue left behind. Spare energy boiled off my skin, rattled through me, set my teeth buzzing in their sockets, my hair seeming to float up around my head. Something was wrong with me, broken, I couldn't slow down if I wanted to.

Ahead the street forked, starlight offering just the lines of the building that divided the way. I veered from one side of the street to the other, unsure which path to follow. Moving to the left made me worse, my speed increasing, sprinting, my hands almost glowing as they pumped, head aching, ready to split, bright light fracturing across my vision. Veering right restored a touch of normality. I took the right fork. Suddenly I knew the direction. Something had been tugging at me since I picked myself up off the cobbles. Now, as if a lamp had been lit, I knew the direction of its pull. If I turned from it then whatever malady afflicted me grew worse. Head toward it and the symptoms eased. I had a direction.

What the destination might be I couldn't say.

It seemed to be my day for charging headlong down the streets of Vermillion. My path now followed the gentle gradient toward the Seleen where she eased her slow passage through the city. I started to pass the markets and cargo bays behind the great warehouses that fronted the river docks. Even at this hour men moved back and forth, hauling crates from mule-drawn trolleys, loading wagons, labouring by the mean light of lanterns to push the stuff of commerce through Vermillion's narrow veins.

My path took me across a deserted marketplace smelling of fish and fetched me up against a wide expanse of wall, one of the city's most ancient buildings, now co-opted into service as a docks warehouse. The thing stretched a hundred yards and more both left and right, and I had no interest in either direction. Forward. My route lay straight ahead. That's where the pull came from. A broad-planked door cracked open a few yards off and without thought I was there, yanking it wide, slipping past the bewildered menial with his hand still trying to push. A corridor ran ahead, going my way, and I gave chase. Shouts from behind as men startled into action and tried to catch me. Builder globes burned here, shedding the cold white light of the ancients. I hadn't realized quite how old the structure was. I charged on regardless, flashing past archway after archway each opening on to Builder-lit galleries, all packed with green-laden benches and walled with shelf upon shelf of many-leaved plants. When, about halfway through the width of the warehouse, a plank-built door opened, slamming out into my path, all I had time to think before blacking out was that hitting Snorri Snagason had hurt more.

I came back to consciousness lying horizontal once again, and hurting in so many places that I missed out the blissful ignorance stage and went directly into the asking of stupid questions.

'Where am I?' Nasal and hesitant.

The bright but flickering light and the faint unnatural whine helped me to remember. Somewhere with Builder-globes. I made to sit up and found myself tied to a table. 'Help!' A little louder. Panicked, I tested my strength against the ropes and found no give in them. "Help!"

'Best save your breath!' The voice came from the shadows by the door. I squinted. A thickset ruffian leaned against the wall, looking back at me.

'I'm Prince Jalan! I'll have your fucking head for this! Untie these ropes.'

'Yeah, that's not going to happen.' He leaned forward,

chewing something, the flickering light gleaming on his baldness.

'I'm Prince Jalan! Don't you recognize me?'

'Like I know what the princes look like. I don't even know the princes' names! Far as I'm concerned you're some toff who got juiced up and went swimming in a sewer. Just your bad luck to end up here. Horace though, he did seem to know you from somewhere. Told me to keep you here and off he went. "Keep an eye on that one, Daveet," he said. "Keep a good watch." You must be some kind of important or you'd be floating down the river by now with your throat cut.'

'Kill me and my grandmother will raze this quarter to the ground.' A blatant lie but, spoken with conviction, it made me feel better. 'I'm a rich man. Let me go and I'll see you're fixed up for life.' I'll admit I have a gift for lying. I sound least convincing when I tell the truth.

'Money's nice an' all,' the man said. He took a step away from the wall and let the flickers illuminate the brutality of his face. 'But if I let you go without Horace's say-so then I wouldn't have no fingers to count it all with. And if it turned out you really were a prince and we let you go without the boss's say-so, well me and Horace would think having our fingers taken was the easy part.' He bared his teeth at me, more gaps than teeth, truth be told, and settled back into the shadow.

I lay back, moaning from time to time, and asking

82

questions that he ignored. At least the strange compulsion that had me running headlong into this mess in the first place had now faded. I still had that sense of direction, but the need to pursue it had lessened and I felt more my old self. Which in this instance meant terrified. Even in my terror though I noticed that the direction that nagged at me was changing, swinging round, the urge to pursue it growing more faint by the minute.

I drew a deep breath and took stock of my surroundings. A smallish room, not one of those long galleries. They'd been growing plants there? That made no sense. No plants in here though. The broken light probably meant it wasn't suitable. Just a table and me tied to it.

'Why—' The door juddered open and cut through my nineteenth question.

'Good lord it stinks in here!' A calm and depressingly familiar voice. 'Stand our guest up, why don't you, and let's see if you can't sluice some of that filth off him.'

Men loomed to either side, strong hands grasped the table and the world turned through a right-angle, leaving the table standing on end, and me standing too, still bound to it. A bucket of cold water took my breath and vision before I had a chance to look around. Another followed in quick succession. I stood gasping, trying to get a breath – no mean task with your nose clogged with blood and water everywhere – whilst a fragrant brown pool began to spread around my feet.

'Well bless me. There seems to be a prince hidden

under all this unpleasantness. A diamond in the muck as they say. Albeit a very low-carat one.'

I shook the wet hair from my eyes, and there he stood, Maeres Allus, dressed in his finest as if bound for high company ... and an opera perhaps?

'Ah, Maeres! I was hoping to see you. Had a little something to hand over toward our arrangement.' I never called it my debt. Our arrangement sounded better. A little more as if it was both our problems, not just mine.

'You were?' Just the slightest smile mocking at the corners of his mouth. He'd worn that same smile when one of his heavies snapped my index finger. The ache of it still ran through me on cold mornings when I reached for the flagon of small beer they put by my bed. It ran through that same finger now, secured at my side.

'Yes.' I didn't even stutter. 'Had it with me at the opera.' By my reckoning the business with Snorri had bought me in the region of six months' grace but it never hurts to sound willing. Besides, the main thing when tied to tables by criminals is to remind them how much more valuable you are to them when not tied to a table. 'The gold was right in my pocket. I think I must have lost it in the panic.'

'Tragic.' Maeres lifted a hand, cupped his fingers and a man came from the shadows to stand at his shoulder. A dry rustling accompanied his advance, and stopped when he did. I didn't like this one at all. He looked too pleased to see me. 'Another fire with no survivors.'

'Well...' I didn't want to contradict Maeres. My eyes slid to the man beside him. Maeres is a slight fellow, unremarkable, the kind of little man you might find bent over the ledgers at some merchant's office. Neat brown hair, eyes that are neither kind nor cruel. In fact remarkably similar to my father in age and appearance. Maeres' companion though, he looked like the sort of man who would drown kittens recreationally. His face reminded me of the skulls in the palace catacombs. Stretch skin over one and press in some pale staring eyes, and you'd have this man, his smile too wide, teeth too long and white.

Maeres clicked his fingers, snapping my attention back to him. 'This is Cutter John. I was telling him as we came in just how unfortunate it is that you've seen my operation here.'

'O-o-operation?' I stuttered the question out. Victory could be measured now by a lack of soiling myself. Cutter John was a name everyone knew, but not many claimed to have seen him. Cutter John came into play when Maeres wanted to hurt people more creatively. When a broken finger, amputated toe, or good beating wouldn't suffice, when Maeres wanted to stamp his authority, set his trademark upon some poor soul, Cutter John would be the man to do the work. Some called it artistry.

'The poppies.'

'I didn't see any poppies.' Row upon row of green

things growing, here under Builder-lights. My Uncle Hertert – the heir-apparently-not, as Father liked to call him – had made countless initiatives to cut the opium supply. He'd had town-law out on boats patrolling God knows how many miles of the Seleen, convinced it came upriver from the port of Marsail. But Maeres grew his own. Right here. Under Hertert's nose and ready to go up everyone else's. 'I didn't see a thing, Maeres. I ran into a door for godsakes. Blind drunk.'

'You sobered up remarkably well.' He lifted a golden vinaigrette to his nose, as if the stink of me offended him. Which it probably did. 'In any event it's a risk I can't run, and if we have to part company we may as well make it a memorable event, no?' He tilted his head at Cutter John.

That was enough to let my bladder go. It wasn't as if anyone would notice, soaked and reeking as I was. 'C-come now, Maeres, you're joking? I owe you money. Who'll pay if I … if I don't pay?' He needed me.

'Well Jalan, the thing is, I don't think you *can* pay. If a man owes me a thousand crowns he's in trouble. If he owes me a hundred thousand, then I'm in trouble. And you, Jalan, owe me eight hundred and six crowns, less some small amount for your amusing Norseman. All of which makes you a small fish that can neither swallow me nor feed me.'

'But … I can pay. I'm the Red Queen's grandson. I'm good for the debt!'

'One of many, Jalan. Too much of any denomination waters down the currency. I'd call "prince" an over-valued commodity in Red March these days.'

'But—' I'd always known Maeres Allus for a businessman, a cruel and implacable one of a certainty, but sane. Now it seemed that madness might be spiralling behind those dark little eyes. Too much blood in the water for the shark in him to lie quiet any longer. 'But … what good would killing me do?' He couldn't ever tell anyone. My death wouldn't serve him.

'You died in the fire, Prince Jalan. Everyone knows that. None of my doing. And if a hint of a rumour floated behind Vermillion's conversations. A whisper that you might have died elsewhere, in even less pleasant circumstances, over a matter of debt … well then, what new heights might my clients reach in their efforts not to disappoint me in future? Might there be ladies of ill-repute who would recognize Cutter's latest bracelet and spread the word as they spread their legs?' He glanced toward Cutter John who raised his right arm. Dry bands of pale gristle encircled the limb, rustling against each other, dozens of them, starting at his wrist and reaching past his elbow.

'Wh-what?' I didn't understand what I was seeing, or perhaps some part of my brain was sensibly stopping me from understanding.

Cutter John circled his own lips with one finger. The trophies along his arm whispered together as he did so.

'Open wide.' His voice slithered as though he were something not human.

'You shouldn't have come here, Jalan.' Maeres spoke into the silence of my horror. 'It's unfortunate that you can't un-see my poppies, but the world is full of misfortunes.' He stepped back to stand by Daveet at the door – the lights flickering across his face providing the only animation, a shadow smile there and gone, there and gone.

'No!' For the first time ever I wanted Maeres Allus not to leave. Anything was better than being abandoned to Cutter John. 'No! I won't talk! I won't. Not ever.' I put some anger into it – who would believe a sobbing promise of strength? 'I'm saying nothing!' I strained at my ropes, rocking the table back against its legs. 'Pull my nails. I won't talk. Hot pincers won't drag it from me.'

'How about cold ones?' Cutter John raised the short handled iron pincers he'd been holding all this time in his other hand.

I roared at them then, thrashing, useless in the ropes. If one of Maeres's men hadn't been standing on the table legs it would have tipped forward and I'd have gone face first into the flagstones, which bad as it sounds would have been far less painful than what Cutter John had in mind for me. I was still roaring and screaming, working my way rapidly toward sobbing and pleading, when a hot wet something splattered across my face. It was enough to make me unscrew my eyes and pause my bellowing. Although I'd stopped yelling the din was no less deafening, only now it wasn't me screaming. I'd drowned out the crash of the door bursting open, too far gone in my terror to notice it. Only Daveet stood there now, framed in the doorway. He turned as I watched, slit from collarbone to hip, spilling coils of his guts to the floor. To the left a large figure moved at the edge of my vision. As I turned my head the action shifted behind the table, another scream and a pale arm wrapped in bracelets made from men's lips landed on the flag-stones about a foot from where Daveet's head hit the stone when he tripped on his intestines. And in one moment there was silence. Not a sound save for men shouting far down the corridor outside, echoey in the distance. Daveet appeared to have knocked himself out or died from sudden blood loss. If Cutter John missed his arm he wasn't complaining. I could see one more of Maeres's men lying dead. The others might be dead behind me or taking a leaf from my book and sprinting for the hills. If I hadn't been tied to the damn table I would have been overtaking them on the way to the aforementioned hills myself.

Snorri Snagason stepped into view. 'You!' he said.

The hooded robe he'd been wearing when I ran into him was half-torn from his shoulders, blood splattered his chest and arms, and dripped from the scarlet sword in his fist. More of the stuff ran down his face from a shallow cut on his forehead. It wouldn't be hard to mistake him for a demon risen from hell. In fact in the flickering light, blood clad and with battle in his eyes, it was quite hard not to.

'You?' The eloquence Snorri had demonstrated in Grandmother's throne room had wholly abandoned him.

He reached for me, and I shrank back, but not far because that fucking table was in the way. As that big hand came close I felt a tingle on my cheekbones, my lips, forehead, like pins and needles, a kind of pressure building. He felt it too – I saw his eyes widen. The direction that had led me, the destination that had drawn me on … it was him. The same force had led Snorri here, and set him among Maeres' men. We both recognized it now.

The Norseman slowed his hand, fingers an inch or two from my neck. The skin there buzzed, almost crackling with … something. He stopped, not wanting to find out what would happen if he touched me skin to skin. The hand withdrew, returned full of knife, and before I could squeal he set to cutting my bonds.

'You're coming with me. We can sort this out somewhere else.'

Abandoning me amongst loops of sliced rope, Snorri returned to the doorway, pausing only to stamp on someone's neck. Not Maeres's unfortunately. He ducked his head through, pulling back immediately, a quick bobbing motion. Something hissed past the entrance, several somethings.

'Crossbows.' Snorri spat on Daveet's corpse. 'I hate bowmen.' A glance back at me. 'Grab a sword.'

'A sword?' The man clearly thought he was still in the wilds among the overly hairy folk of the North. I cast my eye across the carnage, looking behind the table. Cutter John lay sprawled, the stump of his arm barely pulsing, an ugly wound on his forehead. No sign of Maeres. I couldn't imagine how he'd escaped.

None of them had any weapon more offensive than a six-inch knife, carrying anything larger within the city walls just wasn't worth the trouble from town-laws. I took the dagger and kicked Cutter John in the head a few times. It really hurt my toes, but I felt it a price worth paying.

I hobbled back round the table holding my new weapon and earned a withering look from the Norseman. He picked up the door. 'Catch.' I didn't quite manage it. Whilst I hopped on my good foot, clutching my face and swearing nasally, Snorri quickly hacked the legs from the table and bearing it like a huge shield, advanced toward the corridor. 'Get my back!'

The fear of being left behind, and finding myself in Maeres Allus's clutches again, spurred me into action. With some effort I picked up the door and together we propelled our shields into the corridor before stepping between them. Crossbow bolts thudded into both immediately, iron heads splintering partway through.

'Which direc—' Snorri was already too far away to hear me even if he hadn't been shouting his battle cry. He'd stormed off down the corridor behind me. I followed as best I could, trying to hold the door across my back while I stumbled after him, keeping my head down, reaching over my shoulders to hold the door in place. Shouts and screams ahead indicated that Snorri had got to grips with his hated bowmen but by the time I got there it was all blood and pieces. The main difficulty lay in not slipping over in the gore. Several more bolts hit the boards across my back with powerful thuds, and another skipped between my ankles, letting me know that I'd left a gap. Fortunately I had just ten yards to reach the exit. With the door scraping the floor behind me, and just the tips of my fingers exposed, I broke out into the night air. My traditional moment of triumph at escaping yet again was curtailed by a muscular arm that reached from the darkness and yanked me to one side.

'I've got a boat,' Snorri growled. Normally when you say someone growled something it's just a turn of phrase, but Snorri really put something feral into his words.

'What?' I shook my arm free, or he let it go, a mutual thing, neither of us liking the burning needling sensation where his fingers gripped me.

'I've got a boat.'

'Of course you do, you're a Viking.' Everything

seemed rather surreal. Perhaps I'd been hit in the face one too many times since Alain made a grab for me in the opera house only an hour or two earlier.

Snorri shook his head. 'Follow. Quick!'

He took off into the night. The sounds of men approaching down the warehouse corridor convinced me to give chase. We crossed a wide space stacked with barrels and crates, passed dozens of hanging nets, the sails of riverboats poking up above the river wall beside us. By moonlight we crossed a quay and descended stone steps to the water where a rowing boat lay tied to one of the great iron rings set into the wall.

'You've got a boat,' I said.

'I was a mile downstream, free and clear.' Snorri tossed his sword in, stepped in after it, and picked up an oar. 'Something happened to me.' He paused staring for a moment into his hand though it held only darkness. 'Something … I was getting sick.' He sat and took both oars. 'I knew I had to come back – knew the direction. And then I found you.'

I stood on the step. The Silent Sister's magic had done this. I knew it. The crack had run through us, the light through me, the dark through him, and as Snorri and I separated some arcane force tried to rejoin those two lines, the dark and the light. We had drawn away from each other, the river carrying Snorri west, and those hidden fissures started to open again, started to tear us both apart just so they could be free to run together once more. I remembered what happened when they joined. It wasn't pretty.

'Don't stand there like an idiot. Loose the rope and get in.'

'I...' The rowing boat moved as the current tried to wrest it from its mooring. 'It doesn't look very stable.' I've always viewed boats as a thin plank between me and drowning. As a sensible fellow I'd never entrusted my safety to one before, and close up they looked even more dangerous. The dark river slurped at the oars as if hungry.

Snorri nodded up at the steps, up toward the gap in the river wall they led to. 'In a moment a man with a crossbow will stand there and convince you that waiting was a mistake.'

I hopped in sharp enough at that, Snorri deploying his weight to stop me turning the boat over before I managed to sit down.

'The rope?' he asked. Shouts rang out above us, drawing closer.

I pulled my knife, slashed the rope, nearly lost the knife in the river, tried again, and finally sawed at the strands until at last they gave and we were off. The current took us and the wall vanished into the gloom along with all sight of land.

7

'Are you going to be sick *again*?'

'Has the river stopped flowing?' I asked.

Snorri snorted.

'Then yes.' I demonstrated, adding another streak of colour into the dark waters of the Seleen. 'If God had intended men to go on water he would have given them…' I felt too ill for wit and hung limp over the side of the boat, scowling at the grey dawn coming up behind us. '… given them whatever it is you need for that kind of thing.'

'A messiah who walked on water to show you all it was exactly where God intended men to go?' Snorri shook that big chiselled head of his. 'My people have older learning than the White Christ brought. Aegir owns the sea and he doesn't intend that we go onto it. But we do even so.' He rumbled through a bar of song, '*Undoreth, we. Battle-born. Raise hammer, raise axe, at our war-shout gods tremble.*' He rowed on, humming his tuneless tunes.

95

My nose hurt like buggery, I felt cold, most of me ached, and when I did manage to sniff through my twice-broken snout I could tell that I still smelled only slightly less bad than that dung heap which saved my life.

'My—' I fell silent. My pronunciation sounded comical, 'my nose' would have come out 'by dose'. And although I had every right to complain, it might rile the Norseman, and it doesn't pay to rile the kind of man who can jump on a bear to escape a fight-pit. Especially if it was you who put him in that pit in the first place. As my father would say, 'To err is human, to forgive is divine ... but I'm only a cardinal and cardinals are human, so rather than forgiving you I'm going to err toward beating you with this stick.' Snorri didn't look the forgiving kind either. I settled for another groan.

'What?' He looked up from his rowing. I remembered the remarkable number of bodies he left in his wake coming in and out of Maeres's poppy-farm to get me. All with his weapon hand badly injured.

'Nothing.'

We rowed on through the garden lands of Red March. Well Snorri rowed on, and I lay moaning. In truth he mostly steered us and the Seleen did the rest. Where his right hand clutched the oar he left it bloodstained.

Scenery passed, green and monotonous, and I slumped over the side, muttering complaints and vomiting sporadically. I also wondered about how I'd moved from waking beside the naked delights of Lisa DeVeer to sharing a shitty rowing boat with a huge Norse maniac all in the space between two dawns.

'Will we have trouble?'

'Huh?' I looked up from my misery.

Snorri tilted his head downstream to where several rickety wooden quays reached out into the river, a number of fishing boats tied up at them. Men moved here and there along the shore checking fish traps, mending nets.

'Why should—' I remembered that Snorri was very far from home in lands he had probably only glimpsed from the back of a slave wagon. 'No,' I said.

He grunted and set an oar to angle us into deeper water where the current ran fastest. Perhaps in the fjords of the frozen North any passing stranger was game and you became a stranger ten yards from your doorstep. Red March enjoyed ways a touch more civilized. Due in no small part to the fact that my grandmother would have anyone who broke the bigger laws nailed to a tree.

We carried on past various nameless hamlets and small towns that probably had names but held too few distractions ever to make me care what those names were. Occasionally a field hand would rest fingers on hoe, chin on knuckles, and watch us pass with the same vacancy that the cows used. Urchins chased us from time to time, following along the banks for a hundred yards, some throwing stones, others baring their grimy arses in mock-threat. Washerwomen splatting husbands' second smocks against flat stones would raise their heads and hoot appreciatively at the Norseman as he flexed his arms against the oars. And finally on a lonely stretch of river where the Seleen explored her floodplain, with the sun hot and high, Snorri deflected us beneath the broad fringe of a great willow. The tree leaned out across lazy waters at the extreme of a long meander and encompassed us beneath its canopy.

'So,' he said, and the prow bumped up against the willow trunk. The hilt of his sword slipped from the bench and clunked on the planks, blade dark with dried blood.

'Look … about the fight-pits … I—' Much of the morning my maiden voyage had been spent planning the smooth denials that now refused to stutter from my tongue. In between the vomiting and the complaining I'd been rehearsing my lies, but under the focused gaze of a man who appeared to be more than ready to slaughter his way through any situation, I ran out of the spit required for falsehoods. For a moment I saw him staring up at Maeres from the pit floor. 'Bring a bigger bear?' I remembered the smile he had on him. A snort of laughter broke out of me and, fuck, yes it hurt. 'Who even says that kind of thing?'

Snorri grinned. 'The first one was too small.'

'And the last one was just right?' I shook my head,

trying not to laugh again. 'You beat Goldilocks to the punchline by one bear.'

He frowned at that. 'Goldilocks?'

'Never mind. Never mind. And Cutter John!' I sucked in a huge breath and surrendered to the joy of the memory, of escaping that goggle-eyed demon and his knives. The mirth bubbled out of me. I doubled up, gasping with hysterical laughter, beating the side of the boat to stop myself. 'Ah, Jesu! You took the bastard's arm off.'

Snorri shrugged, holding back another grin. 'Must have got in my way. Once your Red Queen changed her mind about letting me go she put her city at war with me.'

'The Red Qu—' I caught myself. I'd said it was the queen's order that he be sent to the pits. He had no reason not to believe me. Remembering the anchor points of any web of lies is part of the basics when practising to deceive. Normally I'm world class at it. I blamed my failure on extenuating circumstances. I had, after all, escaped from Alain DeVeer's frying pan into the fire of the opera only to plunge from that into some-thing even worse. 'Yes. That was … harsh of her. But my grandmother is known as somewhat of a tyrant.'

'Your grandmother?' Snorri raised his eyebrows.

'Um.' Shit. He hadn't even noticed me in the throne room and now he knew me for a prince, a prize hostage. 'I'm a very distant grandson. Hardly related at all really.'

I raised a hand to my nose. All that laughing had left it pulsing with hurt.

'Take a breath.' Snorri leaned forward.

'What?'

He snaked out an arm, catching my head from behind, fingers like iron rods. For a second I thought he was just going to crush my skull, but then his other hand blocked my view and the world exploded in white agony. Pinching the bridge of my nose with finger and thumb he pulled and twisted. Something grated and if I'd had anything left to vomit I'd have filled the boat with it.

'There.' He released me. 'Fixed.'

I hollered out the pain and surprise in one burst, trailing into coherence at the end of it, '...Jesu fuck me with a cross!' The words came out clear, the nasal twang gone. I couldn't bring myself to say thank you though, so I said, 'Ouch.'

Snorri leaned back, arms resting on the sides of the boat. 'You were in the throne room then? You must have heard the tale we prisoners were brought in to tell.'

'Well, yes...' Certainly bits of it.

'So you'll know where I'm headed then,' Snorri said.

'South?' I ventured.

He looked puzzled at that. 'I'd be more at ease going by sea but that may be hard to arrange. It might be I need to trek north through Rhone and Renar and Ancrath and Conaught.'

'Well, of course...' I had no idea what he was talking

about. If there had been a word of truth in his story he wouldn't want to go back. And his itinerary sounded like the trek from hell. Rhone, our uncouth neighbour to the north, was always a place best avoided. I'd yet to meet a Rhonish man I'd piss on if he were on fire. Renar I'd never heard of. Ancrath was a murky kingdom on the edge of a swamp and full of murderous inbreds, and Conaught lay so far away there was bound to be something wrong with it. 'I wish you luck of the journey, Snagason, wherever you're bound.' I held my hand out for a manly clasping, a prelude to a parting of our ways.

'I'm going north. Home to rescue my wife, my family...' He paused for a moment, pressing his lips tight, then shook off the emotion. 'And it went poorly the first time I left you behind,' Snorri said. He eyed my outstretched hand with a measure of suspicion and extended his own cautiously. 'You didn't feel that just now?' He touched his own nose with his other hand.

'Course I bloody felt it!' It was quite possibly the most painful thing I'd ever experienced, and that from someone who learned the hard way not to jump into the saddle from a bedroom window.

He brought his hand closer to mine and a pressure built against my skin, all pins and needles and fire. Closer still, and more slow, and my hand started to pale, almost to glow from within, while his darkened. With an inch between our extended palms it seemed that a cold fire ran through my veins, my hand brighter than the day, his looking as if it had been dipped in dark waters, stained with blackest ink that collected in every crease and filled each pore. His veins ran black while mine burned, darkness bled from his skin like mist, a wisp of pale flame ghosted across my knuckles. Snorri met my gaze, his teeth gritted against a pain that mirrored mine. Eyes which had been blue were now holes into some inner night.

I gave one of those yelps that I always hope will go unnoticed and whipped my hand away. 'Damnation!' I shook it, trying to shake the pain out, and watched as it shaded back to normality. 'That bloody witch! Point taken. We won't shake on it.' I gestured to a gravel beach on the outer edge of the meander. 'You can drop me off there. I'll find my own way back.'

Snorri shook his head, eyes returning to blue. 'It was worse when we got too far apart. Didn't you notice?'

'I was rather distracted,' I said. 'But, yes, I do recall some problems.'

'What witch?'

'What?'

'You said "bloody witch". What witch?'

'Oh nothing, I—' I remembered the fight-pits. Lying to the man on this point would probably be a mistake. I was lying out of habit in any case. Better to tell him. It might be that his heathen ways could lead to some kind of solution. 'You met her. Well, you saw her in the Red Queen's throne room.'

'The old völva?' Snorri asked.

'The old what?'

'That crone at the Red Queen's side. She's the witch you're talking about?'

'Yes. The Silent Sister everyone calls her. Most don't see her though.'

Snorri spat into the water. The current took it away in a series of lazy swirls. 'I know this name, the Silent Sister. The völvas of the North speak it, but not loudly.'

'Well now you've seen her.' I still wondered at that. Perhaps the fact that we could both see her had something to do with her magic failing to destroy us. 'She set a spell that was to kill everyone at the opera I went to last night.'

'Opera?' he asked.

'Better not to know. In any event, I escaped the spell, but when I forced my way through, something broke, a crack ran after me. Two cracks, inter-woven, one dark, one light. When you grabbed hold of me the crack caught up and ran through both of us. And somehow stopped.'

'And when we separate?'

'The dark fissure ran through you, the light through me. When we pull them apart it seems the cracks try to tear free, to rejoin.'

'And when they join?' Snorri asked.

I shrugged. 'It's bad. Worse than opera.' However nonchalant my words might be though, and despite the heat of the day, my blood ran colder than the river.

Snorri set his jaw in that way I'd come to recognize as consideration. His hands quietly strangled the oars. 'So your grandmother sentences me to the fight-pit and then you bring down her witch's curse on me?'

'I didn't seek you out!' The nonchalance I'd been striving for wouldn't come from a dry mouth. 'You stopped me dead in the street, remember?' I regretted using the word 'dead' immediately.

'You're a man of honour,' he said to no one in particular. I looked for the smirk and found nothing but sincerity. If he was acting then I needed lessons from the same place he'd got his. I concluded that he was reminding himself of his duties, which seemed odd in a Viking whose duties traditionally extended to remembering to pillage before raping, or the other way around. 'You're a man of honour.' Louder this time, looking right at me. Where the hell he got that idea I had no notion.

'Yes,' I lied.

'We should settle this like men.' Absolutely the last words I wanted to hear.

'Here's the thing, Snorri.' I eyed the various escape options open to me. I could jump overboard. Unfortunately I'd always viewed boats as a thin plank between me and drowning, and swimming as the same again but without the plank. The tree offered the next best option, but willow fronds aren't climbing material unless you happen to be a squirrel. I selected the last option. 'What's that over there?' I pointed to a spot on the riverbank behind

the Norseman. He didn't so much as turn his head. *Shit.*
'Ah, my mistake.' And that was me out of options. 'As
I was saying. The thing is. The thing. Well, honestly.' The
thing had to be something. 'Um. I'm afraid that when
I kill you the crack will run out of you just the same as
it would if we got too far apart. And then – boom – a
split second later I'd be too far apart. So tempting as it
is to pit my princely fighting skills against those of a …
what is your rank? I never found out.'

'*Hauldr.* I own my land, ten acres from Uulisk shore
to the ridge top.'

'So as much as it tempts me to break with societal
rules and pit the arm of a prince of Red March against
a … a hauldr, I'm concerned that I wouldn't survive your
death.' From his frown I could see that it might be a risk
he was willing to take if no better alternative were on
offer, so to forestall him I added, 'But as it happens I've
always had a hankering to visit the North myself and see
firsthand just how reaving is done. And besides, my
grandmother worries so about these dead ghost-men of
yours. It would put her heart at ease to have the business
sorted out. So I'd best come with you.'

'I mean to travel fast.' Snorri's frown deepened. 'I've
left it too long already and the distance is great. And be
warned: it will be a bloody business when I get there.
Slow me down and … but you were moving pretty quick
when you crashed into me.' His brow smoothed, thun-
derclouds clearing, and that smile lit him up, half-wild,

half-friendly, and all dangerous. 'Besides, you'll know more about the terrain than me. Tell me about the men of Rhone.'

And just like that we were travelling companions. I'd bound myself to his quest for rescue and vengeance in some distant land. Hopefully it wouldn't take too long. Snorri could save his family then slaughter his enemies to the last man, necromancer and corpse monster, and that would be that. I'm good at self-deception but I couldn't manage to make the plan sound like anything other than a suicidal nightmare. Still, the icy North was a long way off – plenty of opportunity to break the spell that bound us together and run away home.

Snorri took up the oars again, paused, then, 'Stand a moment.'

'Really?'

He nodded. I've good balance on a horse and none at all on water. Even so, not wanting to fall out with the man within moments of our new understanding, I got to my feet, arms out to steady myself. He tipped the boat, a sharp deliberate move, and I pitched into the river, grasping desperately at willow twigs as a man about to drown will clutch at straws.

Above the splashing I could hear Snorri having a good old laugh to himself. He was saying something too, '...clean ... together...' But I could only catch the odd word since drowning is a noisy business. Eventually, when I'd given up trying to save myself by swallowing all the water and had slipped below the surface for the third and final time, he snagged my waistcoat and hauled me back in with distressing ease. I lay in the bottom flopping about like a fish and retching up enough of the river almost to swamp the boat.

'Bastard!' My first coherent word before I remembered quite how big and murderous he was.

'I couldn't have you come to the North smelling like that!' Snorri laughed and steered back out into the current, the willow trailing its fingers over us in regret. 'And how can a man not know how to swim? Madness!'

8

The river took us to the sea. A journey of two days. We slept by the banks, far enough back to escape the worst of the mosquitoes. Snorri laughed at my complaints. 'In the northern summer the biters are so thick in the air they cast a shadow.'

'Probably why you're all so pale,' I said. 'No tan and blood loss.'

I found sleep elusive. The hard ground didn't help, nor did the itchiness of anything I used to soften it. The whole business reminded me of the misery that had been the Scorron Campaign two summers earlier. It's true I wasn't there more than three weeks before returning to be feted as the hero of the Aral Pass and to nurse my bad leg, strained in combat, or at least in inadvertently sprinting away from one combat into another. In any event, I lay on the too-hard and too-scratchy ground looking at the stars, with the river whispering in the dark and the bushes alive with things that chirruped and rustled and creaked. I thought then of Lisa DeVeer and suspected that few nights would pass between now and my return to the palace when I wouldn't find occasion to ask myself how I ended up in such straits. And in the smallest hours of the night, feeling deeply sorry for myself, I even found time to wonder again if Lisa and her sisters might have survived the opera. Perhaps Alain had convinced his father to keep them home as punishment for the company they'd been keeping.

'Why don't you sleep, Red March?' Snorri spoke from the darkness.

'We're in Red March, Norseman. It only makes sense to call someone by their place of origin when you're a long way from it. We've been through this.'

'And the sleeping?'

'Women on my mind.'

'Ah.' Enough silence that I thought he'd dropped off, then, 'One in particular?'

'Mostly all of them, and their absence from this riverbank.'

'Better to think of one,' he said.

For the longest time I watched the stars. People say they spin, but I couldn't see it. 'Why are you awake?'

'My hand pains me.'

'A scratch like that? And you a great big Viking?'

'We're made of meat just like other men. This needs cleaning, stitching. Done right and I'll keep the arm. We'll leave the boat when the river widens, then skirt the coast. I'll find someone in Rhone.'

He knew there would be a port at the mouth of the river, but if the Red Queen had marked him for death then it would be madness to go there seeking treatment. The fact that Grandmother had ordered his release and that the port of Marsail was a renowned centre of medicine, with a school that had produced the region's finest doctors for close on three hundred years, I kept to myself. Telling him would unravel my lies and paint me as the architect of his fate. I didn't feel good about it, but better than I would if he decided to trim me with his sword.

I returned to my imaginings of Lisa and her sisters, but in the deepest part of the night it was that fire which lit my dreams, colouring them violet, and I saw through the flames, not the agonies of the dying but two inhuman eyes in the dark slit of a mask. Somehow I'd broken the Silent Sister's spell, escaped the inferno, and borne away part of the magic ... but what else might have escaped and where might it be now? Suddenly each noise in the dark was the slow step of that monster, sniffing me out in the blind night, and despite the heat my sweat lay cold upon me.

Morning struck with the promise of a blazing summer's day. More of a threat than a promise. When you watch from a shaded veranda, sipping iced wine as the Red March summer paints lemons onto garden boughs – that's promise. When you have to toil a whole day in the dust to cover a thumb's distance on the map – that's threat. Snorri scowled at the east, breaking his fast on the last stale remains of the bread he'd stolen in the city. He said little and ate left-handed, his right swelling and red, the skin blistering like that on his shoulders but not burned by the sun.

The river held a brackish air, its banks parting company and surrendering to mud flats. We stood by our boat, the water now fifty yards off, sucked back by tidal flow.

'Marsail.' I pointed to a haze on the horizon, a smear of darkness against the wrinkled blue where the distant sea crowded beneath the sky.

'Big.' Snorri shook his head. He went to the rowing boat and made a slight bow, muttering. Some damn heathen prayer no doubt, as if the thing needed thanking for not drowning us. Finished at last, he turned and gestured for me to lead the way. 'Rhone. And by swift roads.'

'They'd be swifter if we had horses.'

Snorri snorted as if offended by the idea. And waited. And waited some more.

'Oh,' I said, and led off, though in truth my expertise ended with the knowledge that Rhone lay north and a little west. I hadn't the least clue about local roads. In fact past Marsail I would struggle to name any of the region's major towns. No doubt Cousin Serah could reel them off pat, her breasts defying gravity all the while, and Cousin Rotus could probably bore a librarian to death with the populace, produce and politics of each settlement down to the last hamlet. My attentions, however, had always been focused closer to home and on less worthy pursuits.

We left the broad strip of cultivated floodplain and climbed by a series of ridges into drier country. Snorri ran with sweat by the time the land levelled out. He seemed to be struggling: perhaps a fever from his wound had its hooks in him. It didn't take long for the sun to become a burden. After a mile or three of trekking through stony valleys and rough scrub, and with my feet already sore, my boots already too tight, I returned to the subject of horses.

'You know what would be good? Horses. That's what.'

'Norsemen sail. We don't ride.' Snorri looked embarrassed or perhaps it was the sunburn.

'Don't or can't?'

He shrugged. 'How hard can it be? You hold the reins and go forward. If you find us horses we'll ride.' His expression darkened. 'I need to be back there. I'll sleep in the saddle if a horse will get me north before Sven Broke-Oar finishes his work in the Bitter Ice.'

It occurred to me then that the Norseman truly hoped his family might yet survive. He thought this a rescue mission rather than just some matter of revenge. That made it even worse. Revenge is a business of calculation, best served cold. Rescue holds more of sacrifice, suicidal danger, and all manner of other madness that should have me running in the opposite direction. It made breaking whatever spell bound us an even higher priority. By the look of his hand, which seemed worse from one hour to the next, with the infection's spread now marked by a darkening of the veins, any spell-breaking would need to be done soon. Otherwise he might die on me and then my dire predictions concerning the consequence for one of us if the other expired might soon be put to the test. I'd made the claim as a lie, but it had felt true when I spoke it.

We trudged on through the heat of the day, forcing a path through a dry and airless conifer forest. Hours later the trees released us, scratched, and sticky with both sap and sweat. As luck would have it we spilled from the forest's margins directly onto a broad track punctuated with remnants of ancient paving.

'Good.' Snorri nodded, clearing the side ditch with one stride. 'I'd thought you lost back there.'

'Lost?' I feigned hurt. 'Every prince should know his realm like the back of … of…' A glimpsed memory of Lisa DeVeer's back came to me, the pattern of freckles, the knobs of her spine casting shadows in lamplight as she bent to some sweet task. 'Of something familiar.'

The road wound up to a plateau where innumerable springs chuckled from the eastern hills along stony beds and the land returned to cultivation. Olive groves, tobacco, cornfields. Here and there a lone farmhouse or collection of stone huts, slate-roofed and huddled together for protection.

Our first encounter was an elderly man driving a still more venerable donkey ahead of him with flicks of his switch. Two huge panniers of what looked to be sticks almost engulfed the beast.

'Horse?' Snorri muttered the suggestion as we approached.

'Please.'

'It's got four legs. That's better than two.'

'We'll find something more sturdy. And not some plough-horse either. Something fitting.'

'And fast,' said Snorri The donkey ignored us, and the old fellow paid scarcely more attention, as if he encountered giant Vikings and ragged princes every day. 'Ayuh.' And he was past.

Snorri pursed his blistered lips and walked on, until a hundred yards further down the road something stopped him in his tracks. 'That,' he said, looking down, 'is the biggest pile of dung I've seen in my life.'

'Oh, I don't know,' I said. 'I've seen bigger.' In fact I'd fallen in bigger, but as this appeared to have dropped from the behind of a single beast I had to agree that it was pretty damned impressive. You could have heaped a score of dinner plates with it if one were so inclined. 'It's big, but I have seen the like before. In fact it's quite possible that we'll soon have something in common.'

114

'Yes?'

'It's quite possible, my friend, that we'll both have had our lives saved by a big pile of shit.' I turned toward the retreating old man. 'Hey!' Hollered down the road at his back. 'Where's the circus?'

The ancient didn't pause but simply extended a bony arm toward an olive-studded ridge to the south.

'Circus?' Snorri asked, still transfixed by the dung pile.

'You're about to see an elephant, my friend!'

'And this effelant will cure my poisoned hand?' He held the offending article up for inspection, wincing as he did so.

'Best place to get wounds seen to outside a battle-hospital! These people juggle axes and burning brands. They swing from trapezes and walk on ropes. There's not a circus in the Broken Empire that doesn't have half a dozen people who can stitch wounds and with luck a herbman for other ailments.'

A sidetrack turned from the road a quarter of a mile on and led toward the ridge. It bore evidence of recent traffic, and large traffic at that – the hard-baked ground scarred by wheel ruts, the overhanging trees sporting fresh-broken branches. On cresting the ridge we could see an encampment ahead: three large circles of wagons, a scattering of tents. Not a circus set up to entertain but one on the move and enjoying a rest-stop. A dry-stone wall enclosed the field where the travellers had camped.

Such walls were common in the region, being as much a place to put the ubiquitous chunks of rock that the soil yielded as they were a means of containing livestock or marking boundaries. A sour-looking grey-haired dwarf sat guarding the three-barred gate at the field's entrance.

'We already got a strong man.' He eyed Snorri with a short-sighted squint and spat an impressive amount of phlegm into the dust. The dwarf was the kind that resemble common men in the size of their head and hands, but whose torsos have been concertinaed into too small a space, their legs left thin and bandy. He sat on the wall cleaning his fingernails with a knife, and his expression announced him more than happy to stick strangers with it.

'Come now! You'll offend Sally!' I remonstrated. 'If you've already got a bearded lady I can scarce believe she's as comely as this young wench.'

That got the dwarf's attention. 'Well hello, Sally! Gretcho Marlinki at your service!'

I could feel Snorri looming behind me in the way that suggested my head might get twisted off in short order. The little fellow jumped from the wall, leered up at Snorri and unhitched the gate.

'In you go. Blue tent inside the circle on the left. Ask for Taproot.'

I led on in. Thankful that Gretcho was too short to pinch Snorri's backside or we might be owing this Taproot for a new midget.

'Sally?' the Norseman rumbled behind me.

'Work with me,' I said.

'No.'

Most of the circus folk were probably sleeping out the noon heat but a fair number worked at assorted tasks around the wagons. Repairs to wheels and tack, tending animals, stitching canvas, a pretty girl practising a pirouette, a heavily-pregnant woman tattooing the back of a shirtless man, the inevitable juggler throwing things up and catching them.

'Utter waste of time.' I nodded at the juggler.

'I love jugglers!' Snorri's grin showed white teeth in the cropped blackness of his beard.

'God! You're probably the sort that likes clowns!'

The grin broadened as if the mere mention of clowns was hilarious. I hung my head. 'Come on.'

We passed a stone-walled well beyond which, away down the slope, a scattering of headstones stood. Clearly generations had used this place to pause their travels. And some had never left.

The blue tent, though faded almost to grey, proved easy to spot. Larger and cleaner and taller than the rest it stood centrally and sported a battered painted sign outside on two posts.

'Dr Taproot's famous circus
Lions, ~~tigers~~, bears, oh my!
By appointment to the Imperial Court of Vyene'

117

Since knocking is difficult with tents I leaned in toward the entrance flap and coughed.

'...couldn't just paint some stripes on the lion?'

'......'

'Well, no ... but you could wash them off again before that?'

'......'

'No, it's been a while since I last gave a lion a bath but—'

My second, more theatrical cough, caught their attention.

'Come!'

And so I ducked, Snorri ducked lower, and we went in.

It took a moment for my eyes to adjust to the blue gloom within the tent. Dr Taproot I judged to be the skinny figure seated behind a desk, and the more substantial form leaning over at him, hands planted firmly on the papers between them, must be the fellow objecting to bathing lions.

'Ah!' said the seated figure. 'Prince Jalan Kendeth and Snorri ver Snagason! Welcome to my abode. Welcome!'

'How the hell—' I caught myself. It was good that he knew me. I'd been wondering how to convince anyone that I was a prince.

'Oh, I'm Dr Taproot, I know everything, my prince. Watch me!'

Snorri passed me and snagged an empty chair. 'Word gets around. Especially about princes.' He seemed less impressed than I was.

'Watch me!' Taproot nodded, bird-like, a sharp-featured head on a thin neck. 'Message-riders on the Lexicon Road carry gossip along with their sealed scrolls. And what a story! Did you truly jump an arctic bear, Mr Snagason? Do you think you could jump one of ours? The pay's good. Oh, but you've injured your hand. A hook-knife I hear? Watch me!' Taproot's chatter came so rapid and moved so fast that without your full attention the flow of it would hypnotize you.

'Yes, the hand.' I latched onto that. 'Have you a chirurgeon? We're light on funds—' Snorri scowled at that, '—but I'm good for credit. The royal coffers underwrite my purse.'

Dr Taproot offered a knowing smile. 'Your debts are the stuff of legend, my prince.' He raised his hands as if trying to frame the enormity of them. 'But fear not, I am a civilized man. We of the circus do not let a wounded traveller go untended! I shall have our sweet Varga see to the matter presently. A drink perhaps?' He reached for the desk drawer. 'You may go, Walldecker. He shooed away the scar-faced man who had stood in silent disapproval through our conversation. 'Stripes! Watch me! Good ones. Serra has black paint. See Serra.' Returning his attention to me he fished out a dark glass bottle, small enough for poison. 'I have a little rum. Ancient stuff from

119

the wreck of the Hunter Moon, dredged up by scallop men off the Andoran coast. Try it.' He magicked three tiny silver cups into being. 'I'm always one to sit and chat. It's my burden. Watch me. Gossip runs through my veins and I must feed the habit. Tell me, my prince, is your grandmother well? How is her heart?'

'Well she's got one, I suppose.' I didn't like the man's impertinence. And his rum smelled like the stuff the herbmen rub on chill-blains. Now that I had a chair under my arse and a tent about me and my name and station recognized I began to feel a little more my old self. I sipped his rum and damned him for it. 'Don't know anything about how it's ticking though.' The idea of my grandmother suffering any frailties of the flesh seemed alien to me. She'd been carved from bedrock and would outlast us all. That's how Father had it.

'And your elder brothers, Martus isn't it, and Darin? Martus must be coming up to twenty-seven now? Yes, in two weeks?'

'Um.' Damned if I knew their birthdays. 'They're well. Martus misses the cavalry of course, but at least he got a damn chance at it.'

'Of course, of course.' Taproot's hands were never still, plucking at the air as if snatching scraps of information from it.

'And your great-uncle? He was never a well man.'

'Garyus?' Nobody knew about the old man. I didn't even know he was a relative for the first few years after I took to visiting him in the tower where they kept him. I climbed in through the window so nobody saw me come and go. It was Great-uncle Garyus who gave me Mother's picture in a locket. I must have been about five or six. Yes, not long after the Silent Sister touched me. The blind-eye woman I called her back then. Gave me a lepsy. Fits and shakes for a month. I found old Garyus by accident when I was small, clambered in before I noticed the room wasn't empty. He scared me, hunched on his sickbed, twisted in ways a man shouldn't twist. Not evil, but wrong. I feared catching it, that's the honest truth. And he knew it. Good at knowing a man's mind was Garyus, and a boy's.

'I was born this way,' he had said. Not unkindly, though I had stared at him as if he were a sin. His skull bulged as if over-filled, misshapen, like a potato.

He lay propped up in his bed, a jug and goblet on the table close at hand, lit by dusty sunlight. No one came to him in this high tower, just a nurse to clean him, and sometimes a small boy clambering through the window.

'Born broken.' Each sentence gasped between breaths. 'I had a twin, and when we were birthed they had to break us apart. A boy and a girl, the first joined twins that weren't both boys or both girls, they say. They broke us apart. But we didn't break even. And I got … this.' He lifted a twisted arm as if doing so were a labour of Hercules.

He had reached out from his sheets – a grave shroud, that's what those sheets made me think – he had reached out and given me that locket, a cheap enough thing but with my mother's picture inside, so fine and real you'd swear she was looking right at you.

'Garyus,' Taproot agreed, breaking a silence I'd not noticed.

I shook off the memory. 'He's well enough.' None of your damn business, I wanted to say, but when you're far from home and poorer than church mice it pays to curb your pride. Garyus was the only one of them I had time for really. He couldn't leave his room. Not unless someone carried him. So I visited. Possibly it was the only duty I'd ever kept. 'Well enough.'

'Good, good.' Taproot wrung his hands, squeezing out his approval, a pale wrestling of too-long fingers. 'And Hauldr Snagason, how stands the North?'

'Cold, and too far away.' Snorri set down his empty cup, licking his teeth.

'And the Uuliskind? Still fair? Red goats for milk on the Scraa slopes, black for wool on the Nfflr ridges?'

Snorri narrowed his eyes at the circus-master, perhaps wondering if the man was reading his mind. 'Have you … *been* to the Uuliskind? The Undoreth would remember a circus, and yet I'd never heard of an effelant before today. And that reminds me. I must see this beast.'

Taproot smiled, narrow, even teeth behind thin lips. He uncorked the rum again, moving to replenish our cups. 'My apologies, but you can see how it is with me. I pry. I question. I devour travellers' tales. I store each snippet of information.' He tapped his forehead. 'Here. Watch me!'

Snorri took the little cup before him in his good hand. 'Aye. Red goats on the Scraa, black on the Nfflr. Though none to tend them most like. The black ships came. Dead things from the Drowned Isles. Sven Broke-Oar brought this doom upon us.'

'Ah.' Taproot nodded, steepled his fingers, pursed his lips. 'He of the Hardassa. A hard man. Not a good one I fear.' Pale hands shaped his opinion. 'Perhaps the goats, the red and the black, have new herders now. Boys of the Hardassa.'

Snorri drank off his rum. He set his poisoned hand upon the table, the knife-wound a livid and weeping slot between the tendons. 'Mend me and you'll have to change that tale, Circus-master.'

'Of a certainty.' A quick smile lit Taproot's face. 'Kill or cure, that's our motto. Watch me.' His hands moved around the Norseman's, never touching, but framing it, following the line of the incision.

'Go to Varga's wagon. The smallest, with a red circle upon the side. In the grouping close to the gate. Varga can clean a wound, pack it, stitch it. Best poultices you ever saw. Watch me! Even a sour wound may yield to them.'

Snorri stood and I rose to go with him. It had become a habit.

'You might stay, Prince Jalan?' Taproot did not look up but something in his tone kept me there.

'I'll find you later,' I told Snorri. 'Save you the shame of weeping before me when this Varga sets to his work. And watch out for that effelant. They're green and like the taste of Vikings.'

Snorri answered with a snort and ducked out into the blinding brightness of the day.

'A fierce man. Watch me!' Taproot eyed the tent-flap, swaying in Snorri's wake. 'Tell me, Prince. How is it that you travel together? I didn't imagine you as one for the hardships of the road. How is it that the Norseman hasn't killed you for the pits or that you haven't fled for your home comforts?'

'I'll have you know I learned a sight more about hardship in the Scorron Heights than—' Something in the slow regret with which Taproot shook his head took the bluster from my sails. I feared if I mentioned my heroism at the Aral Pass he might laugh at me. That's the trouble with men that know too much. A sigh escaped me. 'In truth? We're bound by some enchantment. A damned inconvenient one. You wouldn't happen to have a—'

'A mind-sworn wizard? A hidden hand that might separate you? Watch me! If I had such this circus would be a gold mine and me the richest of all rich men.'

I had expected him to laugh at my claims of enchantment, so to be taken seriously was a relief, though hearing how hard it might prove to undo the magic was less pleasing.

Taproot finished his drink and put the little bottle back in the drawer. 'Speaking of rich men, you might care to know about one Maeres Allus.'

'You know—' Of course he knew. Taproot knew of the Red Queen's secret brother, too broken for the throne. He knew about goats chewing on the slopes of distant fjords. He would hardly not know of Vermillion's greatest crime lord.

'Watch me.' Taproot laid a slim finger alongside his slim nose. 'Maeres has secrets that even *I* don't know. And he is not best pleased with you.'

'Perhaps a journey north would be good for my health in any case then,' I said.

'True enough.' And Taproot waved me out, fluttering his hands as if I were a tumbler come to beg more sawdust for the centre ring and not a prince of Red March. I let him do it too, for when a man who knows too much knows not to waste his manners on you it's best to be moving on.

9

The pregnant woman, done for the moment with her tattooing, led me to Varga's wagon. She waddled ahead of me looking fit to pop at each step, though she said her time lay weeks ahead.

'Daisy,' she told me. Her name, or perhaps what she planned to call the whelp if it proved female. I hadn't been listening too hard. We'd passed a wagon where a woman in tight silks sat with her ankles crossed behind her head, and my attention had wandered.

'Daisy? A fine name.' For a cow.

I spotted the elephant, corralled by a fence that it could swat aside, tethered to a thick post by a length of chain. A number of circus men, showing off lean and muscular bodies, lounged around a bar made of two barrels and a plank, watching the elephant and whatever else might pass. Behind them a well-laden beer-wagon provided shade. Circuses always came amply provisioned with ale for the audience. I guess it must be easier to impress a drunken crowd.

Further on we passed a shabby tent stitched with moon and stars, symbols of the horoscope dotted among the faded heavens. An ancient sat outside on a three-legged stool, snaggle-toothed and liver-spotted.

'Cross my palm, stranger.' I couldn't tell if the creature was man or woman.

'Don't humour her.' Daisy increased the speed of her waddle. 'Cracked, that one is. Everything's doom and gloom. Drives the punters away.'

'You're quarry.' The old woman called after us, then coughed as if a lung had burst. 'Quarry.' I couldn't tell which of us she'd aimed the words at.

'Save it for the peasants,' I called back, but it left a chill. Always does. I expect that's why prophecy sells.

We walked on until the hacking cough faded behind us. I laughed, but in truth I *had* felt hunted since we left the city. Though by what I couldn't say. More than the Silent Sister, more than Maeres' terrors even, it was the eyes behind that enamel mask that watched me from my quiet moments. Just a glimpse at the opera, just a glancing encounter, and yet it haunted me.

'Varga.' Daisy pointed at a wagon much as Taproot described. She drew in a deep sigh and started to waddle off, back the way we'd come. I offered no thanks, distracted now by the small crowd of scantily-clad young women clustered around the open end of Varga's wagon. Dancers, by the litheness of them and the snatches of silk they wore.

'Ladies.' I approached, flashing them my best smile. It seemed however that a tall blonde prince of Red March was less interesting than a huge dark Norseman bulging with muscle as if his arms and legs had been crammed with boulders. The girls pointed into the gloom beneath the awning, giggling behind their hands, exchanging appreciative whispers. I leaned around and stepped up onto the buckboard.

'You didn't need to take his shirt off,' I said. 'It's his hand that needs removing.'

Snorri offered me a dark look from the sloping couch he'd been arrayed upon. He really did have an alarming topology, his stomach ridged and divided by muscle, his chest and arms bursting with power, veins writhing across him to feed blood into the engines of his strength, all tensed now against the pain Varga's investigations were causing him.

'You're blocking my light.' Varga turned from the messy work in hand. She was a woman of middling years, tending to grey, with a homely face of the kind that supports compassion and disapproval in equal measures.

'Will he live?' I asked, my interest genuine though self-motivated.

'It's a nasty wound. The tendons are undamaged but one of the small bones of the hand has been broken, others displaced. It will heal, but slowly, and only if the infection is contained.'

'A yes then?'

'Probably.'

'Good news!' I turned back to the girls outside. 'That calls for a celebration. Let me buy you fine ladies a drink and we can afford my companion a little privacy.' I stepped down amongst them. They smelled of grease-paint, cheap perfume, sweat. All good. 'I'm Jalan, but you can call me Prince Jal.'

At last my old enchantment started to work. Even the sculpted magnificence of Snorri ver Snagason had a hard time competing with the magic word 'prince'.

'Cherri. Please to meet you, your highness.' Some doubt in her voice but I could tell she wanted to believe her prince had come.

I took her hand. 'Enchanted.' And she smiled up at me, pretty enough with a snub nose and wicked eyes, fair hair, curled, streaked with blonde.

'Lula,' said her friend, a petite wench with short black hair, pale despite the summer, and sculpted as if to satisfy a schoolboy's dream.

With Cherri on one arm, Lula on the other, and a clutch of dancers following behind, I led the way back to the beer-wagon. Snorri let out a sharp gasp from under Varga's awning. And life was good.

The afternoon passed in a pleasant haze and parted me from the company of my last silver crowns. The circus men proved remarkably tolerant of my pawing their women, as did the circus women, and we sprawled on cushions before the beer-wagon drinking wine from amphoras, growing louder as the shadows lengthened.

Annoyingly, the dancers kept asking me about Snorri as if the hero of Aral in their midst wasn't quite enough to hold their attention.

'Is he a chieftain?' Lula asked.

'He's so big.' A red-haired beauty named Florence.

'What's his name?' A tall Nuban girl with copper loops through her ears and a mouth made for kissing. 'How is he called?'

'Snorri,' I said. 'It means wife-beater.'

'No?' Cherri all round-eyed.

'Yes!' I faked sadness. 'Terrible temper – if a woman upsets him he cuts her face.' I drew a line across my cheek with one finger.

'What's the North like?' The Nuban girl wasn't so easily deflected.

I tipped the amphora to my mouth, gulping wine while I held my hand out at a steep angle. 'Like that.' I wiped my lips. 'Only icy. All the northmen slip to the coasts where they congregate in miserable villages smelling of fish. It gets very crowded. Every now and then a bunch more come sliding down from the hills on their arses and the only place for the ones closest to the shore is on a boat. And off they sail.' I mimicked a ship's progression across the waves. I gave Lula my amphora. 'Those horns on their helms?' I made myself two horns, a hand to each side of my head. 'Cuckold's horns. The

130

new arrivals are bouncing abed with the wives left behind. Terrible place. Don't ever go there.'

A small girl and small boy came out to sing for us, a remarkable pair with high clear voices, and even the elephant moved closer to listen. I had to shush Cherri to hear uninterrupted when the children sang 'High-John', but I let her giggle through their rendition of 'Boogie Bugle'. Without warning their voices soared into an aria that drew me back to Father's opera. They sang it sweeter and with more heart, but still the world seemed to close about me and I heard those screams in the fire. And beneath those screams my memory ran a deeper sound, something heard but at the time not understood, a different kind of howling. The roar of something angry rather than scared.

'Enough.' I threw a cushion at them. It missed and the elephant snagged it from the ground. 'Scram!' The little girl's lip wobbled for an instant and they both fled.

'…"give them what they want, dears". That's all he says. With Taproot it's all hips and tits. There's no art in it for him.' Lula looked up at me over her clay goblet, seeking affirmation.

'Well, to be fair, Lula, you *are* mostly hips and tits,' I said, a slight slur to my words now.

They giggled at that. The combination of a title and freely-flowing wine will have people laughing at anything you offer up as funny, and I've never once complained about it. A sharp oath rang out from the direction of

Varga's wagon. I put an arm around Cherri, another around Lula, and drew them close. Enjoy the world while you can, I say. A shallow enough philosophy by which to live, but shallow is what I've got. Besides, deep is apt to drown you.

The first evening stars watched me being taken for a guided tour of the dancers' wagon, supported on either side by Cherri and Lula, though who was doing the most supporting would be hard to say. We tumbled inside and strange to say that in the dark nearly everything we wanted to do required three pairs of hands.

In the dead of night a commotion interrupted proceedings within the dancers' wagon. At first we ignored it. Cherri was making her own commotion and I was doing my best to help. We ignored it until the wagon's rocking stopped dead, moving Cherri to draw breath. Until that point I'd heard little above her exclamations and the creaking of axles and supports.

'Jalan!' Snorri's voice.

I stuck my head out through the flaps into the starlight, far from pleased. Snorri stood with one thick arm gripping the wagon bed, arresting its motion. 'Come.'

I hadn't the breath to tell him that's what I was trying to do. Instead I slipped out, lacing up what needed to be laced. 'Yes?' Not keeping the temper from my voice.

'Come.' He led off between the nearest wagons. I could hear weeping now. Wailing.

Snorri followed the field's gradient, letting it lead us a little way out from the wagons and carts encircling Taproot's tent. Here several dozen of the circus folk huddled before a bright fire.

'A child died.' Snorri set a hand to my shoulder as if offering comfort. 'Unborn.'

'The pregnant woman?' A foolish thing to say – it had to be a pregnant woman. Daisy, I remembered her name.

'The babe's buried.' He nodded to a low mound in the dirt out past the fire, snug between two old grave markers. 'We should show our respects.'

I sighed. No more fun for Jal tonight. I felt sorry for the woman of course, but the troubles of people I don't know never reached that far into me. My father, in one of his rare moments of coherence, declared it to be a symptom of youth. My youth at least. He called on God to visit compassion upon me as a burden to be carried in later life. I was just impressed that he'd noticed me or my ways this once, and of course it's always nice for a cardinal to remember to call on God every now and then.

We sat a little apart from the main group, though close enough to feel the fire's heat.

'How's the hand?' I asked.

'Hurts more, feels better.' He held out the appendage in question and flexed it slightly, wincing. 'She removed a lot of the poison.'

133

Thankfully Snorri omitted greater detail. Some folk will seek to entertain you with the gory details of their ailments. My brother Martus would have painted each glistening drop of pus for me in one of his woe-is-me monologues for which the only remedy is a swift exit.

The night held enough warmth, combined with the fire and my recent exercise, to leave me pleasantly sleepy. I lay back on the ground, without complaint for the hardness of it or the dust in my hair. For a moment or three I watched the stars and listened to the soft weeping. I yawned once and sleep took me.

Strange dreams hunted me that night. I wandered an empty circus haunted by the memory of the eyes behind that porcelain mask but finding only the dancers, each sobbing in her bed, and breaking into bright fragments as I reached to touch them. Cherri was there, Lula too, and they broke together, speaking a single word. *Quarry.* The night fractured, cracks running through tents, wheels, barrels; an elephant bellowed unseen in the darkness. My head filled with light until at last I opened my eyes to keep from being blinded.

Nothing! Just Snorri's bulk, seated beside me, knees drawn up. The fire had fallen to red embers. The circus folk gone to their beds taking their sorrow with them. No sound but for the whirr and chirp of insects. My heart's pounding slowed. My head continued to ache as if it were cracked through, but the blame for that lay with a quart of wine gulped down in the heat of the day.

'It's a thing to make the world weep, the loss of a baby.' Snorri's rumble almost too deep to make sense of. 'In Asgard Odin sees it and his unblinking eye blinks.'

I thought it best not to mention that technically a one-eyed god can only wink. 'All deaths are sad.' It seemed like a good thing to say.

'Most of what a man is has been written by the time his beard starts to prickle. A babe is made of maybes. There are few crimes worse than the ending of something before its time.'

Once more I bit my tongue and made no complaint that this was exactly what he had accomplished at the dancers' wagon earlier. It wasn't tact that held me silent so much as the desire not to get my nose broken yet again. 'I suppose some sorrows can only truly touch a parent.' I'd heard that somewhere. I think perhaps Cousin Serah had said it at her little brother's funeral. I recall all the grey heads nodding and exchanging words about her. She probably fished it from a book. Even at fourteen she was scheming for Grandmother's approval. And her throne.

'When you become a father it changes you,' Snorri spoke toward the fire's glow. 'You see the world in new ways. Those who are not changed were not properly men to begin with.'

I wondered if he were drunk. That's when I tend to speak profundities to the night. Then I remembered that Snorri was a father. I couldn't picture it. Wee ones bouncing on his knee. Tiny hands tugging at his battle braids. Even so, I understood his mood better now I could guess what he might see among the embers. Not this unborn child, but his own children, fleeing horrors in the snows. The thing that drew him North against all sense.

'Why are you still here?' I asked him.

'Why are you?'

'I passed out.' Mild exasperation coloured my voice. 'I'm not sitting vigil! In fact, now that I'm awake I'll find a better place to sleep.' Perhaps one with more interesting contours and a snub nose. I stood, aching along my side, and stamped to get some life back into my legs.

'Can't you feel it?' he said as I turned to go.

'No.' But I could. Something wrong. A sense of brokenness. 'No, I can't.' Even so, I didn't step away.

With one breath the insects ceased their chorus. A deep noise reached me, rumbling up through the soles of my feet, still bare. 'Ah hell.' My hands trembled, with the customary terror of the unknown, but also with something new, as if they were full of fractured light.

'Hel's about right.' Snorri stood too. He had his stolen sword in hand. Had he held it all the time or gone to fetch it while I slept? He pointed the blade toward the baby's grave. The noise had come from there. A burrowing, a scratching, the sound of roots pushing blind paths through soil. The headstone to the left tilted as the ground sunk beneath it. The one to the right toppled forward, coming to rest with a dull thud. All around the child's mound the soil cracked and heaved.

'We should run,' I said, having not the least idea why I was not already doing so. The word 'quarry' repeated over and again behind my eyes. 'What's happening down there?' Perhaps a sick fascination kept me there, or the immobility of the rabbit beneath hawk's claws.

'Something is being built,' Snorri said. 'When the unborn return they take what they need.'

'Return?' I sometimes ask even when I really don't want to hear the answer. Bad habit.

'It's hard for the unborn to return. They are not like fallen that rise from the deaths of men.' Snorri began to swing his sword left-handed, blurring it around him in fire-glow glimmers, making the air sigh. 'They are uncommon things. The world must be cracked open to admit them and their strength is surpassing. The Dead King must want us very badly indeed.'

I found my feet at that and ran. As the ground heaved and some dark thing rose, shedding dry clods of earth and shrugging off gravestones, I raced five full steps before tripping on an abandoned wine jug – possibly one I'd brought with me – and sprawling face first.

I rolled and saw, edged by the radiance of stars and the faint light of embers, a horror still knee-deep in the earth and yet towering above the Norseman, a thin thing of old bones, tattered cloth, encompassing arms with talons built from too many finger-bones to count. And about these dry and creaking remains, something wet and glistening, some vital freshness running along a golem built of long-dead grave litter, knitting this to that, bleeding quickness into the construct.

Snorri bellowed his wordless challenge but he held his ground: no charging against this foe. It overreached him by a yard and more. The dead thing extended an arm, talons questing for Snorri, then snatched the hand back. A grey skull, filled with new wetness, craned down on a neck that was once the entirety of a man's spine. And it spoke! Though it had no lungs for bellows, no tongue to shape its words, it spoke. The unborn's voice squealed like tooth on tooth, grated bone on bone, and somehow carried meaning.

'Red Queen,' it said.

Snorri took a pace back, sword raised. The skull swivelled and those awful wet pits that served for eyes found me, barefoot, weaponless, and scooting away on my backside.

'Red Queen.'

'Not me! Never heard of her.' The strength went from my legs and I stopped trying to escape, although it was the only thing I wanted to do.

'You carry her purpose,' it said. 'And her sister's magic.' It swung its head toward Snorri and I could breathe again. 'Or you,' it said. 'And you?' The unborn returned its gaze to me, now on my feet. Under that inspection I started to die once more. 'Hidden?' The skull tilted in query. 'How is it hidden?'

Snorri attacked. As the unborn's attention pinned me he leapt forward, sword in his off-hand, and hacked at its narrow waist of bone, dry skin, old gristle. The thing lurched alarmingly, recovered itself and slapped him away with a lazy backhand that lifted the Norseman from his feet and sent him sprawling, his sword flying past me, lost in the night.

Battles are all about strategy, and strategy pivots on priorities. Since my priorities were Prince Jalan, Prince Jalan, and Prince Jalan, with 'looking good' a distant fourth, I took the opportunity to resume running away. I find that the main thing about success is the ability to act in the moment. A hero attacks in the moment, a good coward runs in it. The rest of the world waits for the next moment and ends up as crow food.

I made it ten yards before nearly slicing my foot off on Snorri's sword, which had ended its trajectory point first. Nine inches of the blade lay buried in the hard earth, the rest jutting up dangerously. Even in my terror I recognized the value in three foot of cold steel and paused to haul it clear. The action spun me around and I could see the unborn looming over Snorri, ghostly in the starlight. Weaponless, he refused to run and held what looked to be a gravestone above him like a shield. The stone shattered beneath the unborn's descending fist. A thin hand of many bones encircled the Viking's waist – in another moment he would be gutted or have his head torn off.

Something huge and dark and wailing like a banshee swept toward me from the camp. Rather than be flattened beneath its ground-shaking bulk I ran, selecting the direction I happened to be pointing in. I needed all my speed to keep clear of the massive pounding feet behind me, and screaming, I charged directly at the unborn, desperately trying to find the extra legs to veer to the side.

At the last moment, with pants-wetting haste, I dived left, narrowly missing Snorri, rolled, rolled again, and somehow avoided skewering myself on the sword. I rose to watch in astonishment as Cherri bounced past atop an enraged elephant. The unborn went down with the sound of a hundred wet sticks snapping, ground to pieces beneath blunt feet the size of bucklers. The elephant thundered on into the night, still bearing the girl, and trumpeting loud enough to wake the dead, if any had still been asleep.

Snorri landed close by with a thud that made me wince. He lay without moving for five beats of my heart then levered himself up on thick arms. I held his sword out to him and he took it.

'My thanks.'

'Least I could do.'

'Not every man would run off to recover a comrade's weapon then charge an unborn single-handed.' He got to his feet with a groan and stared off into the night. 'Elephant, eh?'

'Yup.'

'And a woman.' He went to the fire and started kicking embers over the unborn's remains.

'Yup.'

Circus folk were streaming toward us now, dark shapes against the night.

'Think she'll be all right?'

I considered the matter, having spent some time between her thighs myself. 'I'm more worried for the elephant.'

10

By first light the circus camp had been half–packed away. None of them held any desire to remain and I expected Dr Taproot would have to find a new stopover the next time they passed this way.

Cherri returned with the elephant as I waited for Snorri by the field gate. The dwarf had returned to his post and we were both trying to cheat each other at cards. I stood and waved. Cherri must have had to wait for dawn to find her way back. She looked worn out, her face paints smeared, dark streaks around her eyes. A gentleman pretends not to notice these things and I hastened over to catch her as she slipped from the creature's back. She felt good enough in my arms to make me regret the need to leave.

'My thanks, lady.' I set her down and backed away from the elephant's questing trunk. The beast made me seven kinds of nervous and smelled of farms to boot. 'Good boy!' I slapped its wrinkled flanks and dodged toward the gate again.

'She's a girl,' Cherri said. 'Nelly.'

'Ah. What else could she be called?' Saved by a dancing girl on a female elephant. I wouldn't be adding that to the tale of the Hero of Aral Pass.

Cherri took the elephant's halter rope and led her off into the camp, shooting me one last wicked glance that made me wish for another night, at the least.

Snorri arrived moments later. 'Hell of a thing.' He shook his head. 'Elephants!'

'You could take one home,' I suggested.

'We have mammoths! Even bigger, but in fur coats. I've never seen one, but I want to now.' He looked back into the camp. 'I paid my respects to the mother. There's nothing to say at such times but it's better to say something than nothing even so.' He slapped an overly familiar hand to my shoulder. 'We should go, Jal, our welcome's worn thin. Unless you wanted to barter for horses?'

'With what?' I pulled out my pockets. 'They sucked me dry.'

Snorri shrugged. 'That locket you're always fiddling with would buy ten horses. Fine ones.'

'I hardly ever touch it.' I blinked at him, telling myself to remember his sharp eyes. I didn't recall looking at it once since we met. 'And it's of no value.' I doubted the old man on the road would have swapped his donkey for the locket and a silver crown.

The Norseman shrugged and made to leave. I nudged his arm as he passed. 'Taproot's come to see us off.'

Dr Taproot approached. He looked uncomfortable in the open air, removed from his desk. Two men flanked him, leading their horses, a pale gelding and a dun mare. The first the lion tamer we met in the blueness of Taproot's tent, the second a hugely-built man who was obviously occupying the strongman job that Snorri had initially been taken to be an applicant for. I wondered if the good doctor was expecting trouble of some kind.

'Taproot.' Snorri inclined his head. The stolen sword hung at his hip now, depending from an arrangement of rope and leather strips.

'Aha! The travellers!' Taproot looked up at his strongman as if weighing him in the balance with Snorri. 'Heading north now. Watch me!'

Neither of us had an answer to that. Taproot continued. 'Dogged by ill-fortune perhaps? The kind of misfortune that fills and empties graves. Watch me!' His hands moved as if performing each task while he described it. 'That would have been valuable information. At yesterday's noon that information would have earned its keep.' The sorrow on his long features seemed almost too perfect, almost caricature. It worried me that I couldn't tell if the baby's death had meant anything to him or not. 'In any case the milk was spilt.' He trailed off then turned to go, but caught himself and spun once more to face us. 'Unborn!' Almost a shout now. 'You bring unborn into the world? How—' He found his control once more and carried on, his voice conversational again. 'This was not well done. Not well done at all. You must go far from here. And fast.' He indicated the two horses and his companions stepped forward holding the reins out toward us. I took the gelding. 'Twenty crowns on your debt slate, my prince.' Taproot inclined his head a fraction. 'I know you will be good for it.'

I looked my steed over, patted his neck, felt the meat over his ribs. A decent enough nag. Snorri stood woodenly beside his as if worried she might bite him.

'My thanks,' I said, and swung up into the saddle. Twenty in gold was a fair enough price. A touch steep, but fair under the circumstances. I felt better, mounted. God gave us horses so we could run away faster.

'Best be quick on your path – you're at the centre of a storm, young prince, and no mistake.' Taproot nodded as if it had been me talking and him agreeing. 'There are hands aplenty in this matter, many fingers in the pot. All stirring. A grey hand behind you, a black hand in your path. Scratch a little deeper though and you might find blue behind the black, red behind the grey. And deeper still? Does it go deeper? Who knows? Not this old circus-keeper. Perhaps everything goes deeper than deep, deep without end. But I'm old, my eyes grow dim, I only see so far.'

'Um.' It seemed the only sensible reply to his outpouring of nonsense. I could see now who trained up the circus fortune-teller.

145

Taproot nodded at my wisdom. 'Let us part friends, Prince Jalan. The Kendeths have been a force for good in Red March.' He held out his thin hand and I took it quick enough for I guessed it pained him to keep it still so long. 'There!' he said. 'I was sorry to hear of your mother's death, my prince.' I released his hand. 'Too young – too young she was for the assassin's blade.'

I blinked at him, nodded, and nudged my new horse on down the lane. 'Come on, Snorri.' Over my shoulder. 'It's like rowing a boat.'

'I'll walk a little first,' he said, and followed on, leading his nag by the reins.

I'll admit some regret in leaving the circus behind. I liked the people, the air of the place, even on the move. And of course the dancers. Despite that, I had a small smile on my lips. It was good to know that even Taproot's vast stock of information failed him from time to time. My mother died of a flux. I touched the lump made by the locket under my jacket, Mother's picture inside. A flux. The contact made me uneasy all of a sudden, my smile gone.

We got to the main road and turned back along the path we'd first taken, guided by directions from the midget card-sharp at the gate. Neither of us spoke until we reached the pile of elephant dung that had first alerted me to the circus' proximity.

'So, you can't ride then?'

'Never tried,' he said.

'You've never even sat on a horse?' It seemed hard to credit.

'I've eaten plenty,' he said.

'That doesn't help.'

'How difficult can it be?' he asked, making no move to find out.

'Less difficult than jumping onto bears and off again, I suspect. Luckily I'm the finest horseman in Red March and a great teacher.' I pointed at the stirrup. 'Put your foot in there. Not the foot you first thought of – the other one. Step up, and don't fall off.'

Lessons continued slowly and to his credit Snagason did not fall off. I did worry that he might cave in the horse's ribs with those oh-so-muscly legs of his but in the end Snorri and the horse reached an uneasy truce where they both adopted a fixed grin and got on with moving forward.

By the time the sun had passed its zenith I could tell the Norseman was suffering.

'How's the hand?'

'Less painful than the thighs,' he grunted.

'Perhaps if you loosened your grip a little and let the poor horse breathe…'

'Tell me about Rhone,' he said.

I shrugged. We wouldn't reach the border until the next evening and the last mile would suffice to tell him anything worthwhile about the place, but it seemed he needed distraction from his aches and pains.

'Not so much to tell. Awful place. The food's bad, the men surly and ignorant, the women cross-eyed. And they're thieves to a man. If you shake a Rhonish hand, count your fingers afterward.'

'You've never been there, have you?' He shot a narrow look back at me then lurched to keep his place in the saddle.

'Did you not listen to what I said? Why would I go somewhere like that?'

'I don't understand it.' He risked another glance back. 'Rhonish kings founded Red March did they not? Wasn't it the Rhonish who saved you from Scorron invasion? Twice?'

'I hardly think so!' Now he mentioned it though it did trigger a faint memory of too-hot days in the Grey Room with Tutor Marcle. 'I suspect a prince of Red March knows a little more about local history than some … *hauldr* off the frozen slopes of a fjord.' I'll admit to sleeping through most of Marcle's history lessons but I probably would have noticed a thing like that. 'In any event, they're a bad sort.'

To change the topic of conversation, and because every time I glanced back my imagination hid monsters in the shadows, I bought up the topic of pursuit.

'When I ran into you, the fissure, the crack that was chasing me … it came from the Silent Sister's spell.'

'You told me this. The spell she placed to kill everyone at this opera of yours.'

'Well … it would have killed everyone, but I don't think that was the reason she cursed the place. Maybe she wasn't out to destroy us all – maybe she had her target and the rest of us were just in the way. Could whatever she was after have chased us to the circus?'

Snorri raised his brows, then frowned, then shook his head. 'That unborn was new-formed, from Daisy's child. It didn't follow us there.'

That sounded a touch more hopeful. 'But … it didn't just happen by chance, surely? Aren't these things supposed to be very rare? Someone made that happen. Someone trying to kill us.'

'Your Red Queen was gathering tales of the dead. She knows Ragnarok is hard upon us – the last battle is coming. She's drawing her plans against the Dead King and likely he's drawing his plans against her. The Dead King may know about us, he may know we're headed north, dragging the witch's magic with us. He may know we're bound for the Bitter Ice where his dead are gathering. He may want to stop us.'

Whilst I'd successfully steered the conversation away from Rhone Snorri had told me absolutely nothing to ease my mind. I chewed on all that he'd said for the next few miles and very sour it tasted. We were pursued, I knew it, blood to bone. That thing from the opera stalked us, and in running before it we plunged headlong into whatever the Dead King placed in our path.

A day later we met our first examples of the type of Rhonishmen I'd been warning Snorri against. A guard post of five Rhone soldiers attached to a sizeable inn that straddled the border. Red March's own guard post of four men adjoined the opposite end of the inn and the two groups dined together most evenings on opposing sides of a long table through which the border ran, marked across the planks by a line of polished nail heads.

I introduced myself as a down-at-heels nobleman since none of them would recognize a Red March prince and, thinking themselves mocked, would take offence. I suppose I could have held up a gold crown with Grandmother's face on it and remonstrated about the family resemblance, but I didn't have one. Or a silver crown. And the coppers mostly had the Iax Tower on them or King Gholloth who reigned before Grandmother and looked nothing like his daughter or me.

Snorri said little at the inn, his tension clear, worried that word might have been sent to secure the borders against him. We spent the remainder of my coppers on a small meal of cabbage soup and mystery meat before moving on into Rhone, which despite my misgivings, seemed very much like Red March, except that the people tended to roll out their 'r's in an annoying manner.

The first Rhonish town we came to coincided with

our first evening. A sizeable place with the dull but worthy name of Milltown. We rode at gentle pace along the muddy high street, a thoroughfare crowded with traders, travellers, and townsfolk. Snorri reined in toward a smithy open to the street and loud with hammers.

'We should get you a sword, Jal.' He'd taken to calling me Jal, not 'my prince', or 'Prince Jalan', or even 'Jalan', but 'Jal'. I didn't let him know it annoyed me because he'd just do it exactly the same amount of times but with a broader grin. 'How are you with a blade?'

'Better than you are with a horse,' I said.

Snorri snorted and his mare joined in. He'd called her Sleipnir after some heathen nag and they seemed to be getting on despite him riding like a big log stuck on a saddle, and weighing about the same as his steed. He dismounted, the effect not dissimilar to the aforementioned log falling off its perch.

'Show me?' He pulled out his sword and offered it hilt first.

I looked around. 'You can't just go swinging swords on the main street. Someone will lose an eye! And that's only if the town-law aren't on you first.'

Snorri looked puzzled, as if on the ice-coated slopes of the North it would be the most natural thing in the world. 'It's a blacksmith's.' He waved to the ironmongery laid out beside us. 'The smith makes swords. People must try them out here all the time.' The sword hilt poked my way again.

'I doubt it.' Hands firmly on the reins. I nodded down to the display tables – scythe blades, bailing hooks, nails, and other domestic goods were all that lay before me. 'Town this size might have a weapon-smith somewhere. This ain't it though.'

'Ha!' Snorri pointed to a sword hanging up back in the gloom under the awnings. 'Smith!'

The smith emerged at Snorri's booming, a short man, ugly with sweat, thick in the arms of course but with a surprising bookish look to him. 'Evenin'.'

'I'll test that blade.' Snorri pointed to the hanging sword.

'Repairing that for Garson Host,' the smith said. 'Taking out the notches, putting a fresh edge on it. T'aint for sale.'

'Don't humour him.' I nodded my approval at the man.

The smith bit his lip. I'd forgotten that Rhonish men always look for a chance to put a Red March man on his arse, and that common men like nothing better than seeing their betters knocked about. I would have been wiser to hold my tongue. Snorri might be a foreigner but at least he hadn't committed the cardinal sin of being a foreigner from the country next door.

'Don't s'pose Garson'll mind if it's three notches I knock out of the blade or five notches.' The smith went back and reached up to retrieve the sword.

Resigned to my fate, I dismounted and took the hilt

152

that Snorri poked at me again. It happens that I'm not that bad a swordsman when my life's not in danger. In the practice yard with dull blades and sufficient padding I could always hold my own well enough. More than well. But all those lessons went running down one leg on the only day I was ever called on to swing a sword in earnest. Crashing in amongst those Scorron soldiers up in the Aral Pass raw terror washed away all my training in an instant. Those were great big angry men with sharp swords actually wanting to cut pieces off me. It's not until you've seen a red gaping wound and all the complex little bits inside a man all broken up and sliced open, and known that they weren't ever getting back together again, and vomited your last two meals over the rocks … it's not until then that you understand the business of swords properly and, if you're a sensible man you vow to have nothing to do with it ever again. I remember nothing from the battle in the Aral Pass but frozen moments shuffled together – steel flashing, crimson arcs, horrified faces, one man choking on blood as he backed away from me … and the screaming of course. I still hear that today. Everything else about the battle is a blank.

Snorri took his new sword in his uninjured hand and jabbed at me. I swatted it away. He grinned and came at me again. We traded thrusts and parries for a few moments, the clash of steel bringing much of the street to a halt, heads turning our way. Usually strength, while important, is not the prime factor in sword-work, even with heavier blades of the type we employed. The rapier is all about quickness but even the longsword is more about quickness, once you have the strength to swing it, than it is about excess strength. Properly trained, a swordsman will benefit more from a small increase in skill and speed than from a large increase in strength. The sword is, after all, a lever. With Snorri, however, strength *was* a factor. He used basic enough moves but blocking them made my hand hurt and the first blow he put any real effort into nearly took the blade from my grasp. Even so, it was clear quite early on that I had more sword skills in my right hand than the Norseman had in his left.

'Good!' Snorri lowered his weapon. 'You're very good.'

I tried not to simper under his praise. 'Grandmother requires that all her family be well-versed in the arts of war.' Whether they want to be or not… I recalled endless training as a young prince, gripping a wooden blade until I got blisters, and being beaten mercilessly by Martus and Darin who saw it as part of their duties as elder brothers.

'Keep the sword,' Snorri said to me. 'You'll make better use of it than me.'

I pursed my lips. As long as having the sword didn't mean I had to use it then I was fine with the arrangement. I certainly cut a better swagger with a longsword at my hip. I tilted the blade and let the light run along it. At one point the metal had taken on a dark stain. Perhaps where it had bit into the unborn when Snorri swung at its body. I pushed the memory away.

'What about you?' I asked, concerned with my safety rather than his.

'I'll buy a replacement.' He turned to the smith, who made no effort to hide his disappointment at not seeing the giant Viking squash me.

'You can't afford another sword!' He couldn't afford anything – he'd been a prisoner for months until his recent escape. Not the most lucrative of occupations.

'You're right.' Snorri handed the smith's sword back. 'It's not for sale in any case.' He nodded into the forge. 'Do you have a good axe? A war-axe, not something for cutting wood.'

As the smith headed in to delve through his stock, Snorri pulled a pouch on a string from about his neck. I crowded over to see what he had. Silvers! At least five of them.

'Who'd you murder for those?' I frowned, more at the thought of Snorri being richer than me than at the thought of robbery with violence.

'I'm not a thief.' Snorri lowered his brows.

'All right, we'll call it pillage,' I said.

Snorri shrugged. 'Viking lands are poor, the soil sparse, winters cruel. So some do reach out and take from the weak. It's true. We Undoreth, however, prefer to take from the strong – they have better stuff. For each longboat launched against distant shores there are ten and more launched to raid close neighbours. The Viking nations waste their main strength on each other and have always done so.'

'You still haven't answered the question.'

'I took from the strong!' Snorri grinned and reached out to take the axe the smith brought him. 'That big man with Taproot when we left? The Amazing Ronaldo! Circus strongman.' No Norse axe this, but a serviceable footman's axe, a single triangular blade, the ash haft iron-banded and dark with age. The axe was ever a peasant's weapon but this one at least had been made for a peasant signed to some lord's levy. Snorri twirled it, coming alarmingly near to the stock tables, me, and the smith. 'The Amazing Ronaldo made a wager with me regarding a feat of strength. He didn't win. That dwarf said they'll call him the Amazed Ronaldo now!' Snorri hefted the axe and held the blade close to his ear as if listening to it. 'I'll take it.'

'Three.' The smith held up the appropriate number of fingers as if Snorri hadn't been speaking the Empire Tongue.

'He's robbing you! Three silvers for what's basically a farm implement?'

But Snorri paid over the coins. 'Never haggle over a weapon's price. Buy or don't buy. Save the arguments for when you own it!'

'We'll have to get you a sword,' I said. 'When funds allow.'

Snorri shook his head. 'An axe for me. Swords trick you into thinking you can defend. With an axe all you can do is attack. That's what my father named me. Snorri. It means "attack".' He lifted the axe above his head. 'Men think they can defend against me – but when I knock, they open.'

'What the hell *are* unborn?' It took three days for me to ask the question. We'd come riding into the town of Pentacost, covering about a hundred miles from the border. Snorri still rode like a log, but fortunately he also endured like a log and hadn't murmured a word of complaint. Rain found us on the road and poured on our heads for the last ten miles so we came dripping from the stables and now sat at the centre of our own little lakes, steaming gently before an empty hearth in the King of Rhone tavern.

'You don't know?' Snorri raised wet eyebrows at that and plastered his hair further up his forehead, shaking the excess water from his fingers.

'No.' I'm often like that. I have a bad habit of blanking unpleasantness from my mind – something I've done since I was a child. Genuine surprise is a great help when faced with an unwelcome duty. Of course when it's the paying of debts you're forgetting then that can lead to broken fingers. And worse. I guess it's a form of lying – lying to oneself. And I'm very good at falsehoods. They often say the best liars half believe their lies – which makes me the very best because if I repeat a lie often enough I can end up believing it entirely, no half measures involved! 'No, I don't know.'

During our travels, down dull and muddy tracks in the main and past innumerable dreadful little farms, I'd spent a lot of time reminiscing to myself about Cherri's charms and Lula's pleasing sense of exploration, but of the incident at the graves … nothing, just a brief memory of Cherri riding to the rescue. A dozen times I'd pictured the bouncing of her breasts as she'd thundered past. It took a three-hour soaking at the end of a three-day ride for the unborn to at last surface with a nagging insistence that finally made me ask. The truth could scarcely be worse than what my imagination had begun to suggest. I hoped.

'How can you not know?' Snorri demanded. He didn't thump the table but I knew he wanted to.

Snorri proved the ideal travelling companion for a man like me who didn't want to dwell on past mistakes and the like. As far as Snorri was concerned all his goals, ambitions, loves and dangers lay ahead – anything in our wake, Red March and all its peoples, Grandmother and her Silent Sister, the unborn, all these things of the South, were to be left behind, outpaced, no longer of concern or consequence.

'How can you not know?' he repeated.

'How can you not know what eleven times twelve is?'

'A hundred and thirty-two.'

Damn. 'I'm just more interested in the finer things in life, Snorri. If you can't ride it – one way or another – and it doesn't play dice, or cards, or pour from a wine bottle, then I'm really not that bothered. Especially if it's foreign. Or heathen. Or both. But this … thing … said something that worried me.'

'Quarry.' Snorri nodded. 'It was sent after us.'

'By? The other day you said it might be the Dead King, but couldn't it be someone else?' I wanted it to be someone else. 'Some necromancer or—'

'The Dead King is the only one who can send the unborn anywhere. They laugh at necromancers.'

'So. This Dead King. I've heard of him.'

Snorri spread his hands, inviting more of my wisdom on the subject.

'A Brettan lord. Some godless island-hopper from the Drowned Lands.' I sipped my wine. A Rhonish red. Vile stuff, like vinegar and pepper. Other countries wouldn't be so bad if they weren't crammed with foreigners and all their stuff. This Dead King was a case in point.

'That's it? That's what you know about the Dead King? "He's from the Drowned Isles".' It seemed to me that the steam was coming off Snorri rather more rapidly now.

I shrugged. 'So why would some Brettan send a

monster after us? How would he even know? I bet Maeres Allus put him up to it. Six will get you ten. Maeres Allus!'

'Ha!' Snorri drained his ale, wiped the foam from his moustache and made to order another before remembering our poverty. 'That, Jal, would be like a minnow ordering a whale. This Allus of yours is nothing. Get ten miles from the walls of your city and nobody knows the man.'

Prince Jalan, damn it! Ten miles outside my city and nobody knows I'm a prince. 'So why send the monster?'

'The Dead King and this Silent Sister, they're hidden hands, they play a game across the empire, them and others, pushing kings and lords across their board. Who knows what it is they want in the end? Perhaps to remake the empire and give it an emperor with strings by which he can be made to dance, or perhaps to wipe the board clear and start the game anew. In any event the unborn said we carried the Red Queen's purpose, and then it said we carried magic. Which we do.' He jabbed a finger at my shoulder and that unpleasant crackling energy built immediately, remaining until he withdrew the offending digit.

'But that was some kind of accident! We're not on anyone's purpose! Certainly not my grandmother's.' Not unless the Silent Sister's blind eye saw into the future and selected an unlikely chance. An unsettling thought. She was after all, battling the dead, and Snorri was dragging both me and the witch's magic North to where his foes worked alongside corpse-men brought in on the black ships of the Drowned Isles. 'It's just coincidence!'

'So maybe the unborn was wrong, the Dead King too. Maybe we've got them, the Silent Sister, and even your weasel Allus on our trail. Let them come. We'll see how much staying power they have! It's a long way to the North.'

'So,' I said, returning to my theme. 'What the hell is an unborn?' I had a vague memory of the name from before the nightmare journey began. I think the first time I heard it I had rather hoped they were just risen corpses, which given their size would be easily dealt with. Not that I'm keen to stamp on babies, dead or otherwise, but it'd be a sight less dangerous than what happened at the circus. 'And how the hell is an "unborn" a huge grave-horror that takes a charging elephant to put down?'

'Potential, that's what the unborn are. Potential.' Snorri picked up his empty tankard, checked its emptiness and put it down again. 'The one we faced wasn't so dangerous as it had only been dead a few hours. All that potential for growth and change a child has – all that goes to the deadlands if the child dies unborn. It becomes twisted there. Soured. Time passes differently there, nothing stays young. The unborn child's potential is infected with older purpose. There are things that have always been dead, things that dwell in the Land Beyond Death, and it's those ancient evils which ride the unborn potential, possess and haunt it, hungry to be born into the world of life. The longer the unborn stays in the deadlands the more strength it draws from that place but the less it can change, the harder it becomes to return. No common necromancer can summon an unborn. Even the Dead King is said to have been able to bring through only a handful and seldom in a place of his choosing. They serve as his agents, his spies, able to grow into new forms, disguise themselves, walk among men unseen for what they are.'

'New ones are not so dangerous?' I'd latched on to that and repeated it to myself in disbelief whilst the rest of what he said washed over me. 'It would have ripped you in half if not for a handy elephant! Let's hope we don't ever meet another one, because elephants are in short supply around here if you hadn't noticed. Christ!'

Snorri shrugged. 'You did ask.'

'Well I wish I hadn't. Remind me not to in future.' I took a deep draft of my wine, regretting we lacked the wherewithal to buy enough to get roaring drunk and wash the whole business back into convenient amnesia.

'There was *something* there that night at the opera.' I didn't want to speak about it but things could hardly get worse.

'This demon of yours?'

I nodded. 'I broke the spell.' Cracked it. 'Anyway. There was *something* in there with us. A demon. It looked like a man. Or its body did – I never saw the face. But there was something wrong. I know it. I saw it as clear as I see the Silent Sister when everyone else looks past her.'

'An unborn, you think?' Snorri frowned. 'And now you say it's following us?' He shrugged. It's not doing a very good job of catching up. I'd worry more about what lies ahead than behind.'

'Hmmm.' Stop worrying about the frying pan because the fire's hotter? I shrugged but couldn't get those eyes out of my imagination. 'But what if it did catch us up?'

'That would be a bad thing.' Snorri studied his empty tankard again.

I looked out at the rain, and at the sky darkening with a gathering storm, and at the night's approach. Whatever Snorri said, out there something that loved us not was following our trail. *Quarry* it had called us. I picked my wet cloak off the floor, still dripping. 'We should press on to the next town. No point dawdling.' Nice as a night under a good roof would be it was time to be off.

Keep still and your troubles find you. I might not have known much about the unborn, but I sure as hell knew about running!

11

'It's not raining!' I hadn't noticed at first. My body still huddled as if against the downpour, but on this evening, beside the muddy trail and close enough to our fire to make my clothes steam, there wasn't a drop of rain to hide from.

'Stars.' Snorri stabbed a finger at the midnight-blue heavens.

'I remember those.' Not long ago I'd been watching them on a hot night, leaning out from Lisa DeVeer's balcony and lying. 'Those there are the lovers,' I had told her. Pointing at some random piece of sky. 'Roma and Julit. It takes an expert to spot them.'

'And is it good luck when they shine on us?' Lisa had asked, half-disguising a smile that made me think she might well know more astrology than I'd given her credit for.

'Let's find out,' I had said, and reached for her. And they did turn out lucky that night. Even so, I suspected myself a victim of Grandmother's insistence on education

164

for all. It's hard on a chap when the women he wishes to impress are better schooled than he is. I suspect my cousin Serah could name every constellation in the sky while penning a sonnet.

'I wasn't captured on the Uulisk slopes,' Snorri said.

I frowned at the stars trying to make sense of that. 'What?'

'What I told your queen would lead her to believe that I had been.'

'Had been what?' I was still trying to see what this had to do with stars.

'I said Broke-Oar sailed up the Uulisk. That they fell upon us there, that the Undoreth were broken, my children scattered. I said he took me to his ship in chains.'

'Yes,' I said, trying to remember any of it. I recalled the throne room had been stuffy, that my legs ached with standing, that I'd lost a night's sleep and found a hangover. The details of Snorri's tale – not so much – except that I had thought he'd been lying the horns off his Viking hat and now he seemed to be telling me that he really had been.

'When the spring comes to the Uulisk it comes in a rush, ready for war!' Snorri said, and he told his story, with the fire crackling at our backs and our eyes upon the innumerable stars. He spun the tale out into the darkness, weaving pictures with his voice, too bright, too vivid to look away from.

★   ★   ★

He had woken that morning to the groaning of the ice. For days black water had glimmered at the fjord's centre. Today though, today the thaw would come in earnest and with the sun's first touch, reaching down across the high ridges of Uuliskind, the shore ice groaned in protest.

'Get up! Up you big ox!' And Freja pulled the furs from the cot, letting cold air nip at his flesh. Snorri groaned as the ice had groaned. Some forces of nature cannot be resisted. Outside, the ice grumbled and surrendered to the authority of the spring thaw, inside a husband gave way before a mother ready to sweep away a whole winter's worth of filth and to throw the shutters wide. Neither were to be withstood.

Snorri reached for his shirt and breeches, yawning wide enough to crack his jaw. Freja worked around him, twisting aside with practised ease when his hands sought her hips.

'You behave, Snorri ver Snagason.' She started to lift the bed-skins and tug out the heather beneath. 'There's those pens want fixing on the Pel slope. Spring'll have the he-goats nosing around the she-goats.'

'This he-goat wants his she-goat.' Snorri snorted, but he stood and made for the door. Freja was right, as always. The fences wouldn't keep kids in or wolves out. Not as they stood. Not how the winter had left them. He took his iron-toothed saw from the wall. 'Ver Magson will have staves. I'll promise him a barrel of salted hake.'

'You'll promise him half a barrel, and check the timber first,' Freja said.

Snorri shrugged and kept his mouth pressed closed on a smile. He took a roll of seal hide, his steel knife, a whetstone. 'Where are the children?'

'Karl's off string-fishing with the Magson boy. Emy went out to look for her peg doll, and Egil—' Freja toed a lump in the bed furs up against the wall, '—Egil is still sleeping and needs to wake up!' Her voice rose into a command and the lump shifted, muttering some complaint, a shock of red hair now just visible at the far end of the furs.

Snorri tugged on his boots, took his sheepskin from the hook, patted his battleaxe secured high above the lintel, and pushed open the door. The cold hit him at once, but it lacked its winter bite – this was a wet cold and, soon enough, spring would wrestle it round to mild.

The rocky slope ran from his doorstep past a half dozen other stone-built huts to the Uulisk's ice-locked shore. The fishing boats slouched in their winter berths, cradled in timber above the worse of the snow. Eight quays led out over the ice, strutting on pine legs, planking warped by too many harsh seasons. The town had been named for them, Eight Quays, back in an age when eight was a number to boast of. Einhaur six miles seaward had twenty and more, but Einhaur had been nothing but ice and rock when Snorri's grandfather's grandfather had settled the shore at Eight Quays.

A small figure was making its way out along the longest of those quays as Snorri watched.

'Emy!' Snorri's shout had heads thrusting from doorways, window hides lifting. The little girl almost fell from the long-quay in shock, which had been precisely the threat that had scared the shout out of him in the first place. But she caught herself after jolting forward, and hung to an upright, little fingers clutching the icy timber, white hair falling across her face and reaching for the dark waters a couple of feet below. One slip and the fjord would swallow her, the cold stealing both breath and strength.

Snorri dropped his gear and ran out along long-quay, sure footed, stepping where it would bear his weight and losing no time over the choices. He'd run the long-quay all his life.

'Fool girl! You know you're not to—' Fear made his voice harsh as he fell to his knees and scooped Emy into his arms. He bit back the anger. 'You could have fallen, Einmyria!' A child raised to the Undoreth should have more sense, even at five. He held her tight to his chest, still careful not to crush her, his heart hammering. Emy had been a babe at her mother's breast when Jarl Torsteff led the Undoreth against Hoddof of Iron Tors. At no point in that battle – not charging the shield wall, not wet with Edric ver Magson's blood, not pinned by stockade timber with two men of Iron Tors approaching – had Snorri known fear such as that which seized him seeing his own child hanging over dark waters.

Snorri held Emy away from him. 'What were you doing?' Soft now, almost beseeching.

Emy bit her lip, struggling to hold back the tears filling her eyes – the same cornflower-blue as her mother's. 'Peggy's in the water.'

'Peggy?' Snorri tried to recall a child of that name. He knew all the children by sight of course but … it came to him, a wash of relief erasing any exasperation. 'Your doll? You're out here looking for a peg doll you lost before the snows?'

Emy nodded, still close to tears. 'You find her! You find her, Papi.'

'I don't— She's lost, Einmyria.'

'You can find her. You can.'

'Some lost things can be found again and some can't.' He broke off his explanation, seeing in his daughter's eyes the exact moment that a child first understands there are limits on what her parents can do, rather than just limits on what they choose to do. He knelt before her in a moment's silence, somewhat less than he had been just seconds before, and Emy a half-step closer to the woman she would one day become.

'Come on.' He stood, lifting her. 'Back to your mama.' And he walked back, careful now, watching the planks, placing each foot with precision. Carrying Emy up the slope, Snorri echoed with an old pain, the hurt of every parent separated from their child, whether by a sudden slip into deep and hungry water, or by slow steps along divergent paths bound for the future.

They came that night.

Snorri had often said that Freja saved his life. She took from him the rage that had forged his skill with axe and spear, setting in its place new passions. He said she had given him purpose where all he had before was confusion that he hid, as most young men do, behind an illusion of action. Perhaps she saved his life again that night, some dream-murmured warning thinning his sleep.

What woke him Snorri couldn't say. He lay in the dark and the warmth of his covers, Freja close enough to touch but not touching. For long moments he heard only the sound of her breathing and the creak of ice reforming. He had no concern over attack – the jarls had settled the worst of their squabbles, for the now. In any case only a fool would risk a raid with the season barely starting to turn.

Snorri set a hand to the smoothness of Freja's hip. She muttered some sleepy rejection. He pinched.

'Bear?' she asked. Sometimes a white bear would nose around, take a goat. The best thing to do was to let it. His father advised 'never eat a white bear's liver'. As a boy Snorri had asked why, were they poisonous? 'Yes,' his father had said, 'but the main reason is that if you try to, the bear will be busy eating yours, and he has bigger teeth.'

'Maybe.' *Not a bear.* Where his surety came from Snorri didn't know.

He slid from the furs and the cold gripped him. Clad only in skin, he took down his axe, Hel. His father had given him the weapon, a single broad blade, half-moon cutting edge. 'This blade is the start of a journey,' his father had said. 'It has sent many men to Hel, and it will send her more souls before its time is done.' With the axe in his hand Snorri felt clothed, the cold laying no finger upon him for fear he might hack it off.

Someone stumbled outside, close by the hut, yet not so close that it left no room for doubt. 'That you, Haggerson? Taking a piss on the wrong ground?' Sometimes Haggerson would drink with Magson and Anulf the Ship then stumble off in search of home – lost even though he had but forty huts to choose from.

 A soft but penetrating cry went up, almost the call of a loon, but not quite and in any case the birds were silent before the ice left. Snorri slipped the latch, set the ball of his foot to the timber, and kicked his door open as hard as he could. Someone howled in pain and staggered back. Snorri barrelled through, into a moonless night pierced by lantern-light, more lanterns being unhooded by the moment. Snow lay thick on the ground. It fell in fat and heavy flakes: spring snow, not the tiny crystals of winter. Snorri's bare feet nearly slid from beneath him but he kept his balance, swung, and sunk his axe into the spine of the man still clutching his face after kissing the door. A savage tug ripped the blade free of the man's lower back as he collapsed.

'Raid!' Snorri bellowed it. 'To arms!'.

Lower down the slope a fire struggled to keep burning on the turf roof of a hut closer to shore. Dark shapes hurried past amid white flurries, caught in the glow for a moment, then swallowed by the night once more. Foreigners then: Vikings might set torch to thatch when raiding in warmer climes, but none of them would waste time on that in the North.

Figures converged on Snorri, three rounding the hut, half-running, one tripping over the log stack. Others came up the slope. Smaller, scrawny shapes that made no sense to the eye. Snorri rushed the closest trio. Darkness, flame, and shadow offered little chance to pick out the glimmer of weapons and defend himself. Snorri made no attempt at it, relying instead on the logic that says if you kill your foe immediately you have no need of shield or armour, no need to parry or to evade. He swung, double-handed, arms extended, body turning with the blow. Hel sheared through the first man's head, hit the second in the shoulder and buried deep enough to leave his arm swinging on threads. Snorri reversed his turn, feeling but not seeing the hot spray of blood across his shoulders as he spun. The rotation brought him level with the third man, rising with an oath among the scattered logs. Snorri's shin caught the man's face, his momentum wrenched Hel free and he brought the axe down, overhead, as he had so many times before in this very spot – a different axe, splitting logs for the fire. The result was much the same.

Something hissed past his ear. Cries and screams went up across Eight Quays now, some terrified, some the terminal sounds men make when wounded beyond repair. He could hear Freja shouting at the children inside the hut, getting them to stand behind her by the stone hearth. Something sharp struck him between the shoulders, not hard, but sharp. He turned, sighting figures atop Hender's hut, straddling the roof, dislodging the snow to fall in miniature avalanches, some kind of sticks in their hands… A dart struck him in the shoulder, no longer than his finger. He pulled at it, running for the Hender's doorway where he would be out of sight from the roof. The dart resisted, its barbs hooked deep in his flesh, and yet there was no pain, just a numbness. Snorri ripped the thing free, careless of the damage.

Hender's door hung from one leather hinge, men in black rags huddled over something at the far end of the main chamber, hinted at by the glow of a dying fire. The place stank of rot, so bad it made Snorri's eyes sting, rotten meat and an acrid bog stench. Dark footprints marked the floor around a pool of blood before the hearth.

A roar from behind brought Snorri twisting back to

173

the scene outside. Before Magson's hut Olaaf Magson laid around him with the broadsword his father won from a Conaught prince. His son, Alrick, beside him with a torch flaring in one hand and a hand-axe in the other. Ragged men pressed in on all sides, weaponless, their flesh sunken, skins stained dark, hair in black ropes. They came forward, even without hands, even with Alrick's hand-axe buried in the join between neck and shoulder. A huge figure strode past the melee, wolfskins trailing from his shoulders, a double-headed battle-axe in one hand, small iron buckler in the other. Two Vikings kept at his side.

'Broke-Oar.' Snorri breathed the name, pressing back against the log wall. Few men over-topped Snorri and only one was renegade and traitor enough for this night's work. Though had anyone accused the Broke-Oar of sailing with necromancers Snorri would have laughed at the notion. Until now.

Small darts stood from Olaaf Magson's neck. Snorri saw them in the torch light as Alrick went down, grappled by his attackers. Magson tried to lift his sword, arms trembling, then vanished beneath his foes. Snorri reached up between his shoulders and pulled the dart there clear. He had pressed it deeper against the wall and not felt it. Even now a weakness ran through him.

Dead men moved toward the door of Snorri's hut, stepping frozen-footed through the snow. Between the ver Lutens's huts a hundred yards up-shore the Broke-Oar

174

and a handful of his men stood with torches raised. Around them mire-ghouls found the rooftops, blow-pipes ready.

From the shoreline voices barked orders, their accents strange, clipped like those of Brettan men. The Drowned Isles then, a raid from the Drowned Isles, guided in by Sven Broke-Oar. It made no sense.

The first dead man set his frost-black hands upon Snorri's door. When Snorri had seen Emy that morning walking with a five-year-old's lack of guile along the long-quay he'd known a terror like no other. His child had been, in that moment, out of reach, alone with her danger. It hadn't been the danger that unmanned him, but his inability to stand between it and her.

'Thor. Watch me.' Snorri had never had much time for calling on gods. He might raise a flagon to Odin on feast day, or swear by Hel when they stitched his wounds, but in general he saw them as an ideal, a code to live by, not an ear to moan and complain into. Now though, he prayed. And launched himself into the corpse crowd before his door.

As Snorri broke cover he heard nothing above his own battle-roar: not the ghouls' sharp exhalations or the hissing flight of their darts. Even the sting as they punctured his shoulder, arm and neck he barely noticed. He took the head from the closest of the dead men, the arm that reached for him, a hand, another head. All the time Hel felt heavier in his hands, as if the axe were stone. Even his arms grew heavy, muscles almost unable to bear the weight of the bones they wrapped. A black fist struck him, frost-bitten knuckles hammering his temples. Hands caught hold around his knees, some fallen opponent still unable to die despite grievous wounds. Snorri started to fall, toppling to the side. With the last of his strength he launched himself to break the grip around his legs, rolling heels over head along the icy margins of his hut. The invaders pressed on toward the hut's door in a tight huddle, leaving only the pieces of bodies shorn by his axe and a corpse near-severed at the spine but hauling itself towards him hand over hand.

A numbness ran through Snorri, deep as any that cold will put in a man. He couldn't feel his limbs, though he saw his arms before him corpse-white and smeared with the dark ichor that lay still in the dead men's veins. No part of him would move though every fibre of his will demanded it. Only the sound of door planks splintering shocked his traitor body into rising. An avalanche hammered him back to the ground. Something on the roof of his hut – ghouls, shifting the snow as they scampered into position – and in one mass it fell, pressing him down with a soft but implacable hand.

Snorri lay helpless, the last of his strength gone, his naked body entombed in snow, waiting for death, waiting for the strangling grip of dead hands or the teeth of ghouls or the axe of one of the Broke-Oar's reavers. No matter what the Broke-Oar was being paid he would want no witnesses to this night's shame.

A high shriek reached him, even through his cocoon of snow. Emy! Then Freja's screams, her battle-cry, a mother's rage, the roar from Karl, his eldest, as he attacked. Every part of his mind howled for motion, every ounce of his will trying to force his arms to reach, legs to pump … but no piece of him moved. All that anger and desperation, yet only a sigh escaped the numbness of his lips, drooling into the blind white all about him.

The incessant tapping had woken him. The tap tap tap of rain. Rain pouring off the eaves, washing away the snow, taking the ice from his eyelids so he could open them to the day. He turned his head and the water ran from his eyes. The remains of the snow heap lay around him, a touch whiter than the marble of his flesh.

Snow makes a soft bed, but no man wakes from it. That was the wisdom of the North. Snorri had seen enough drunks frozen where they slept to know the truth of it. A groan escaped him. This was death. His dead body would shamble after the corpse legions, his mind trapped within. He had never thought that good men might watch helpless from behind dead eyes, in thrall to necromancers.

Still the water splattered across him, gushing from behind the fascia board, falling in a grey curtain all along the roof's edge. It beat at his ear, ran across his chest, almost warm though icicles fringed the eaves, defying the thaw. He rolled clear across half-frozen ground. The motion took him by surprise, left him unsure whether he owned it or not.

The raid! As if Snorri's mind were thawing too memory began to leak behind his eyes. In a moment he found his feet, rain starting to clean the mud from his side. He stood, unsteady, a tremble running through him, the cold reaching him for the first time. 'Gods no!' He stumbled forward, reaching for the wall for support, though his hands had no more sensation in them than his feet.

The door lay flat, torn off its leather hinges, the interior beyond strewn with bed furs, broken pots, scattered corn. Snorri staggered in, searching through the furs with blunt fingers, seized by a shivering beyond his control, tossing the bedding aside, dreading to find nothing, dreading to find something.

In the end he discovered only a pool of blood on the hearthstone, dark and sticky and smeared by feet. Against the whiteness of his fingers the blood regained its crimson vitality. Whose blood? How much spilled? Nothing left of his wife, of his children, but blood? At the door, a clump of red hair caught his attention, snagged by a crack in the support, made to dance by the wind. 'Egil.' Snorri reached for his son's hair with bloodstained hands. Convulsions overtook him and he fell back, thrashing and trembling among the hides of grey wolf and black bear.

How many hours it took for the ghouls' poison to leave him Snorri could not have said. The venom that had preserved him in the snow, slowing his heart and drawing back life into the tightest core now restored all sensation as it left his system. It put an edge on each of the senses, heightening the pain of returning circulation, making a misery of the cold despite being wrapped with many furs, even putting fresh barbs on a grief that already seemed beyond enduring. He raged and he shook and by slow degrees both warmth and strength returned to his limbs. He dressed, tying laces with still-numb fingers in an ecstasy of fumbling, pulled his boots on, crammed the last of the winter stores into his travel pack, dry hake and black biscuit, salt in a wrap of sealskin, fat in an earthenware jar. He took his travelling skins, seal in two layers, trapping the down of the cliff-gull. Above it he wore a wolfskin, a grey beast that like the dark bears travel north with the summer and retreat before the snows. It would be enough. Spring had won her war, and like the summer-wolf Snorri would strike north and take what he needed.

'I will find you,' he promised the empty room, promised the dent in the bed where his wife had slept, promised the roof above them, the sky above it, the gods on high.

And ducking the lintel, Snorri ver Snagason left his home to find his axe amid the thaw.

'And did you find it?' I asked, imagining his father's axe lying there in the melting snow, and Snorri lifting it with awful purpose.

'Not first.' The Norseman's voice put so much despair into just two words I couldn't ask him to speak more and held my peace, but a moment later he spoke on unprompted.

'I found Emy first. Discarded on a midden heap, limp and ragged, like a lost doll.' No sound but for the crackle of the fire beside us. I wanted him to keep silent, to say nothing more. 'The ghouls had eaten most of her face. She still had eyes though.'

'I'm so sorry.' And I was. Snorri's magic had reached into me again and made me brave. In that moment I wanted to be the one to stand between the child and her attackers. To keep her safe. And failing that, to hunt them to the ends of the earth. 'Death must have been a kindness.'

'She wasn't dead.' No emotion in his voice now. None. And the night felt thick around us, the dark deepening into blindness, swallowing stars. 'I pulled two ghoul-darts from her and she started to scream.' He lay down and the fire dimmed as if choked by its own smoke, though it had burned clean enough when set. 'Death was kind.' He drew a sharp breath. 'But no father should have to give such a kindness to his child.'

I lay down too, no care for the hard ground, damp cloak, empty stomach. A tear made its way along the side of my nose. Snorri's magic had left me. My only desire lay south, back in the comforts of the Red Queen's palace. An echo of his misery rang in me and confused itself with my own. That tear might have been for little Emy – it might have been for me – it probably was for me, but I'll tell myself it was for both of us, and perhaps one day I'll believe it.

12

On the morning after Snorri's tale of horror in the North we neither of us spoke of it. He broke his fast in a sombre mood but by the time it came to ride on his good humour had returned. Much of the man was a mystery to me but this I understood well enough. We all practise self-deception to a degree: no man can handle complete honesty without being cut at each turn. There's not enough room in a man's head for sanity alongside each grief, each worry, each terror that he owns. I'm well used to burying such things in a dark cellar and moving on. Snorri's demons might have escaped into a quiet moment the night before while we sat watching the stars, but now he'd harried them back into some cellar of his own and barred the door once more. There's tears enough in the world to drown in, but Snorri and I knew that action requires an uncluttered mind. We knew how to set such things aside and move on.

Of course he wanted to move on to daring rescue

and bloody revenge in the North whilst I wanted to move on to sweet women and soft living in the South.

Another day's travel, damp, muddy, grey skies and a stiff wind. Another roadside camp with too little food and too much rain. I woke the next morning at dawn, disappointed to find myself beneath the same dripping hedge and wet cloak I'd shivered myself to sleep under the evening before. My dreams had been full of strangeness. At first the usual horror of the demon from the opera stalking us through the rain-dark night. Later though my nightmare became full of light and it seemed a voice addressed me from a great distance at the heart of all that brilliance. I could almost make out the words … and finally as I opened my eyes to the first grey hints of the day it seemed I saw, through the blurry lash-filled slit of my eyes, an angel, wings spread, outlined in a rosy glow, and at last one word reached me. *Baraqel.*

Three more days riding through the continuous downpour that served as a Rhonish summer and I was more than ready to gallop back south toward the myriad pleasures of home. Only fear bound me to our course. Fear of what lay behind and fear of what would happen if I got too far from Snorri. Would the cracks run through me from toe to head spilling out light and heat until I crisped? Also fear of his pursuit. He would know the direction I took, and though I trusted my riding skills to keep me safely ahead in the chase I had less faith in the city walls, town guard, and palace security to keep the Norseman out once I'd stopped running.

Twice over the next three days I saw a figure, half-imagined through miles of rain, on distant ridges, dark against the bright sky. Common sense said it was a herder following his flock or some hunter about his business. Every nerve I owned told me it was the unborn, escaped from the Sister's spell and dogging our heels. Both times I urged my gelding into a canter and kept Snorri bouncing along behind me until I'd outrun the worst of the cold terror the sight put in me.

With dwindling resources we ate mean fare in small portions, cooked by peasants I wouldn't trust to feed my horse. We spent two more sleepless nights huddled beneath lean-to shelters of branches and bracken that Snorri constructed against the hedgerows. He claimed it to be all a man needed for slumber and proceeded to snore all night. The downpour he proclaimed to be 'fine damp weather'.

'North of Hardanger the children would run naked in warm rains like these. We don't sew our bearskins on until the sea starts to freeze,' he said.

I nearly hit him.

I slept better in the saddle than I had in his shelter, but wherever sleep found me dreams came too. Always the same theme – some inner darkness, a place of peace and isolation, violated by light. First bleeding through a hairline fracture, then brightening as the crack forks and divides, and beyond the thin and breaking walls of my sanctum, some brilliance too blinding to look upon … and a voice calling my name.

'Jal … Jal? … Jal!'

'Wh-what?' I jerked awake to find myself cold and sodden in the saddle.

'Jal.' Snorri nodded ahead. 'A town.'

The sixth night out from Pentacost saw us in through the gates of a small, walled town named Chamy-Nix. The place sounded vaguely promising but proved to be a big let-down, just another wet Rhonish town, as dour and worthy as all the rest. Worse still, it was one of those damnable places where the locals pretend not to speak the Empire Tongue. They do of course, but they hide behind some or other ancient language as if taking pride in being so primitive. The trick is to repeat yourself louder and louder until the message gets through. That's probably the one thing my military training was good for. I'm great at shouting. Not quite the boom that Snorri manages, but a definite blare that comes in handy for dressing down unruly servants, insubordinate junior officers, and of course as a last ditch means of intimidating men who might otherwise put a sword through me. Part of the art of survival as a coward is not letting things get to the point where that cowardice is exposed. If you can bluster your way through dangerous situations it's all to the good, and a fine shouting voice helps immensely.

Snorri led us to a dreadful dive, a low-roofed subterranean tavern thick with the stink of wet bodies, spilled ale, and wood-smoke.

'It's a touch warmer and slightly less damp than outside, I'll grant you.' I elbowed my way through the crowd at the bar. Local men, dark-haired, swarthy, variously missing teeth or sporting knife scars, packed around small tables toward the back in a haze of pipe-smoke.

'At least the ale will be cheap.' Snorri slapped what might be our only copper on the beer-puddled counter.

'*Qu'est-ce que vous voulez boire?*' the barkeep asked, still wiping someone's spit from the tankard he intended to serve in.

'Kesquer-what?' I leaned in over the counter, natural caution erased by six days of rain and the foul mood that torrent had exposed. 'Two ales. The best you have!'

The man favoured me with the blankest of stares. I drew breath to repeat myself rather more loudly.

'*Deux biéres s'il vous plaît et que vous vendez repas?*' Snorri answered, sliding his coin forward.

'What the hell?' I blinked at him, talking over the barkeep's reply. 'How— I mean—'

'I wasn't raised speaking the Tongue, you know?' Snorri shook his head as if I were an idiot and took the first full tankard. 'When you've had to learn one new language you develop an interest in others.'

I took the tankard from him and eyed the beer with suspicion. It looked foreign. The floating suds made an island that put me in mind of some alien place where they'd never heard of Red March and cut princes no slack. That put a bad taste in my mouth before I'd even sipped it.

'We of the North are great traders, you know?' Snorri continued, though what sign I'd given that I might be interested I could not imagine. 'Far more comes in through our ports on Norse cargo ships than in the holds of longboats returning from raids. Many a Norseman knows three, four, even five languages. Why I myself—'

I turned away and took my foul-tasting beer off toward the tables, leaving Snorri to negotiate the food in whatever mangled tongue was required.

Finding a space proved problematic. The first burly peasant I approached refused to move despite my obvious station, instead hunkering over his huge bowl of what looked to be shit-soup, but smelled infinitely worse, and ignoring me. He muttered something like 'murdtet' as I moved off. The rest of the ill-mannered louts kept to their seats and in the end I had to squeeze into place beside a nearly spherical woman drinking gin from a clay cup. The soup-man then proceeded to give me the evil eye whilst toying with his wicked-looking knife – an implement generally not required for the consumption of soup – until Snorri came up with his beer and two plates of steaming offal.

'Budge up,' he ordered, and the whole row of locals edged along, my neighbour wobbling like gelatine as she undulated to the left, leaving sufficient room for the new addition.

I eyed the plate before me. 'This is what any decent butcher removes from the ... what I'll generously assume was a cow ... before sending it to the kitchens.'

Snorri started tucking in. 'And what you leave will make a meal for someone who's really hungry. Eat up, Jal.'

Jal again! I would have to sort that out with him sometime soon.

Snorri cleared his plate in about the same time it took me to decide which bit of mine looked least dangerous. He took a stale hunk of bread from his pocket and started scraping up the gravy. 'That fellow with the knife looks like he wants to stick it into you, Jal.'

'What can you expect from this kind of establishment?' I tried for a manly growl. 'You get what you pay for and soon we won't be able to pay for even this.'

Snorri shrugged. 'Your choice. If you want luxury sell your locket.'

I restrained myself from laughing at the barbarian's ignorance – all the more puzzling as you would think a man accustomed to the business of loot and pillage would have a better eye when it came to appraising which valuables to carry off. 'What is it with you and my locket?'

'You're a brave man, Jal,' Snorri said, apropos of nothing. He poked the last of the bread between his lips and started chewing, cheeks bulging.

I frowned, trying to figure out why he'd said that – was it some kind of threat? I also tried to figure out what the thing dangling from the end of my knife was. I put it in my mouth. Best not to know.

Finally Snorri managed to swallow down his huge mouthful and explained. 'You let Maeres Allus break your finger rather than pay your debts. And yet you could have paid the man off at any time with that trinket of yours. You chose not to. You chose to keep and honour the memory of your mother over your own safety. That's loyalty to family. That's honour.'

'That's nonsense!' Anger got the better of me. It had been a rotten day. A rotten week. The worst ever. I whipped the locket from its hiding place in a small pocket under my arm. Better judgment warned me against it. Worse judgment warned me too, but Snorri had worn both away. Snorri and the rain. 'This,' I said, 'is a simple piece of silver and I've never been brave in my—'

Snorri tapped it out of my hand and it went sailing in a bright and glittering arc that set it splashing down in the soup-man's dish, splattering him with a generous helping of brown muck. 'If it's not worth anything and you're not brave then you won't be going over there to get it back.'

To my astonishment I found myself most of the way

across the intervening space before Snorri had got past his third word. Soup-man rose bawling out some threat in his gibberish: 'murdtet' featured again. His knife looked even more unpleasant up close and in a desperate attempt to stop him sticking it into me I caught hold of his wrist whilst punching him in the throat as hard as I could. Sadly his chin got in the way, but I knocked him back and as a bonus the wall smacked him round the back of the head.

We stood there, me frozen in fear, him spitting out blood and soup through the gaps left by missing teeth. I clung onto his wrist for dear life before realizing that he wasn't making any effort to stab me. At that point I noticed that my dinner knife was still clenched in the fist I had wedged under his chin. A fact that he had already registered. I stared expectantly at his knife hand and he obliged by opening it to let his blade fall. I released his wrist and snagged the chain of my locket from the edge of his bowl, bringing the trinket dripping from the soup.

'If you have a problem, peasant, bring it up with the man who threw it.' My voice and hand shook with what I hoped would be considered suppressed manly rage, and was in fact cold terror. I nodded toward Snorri.

Having kicked the man's knife under the table I withdrew my own from beneath his chin and returned to sit by the Norseman, making sure my back was to the wall.

'You bastard,' I said.

Snorri tilted his head. 'Seems that a man who would come back with my sword against an unborn wasn't going to be scared of a mill worker with an eating knife. Even so, if it were worthless you might have paused for thought before going to reclaim it.'

I wiped at the casing with what had left the city of Vermillion as a handkerchief and was now little more than a grey rag. 'It's my mother's picture you ignorant—' The soup smeared away to reveal the jewel-set platinum beneath. 'Oh.' I'll admit that seen through a coating of muck and the misting in my eyes it was hard to judge the thing's value but Snorri had not been far off. I remembered now the day that Great-uncle Garyus set the locket in my hand. It had glittered then, catching the light within cut diamonds and returning it in sparkles. The platinum had glowed with that silver fire that makes men treasure it above gold. I remembered it now as I hadn't for many years. I'm a good liar. A great one. And to be a great liar you have to live your lies, to believe them, to the point that when you tell them to yourself enough times even what's right before your eyes will bend itself to the falsehood. Every day, year on year, I took that locket and turned it in my hand and saw only cheap silver and paste. Each time my debts grew I told myself the locket was worth a little less. I told myself it wasn't worth selling, and I offered myself that lie because I had promised old Garyus, up there on his bed in that lonely tower, crippled and twisted as he was, that I would keep it safe. And because it held my mother's picture and I didn't want a reason to sell it. Day by day, by imperceptible degrees, the lie became real, the truth so forgotten, so walled away, that I sat there and denied Maeres Allus – the lie became so real that not even when the bastard had his man break my finger did any whisper of the truth reach me and allow me to betray that trust to save my hide.

'Ignorant what?' asked Snorri without rancour.

'Huh?' I looked up from cleaning the locket. One of the diamonds had come loose, perhaps from hitting the bowl. It came free in my fingers and I held it up. 'Let's get some real food.' Mother wouldn't begrudge me. And so it began.

Already the gleam of the thing was attracting attention. A man watched intently from the bar, a man with short iron-grey hair save for a peculiar broad strip, darker than a raven's wing, across the top, as though the years had missed that part. I hid the locket away sharpish and he smiled, but kept on looking as if I'd been the object of his interest all along. For a moment I felt a shudder of recognition, though I'd swear I never met the man. The déjà vu passed as my fingers left the locket, and I busied myself with my ale.

Snorri spent the last of his money on a bigger bowl of slop, more ale, and a few square yards of space on the floor of the tavern's communal sleeping hall. The hall sccmcd to serve as a method to prevent loss of drunks who might otherwise wander off in search of a spot to sleep and wake closer to some competing tavern. By the time we were ready to retire the remaining locals were busy roaring out songs in Old Rhonish.

'Alley wetter, Jonty's alley's wetter!' boomed Snorri, rising from his seat.

'A fine singing voice you have, to be sure.' This from a man close by, nursing a pewter cup that brimmed with dark liquor. I looked up to find it was the fellow with the blue-black strip amid his greying hair. 'Edris Dean I am. Traveller myself. Will you be heading north in the morning?' He stepped from the bar and leaned in to be heard above the song.

'South,' Snorri said, the humour gone from him.

'South. Do you say so?' Edris nodded and sipped his drink. He had a hard look about him under the smile. A smile that not only reached his eyes but filled them with good humour – which is a difficult trick to pull if you don't mean it. Even so, something in the thin-seamed scars along his arms, pale through the dirt, made me nervous. That and the quick but solid build of the body wrapped by the worn leather jerkin, and the knives at each hip – and not the kind for eating, more the kind for opening a bear from gut to growl. He had a thick ridge of scar on his cheek too, an old one, running along the bone. That one drew my eye and made me hate him, though I couldn't say why.

Edris smacked his lips and called across to two men he'd been with at the bar. 'South he says!'

Both men joined us. 'My associates. Darab Voir and Meegan.' Darab looked to have a touch of Afrique in his mix, swarthy and a bruiser, overtopping me by an inch or so, with the blackest eyes and ritual scar patterns on his neck vanishing down into his tunic. Meegan scared me the most though, smallest of the three but with long ropey arms and pale staring eyes that put me in mind of Cutter John. Beneath a pretence of casual interest all of them studied me with an intensity that set my teeth on edge. They marked Snorri too and I found myself wishing he hadn't stowed his axe with the horses.

'Stay. Have another ale. This lot are only getting warmed up.' Edris waved at the tables where the singing had reached a whole new level.

'No.' Snorri didn't smile. Snorri had smiled at the bear – now he looked grim. 'We'll sleep well enough, song or no song.' And with that turned his broad back on the trio and walked off. I managed an apologetic grin, spread my hands, and backed away after him, instinct not allowing me to present the space between my shoulder-blades to them.

In the gloom of the next hall it was easy enough to find Snorri – he made the largest lump.

'What was that about?' I hissed at him.

'Trouble,' he said. 'Mercenaries. They've been watching us half the night.'

'Is this about the locket?' I asked.

'I hope so.'

He was right, any alternatives I could imagine were worse than robbery. 'Why would they tip their hand? Why be so obvious?' It made no sense to me.

'Because they don't mean to act now. They might hope to spook us into unprepared action, but failing that it's just to give us a night or two without sleep – to wear at our nerves.'

I settled down close by, kicking aside the outstretched arm of a rather pungent human-shaped lump and the legs of another. Tomorrow I'd sell that diamond and put an end to this nightly misery of choosing between stench and lice, or cold and rain. I made a pillow of my cloak and set my head on it. 'Well,' I said. 'If they meant to spook us it's working.' I kept my eyes on the arch into the bar-room and the shapes in silhouette that passed back and forth. 'Damned if I'm sleeping. I wo—'

A familiar rumbling snore cut across me.

'Snorri? Snorri?'

13

*Never having been troubled by a conscience before I
was far from sure what to expect of one, and so when
for a minute or two each day at dawn a voice began
to whisper to me to be a better man I decided the
shock of recent events had finally woken mine. My
conscience had a name – Baraqel. I didn't like him
much.*

From the moment I jerked into the waking world that
morning, suddenly terrified that I'd fallen asleep with
Edris and his murderers waiting close by, to the moment
we left town under a brightening sky, I had been looking
over my shoulder.

'You won't miss them,' Snorri said.

'No?' There was no part of Rhone I would miss.
Though perhaps now with my purse fat and jingling
once more the nation might open her arms to me and
deign to show a visiting prince a good time.

'There'll be too many to hide.' Snorri's voice wobbled

with the gait of his steed, jolting up and down when the mare picked up the pace.

'How do you know that?' Annoyance coloured my question. I didn't like the open reminder of our troubles. With Snorri troubles were always put front and centre and dealt with. My style was more to shove them under the rug until the floor got too uneven to navigate, and then to move house.

'He was too confident, that Edris. There'll be a dozen of them at least.'

'Shit.' A dozen! I squeezed my nag along that little bit faster. I'd named the gelding Ron, after the Amazing Ronaldo whose ill-advised bet with Snorri had financed the early part of our trip.

We rattled along up the valley at a decent pace, fast enough to startle the sheep in successive fields into waves of woolly panic. It had to be said that, as uninspiring as Chamy-Nix was, the surroundings viewed with the morning coming up red and rosy behind them were quite stunning. Rhone gets hilly as you work your way north. Hills become mountains, mountains become peaks, and from Chamy-Nix you can see the white heights of the Aups, mountains so tall and so legion that they divide the empire more surely than a blade. In many senses the empire had always been broken and the Aups were the sword that divided it.

An hour later, gaining height and with our path back to Chamy-Nix laid out behind us I spotted the pursuit.

'Hell, that looks like a lot more than a dozen!' And a dozen was a lot more than we could handle. In fact if it had been only Edris, Darab and Meegan that would have been too many. My stomach folded around itself in a cold knot. I remembered the Aral Pass. There's no way any sensible person could view the prospect of someone else attempting to open them with a sharp edge as anything but terrifying. I found myself eyeing up the larger rocks in the hope I might hide beneath one of them.

'Twenty. Near enough.' Snorri looked back up the track and nudged Sleipnir on. He'd told me the original bearer of the name in his heathen tales had sported eight legs. It's possible that on such an over-endowed beast even Snorri stood a chance of outpacing the band on our trail. On any regular mount, though, it was never going to happen.

'Maybe if we just left the locket here...' It took about three seconds for my resolve to fail. I could abandon Snorri and set Edris's band a stiffer test. By rights I would win clear, but Ron was far from the best of horses and in such mountainous terrain it's easy to lame an animal if you push too hard. That would leave me meeting the band alone – if, of course, I managed to survive Snorri's death given the magics binding us. Abandoning the locket to them seemed the easiest of paths.

Snorri just laughed as if I'd made a joke. 'We should

keep one of them alive,' he said. 'I want to know who set them on us.'

'Oh, right.' A madman, I was riding with a madman. 'I'll try to keep a small one for later.' Snorri, it seemed, was as capable of deluding himself about upcoming battles as I was about the value of my locket. Perhaps that's all bravery was – a form of delusion. It certainly made it much easier to understand if that were the case.

'We need a good place to make a stand.' Snorri cast about as if this might be such a place. I could have told him with some confidence that no such place existed, anywhere. Instead I tried a different tactic.

'We need to get higher up.' I pointed to the barren slopes above us where the mean grass lost its footing and bare rock cut a path toward the heavens. 'We'll have to abandon our horses, but so will they, and then the fact you can't ride for shit won't matter any more.' And if I had my way we'd lose Edris' party among the confusion of ridge and gorge, then win free to buy better horses somewhere else.

Snorri rubbed his short beard, pursed his lips, looked back at the distant band, and nodded. 'Better if everyone is on two feet.'

I led the way, urging Ron off the track and up toward the ridges impossibly far above us. Beyond those ridges peaks rose, white with snow and brilliant in the sunshine. A fresh breeze followed us up the side of the valley, offering a helpful push, and for a while I felt hope sinking its cruel hooks into me.

Tough mountain grass gave way to boulderfields and scree, Sleipnir's hooves skittered out from under her and she fell, legs flailing, looking for a moment as if she might actually have eight of them. Snorri grunted as he hit the ground, pulling clear while Sleipnir struggled to right herself.

'That hurt.' He brushed his thigh where the horse's weight had pressed, then used his fingers to pry loose the small stones bedded into his flesh. 'I'll walk from here.'

I stayed in the saddle for another five or ten minutes, while Snorri hobbled along without complaint. At last though, even with my expert guidance, the going became too steep for Ron. Rather than wait for the inevitable tumble, which would probably see us both rolling down the slopes to where Snorri had had his own fall, I dismounted.

'Off you go, Ronaldo.' The climb ahead of us would test a mountain goat. I gave his flank a sound slap and moved on, burdened once more beneath my few possessions. The sword that Snorri had given me was the heaviest of my loads and kept trying to trip me. I held on to it mainly to please the Norseman, though my ultimate plan was to throw it away and beg for mercy if cornered.

The wind became less friendly as we gained height,

colder and capricious, seeming to press us to the rocks one moment then in the next try to yank us clear so that we might tumble back the way we'd come. I paused frequently to check the progress of our pursuit. They had ridden harder than us and abandoned their horses later. A bad sign. These were driven men. Ahead of me, Snorri crested the ridge we'd been aiming for during the long climb. He still hobbled but his injury seemed no worse than it had been at the start.

'Crap.' The Aral Pass ran between two huge mountains in the Auger range on the Scorron borderlands. I had always felt that mountains could come no larger – the rocks at the bottom would surely be unable to support the weight. I had been wrong. The Aups above Chamy-Nix deceive the eye. It's not until you get among them that you understand just how ridiculously big they are. A whole city would be little more than a stain on the flanks of the tallest. Beyond the ridge we now clung to, defying a murderous wind, rose a second ridge and a third and a fourth, each separated by deep-cut gorges, the slopes between variously lethal with scree or unclimbably steep. And all the ways open to us lay divided by smaller gorges and littered with boulders the size of buildings, each poised to fall.

Snorri set off down, grunting once as his foot tried to slip out from under him. I knew if he started to slow me I would leave him behind. I wouldn't want to, and I would dislike myself for doing so, but nothing would

201

compel me to stand against twenty mercenaries. It sounded better like that. More reasonable. Twenty mercenaries. The truth was that nothing would compel me to stand against one mercenary, but twenty sounded like a better excuse to leave a friend in the lurch. A friend? I pondered that one on the way down. An acquaintance sounded better.

By the time we needed to start heading up again there were few parts of me that didn't hurt. I've developed a good degree of resilience when it comes to riding. Walking, not so much. Climbing, none at all. 'W-wait a minute,' I panted trying to snatch a breath from the wind – less fierce in the valley but still insistent. The air seemed thinner, unwilling to replenish my lungs. Snorri didn't appear to notice, his breathing scarcely harder now than when we started the climb.

'Come,' he said it with a grin, though he had grown more sombre as we went on. 'It's good to make a stand in a high place. Good for the battle. Good for the soul. We'll make an end of this.' He looked back at the ridge we descended from. 'I had dark dreams last night. Of late all my dreaming has been dark. But there's nothing of darkness in warriors met for battle on a mountainside beneath a wide sky. That, my friend, is the stuff of legend. Valhalla awaits!' He thumped my shoulder and turned to the climb. 'My children will forgive their father if he dies fighting to be with them.'

Rubbing at my shoulder and at the stitch in my side,

I followed. His 'warriors met beneath a wide sky' nonsense was full of darkness as far as I was concerned, but as long as we were still doing our best not to meet the mercenaries anywhere at all then we were in accord.

We had to scramble in places, leaning so far forward we practically kissed the mountain, reaching for crevices in the folded bedrock to haul ourselves up. My breath came ragged, the cold air filling my lungs like knives. I watched Snorri path-finding, sure, measured, no fatigue, but favouring his uninjured leg. He had spoken of his dreams but he didn't have to. I'd slept alongside him, heard his muttering, as if he argued the night away with some visitor and when he woke that morning on the tavern floor his eyes, usually a Nordic blue, sky pale, were black as coals. By the time he rose to break fast no trace of the change remained and I could pretend it a trick of shadows in a hall lit only by borrowed light. But I had not imagined it.

I sighted the first of the pursuit cresting the ridge behind us while we closed the last hundred yards to the ridge above us. Losing sight of them as we descended the next gorge gave me some comfort. Troubles are troublesome enough without having to look at them all the time. I hoped they'd find the going as tough as I had and that at least a few of the bastards would take the last tumble of their lives.

The shadows started to reach, striating the slopes. My body told me we'd been climbing for a month at the least, but my mind was surprised to discover the day almost over. Night would at least offer a chance to stop – to snatch some rest. Nobody could navigate slopes like these in the dark.

Mountains are pretty at a distance but my advice is to never let them get to be more than scenery. If you have to crane your neck to look at something you're too close. By the time we were approaching the top of the third ridge I was practically crawling. Any disloyal thoughts about abandoning Snorri with his injured leg were cast aside far below us. I had promoted him to best friend and to man most likely to carry me. In places it wasn't the steepness that had me crawling but sheer exhaustion, my raw lungs unable to draw sufficient breath to work my limbs. We threaded our way along a series of broad ledges littered with boulders from man-size to ones that dwarfed elephants, hunting along each ledge for climbable access to the next.

'Come. It's easy.' Snorri looked down at me from the level above, holding out a hand. I'd come to a halt about two-thirds of the way up, caught on a steep field of loose, frost-shattered stone resting on solid rock beneath. I took a step toward him, reaching for the offered hand.

'F—' I started to say 'fuck' but as my boot continued to slide the word drew out into a wail that turned into a scream and ended with an 'Ooffff!' and me on my arse.

'Try again.' Snorri. Ever helpful.

'I can't.' I said it through gritted teeth. My ankle had filled with a hot, liquid pain. I'd felt the joint flex past the angle any ankle should make. There might have been a snapping under my scream, or perhaps just a tearing, but either way the idea of putting weight on it was not one I could entertain.

'Get up!' Snorri roared it at me as if I were a common soldier on parade. He would have made a good drill sergeant because I was on my feet before better judgment could stop me. I toppled forward and collapsed screaming, hiking my breath in to vent in successively louder outbursts.

When I fell silent I could hear a slithering of stones and a second later Snorri loomed above me, blocking out the day.

'I don't abandon comrades,' he said. 'Come on, I'll help you.'

Now, I'm not a man who takes his pleasure in other men, but in that moment Snorri's over-muscled and sweaty embrace was a thousand times more welcome than any I might get from Cherri or Lisa. He hefted me over one shoulder and started walking. The proximity caused that strange crackling energy to begin building between us but I was prepared to risk it being less fatal than Edris and his murderers.

'Thank you,' I burbled, half-delirious with the pain. 'I knew you wouldn't leave me. I knew—' Snorri stopped and set me with my back to a boulder, propped up on one foot. 'What?'

'It's fine.' Snorri cast about, studying the layout of the boulders, the width of the ledge. 'This will do, here. I'm not leaving.'

'I *want* you to leave!' I hissed the words past gritted teeth. 'Keep going, you big lummox.' *Just take me with you!* I kept that last part behind my teeth. Not because Snorri might think badly of me, but just because I didn't think it would change his mind. Of course, if he actually made to leave I would be immediately addressing the issue of being hauled along too. For the now, me play-acting the bluff hero would at least keep him happy and more likely to put some effort into defending me in my incapacitated state.

Snorri unlimbered his axe. He would have been more content with the broad crescent of a Norse axe suited to the shearing off of limbs. The weapon he carried sported a heavy wedge of a blade designed to punch a hole in armour. If the mercenaries had any significant armour and yet had managed to climb to where we were, then we might as well give up since they'd have to be supermen.

A short way back the ledge narrowed and a huge rock sealed off all but two or three feet of it, leaving a harrowing stretch where we had had to edge along the boulder beside a drop of ten yards to the ledge below. Snorri crouched down where he would be out of sight of the men as they came along that open and narrow path.

'That's the plan? You surprise the first one and then it's just the other nineteen to deal with?'

'Yes.' He shrugged. 'I was only running because I knew you'd stay with me and I didn't want your death on my hands, Jal. Now we're in it together as the gods must have wanted from the start.' The smile he offered made me really want to punch him.

'We're out of sight. We could hide. They go past, spread out, lose us, give up. They can't track us on rock!' I didn't mention he'd have to carry me.

Snorri shook his head. 'They could wait us out. If we tried to leave the ledges they'd see us on the more exposed slopes. Better this way.'

'But...' *There's fucking twenty of them, you moron!*

'They're strung out, Jal. A proper leader would have kept them together, but they're too confident, eager for the kill. The four or five at the front are nearly a quarter of a mile ahead of the last man.' He spat as if to show his disgust for their poor tactics. I would have spat too but my mouth was too dry.

'Steady on, let's think this one through—'

Snorri cut me off with a hiss and a raised hand. A clatter of rock on rock from the ledge below. An oath. I hadn't realized how much I'd been slowing the Norseman down: our pursuers were only minutes behind. I lay back against the cold rock. My final resting place? I would likely die within a yard of it. At our elevation the mountain held nothing in common with the world I knew, just bare fractured stone, too exposed and too high for lichen or moss, not a twig or scrap of grass or any hint of green to rest the eye upon. As lonely a spot as I'd ever seen. Nearer to God perhaps but Godforsaken.

In the west the sun dropped toward high and snow-capped peaks, the sky crimson all about them.

Snorri grinned across at me, eyes clear and blue once more, the wind playing raven hair around his neck, across his shoulders. He saw death as a release. I could see that now. Too much had been taken from him. He wouldn't ever surrender but he relished the impossibility of the odds. I grinned back – it seemed the only thing to do – that or start crawling away.

The wind brought faint sounds of men climbing now. Stones slipping beneath boots, weapons clattering, curses offered to each other and to the world in general. I tested my ankle and nearly bit my tongue off, but only nearly – so sprained rather than broken. I took the quickest of steps on it and found myself back against the rock having blacked out for a moment. Perhaps I could hop and stumble on a bit further, buoyed up with terror, but I'd be caught soon enough and without Snorri for protection. The moment he fell though, I'd be off, hope or no hope.

Find a happy place, Jalan. I hopped around my

boulder, trying to remember my last moments with Lisa DeVeer. Footsteps sounded along the narrow path between the drop and the boulder. The fall was the least of their worries, though they didn't know it. Crouching and biting back on the pain I peered around the edge of my rock to see them arrive. I would have wet myself but the mountain air is very dehydrating.

The first man to come into view was Darab Voir, just as I recalled him from the tavern, a bald-headed bruiser, scar-patterned in the traditions of some Afrique tribes, sweat glistening on his dusky skin. He never saw Snorri. The Norseman's axe descended in an arc, paralleling the side of the rock as Darab emerged. I've always considered a head to be a solid object, but as Snorri's axe passed through the mercenary's I had to reconsider. The wedge of his blade entered Darab's skull at the back, near the top, and emerged beneath his chin. The man's face literally bulged, the sides of his head seemed to flow outward, and as he toppled away over the drop, without cry or protest, the rocks were drenched with him.

Snorri roared then. The ferocity in it would have given Taproot's elephant pause, but that wasn't where the terror lay. The horror was in the simple unabashed joy of it. He didn't wait for anyone else to emerge. Instead he rounded the corner swinging his axe to cave in the side of the next man's head and smash him against the rock wall. He ran then, literally ran through them, striking quick short blows as if his axe were a rapier, light as a willow switch. Two, three, four men variously pitched into empty space or slammed against the rock, all of them with a hole in them big enough to put your fist into.

Somewhere out of sight Snorri found a pause and started to declaim, not some Norse battle dirge but ancient verse from the 'Lays of Rome'.

> *Then out spake brave Horatius,*
> *the Captain of the Gate:*
> *'To every man upon this earth*
> *Death cometh soon or late.'*

Another grunt of exertion, a clatter of metal on rock. The thump of bodies falling.

> *'And how can man die better*
> *than by facing fearful odds,*
> *For the ashes of his fathers,*
> *And the temples of his gods.'*

Damn the barbarian. He was enjoying this madness! He thought himself Horatius on the narrow bridge before the gates of Rome, holding back the might of the Etruscan army! I started to crawl away. It's shame that gets us killed. Shame is the anchor, the heaviest burden to carry from the battlefield. Fortunately shame was an affliction I'd never suffered from. I did wonder though, hearing Snorri move on to the next verse of his epic, whether he might not be able to hold out there indefinitely. Providing they didn't have bows with them... Of course, if that Edris were any kind of a leader he'd have sent men to flank his enemy. No single man can stand against many when they come at him from two sides. I would have flank—

'Hello. What have we here?'

I looked up into the pale staring eyes of Meegan – Edris' second companion from the night before. The setting sun framed him with a bloody light. He'd struck me back at the tavern as one of the last men on earth I'd want to meet in a dark alley. Like Cutter John he had the look of a man who kept a distance from the world, as if viewing us all from behind the confessional screen. Such men make good torturers.

At Meegan's shoulder stood a hard-bitten warrior tending to grey with a longsword ready in his hand. More men sent to flank us probably approached along the ledge as Meegan and I blinked at each other, me on all fours, him leaning forwards as if in enquiry.

Whatever you do in dangerous situations the main thing is to do it quickly. I've always maintained just because it's given to you to be a coward doesn't mean it's something you can't strive to do well. My father used to admonish me to excel in all things. Excellence in cowardice means being quick off the mark. If you want

211

to run away fast then the first thing to do is take off in whatever direction you happen to be facing.

'Ooof' was the only remark Meegan had an opportunity to make as I ran through him, and that utterance was chosen for him by the fact a lot of air needed to vacate his lungs in a hurry. I launched forward off my good ankle and put my shoulder into the little bastard. Being a big bastard helps in these exchanges. The man behind him staggered back, tripping.

One good thing about falling over on a mountain – good at least when it's other people – is that you're pretty much guaranteed to hit your head on a rock. Meegan showed no signs of wanting to get up again. The other man managed to land on his arse though and sprang back up sharpish with a curse. We both found ourselves looking at the gleaming length of my sword between us, held at one end by my hand on the hilt and at the other by the ribs he had wrapped around the blade. I had no memory of drawing it, let alone pointing it at him.

'Sorry.' Don't ask me why I apologized. In the heat of the moment my ankle's complaints were ignored and I hurried on past the mercenary, yanking my steel clear of his flesh with a sick-making wet tearing sound and the grate of cutting edge against bone. I saw more figures negotiating the boulder-strewn ledge ahead of me, and executed a swift turn on my good ankle before hobbling at speed back toward the ambush point where I'd last seen Snorri.

I met him coming in the opposite direction. Or more accurately I threw myself to the ground when he came charging around a corner, drenched in blood, axe held blade to ear, haft to chest. The silent purpose in him was terrifying – and then he roared his battle-cry and all of a sudden the silence of his purpose would have been fine. A moment later I worked out that he had been shouting, 'Behind you!'

Four men had been practically within stabbing range of my heels. Snorri burst amongst them with reckless disregard for everyone's safety, including mine and his. His axe head buried itself in one man's solar plexus on a rising arc that split his sternum. He shoulder-charged another man, a hefty fellow, lifting him off his feet and mashing him against a sharp corner of rock. A third man thrust at Snorri but somehow the twisting giant conspired not to be in the way – the mercenary's sword tip lancing between the Norseman's elbow and chest. Snorri's continuing turn trapped the blade and wrenched the weapon free from his attacker's grasp. The last of the four had Snorri cold. Axe bedded in one foe, tangled with another, he stood open to the man's spear thrust.

'Snorri!' Why I shouted a useless warning I don't know. Snorri could see the problem well enough. The spearman hesitated for a split-second. I don't think my cry distracted him. Most likely he was intimidated by the blood-soaked giant before him, his scarlet battle-mask divided by a fierce and broad grin. A split-second should not have been enough but with a roar Snorri impossibly powered his axe through his victim's chest, splattering the varied insides of the man in the process, and cut away the spear's head just before it reached his neck. The backswing broke open the spearman's face with the blunt reverse of the blade. And I swear to you the iron trailed darkness as it cut the air. Swirls of night left in its wake, fading like smoke. The last man, now swordless, spun away and ran for it. Snorri turned to me, eyes wholly black, panting, snarling, unseeing.

I rolled to my feet – well, foot – sword hanging from my hand, and for a moment we faced each other. Over Snorri's left shoulder the last burning scrap of the sun fell behind the mountains.

'You've got a bit of…' I mimed with my hand, scraping at my chin. 'Um … something in your beard. Lung I think.'

He reached up, a slow movement, eyes clearing as he did so. 'Could be.' He flicked the gobbet of flesh away. A grin. Snorri again.

'There are more coming?' I asked.

'There are more,' he said. 'Whether they're coming or not is yet to be decided. I think there are eight remaining.' He wiped his face, smearing the crimson. Where clean skin showed he looked far too pale – even for a Norseman. The dark and flowing nature of the gore beneath his ribs on the left suggested that not all the blood belonged to our enemy.

'Edris?' I asked.

Snorri shook his head. 'Him I would remember putting down. He'll be bringing up the rear, making sure none of his stragglers decide the mountain's too steep.' He leaned back against the rock, axe dangling from his hand, flesh white beneath the scarlet now, veins curiously dark.

'We should give them something to think about,' I said. I knew the power of fear better than most men, and Snorri had left a frightful mess. I took hold of the man Snorri had ripped his axe out of to save himself from the spear thrust. His left boot proved the least slippery part of him and I tugged him toward the drop where our ledge fell away to the next. I'd moved him about six inches before discovering that while blind terror is a great anaesthetic in the moment, once the immediate danger is passed the effect wears off rapidly. I fell back clutching my ankle and inventing new swear words that might more effectively convey my distress. 'Bollockeration.'

'Toss the corpses over?' Snorri asked.

'It might make them think twice.' It would make me think just the once, and the thought would be 'I'll come back later.'

Snorri nodded and, taking two men by the ankle, threw them over the edge. They landed with a sound that was wet and crunchy at the same time, and my stomach lurched. It would be the path the mercenaries' rearguard would likely take – the route we had taken. Meegan and his companions had only been inspired to the alternative and more difficult ascent by the sounds of battle. The sensible desire to flank Snorri rather than face him one by one in the narrow defence point he'd chosen had driven them up a more dangerous path.

Still sat on my backside, I grabbed another man by the wrist, braced my good leg against a ridge of rock and started to tug him by inches toward the drop. I moved him about a yard in the time it took Snorri to toss all but one of the rest in the area.

'This one's still alive.' Snorri leaned over Meegan and kicked him in the ribs. 'Out cold though.' He looked over at me with an appreciative grin. 'You saved a small one for questioning like you promised.'

'All part of the plan,' I grunted, shifting my corpse another three inches. He was the spearman. Thankfully he lay face down. His passage across the rocks had left a red smear where I'd dragged him. I clutched him below the hand, not wanting to touch his warm dead fingers.

'I'll sort out the others.' And Snorri headed off to deal with any of the fallen from his initial attack who hadn't yet fallen far enough.

'No, I'm fine. Don't trouble yourself.' I got no reply – with Snorri already out of earshot and the rest of my audience dead or unconscious my sarcasm was wasted. 'Heave!' and I heaved again. The corpse slid forward another three inches. Dead fingers moved against my skin, a convulsion of them like spider legs flexing, stroking down the veins and tendons in my wrist. I nearly let go fast enough but the hand clasped me as I unclasped it, the dead man lifted his head, the ruin of his face gaped a crimson grin at me, white skull visible beneath flapping flesh. Fear lends a man strength but so too does being dead, apparently. I wrenched hard enough to drag the spearman a whole extra yard, but it didn't win me free, just brought him close enough to reach for my throat. I managed half a scream before dead fingers, still warm, cut it off with an iron grip.

It's not until you've actually been throttled that you realize how terrible it is. It doesn't take enormous strength to seal your air off completely – and the dead man's strength *was* enormous. When you're denied a breath then all of a sudden breathing is the *only* thing you're interested in. I clawed at the wrist beneath my chin, dug at the fingers, but if a face can kiss Snorri's axe and still find a smile then fingernails aren't going to mean much. I planted a foot on the dead thing's shoulder and pushed for all I was worth. It felt as though my throat would be ripped from my neck, but the grip wasn't released. Black spots began to grow in my vision, joining at the edges to make a wall of darkness. Blinding cracks ran through the black, my heart hammered behind its cage of ribs, and the stink of burning flesh filled my nostrils even though I could draw no air into them.

And then, as suddenly as the hand had seized me, it was gone. Snorri loomed over me, gripped under my armpits and hauled me clear. If my throat hadn't been so well lubricated with terror-sweat I suspect I would have seen it still clutched in the dead man's fingers, red and dripping.

Snorri snatched up his axe while I sucked air through the straw that being choked had left me with. The dead man stood, still grinning amid the butchered remains of his face, and raised his hands toward us, the wrists and forearms curiously burned, wisps of smoke still lifting from them. Snorri made to advance but two figures tackled him from the rear. He staggered, desperate to keep his footing. Two of his victims clung to him, blood still oozing from the fatal wounds his axe had given them.

Gasping and weak, I backed away from the spearman, still on my arse, shuffling among the rocks, retreating before his unhurried advance. Snorri looked in trouble too, with one of the things clinging to his back, the other encircling his waist with both arms and trying to eat its way into his stomach.

'Help.' I only managed to squeak it out as a whisper. I don't think Snorri noticed. He'd just thrown himself back against the rock wall to the next ledge, sandwiching the corpse on his back between the broadness of his shoulders and the stone. *He* might not have heard my cry for aid, but *I* heard the resulting cracking of ribs and vertebrae loud and clear.

'Mffgl.' The dead spearman tried to speak just before he fell upon me. Torn flesh and a broken jaw rendered him incomprehensible.

'Help!' I managed a touch more volume, and this time, expecting to be throttled again, I caught both the creature's wrists. The thing's strength was shocking, and the burned flesh slid and tore beneath my grip.

Across the way, just behind my attacker's head, I saw Snorri butcher the corpse-man he'd crushed, not severing its head but pulverizing its neck with two quick axe-blows. With the second blow a horrifying change came over my opponent. Its strength multiplied and where it had been inexorably pressing my arms back it now brushed aside any attempt at defence and sealed both hands around my bruised neck once more.

The ruined face came close to mine, dripping, tongue writhing over shattered teeth and a hideous intelligence in its eyes. Yards behind, Snorri caught the head of his last opponent in both hands and with an oath pushed it away from his side. It took all his strength as if his enemy had also grown in power, and the scarlet mouth he tore from his hip trailed skin and strands of flesh from its jaws. Snorri drove his knee right into the thing's face, booted it away, then pursued, raising a big rock on high to pulp its head.

Again, as if some necromantic vitality had been shared among the corpses and now flowed from the destroyed corpse into the last available vessel, my enemy's strength redoubled. It stood, lifting me as if I were nothing. By rights it should have snapped my neck but although the strength of its arms had grown the creature's grip actually weakened.

I looked down and where my hands fastened upon the dead skin a blinding light burned. The white heat of a desert sun bled between my fingers, my bones just shadows in a rosy haze of pumping blood and living flesh. The dead thing crisped where I touched it. Fats bubbled, flesh burned back, exposing sinews that smouldered then shrivelled.

I nearly let go in shock.

Snorri came running, axe recovered and ready. He whirled it in a blow toward the monstrosity's head but somehow it took one hand from my throat and caught the weapon beneath its blade. The haft thunked against its palm with a dull and wooden sound. Snorri struggled to pull his axe free but though he dragged the dead man several yards, and me too, still held in its choking fingers, he couldn't defeat the thing's strength.

The Norseman paused, slipped his grip to the end of the axe haft and to the head, and used the weapon as a lever to twist the spearman's wrist. Bones snapped with loud retorts, tendons gave, flesh tore. Leaving his axe in the broken hand Snorri bore his foe to the ground and proceeded to pulp the grinning face with a large chunk of rock.

Released, I rolled clear, struggling for air. The hand that had held me now rested on two blackened arm bones jutting from the dead man's forearm. Even now my breath wouldn't draw. I fell into unconsciousness reflecting rather abstractly that I'd never even known that there were two bones in a man's forearm.

14

'Wake up.'

I don't want to.

'Wake up.' A slap this time. Perhaps there had been one the first time too.

Not if I'm still on that sodding mountain. Someone had packed my throat with brambles and my chest hurt.

'Now!'

I opened one eye. The sky still kept an echo of the day though the sun had set. Already the cold had rolled down from the peaks. Damn. Still on the mountain. 'Bugger.' The word came out in thin slivers. Snorri let my head slide back onto my pack and moved away.

'What are you doing?' Not enough of the question emerged for him to respond. I gave up and let the air wheeze back into my lungs. A charred hand rose before my face and I yelped, flinching from it before realizing it was my own. The strange disconnected feeling persisted as I edged into an upright position and started to pick pieces of blackened skin from my palm. Not my skin, but fragments from the dead thing that had tried to kill me. The pieces of skin, part crispy, part wet, fell among the rocks, too heavy for the wind to take. Memories of the attack were just as broken and unwelcome. Trying not to think about it didn't help. I kept seeing the light bleeding out from beneath my hand, blinding and without heat. *How did it burn without heat?*

'What are you doing?' Perhaps Snorri would distract me. My voice came louder this time and he looked up.

'Cleaning the wound. Damn thing bit me.'

I could see teeth marks in the flesh above his hip. 'The sword cut looks worse.' A red furrow sliced through the ridged topography of his abdomen.

'Bites are dirty wounds. Better to be skewered through the arm by a sword than bitten on the hand by a hound.' Snorri squeezed the damaged flesh again, producing a rush of blood that ran down over his belt. He grimaced and reached for his water flask, tipping some of our last reserves over the injury site.

'What the hell happened?' Most of me didn't want to know, but apparently my mouth did.

'Necromancy.' Snorri took a needle and thread from his pack, something he must have acquired at the circus. Both were covered in an orange paste. Some heathen conceit to keep ill humours out of the wound no doubt. 'No unborn here,' he said. 'But a powerful necromancy to return the dead so soon after death.'

Another stitch placed. My stomach lurched. 'And for the necromancer to not even be present!' He shook his head then nodded to a spot behind me. 'I expect our friend knows more.'

'Buggeration!' Twisting my neck to look reminded me that someone had filled it with broken glass. I edged my whole body around by degrees, keeping my head facing front and centre. Finally Meegan came into view, pale eyes goggling at me over a gag of knotted cloth. Snorri had bound him hand and foot and sat him with his back to a boulder. Saliva clung to the stubble on his chin and his arms trembled, from fear or the cold, or both.

'So how are you going to make him talk?' I asked.

'Beat him about, I expect.' Snorri glanced up from his stitching. The needle looked ridiculously small in the great paws of his hands, and at the same time far larger and more pointy than anything I'd want to have to push through my own flesh.

I sniffed. The place stank of death and the wind couldn't scour it clean. 'Edris!' The memory hit me like cold water. I reached for my sword and couldn't find it.

'Gone.' Snorri sounded a touch disappointed. 'The bodies we threw down got up again and scared his lot off. I watched them go.'

'Hell! More of those things?' I'd rather Edris than another of those grinning corpses with their refusal to play dead and their penchant for throttling me.

Snorri nodded, dipped to bite through the thread,

then spat it out. 'Can't climb though. They weren't great at it when they were alive. Now?' He shook his head.

I had no desire to look over the edge and see their faces staring up at me, raw fingers clutching at the rocks, climbing, sliding back, climbing again. I remembered the look in those eyes as the thing choked me. Bile rose at the back of my throat. Something different had watched me from those eyes, something far worse than whatever had looked out through them for all the years prior to those last minutes.

Meegan might have scared me back in the tavern, studying me as if I was an insect he would enjoy pulling legs off, but on the mountain he proved one of the least worrying things to look at. 'Beating him's apt to knock him senseless again. And your idea of a beating would probably kill an ox.'

'We can't kill him,' Snorri said. 'Who knows what we'd get?'

'*I* know that.' I set my forehead in my hand, reminding myself just how much bigger Snorri was than me. 'And now *he* does too. Which isn't helping our cause.'

'Oh.' Snorri placed another stitch, drawing two ragged edges of his belly together. 'Sorry.'

'I say we take his boots off and light a small fire under his feet. He'll know his only chance of getting off this mountain is to be able to walk. And it won't take long to loosen his tongue.'

'Look around.' Snorri gestured with the knife he was

using to trim a bandage. 'No wood. No fire.' He frowned. 'That last corpse I threw over though … the arms were burned. How did you do that?' Narrowed eyes focused in on my hands, still blackened.

'It wasn't me.' It almost sounded true. It *couldn't* have been me. 'I don't know.'

Snorri shrugged. 'Calm down. I'm not one of your Roma Inquisitors. Just thought it might be useful with Goggle there.' He pointed his knife at Meegan.

I looked at my hands and wondered. It's often said that cowards make the best torturers. Cowards have good imaginations, imaginations that torment them with all the worst stuff of nightmare, all the horrors that could befall them. This provides an excellent arsenal when it comes to inflicting misery on others. And their final qualification is that they understand the fears of their victim better than the victim does himself.

All this might be true but I've always found myself too scared that somehow, some way, any victim of mine might escape, turn the tables, and work the same horrors on me. Basically the cowards who make good torturers are less cowardly than me. Even so, Meegan did need some encouragement and I needed to understand what had happened with the corpse-man. Snorri had mentioned the Roma Inquisitors, without doubt the most accomplished torturers in the Broken Empire. If I wanted to avoid discussing 'my witchcraft' with those monsters then I would be best advised to understand it myself so as to be rid of it as quickly as feasible and to be able to hide it as effectively as possible.

Meegan had an ugly-looking cut on his arm, just below the shoulder. Some edge of the rock had ripped through his padded jerkin and chewed on into his flesh. I reached out toward it. Always start with a weak point.

'Myltorc! Myltorcdammu!' He chewed at the gag trying to get the words out.

I have to admit a small thrill at having the upper hand after what seemed like weeks of nothing but running, sleeping in ditches and being terrified. Here at last was a foe I could handle.

'Oh, you'll talk all right!' I used the menacing voice I used to scare my younger cousins with when they were small enough to push around. 'You'll talk.' And I slapped my palm to his wound, willing him to burn!

The results were … underwhelming. At first I felt nothing but the decidedly unpleasant squishiness of his injury as he writhed and jerked beneath my touch. I had to press hard to keep him from twisting away. At least it seemed to be hurting him, but that turned out to be more by way of anticipation than anything else and he quieted down soon enough. I tried harder. Who knows what working magic is supposed to feel like? In the games we used to play in the palace, the sorcerer – always Martus, by dint of being the eldest brother – cast his spells with a strained face, as if constipated, squeezing his reluctant magic into the world through a small ... well, you get the picture. Lacking any better instruction, I put into practice what I'd learned as a child. I crouched there on the mountain, one hand on my hopefully terrified victim, my face constipated with the awesome power I was straining to release.

When it actually happened nobody there was more surprised than me. My hand tingled. I'm sure all magic tingles – though it may have been pins and needles – then a peculiar brittle feeling stole from each fingertip, joining and spreading to the wrist. What I first took to be a paling of the flesh became a faint but unmistakable glow. Light started to leak around my fingers as if I were concealing something brighter than the sun within my grip, and a faint warmth rolled beneath my palm. Meegan stopped struggling and stared at me in horror, straining at his bonds. I pushed harder, willing hurt into the little bastard. Bright fracture lines started to spread across the back of my hand.

The light and the warmth seemed to draw on me, flow from my core to the single extremity where they burned. The day grew colder, the rocks harder, the pain in my ankle and throat sharp and insistent. The spreading cracks frightened me, too strong a reminder of the fissure that had chased me when I broke the Silent Sister's spell.

'No!' I jerked my hand back, and the weight of exhaustion that settled on me nearly pressed me to the rocks.

A shadow loomed across us. 'Have you broken him yet?' Snorri squatted beside me, wincing.

I lifted my head. It weighed several times more than it should. The rip in Meegan's jerkin showed pale and unbroken skin beneath the blackening smears of blood, a faint scar recording where his wound had been. 'Shit.'

Snorri tugged at the man's gag. 'Ready to talk?'

'I been ready since I came round,' Meegan said, trying to roll back into a sitting position. 'I was trying to tell that one. No need for any rough stuff. I'll tell you everything I know.'

'Oh,' I said, vaguely disappointed, though it was exactly what I would have done in his position. 'And we're supposed to let you go after that, are we?'

Meegan swallowed. 'It'd be right fair of you.' He had a nervous, sweaty way about him.

'Fair as twenty against two?' Snorri rumbled. He'd brought his axe with him and ran his thumb along its edge as he spoke.

'Ah, well.' Meegan swallowed again. 'Weren't anything personal. That's just how many she paid for. Was just business for Edris. He spread her coin around and got together a bunch of us local men, fellas who'd seen some trouble, fellas who'd fought a battle or hired their-selves out for sharp-work before, that kind o' thing.'

'She?' I knew plenty of women who'd like to see me take a beating, and not a few who might pay to have it

229

done, but twenty men was excessive, and most of them would probably not want the castigation to be fatal.

Meegan nodded, eager to please, spittle drying on his chin, snot on his upper lip. 'Edris said she were a fine-looking woman. Didn't say it all polite like that though, no sir.'

'You didn't see her?' Snorri leaned in.

Meegan shook his head. 'Edris made the deal. He ain't local. Knows a lot of bad folk. Passes through once, twice a year.'

'She'll be the necromancer. Did she have a name?' Snorri asked.

'Chella.' Meegan licked his lips. 'Had Edris scared, she did. Never seen him scared afore. I didn't want to meet her, not after that. Don't care how tasty she were built.'

'And would you know where to find this Chella now?' Snorri's great hands closed around the haft of his axe as if imagining it the necromancer's throat.

Meegan shook his head, a quick shake like a dog flinching off water. 'Ain't from around here. A northerner, Edris said. Had a bottle of liquor off her, he did, for us all to toast the mission with. Some Gelleth brew, I think Darab said it was. Strange burn to it.' He smacked his lips. 'Passing strange. Made you want more of it though. Most like she's from Gelleth. Perhaps she went back. Perhaps she's watching us right now. Something stood the boys back up after you knocked 'em down.'

230

'What should we do?' I didn't like the idea of some necromancer witch watching from the ridges, ready to send her dead men after us. The whole idea had sounded faintly ridiculous back in Grandmother's court. I'd been sure most of it was lies, and whatever parts of it might have held truth didn't seem so scary. Mouldy old corpses jerking witlessly after frightened peasants seemed no threat to proper soldiery. But miles from civilization – and Rhonish civilization at that – outnumbered by the dead on treacherous ground, my view of things had suffered an about turn. 'I mean, we should do something.'

'With him?' Snorri kicked Meegan's bound feet.

'About her,' I said.

'My goal is in the north. If anything gets in my way, I'll put a hole through it. If not, I'll leave it behind.'

'We pick up the pace, keep heading north. I like it.' When a plan involves running away, I'm in.

'And him?' None of the solutions for Meegan looked good. I didn't want to let him go, I didn't want to keep him, but whilst I'll do my fellow man down at every turn, I've no murder in me.

'Let him join his friends.' Snorri knotted a hand in the ropes around Meegan's wrists and hoisted him to his feet.

'Hey now, that hardly seems fair. He was going to kill—'

Snorri took three strides, dragging Meegan to the edge where the rock fell away in a single steep step … and pushed him over. 'Those friends.'

231

Meegan's wail of despair ended with a wet thunk and the sound of something, or things, running toward the place he hit. Snorri met my shocked gaze. 'I try to be a fair man, to live with honour, but come against me armed and looking to take my life, and you will not walk away again.'

15

Nights spent on mountains are not to be recommended. Nights where the dark is full of the sounds of dead men trying to climb up to where you're shivering under thin blankets, even less so.

In the end the morning came. That's what matters.

'So you healed that man.' Snorri led the way across the mountain face, looking for a way down that would not be accessible to the corpses in our wake.

'No I didn't.' Deny everything was a policy I'd adopted at an early age. 'Shit!' I missed my footing and set my boot down harder than intended. The white-hot needles of pain lancing up from my ankle let me know that getting down off the mountain was going to hurt.

'He had a rip in his arm deeper than the cut I've got on my belly.'

'No. Just his jerkin. Big hole in his jerkin, little scrape on his arm. He bled a lot. That's probably what fooled you. I just wiped the blood away some.' I could see where this was going. Snorri wanted the same treatment.

Well, no. The cut on Meegan's arm had sucked out too much of my energy as it was. A whole night with the DeVeer sisters might have left me more go in my legs. Snorri's injuries would leave me crawling. 'Sorry but I— Ouch! Christ bleeding that hurt!' A light knock of ankle against boulder.

'Of course,' said Snorri, 'a man that could erase a gash like that would have mended his own ankle by now. I must have been mistaken.'

I took three more painful steps whilst that one sunk in, then sat on the nearest suitable boulder, 'You know, it does hurt quite a lot. I'll just try to rub some life back into it.' I tried to be surreptitious about it, but he just stood there watching, with his arms folded, like some big suspicious Norseman. The thought of walking down on a sound ankle proved too much temptation. With teeth gritted and jaw set I bound both hands around the joint and strained. Snorri raised a brow. I reached for whatever magic had burned in me and pushed harder.

'I, erm, can leave you to it if you need a quiet moment.' The tight line of his lips in that black beard gave no indication that he was mocking me.

'You're mocking me aren't you?'

'Yes.'

I let go and gave my ankle an experimental wiggle. 'Motherf—' words became an inarticulate howl.

'Not fixed then?' Snorri asked.

I stood up slowly. It seemed that whatever I'd done

234

to Meegan was, like tickling, something you can't do to yourself. And all in all healing Meegan had been a complete waste of effort given that Snorri had pushed him over the ledge a minute or two later. Perhaps it had been a one-off thing. I hoped so.

'You want some?' I held out a hand toward Snorri's waist.

He took a sharp step back. 'Best not. Bad stuff happens if we touch and I've got a feeling it would be worse than last time.'

I remembered reaching for his hand as I slipped down the mountain. In retrospect the damage done to my ankle might have been the lesser of two evils. If I had managed to grab hold we might just have burned up like the dead man.

'What's going on?' I held my hands up, palms toward me. 'That dead man fried where I touched him. And you.' I looked back up at Snorri, angry now, scared and angry and in that moment not caring if he took offence. 'You! There's something wrong with you, Norseman. I've seen those black eyes. I saw ... smoke, hell, I'll call it what it is, I saw darkness swirl around you when you killed those men, like your axe was cutting the stuff out of the air.' I made the connection then. I should have seen it before. 'And that's what's in you isn't it? Dark eyes, dark dreams. Darkness!'

Snorri hefted his axe, running a speculative eye along its length. For a moment I thought he might strike me

235

down, but he shook his head and offered a grim smile. 'It took until now to for you understand? It's the curse you brought on me. On us. Your witch, the Silent Sister. Her curse. That broken spell, that twin crack, running after you, dark and light. I got darkness – you got light – both whispering to us, and both of them wanting to get out.

'In the North the wise women say the world is a cloth, woven from many strands and stretched across what is real. The world we see is thin.' He held up a thumb and finger, almost touching. 'Where it tears deeper truths escape. And we are torn, Jal. We're carrying wounds we can't see. We're carrying it north and the dead want to stop us.'

'Look, we'll go back. My grandmother is the Red Queen, dammit. She can have this made right. We'll go back and—'

'No.' Snorri cut me off. 'I took the prince out of the palace but the palace is still crammed firmly up the prince's arse. You need to stop moaning about every hardship, stop chasing every woman you lay eyes on, and concentrate on surviving. Out here—' He waved the axe at the bleakness of the mountains. 'Out here you need to live in the moments. Watch the world. You're a young man, Jal, a child who's refused to grow up. Do it now, or you'll die a young man. Whatever is behind this pursuit it all started in Vermillion. Whatever war is being fought there is being lost. The Dead King is trying to kill us because we're taking the Sister's strength north.'

I got to my feet. 'So we stop going north! Go back. Make this right! It's nonsense anyhow. It was all an accident. Just ill-fortune. Nobody could have planned it. It's all a mistake.'

'I saw her too, Jal. This Silent Sister of yours.' Snorri set the tip of his index finger just above his cheekbone. 'She had one white eye.'

'Half-blind, yes.' One pearly eye. I'd called her the blind-eye woman for years before I knew any other name.

Snorri nodded. 'She sees the future. She looked too far and it blinded her. But she still has a second eye to look with. She looked through the might-have-beens and saw far enough to know you would escape, meet me and take her power north.'

'Hell.' There didn't seem much else to say.

We found a route down from the mountains that did not allow the dead men to follow us, though it could be argued that it came closer to killing us both than they might have. I say 'we' but Snorri led the way. My navigational skills are more suited to the city where I can find a low dive with unerring skill. On mountains I'm more like water. I head down, tumbling over rocks where necessary.

In their haste the retreating mercenaries hadn't collected all of their fallen comrades' mounts, and better still, we found Ron and Sleipnir browsing on the lower slopes. Neither horse was anything to boast about, but they were used to us, and we loaded them with the most useful items we'd managed to steal off the strays before driving them off. Sleipnir continued her placid munching at the saw-grass while Snorri heaped his loot upon her, flinching only when he climbed aboard. To be fair it looked as if they should take turns – I thought the Norseman fully capable of carrying his mare up the valley.

'We should look out for Edris and his friends,' I said. Not that I'd stopped doing exactly that at any point. 'Oh, and that necromancer bitch.' The idea of some death-sworn beauty lurking out among the rocks was unsettling. That she could frighten Edris with just a look, return the dead, and might well slip into our camp in the middle of night, was the stuff of nightmare – not that I planned to sleep again. Ever. 'And Maeres might yet have an agent on our tail ... and if those corpses know where to—'

'How about we just look out for trouble?' And Snorri led the way north.

We spent another night on high ground, our beds as cold and stony as the one before, the shadows just as threatening. Worse – if it could get worse – as the sun set Snorri grew distant and strange, his eyes drinking in the gloom and growing even blacker than they had been when slaughtering his foe and painting the slopes red.

The way he looked at me just before the last burning piece of the sun fell behind the mountain's shoulder made me consider hobbling away as soon as he slept. Though minutes later he seemed returned to his old self and reminded me to aim down slope if nature called in the night.

With the mountains demoted to scenery we followed the borderlands, first along the border with Scorron, which would soon be the border with Gelleth. Snorri kept his eyes always fixed on the horizon, hunting the north, mine always turned south, toward home, and to look for what dangers might be on our heels. Borderlands offer swift travel to those not seeking to cross over as the folks there are often occupied with their neighbours and not so keen to question travellers, to detain them, or to seek taxes from them. Such lands are, however, unhealthy places to linger. Many of my own worst experiences occurred on Red March's border with Scorron – all of them in fact, until I met Snorri.

In the province of Aperleon the kingdom of Rhone meets the duchy of Gelleth and the principality of Scorron. Monuments to the dead of a hundred battles crowd the elevations, most in ruin, but the land is lush and people return to resettle it time and again, as people are wont to. Snorri led the way along the approach to the town of Compere, famed for its cider and for the quality of tapestries woven there. Where he learned this stuff I couldn't say, but the Norseman would always win some new fact or other from even the shortest of exchanges with passersby.

The summer found us at last and we rode in bright sunshine, sweating beneath our travel-stained rags, throwing dark shadows and swatting at flies. We saw few people, then fewer still, all steering away upon their own paths, drawing back as if we might carry contagion.

Further on, the land took on a neglected air. Ron and Sleipnir plodded placidly between high hedgerows, Snorri's white skin turned red in the sun, and for a moment I started to feel at ease, lulled by the heat and the arable peace. It didn't last. We soon found fields untended and overgrown, farmhouses empty, their animals gone. In one place churned earth, an abandoned helm, a crow-pecked hand. A chill returned to me, despite the warmth of the day.

The castle of Rewerd's Curse – the ancestral seat of the House Wainton – stands on a high bluff of pale rock some miles from Compere Town. It watched us with empty eyes, the walls black with smoke, the cliffs beneath it still stained a rusty colour as if the blood of the last defenders had poured from the gates and overflowed the plateau. The sun had started to sink behind the fortification, making serrated silhouettes of the battlements and sending its shadow questing toward us, an accusing finger, long and dark.

'This is fresh.' Snorri drew a long breath through his nose. 'You can smell the char.'

'And the rot.' I regretted sniffing so deeply. 'Let's find another path.'

Snorri shook his head. 'You think any path is safe? Whatever happened here has passed.' He pointed to a faint haze ahead, indistinct trails of smoke rising to join it. 'The fires have all but burned out. You'll find more peace in ruins than in any other place. The rest is all waiting to be ruins. Here it's already happened.'

And so we rode on and came by evening to the desolation of Compere.

'This was vengeance.' The walls had been toppled, standing nowhere higher than three stones atop each other. 'Punishment.' I stepped over the rubble. Heat still rose from the ground. Beyond a forest of blackened spars a carpet of cinders marched into the distance until the drifting smoke overwrote it.

'Murder.' Snorri towered at my shoulder, a stillness in him.

'They never meant to hold this place,' I said. 'Whoever "they" were.' It could have been Gelleth troopers, a raid out of Scorron, or even a Rhonish army reclaiming what had been taken. 'I've never seen the like.' I knew the Hundred's squabbles left such damage in their wake but I'd not seen it, not like this.

'I have.' Snorri passed me by, striding on into the remnants of what had once been Compere.

We made camp in the ruins. Swirls of ash and cinder

stung our eyes and made the horses cough but night was upon us and Snorri proved unwilling to press on. At least we didn't have to choose between the risk of a fire and a cold camp. Compere came with its own fires. Dying beds of embers in the main, but giving off a great heat.

'I've seen worse.' Snorri repeated himself pushing aside the stew he'd prepared. 'At Eight Quays the Islanders made swift work and moved on. At Orlsheim, further up the Uulisk, they took their time.'

And in the ruins Snorri once more stole me away to the North, winding his tale around the night.

Snorri followed the raiders' tracks through the thaw. Their ships had gone, perhaps to some secluded cove to shelter from both storm and hostile eyes. He knew they would be planning a return to collect the Drowned Isles necromancers, their troops, and their captives. Even in the spring the interior was an inhospitable place this far north. The Broke-Oar would have told them that. How many of the captives might be on the ships and how many with the raiders Snorri couldn't tell. The raiders though, he could follow, and eventually they would lead him to their ships.

Orlsheim lay three miles further inland on the edge of the Uulisk where the fjord started to taper and pine forests reached almost to the water on gentler slopes than those at Eight Quays. The Brettans had left a broad trail, burdened as they were by many captives. Apart from Emy there had been only a handful of dead: three babes-in-arms, chewed and discarded, and Elfred Ganson, missing a leg and left to bleed out. Snorri guessed any others killed in the fighting would just have been added to the ranks of the necromancers' servants and set stumbling ahead to Orlsheim. How Elfred came to lose a leg Snorri couldn't guess but it had at least saved him the horror of a living death.

Where the settlement at Eight Quays had been stone-built the houses of Orlsheim were timber, some rude constructions of logs and wattle, others clinker-built of planks like the longboats themselves, defying the weather with the same obstinacy that the Vikings' ships offered the sea. Smoke had signalled Orlsheim's destruction even from the doorstep of Snorri's home, but not until the last few hundred yards had he imagined the fire to be so all-consuming. Even the great mead-hall of Braga Salt had left no more than a heap of embers, every roof beam consumed, its eighteen pillars each thicker than a mast and deep carven with saga tales, all devoured by the flames.

Snorri pressed on, leaving the Uulisk shores when the raiders' tracks turned to skirt Wodinswood, a dense and unwelcoming forest that reached for fifty miles and more until the foothills of the Jorlsberg defeated it. Men called Wodinswood the last forest. Turn your face north and you would find no more trees. The ice would not admit them.

And on the margins of that forest, where he had so often come in search of the reindeer who browse the tree-moss, Snorri found his eldest son.

'I knew him the moment I saw him,' Snorri said.

'What?' I shook my head, ridding myself of the dream the Norseman had woven. He addressed me directly now demanding a response, demanding something – perhaps just my company in this moment of rediscovery.

'I knew him, my son … Karl. Though he lay far ahead. There's a deer trail up alongside the Wodinswood from the Uulisk, broadened into mud by the raiders, and he lay sprawled beside it. I knew him from his hair, white-blonde, like his mother. Not Freja, she bore me Egil and Emy. Karl's mother was a girl I knew when I wasn't much more than a boy myself: Mhaeri, Olaaf's daughter. We weren't but children but we made a child.'

'How old?' I asked, not really knowing if I meant him or the boy.

'We must have been fourteen summers. She died bringing him into the world. He died just stepping into his fifteenth year.' The wind changed and shrouded us in thicker smoke. Snorri sat without motion, head bowed over his knees. When the air cleared he spoke again. 'I rushed to him. I should have been cautious. A necromancer could have left his corpse to waylay anyone trailing them. But no father has that caution in him. And as I came closer I saw the arrow between his shoulders.'

'He escaped then?' I asked, to let him take his pride in that at least.

'Broke free.' Snorri nodded. 'A big lad, like me in that, but more of a thinker. People always said he thought too much, said I'd always be the better Viking however strong he grew. I said he'd always be the better man, and that mattered more. Though I never said it to him, and I wish now that I had. They'd had them in iron shackles, but he broke free.'

'He was alive? He told you?' I asked.

'He had a breath left in him. He didn't use it to tell me how he escaped but I could see the iron marks on him and his hands were broken. You can't escape slave shackles without breaking bones. He only had four words for me. Four words and a smile. The smile first, though I saw it through tears, biting down on my curses so I could hear him. I could have been there quicker, I could have run, found him hours earlier. Instead I'd gathered my belongings, my weapons, as if I were going on a hunt. I should have run them down the moment the snow bank gave up its hold. I—' Snorri's voice had grown thick with emotion and now broke. He bit the word off and ground his jaw, face twitching. He lowered his head, defeated.

'What did Karl say?' I couldn't tell you where along the way I'd started to care about the Norseman's story. Caring was never my strong suit. Perhaps it was the weeks together on the road that had done it, or more

245

likely some side effect of the curse that chained us together, but I found myself hurting with him, and I didn't like it one bit.

'They want the key.' Spoken to the ground.

'What?'

'That's what he said. He used his last breath to tell me that. I sat with him but he hadn't any more words. He lasted another hour, less than that maybe. He waited for me and then he died.'

'A key? What key? That's madness – who would do all that for a key?'

Snorri shook his head and held up a hand as if begging quarter. 'Not tonight, Jal.'

I pursed my lips, looked at him hunched before me, and swallowed all the questions bubbling on my tongue. Snorri would tell me or he wouldn't. Perhaps he didn't even know. Either way it was of no great consequence for me. The North sounded more terrible by the minute and whilst I was sorry for Snorri's losses I had no intention of chasing dead men across the snow. Sven Broke-Oar had taken Freja and Egil to the Bitter Ice. And Snorri seemed to think his wife and son were still alive there now – and perhaps they were. Either way, that was a matter between Snorri and the Broke-Oar. Somewhere between us and the northern ice would be a means to unlock the two of us, at which point I'd be off before the 'G' of 'Goodbye' had cleared the Norseman's beard.

We sat in silence. Or almost silence for it seemed as

if Baraqel's voice spoke just beyond the edge of hearing, gentle and full of music. After a time I lay down and set my head on my pack. Sleep took me quick enough and as it caught hold the voice came more clearly so that in the moments before dreaming washed over both me and the voice I could almost make out the words. Something about honour, about being brave, about helping Snorri find his peace…

'Bugger that,' I replied. Words muttered half asleep over slack lips – but heartfelt nonetheless.

16

We came to Ancrath along the border roads between Rhone and Gelleth. Snorri travelled with a native caution that kept us safe on several occasions, holding us back amid a wood as battle-ragged troops marched south, taking us into the corn when brigands rode by in search of wickedness. I was keener to avoid such encounters than Snorri but my senses were better honed to detecting the approach of trouble across a crowded feast hall or through the smokes of an opium parlour than on horse-back across open country.

In the town of Oppen just a few miles into Ancrath I bought more serviceable travelling clothes. I made sure to buy sufficient quality to mark me out as a man of distinction, though of course normally I'd not be seen dead in sturdy boots and tough-wearing garments made to withstand rough treatment. I'd rejected the idea of letting a Rhonishman fit me for cloak and hat, but decided I could suffer the attentions of an Ancrath tailor. Snorri snorted and stamped so much during the fitting that I had to send him out to find an axe more suited to his tastes.

The moment he'd gone I started to feel an unease. Nothing to do with the slight stretching of the magics that bound us, and everything to do with the certainty that the necromancer who had sought our deaths in Chamy-Nix would still be hard upon our trail. Her or that creature that had watched me from behind its mask at the opera. The Silent Sister's trap had been set for that one. I was certain of it now. She'd been prepared to sacrifice the lives of two hundred, including some of Vermillion's finest – *including me, damn it* – to burn that one monster. I could only pray the crack I'd put in her spell whilst escaping hadn't let it free. And of course other servants of the Dead King might lurk around any given corner. Even in a tailor's shop!

In the end I left Oppen with a sense of relief. Being on the move had become a habit and I wasn't sure I would ever feel entirely comfortable settled in one place again.

We skirted the Matterack Mountains, a dour range with none of the Aups' grandeur, and found our way in time to the Roma Road, which I'd long argued we should have followed the whole way. 'It's better paved, safer, equipped with inns and whorehouses at regular intervals, passes through two dozen towns of note…'

'And is easily watched.' Snorri guided Sleipnir out onto the ancient flagstones. She immediately started to clatter. I think of that noise, horseshoe on stone, as the sound of civilization. In the countryside everything's mud. Give me a clatter over a clomp any day.

'So why are we risking it now?'

'Speed.'

'Will it make—' I bit off the words. Would it make a difference? To Snorri it would. His wife and younger son would have been captive for months now, even before he'd been dragged in chains to Vermillion. And if they had endured all this time, labouring at some task the Drowned Isles necromancers set them to, the chances were that a few days either way wouldn't make much difference to their situation. I couldn't say that to him though. Mostly because I'm fond of my teeth, but also the angel that kept whispering to me wouldn't approve, and you don't want to piss off an angel that lives under your skin. They're the worst sort. 'We've been making good time, pacing ourselves for the journey. Why do we need to travel faster *now* all of a sudden?' I settled on letting him say it himself. It's harder to lie to yourself out loud with an audience. Let him tell me he still truly believed his wife and child lived.

'You know.' He gave me a dark look.

'Tell me anyway,' I said.

'The voices. We need to get this over and done, get that bitch's curse off us, before the voice I'm hearing stops suggesting and starts telling.'

That left me with my mouth open and nothing to

say. Ron clip-clopped his way up another twenty yards of the Roma Road before I found the presence of mind to press my lips together.

'You're trying to tell me you're not hearing a voice?' Snorri leaned around in the saddle to scowl at me. He could manage the sort of scowl that reminded you he named his axes.

I could hardly deny it. The voice that had whispered beyond the edge of hearing in Compere had grown more distinct day by day, and its directives more frequent. It grew loudest each dawn. At first I had imagined that this was what people like Cousin Serah meant when urging me to listen to my conscience. I thought perhaps that too much fresh air and a lack of alcohol had opened me up to the nagging monologue of conscience for once in my life. Morning after morning of pious lecturing had me doubting my theory though. Surely everyone couldn't go around with some sickeningly moral voyeur hectoring them each moment of their life? How would they stay even vaguely sane? Or have fun?

'And what does this voice say to you?' I asked, still not admitting to anything. Snorri returned his gaze to the road ahead, showing me broad shoulders. 'I'm dark-sworn, Jal. Cracked through with it. What kind of secrets do you think the night whispers?'

'Hmm.' That didn't sound good, though frankly I wouldn't have minded swapping. Unsavoury suggestions bubbled out of the darkness at the back of my mind all

251

the time. Most I ignored easily enough. Being upbraided on my own moral shortcomings at every turn on the other hand was proving most annoying. 'Does your voice have a name?'

'She's called Aslaug.'

'She? You got a woman?' I couldn't keep the complaint from my voice. Nor did I try.

'Loki lay with a jötnar, a beauty with a spider's shadow.' Snorri sounded self-conscious, no hint of the story-teller now, hesitating as he repeated unfamiliar details. 'She birthed a hundred daughters in the dark places of the world and none of them ever stepped out into the light. Old Elida used to tell us that tale. Now one of those daughters walks in my shadow.'

'So you got a beauty with a dirty mind, and I got a pious kill-joy. Where's the justice in that?'

'Called?' Snorri glanced back at me.

'Baraqel. I expect my father used to drone on about him from the pulpit. Damned if I know the name though.' I was sure Baraqel would be eager to burden me with his lineage if I gave him the chance. He seemed to be a disembodied voice who liked the sound of his own pronouncements. Fortunately his visitations were limited to the few minutes between the sun cresting the horizon and clearing it – the rest of the time I could pretty much ignore him. And what with me being almost entirely made of sins that needed to be vilified it didn't leave much time for other matters.

'Well,' said Snorri. 'It's pretty clear we need to make haste, before Baraqel makes a decent man of you. And before Aslaug makes a bad one of me. She's not fond of you, Jal, you should know that.'

'You should hear what Baraqel has to say about my choice of heathen travelling companion.' Not a bad return shot but annoyingly my angel held Snorri up as something of a paragon during our morning chats, so it was better that the Norseman didn't hear after all.

We rode all day and for once the sun blazed. It appeared that Ancrath was enjoying the summer so long denied to us on our trail. Perhaps the weather skewed my judgment but I have to say that Ancrath struck me as a fine corner of the empire, free of the Rhonish taint, fertile lands well-farmed, pleasingly humble peasants, and the merchant classes as servile as you like in the hunt for coin.

I kept close watch on Snorri all that day for any signs of evil, though what I'd do about it if I spotted any I hadn't a clue. Being shackled to a battle-hungry Viking on route for a suicidal rescue mission had been harrowing enough. Now I was shackled to one who might become a creature of the night at the drop of anyone's hat.

The day passed peacefully enough and Snorri showed no inclination toward the traditional demonic pursuits, though I did convince myself that his shadow was rather darker than everyone else's and found myself peering into it every now and again, searching for any hint of his new mistress.

My own little blessing from the Silent Sister woke me at the instant of sunrise just as the cocks were throat-clearing for the first crow of the day.

'The heathen has become a servant of darkness. You should denounce him to some suitable member of the church inquisition.' Baraqel spoke quiet enough but there's something about a voice behind your eardrum that's hard to ignore. Also he had a very irritating tone about him.

'Wh— what?'

'Have him arrested.'

I yawned and stretched. Pleased to find myself in a bed for once, albeit unaccompanied. 'I thought Snorri was your golden boy. Everything I should strive to be?'

'Even a heathen can embody character traits that may be admired and good role models are hard to come by in the wilds, Prince Jalan. However, his lack of true faith left him open to possession and he has been tainted beyond salvation. The rack and fire are his last best chance to lessen his sentence in hell now.'

'Hmmm.' I scratched my balls. Unfamiliar fleas were a small price to pay for the comfort of a bed. 'I doubt he'd thank me for the favour.'

'Snorri's wants are not of importance, Prince Jalan. The evil that has possessed him must be burned out. She must be cast into the fire and—'

'She? So you know Snorri's passenger do you? Old friend of yours?'

'You endanger your soul each time you mock me, Jalan Kendeth. I am God's servant on earth, descended from Heaven. Why wou—'

'Why would God create fleas? Did he ever tell you? Ah! Got one, you little bastard!' I cracked it between two fingernails. 'So, what's coming up today, Baraqel? Anything useful I should know? Let's hear some of that divine wisdom.' It wasn't so much that I didn't believe he was an angel and I certainly wasn't about to dispute the existence of such – my neck still bore the trace of bruises where a dead man tried to throttle me – it was just that I felt Baraqel must be a rather poor example. After all, angels should tower above you in gold and feathers carrying flaming swords and speaking wisdom in tongues. I didn't expect them to hide away and nag me to get up each morning in a voice suspiciously like my father's.

Baraqel remained silent for several moments, then a cockerel let out a raucous hallelujah to the morning close by and I decided my angel had taken his leave.

'Dark travellers on the road. Born of flame. A prince has sent them. A prince of evil, of darkness and revenge, a prince of lightning. A thorn prince. They are his work. Messengers of the doom to come.'

The pronouncement startled me awake again. 'That's the sort of nonsense I could have off Dr. Taproot's old fortune-teller for half a copper.' More yawning, more scratching. 'What prince? What doom?'

'The thorn prince. He whose line will spill heaven into hell and rip the world asunder. His gift is the death of angels, the death of...' And blessedly he trailed off, the sun having cleared the horizon somewhere out beyond the musty confines of my room.

I stretched, yawned, scratched, contemplated the end of all things, and went back to sleep.

We left the inn after a breakfast of liver and fried potatoes washed down with small beer. So far the famed cuisine of Ancrath had proved the least appealing aspect of the country, but riding a horse day in day out for weeks on end gives a man an appetite of the kind that's ready to try anything. Even horse.

Joining the Roma Road once more from the dirt track to the inn, I fell into my customary daydreaming, the sort that's apt to get you killed in the wilds but is the kind of luxury civilization affords us. I realized simultaneously that I had no idea what a liver was for and that I also didn't ever want to eat one again, especially not for breakfast with garlic.

Snorri stopped me pursuing that line of thought any further by drawing up in the road directly ahead of me. A ragged group of travellers were heading north toward Crath City, blocking the road, some pulling handcarts, others labouring under their possessions, others still flapping along in just the tatters they wore. And among them not a clean limb showed: all were black with filth of some kind.

'Refugees,' Snorri said.

*Dark travellers. A*n echo of Baraqel's prophecy ran through my mind.

As we caught them up I saw many bore wounds, still raw and open, and each of them – man, woman, child – was black with soot, or with dried mud, or black with both. Snorri nudged Sleipnir in amongst them, offering apologies. I followed, trying not to let any of them touch me.

'What happened here, friend?' Snorri leaned from his saddle toward a tall fellow, peasant-thin, an ugly rip along the top of his scalp.

The man offered a blank-eyed stare. 'Raiders.' Little more than a mutter.

'Where away?' Snorri asked, but the man had turned from him.

'Norwood.' A woman on the other side, grey-haired and hobbling. 'They burned it down. There's nothing for us now.'

'Baron Ken's troops? Is Ancrath at war?' Snorri frowned.

The woman shook her head and spat. 'Raiders. Renar men. Everywhere's burning. Sometimes it's knights and soldiers, sometimes just rabble. Road scum.' She turned away, head down, lost in her misery.

'I'm sorry.' Snorri didn't try to cheer her or claim

her lot would soon improve – but he said something. More than I would know to do. A shake of reins and he moved on.

We made our passage through the refugees, thirty of them maybe, and picked up speed. It was a relief to be clear of the stink. I'd been poor for a day or three and hadn't liked it one bit. The survivors of Norwood had been poor enough to start with and now they had nothing but need.

'They're hoping to throw themselves on the mercy of King Olidan,' Snorri said. 'That's the measure of their desperation.'

It still irked me just how much the Norseman knew about lands that lay across the sea from his. I'd heard of Olidan of course. His reputation had reached even into my cosy world: Grandmother complained of his manoeuvring more than enough for that. But who ruled in Kennick and how relations stood between Ancrath and its muddy neighbour I had no idea. Snorri had upbraided me about my tenuous grasp of Empire history but I told him history's just old news, prophecy that's well past its sell-by date. Current affairs were more my thing. Especially my current affairs, and Crath City could improve those no end. There would be wine, women, and song, all much missed on our long and miserable trek so far – women in particular. In addition where better to find some wisemen to strike off the shackles the Silent Sister had bound me to Snorri with?

The Roma Road bore us swifter than a river and we came in sight of Crath City as the sun plunged behind its towers, making a black architecture of spires and spans. I'd heard Olidan's capital rivalled Vermillion for the grandness of its buildings and the wealth spent there in bricks and mortar. Martus visited on an embassy two years previously and described the Ancrath palace as the stump of some Builder-tower, but my brother was ever full of lies and I'd be able to make my own judgment on that soon enough.

'We should skirt around.' Snorri had fallen behind and when I turned all his face lay in shadow, only the ridges of his brow and cheekbones catching the redness of the sunset.

'Nonsense. I'm a prince of the March. We have agreements with the Ancraths and it's my duty to call in on the king.' Duty had nothing to do with it. Crath City was my last best chance to break the Silent Sister's curse. With luck King Olidan could be persuaded to help. He would have magicians in his service. And even without his help there were always spell-smiths of one kind or another tucked away in such an ancient city. I'd never set much store by such things before. Smoke, mirrors and old bones I'd called it. But even a prince of Red March may have to revise his opinion on occasion.

'No,' Snorri said. I couldn't see his eyes in the half-light, and as the shadows stretched out across the road I remembered that this would be the time she spoke to

259

him. Aslaug, his dark spirit, would be whispering her poison while the sun fell from the world.

'Rushing in unprepared didn't work so well for you the first time did it? You want to save Freya? Little Egil? Cut Sven Broke-Oar into several pieces? It's time to use your head, to understand what we're up against and formulate a plan.' I had to move him somehow, even if it risked provoking the Viking in him and daring the consequences. 'This is Crath City. How much of the world's lore came from this very spot? Dig down far enough into anything the wise say and there's a document from the vaults of the Loove at the bottom of it.' I paused for breath, having exhausted everything I could remember my tutors saying about Crath City. 'Wouldn't time here be well spent? Advice on the nature of your foe? Maybe an antidote to ghoul poison. Or even a cure for the curse on us. You're risking the Roma Road, rushing north at full tilt, hoping to make it before the dark seduces you ... and the solution might be just behind those walls. The Silent Sister's not the only witch in the Broken Empire, not by a long shot. Let's find one who can help us.'

We faced each other now, horses nose to nose, me waiting for some reply.

The silence stretched. 'You're right,' Snorri said at last, and nudged Sleipnir into motion toward the city. The sense of relief that washed over me as he passed by proved shortlived. It occurred to me that I didn't know for sure who he was talking to. Me or his demon? I waited a minute then shrugged and rode on after. Who really cared? I got what I wanted. A chance. After all that's all a man really needs; a big city full of sin and sleaze, and a chance.

'Aslaug speaks of you,' Snorri said as I drew level on the road. 'Says the light will turn you – set you in my path.' He sounded weary. 'I doubt Loki's daughter can utter anything that's not half a lie, but she has a silver tongue and even a half-lie is half-true. So listen when I say it would be ... poor advice ... that led you to try and stop me.'

'Ha,' I slapped him on the shoulder and wished I hadn't, my hand crackling with painful magics. 'Can you think of anyone less likely than me to listen to an angel, Snorri?'

Crath City opened her arms and invited us in. We drifted along the riverbank, enjoying the warmth of the night. Everywhere along the dusty path inns lit the way from the right, barges from the left, moored and decked with lanterns. The city folk drank at tables, at barrel tops, standing in groups, lying on the sod, or on the decks of the barges. They drank from clay cups, pewter mugs, wooden trenchers, from jugs, bottles, kegs and ewers, the method of delivery as varied as the brews poured down so many throats.

'A jolly lot, these Crathians.' Already the place had

261

started to feel like home. Any wanderlust had wandered off the moment I smelled cheap wine and cheaper perfume.

A ruddy-cheeked peasant reeled backwards across our path, somehow maintaining his pint mug at an angle that spilled no ale though he stumbled as if at sea on a stormy night. Snorri shot me a grin, the black mood Aslaug had left him with now lifting.

A crowd of men on the nearest beer-barge broke out into the chorus of the 'Farmer's Lament', a bawdy ballad detailing in seventeen verses what amusement one can and can't get up to with livestock. I knew it well, though in Red March it's a Rhonish man who'll have no peace till he grabs a fleece not a Highlander.

'Must be a festival day.' Snorri breathed in deeply: the air came laden with the smell of meat a-roasting. That's a scent that will set your belly growling after a long day's travel. Snorri's stomach practically roared. 'It can't be like this every night.'

'The lost prince is back. Didn't you know?' A woman in her cups, passing by and reaching up to paw at Snorri's thigh. 'Everyone knows that!' She reversed direction and walked alongside Sleipnir, hand still exploring Snorri's leg. 'Oh my! There's a lot of meat down here!'

A husband or suitor managed to snag the woman's hand and pull her away, frowning all the while but hardly in a position to blame Snorri. Which was probably for the best, all things considered. I watched her go. Tempting as the roast in her own way, well-fed, fat some might say, but jolly with it, a twinkle in her eye. She even had most of her teeth. I sighed. I had been entirely too long on the road.

'Lost prince?' Hadn't Baraqel said something about a prince?

Snorri shrugged. 'You're a lost prince. They always seem to turn up again. Some prodigal son has returned. If it puts the locals in a good mood then that makes life easier. We get in, take what we need, leave.'

'Sounds good.' Of course we weren't talking about entirely the same things – but it did sound good.

We crossed the Sane by the Royal Bridge, a fine broad construction sitting on great piles that must have survived the Thousand Suns. Crath City rose from the docks on the opposite bank, sprawling over gentle hills and reaching up to the walls of the Old City where the money lived, looking out over what it owned. The Tall Castle waited in the middle of it all, high above us. I let the gradient guide the way. It took us into an ill-lit quarter where the sewers ran rank and drunks staggered narrow paths along the middle of the alleyways, not trusting the shadows.

'We'll find a place down here tonight,' I said. 'Somewhere unsavoury.' Tomorrow I'd be a prince again, knocking on Olidan's doors. Tonight I wanted to take full advantage of my anonymity and enjoy the benefits of civilization to the full. The benefits of a decadent civilization. If Baraqel was going to wake me up at cockcrow for a lecture on morality I might as well make it worth his while. Besides, if I found a low enough dive and woke amid as much sinning as I hoped to he might just decide not to show.

'There?' Snorri pointed down a thoroughfare broad enough to host taverns, the houses stacked three storeys high, each stage heavy-beamed and over-stepping the one below so they crowded out into the street as they rose. Snorri's thick finger directed me toward one of several hanging signs.

'The Falling Angel. Sounds about right.' I wondered what Baraqel would make of that.

With the horses given over to an ostler and stabled, I followed Snorri into the bar. He had to duck low to avoid the lanterns over the street door and when he stepped aside the place lay revealed to me. A dive indeed, and populated by a collection of the most dangerous-looking men I'd laid eyes on outside of a fighting pit … and quite possibly inside one too. My instinct was to execute a rapid reversal of direction on one heel and find a less intimidating venue but Snorri had already secured a table and having seen him demolish Edris's crew in the mountains I felt it might be safer to stick close to him than try my luck alone outside.

The Angel had that reek to it: sweat, horses, stale beer, and fresh sex. The serving girls looked harried, the three barkeeps nervous; even the whores were keeping to the stairs, peering down between the railings as if no longer sure of their chosen profession. It seemed as though the bulk of the customers crowding the place from front wall to back weren't regulars. In fact as I slid along the bench to sit beside my Viking I noticed that the night's clientele looked every bit as far-flung as a Norseman and a native of Red March. The Nuban close by the hearth had perhaps travelled furthest. A powerfully-built man with tribal scars and a watchful gravitas about him. He caught me staring and flashed a grin.

'Mercenaries,' Snorri said.

I noticed as he said it that almost every man in the place carried a weapon, most of them several weapons, and not the civilized man's poniard or rapier but bloody great swords, axes, cleavers, knives for gutting bears; and the biggest crossbow I've ever seen occupied most of the table before the Nuban. Several of the men wore breastplates, grimy and battered as if from hard service; others old chainmail shirts or quilted armour stitched with the occasional bronze plate.

'We could try that place down the street, the Red Dragon,' I suggested as Snorri raised his arm for ale. 'Somewhere a bit less crowded and...' I raised my voice to compete with a cheer from the next table, '...noisy.'

'I like this place.' Snorri raised his arm higher. 'Beer, woman, beer! For the love of Odin!'

'Hmmm.' I saw cards and dice aplenty but something told me that winning money off any of these men might be a shortlived pleasure. Beside Snorri an old and tooth-less man supped his ale from a saucer, still managing to spill most of it over the grey stubble of his chin. A young fellow sat next to the elder, this one not quite old enough to shave, slim, slight, unremarkable save for a fine quality to his features that might make him hand-some in the right light. He shot me a shy smile but the truth of it was I didn't trust either of them to be what they seemed. Keep the company of brigands such as filled the Angel and you had to have some iron in you, probably a whole parcel of wickedness too.

Our ale arrived, smacked down in earthenware cups and frothing over the sides. They were poorly fashioned, made in a hurry for the lowest cost, the sort of cups that expected to get broken. I sipped from mine – bitter stuff – and wiped away the white moustache. Across the room, through smoke and past the to-and-fro of bodies, a huge man was giving me the evil eye. He had the kind of blunt weapon of a face you could imagine breaking through a door, and he sat head and shoulders above the men beside him. To the giant's left a man who seemed too fat to be dangerous but somehow managed to look scary anyway, with a patchy beard straggling down over multiple chins, piggy eyes assessing the crowd whilst he chomped the meat off a bone. To the right was the only normal-sized man of the trio, looking somehow ridicu-lous in their shadow, and yet I'd be giving him the widest of berths. Everything about him said warrior. He ate and drank with an intensity that unnerved me, and if a man can unnerve you across a crowded room just by cutting his beef then you probably don't want to see him draw steel.

'You know, I really think we'd be better off at the Red Dragon down the street,' I said, putting down my cup half-empty. 'This is obviously a private party … I don't think it's safe here.'

'Of course it isn't.' Snorri gave me that same worrying grin he had offered on the mountain. 'That's why I like it.' He raised his cup, coming dangerously near to splattering another of the band with foam, this one a moustachioed fellow with an unlikely number of knives bound about his person. 'Meat! Bread! And more ale!' I could imagine him now in the mead-hall of his jarl at a gathering of the clans, grasping a drinking horn. He looked more relaxed than I'd seen him since the blood pits in Vermillion.

I caught sight of the ugly giant throwing me another dirty look. 'I'll be back.' I struggled up between bench and table and went out the front to relieve myself. If my admirer across the tavern had stood and come over to make trouble I probably would have wet myself, so getting out of his eyeline to answer nature's call seemed a good move.

The Falling Angel turned out not to be entirely without class. They had a decent purpose-built wall to piss against and a little gutter running down into the street gutter to

267

carry away the used beer. Although the fact that someone was lying face-down in the street gutter and leaking blood into it did detract somewhat from the otherwise pleasant scene of life flowing through the less salubrious arteries of Crath City. Beyond him, bravos and labourers, good-wives with their good-husbands, vendors of food-on-sticks, all came and went, glimpsed in the light of one lantern, lost, then seen again in the light of another, passing by the purveyors of affection on the street corner and lost again never to return.

I finished up and went back in.

'—think that but you'd be wrong.'

I'd been outside for two minutes, three at the most, and returned to find Snorri flanked by mercenaries and swapping stories like old friends. 'No,' Snorri continued, back half-turned to me. 'I'm telling you he's not. I mean, you might think it to look at him, granted. But I hauled him out of this place, they had him tied to a table, wanted some information and the knives were out. And we're not talking a gentle jabbing here – they were about to cut off the kind of bits you'd miss.' Snorri drained off the last of his ale. 'Know what he said to them? Roared at them he did. I heard it out in the corridor. "I won't ever tell!" Shouted it in their faces. "Get the pincers out if you like. Heat them in the coals. I ain't talking." Now that's the kind of man who's got fire in his belly. Might look like there's nothing behind the bluster, but you can't trust your gut with this one. Brave man. Charged an unborn all by himself. Thing must have been twelve foot of grave-horror, had me disarmed, and in came Jal swinging a sword—' Snorri glanced my way. 'Jal! I was just talking about you.' He gestured across the table. 'Make a hole!' And they did, two mean-eyed thugs sliding apart so I could wedge in. 'These fine fellows are Brother Sim—' he pointed out the slight lad, 'Brother Elban, Brother Gains …' he indicated the old man and a tow-haired bully. 'Well they're all brothers. It's like a holy order of the road, only without any "holy".' He waved his half-gnawed bone down the line. 'Brothers Grumlow, Emmer, Roddat, Jobe...' The knife-man, a stern close-shaved fellow, and two younger men, both sallow, one scar-cheeked, the other pock-marked. 'More beer!' And he thumped the table hard enough to make everything on it jump.

Somehow Snorri's loudness had broken the tension and the Angel came alive. The staff relaxed, the girls came down off the stairs to ply their trade, and laughter ran more freely. I may have been the only man there still miserable. It's in my nature to absent myself from danger whenever possible, and relaxed or not, this brotherhood we'd fallen in with sweated danger from every pore. Besides, Snorri's magic hadn't reached all corners of the room. I could still feel the giant's hostile gaze searing across the back of my neck. I snatched up the ale set before me and knocked it back, hoping to deaden the sensation.

Relief came in the instant. An inviting softness squeezed against my neck to replace the feeling of being stared at, hennaed curls flooded over my shoulder, narrow hands massaged my upper arms and the ridges of a whale-boned corset pressed the length of my back.

'Where's your smile, my handsome?' She leaned around me, bodice offering her goods for display. Pale hands ran down across my chest, over the flatness of my stomach. I'll admit weeks of unwanted exercise and privation had stripped me of any padding. 'I'm sure I could find it.' Her fingers slid lower. Years of experience in such situations kept my attention divided between the twin distractions of breasts served up on the bodice and the location of my own valuables. She leaned in and husked into my ear, 'Sally will make it all good.'

'My thanks, but no.' I surprised myself. She still had her youth, and the good looks she'd been born with. Those had yet to be stripped by the bitter wind of experience that blows through the backstreets of such places. But I'm not at my best in a cold sweat and every coward's instinct I had told me I should be running. Under such circumstances my ardour grows softer.

'Truly?' She leaned in, breasts swaying, breathing the word into my ear.

'I've no money,' I said, and in an instant the warmth fell from her expression, her eyes dismissing me to seek out other opportunities. Snorri caught her attention of course but he was well wedged into his corner and attacking a slab of beef on the bone with such ferocity that Sally perhaps doubted she would be able to compete. In a swirl of skirts she was gone. Nervous or not, I still turned to watch her retreat, and found myself the study of two veterans, grey heads, but lean and tough like old leather, the same dispassionate speculation in their eyes that I'd seen when Cutter John took my measure. I turned back to my plate, lacking appetite. Someone had called those two Brothers Liar and Row. I had no desire to find out how they came by their names. A roar of laughter from Snorri overwrote my fears, though I did flinch when he slammed his axe down on the table.

'No. *That's* an axe. What you've got is more by way of a hatchet.'

As Snorri held forth about longboats, axe design, and the price of salt fish I glanced around with as much surreptitiousness as can be achieved over the rim of a beer mug. Aside from the trio of huge, fat, and deadly behind me, one other table seemed set on matters more serious than the emptying of barrels. In an alcove across the room two men debated over a table. The few pieces of armour they still wore were far better quality than anything the Brothers had. Both were tall, both with long dark hair, one straight, one curled, the elder maybe thirty, a generous face perhaps not given to its current sombre look, the other young, very young, maybe not yet eighteen, but dangerous. If the rest of the Brothers set off my warning bells, this sharp-featured boy rang them off their mountings. He cast me a look the moment I found focus on him. A thousand-yard stare that told me to turn away.

Ale continued to flow and gradually my appetite returned, followed by my good humour. Ale has a way of washing away a man's fears. Sure enough he'll find them the next day, sodden and wrapped around his ankles, with a couple of new ones thrown into the mix and a headache fit for splitting rocks, but in the moment ale is a fine substitute for bravery, wit, and contentment. Before very long I was exchanging tales of wenching with the taciturn Brother Emmer wedged beside me. A fairly one-way exchange truth be told, but I do warm to the subject once my tongue's been loosened, as do most young men in good health.

By the time the next whore approached I was ready with a quite different answer to the one I'd given Sally. Mary had pared the corset and gown ensemble down to just corset, and the combination of her long dark hair, mischievous eyes, and the ample portion of recklessness the ale had loaned me, had me getting to my feet. At which point I noticed the giant – the Brothers called him Rike – was inbound, his face heaped up over raw bones into a fearsome scowl. I sat immediately and suddenly found the bottom of my cup to be fascinating.

Relief sighed out of me as the giant's shadow passed over us and moved on. The man was taller than Snorri by at least a hand's width, his arms lacking the Norseman's well-defined muscle but thicker than my thighs. Brothers scattered out of his way as he closed on Snorri: young Sim literally slid under the table to avoid being caught between them – slippery that one, as I suspected. Mary also vanished with commendable speed. Snorri himself seemed unconcerned, placing his ale mug on the next table along and wiping the beard at the corners of his mouth to clean away any of the larger detritus from his meal.

Generally, even when a fight is inevitable, both parties take a short while to warm to the idea. A disparaging remark is aimed, the reply ups the stakes, someone's mother is a whore, and an instant later – whether the mother was in fact a whore or not – there's blood on the ground. Brother Rike favoured a shorter path to violence. He simply let out an animal roar and closed the final three paces at speed.

At the last moment Snorri shifted his considerable weight and the end of the hastily-cleared bench shot up to smack Rike under the chin then jam against his throat. Even with Snorri sitting on it the bench scraped several inches along the floor before arresting Rike's advance. Snorri stood, letting the bench fall as Rike reeled back, then in one quick stride seized the man behind his head with both hands and rammed him face-first into the table. The impact sent my ale vaulting out of its cup and into my lap. Rike himself slid to the floor trailing a long red stain across the beer-soaked boards.

The killer stood behind his fallen companion. Red Kent they called this one. His hand on the hatchet at his side, a question on his brow.

'Ha! Let him sleep it off.' Snorri grinned at Kent and sat down. Brother Kent returned the smile and went back to sit with his fat companion.

Snorri returned to his place and reached across to retrieve his drink from the other table.

I felt much better after that. Rike's sudden downfall filled me with no end of good humour. I snatched another ale from a passing serving girl, tossing a copper onto her tray.

'Well, Brother Emmer.' I paused to quaff – a style of drinking not dissimilar from swigging but which involves spilling rather more of the brew down your chest. 'I don't know about you but I'm in the mood for some more horizontal entertainment.' And as if on cue sweet Mary stood at my side, smile in place. 'Hail Mary, full of grace,' I said, alcohol substituting for wit. 'My father's a cardinal, did you know that? Let's go upstairs and discuss ecumenical matters.' Mary giggled dutifully and with a hand on Brother Emmer's shoulder I found my feet. 'Lead on, dear lady.' I started a bow but thought better of it, most traces of balance having deserted me.

I followed Mary to the stairs, veering from one side to the other but thankfully not managing to spill a Brother's pint or otherwise causing offence, and always drawn back on course by her tempting wiggle. At the bottom of the stairs Mary took a candle from the wall-box, lit it, and led on up. It seemed I'd started a trend as someone else followed us up the steps, boots thudding.

A long passageway divided the second floor, doors to either side. Mary led the way to one of the ones standing ajar. She set the candle in a holder on the wall and turned. Her smile slipped away, eyes widening.

'Get lost.' For a moment I wondered why I'd said that, then realized that the voice had come from behind me.

Mary dodged aside and pattered back down the corridor whilst I wrestled with the business of turning around without falling over. Before I could manage it fingers knotted in the hair at the back of my head and steered me into the darkened room.

'Snorri!' What had been meant as a manly cry for assistance came out more as a squeak.

'We don't need him.' The hand steered me further in. Shadows swung as the candle moved behind me. 'I—' A pause to deepen my voice. 'I don't have any money. Just a copper or two. The Viking carries for me.'

'I don't want your money, boy.'

Even a skinful of ale only allows so much room for optimism. The edge of a bed-frame pressed sharp against my shins. 'Fuck that!' I swung round, fist flailing. The flickering light allowed me a glimpse of Brother Emmer before a two-handed shove sent me tumbling backwards. My fist found only air, and the candle went out.

'No!' It became a wail. The bedclothes engulfed me,

lavender scented to obscure the stink of old sweat. I lashed out again but the blanket tangled my arm. I heard the door kicked shut. The weight of a body covered me.

'Emmer! I'm not like that!' A shout now. 'I'm—' I remembered my knife and started to hunt it.

'Oh, shush.' Much softer tones, close to my face. 'Just behave.'

'But—'

'It's Emma.'

'What?'

'Emma, not Emmer.' An iron grip encircled my wrist as my fingertips found the hilt of my dagger. The body pinning me now stretched out on mine, hard with muscle but shorter than me, and at such close quarters, quite possibly female. 'Emma,' she said again. 'But let that slip outside this room, pretty boy, and I'll cut your tongue out and eat it.'

'But—'

'Just relax. I've saved you half a silver ducet.'

So I did.

17

'Mired in sin!' The annoyingly judgmental voice rang behind my ears and sent shards of white pain into my head. 'Deeper in deed than in thought! I hadn't considered it possible.'

'Oh God!' Someone had turned my stomach inside out and filled it with eels. I was sure of it.

'How dare you call upon Him!' Baraqel's anger carried a hint of delight as if nothing pleased him more than finding good fresh sin to condemn.

'Just kill me!' I rolled over. All of me hurt. I must have slept with my mouth open because by the taste of it the rats had been using it as a latrine all night.

'How a creature such as you came to the light...' Baraqel's imagination or eloquence failed him.

I cracked one eye open. Daylight streamed in like razors, slivers of it reaching through heavy shutters to illuminate a filthy chamber. I ran a hand across my chest, remembering somebody pushing me. Naked? *My locket!* I lurched up, my stomach lurched faster, and for a moment I struggled not to decorate the headboard. My clothes lay strewn over the floorboards and an ill-advised lunge placed my hand over the comforting lump that the locket made in the shirt that I'd been wearing since Oppen. This time my struggle was in vain and I threw up what appeared to be everything I'd eaten the night before, along with a couple of other people's meals and a bag of diced carrots I'd no memory of consuming.

'Cover yourself, man! There's a lady present.' I winced at the angel's voice, roaring like nails down the chalkboard of my soul.

'Uuuurgod,' proved to be my snappiest response. I wiped my mouth and hauled myself up so my head rose above the edge of the bed.

On the far side, across a wrinkled sea of soiled linen and grey wool, Emma was pulling herself back into a pair of worn leather trousers. Even in my delicate state I managed to admire the hard, if grimy, lines of her body before they were entirely hidden away. She turned, buttoning her jerkin over tight-wrapped breasts, her expression a mix of amusement and mild disgust. I took her to be somewhere in her thirties, toward the end of them perhaps. Even with her short hair and broken nose I couldn't understand how I'd not seen her for what she was before.

'My secret.' She grabbed herself between the legs, all traces of amusement dropping from her face. 'Speak of it and I'll cut you to look the same.' Suddenly I couldn't see any trace of a woman in her at all.

'There's no secret, Brother Emmer,' I said.

'That's right.' She flipped a copper crown at me, pulled her knife from where it had been wedging the door shut, and left the room.

Alone in the unsavoury mess, I took a moment to reflect. 'A helluva woman!' I crawled back onto the bed.

'Naked as the devil and clothed in sin!' Baraqel howled – or at least it felt as if he howled it. 'Find a priest, Prince Jalan and—' Somewhere the sun parted company with the horizon and shut him up. The daylight lanced ever more pointedly through the shutters and I pulled the blanket over my pounding head. The pounding got worse. After a few confused minutes of rolling about in misery, holding my temples, I figured out that a fair portion of the pounding was actually coming through the wall as a headboard struck against it repeatedly. I buried my head under my arms, then decided against it, the mattress was a long way from wholesome, several national boundaries away from it probably. Instead I just plugged my ears and hoped for the world in general to go away, and for whoever was having such a good time in the next room to run out of energy. Or die.

An indeterminate amount of time later the stink of the place drove me to stagger to the door, still reeling, half-drunk from the night before, wrapped in a thin blanket and clutching most of my clothes, my boots, my sword. I took Emma's copper too. Waste not, want not. The shirt I left as a gift for the next occupant – minus Mother's locket of course.

'—royally fucked.' A man stood in the doorway to the next room, facing into it. From the back he looked a lot like the older of the two mercenaries in the alcove last night. 'So, are we ready to go?' he asked.

'Tell them an hour. I'll be ready in an hour.' A younger man, inside the room.

The other shrugged and turned to leave, pulling the door behind him. A woman in the room said something about a prince but the rest of it was lost as the door closed. The man – it *was* the fellow from the alcove – strode past me, a slight smile twitching on his lips.

It occurred to me that I might wear my clothes rather than carry them. I dressed, somewhat gingerly, sore in all manner of places, and went down the stairs.

The bar was largely deserted – just a handful of Brothers slumbering at their tables with heads on folded arms, and Snorri in the midst of it all attacking a pewter plate mounded with bacon and eggs. The dark-haired man from the corridor sat beside him.

'Jal!' Snorri shouted, loud enough to split my head, and waved me over. 'You look like hell! Get some food inside you.'

Resigning myself to his good cheer I sat at the table, as close to his breakfast as my stomach would allow.

'This is Makin.' He jabbed a loaded fork at the man beside him.

'Charmed,' I said, feeling anything but.

'Likewise.' Makin nodded politely. 'I see they have fearsome bedbugs in this establishment.' His gaze slid to where my jacket hung open exposing chest and belly.

'Christ on a bike.' Something had bitten me all right. Emma's tooth marks left me looking like I had some kind of giant pox all over.

'One of the women said you had some trouble with Brother Emmer last night?' Snorri shovelled half a sliced pig into his mouth, tucking in stray ends of bacon with a finger.

'That Emmer's a tricky sort,' Makin said, nodding to himself. 'Lightning fast. Some smarts too.' He tapped his forehead.

'No.' I avoided squeaking the denial. 'No trouble.'

Snorri pursed his lips around his mouthful, peering down at my bites. I clasped my jacket closed over them. 'I'm not judging,' he said, one eyebrow elevating.

'Man's free to choose his own path.' Makin rubbed his chin.

I shot to my feet, immediately wishing I'd taken more time over it. 'Damned if I'm sitting here watching you stuff down pig like a ... like...'

'A pig?' Snorri suggested. He lifted his plate and scraped several fried eggs toward his mouth.

'I'm getting some decent clothes and a bath, and a

meal at some half-civilized establishment.' My headache appeared to be trying to split me down the middle and I hated the world. 'I'll meet you at the castle gates at noon.'

'It's noon now!'

'Three hours!' I called it from the doorway and staggered out into the sunshine.

The sun watched from the west as I climbed the long hill to the outer gate of the Tall Castle. I'd soaked off the road-stink at a bath house, leaving the waters black, had my hair cut and tamed, and calmed my head with some powders the barber swore were good for the easing of pain, also beneficial in cases of plague and dropsy. Finally I had purchased a fresh linen shirt, adjusted to my size with a few well placed stitches, a cloak of brushed velvet, trimmed with something claimed as ermine and probably squirrel, and a silver-ish clasp mounted with a piece of ruby-ish glass to round it off. Not quite princely garb, but enough to pass muster as gentry on casual inspection.

Snorri hadn't turned up. I considered going on without him but decided against it. Apart from the show of having a bodyguard, I've always been in favour of having one, for guarding my body. Especially a maniac over six and a half foot tall, packed with muscle and with a vested interest in not letting me die.

It took perhaps another half hour before I saw the

Norseman on the broad street below. He had Sleipnir and Ron in tow but at least hadn't managed to have any of the Brothers tag along.

'You should have left the nags where they were.' I knew better than to upbraid him for being late. He would just grin and slap me on the back as if I were joking.

'I thought only beggars arrived on foot in these flat countries.' Snorri grinned and ran a hand through Sleipnir's mane. 'Besides, I've grown fond of the old girl, and she's carrying all my stuff.'

'Better to let them think I've a decent horse stabled somewhere nearby than to march up to the gates with this mangy pair and suffer the pity of guardsmen.'

'Well—'

'Look, never mind, just pretend they're both yours.' I walked on letting him follow at a respectful distance.

I presented myself at the appropriately named Triple Gate to the most senior of several chain-armoured guards standing to vet potential visitors. There's a certain arrogance expected of aristocracy and a life of service had trained men such as the ones before me to respond to it. My brother Martus had a marvellous way of looking down his nose at even the tallest of underlings and I do a decent job of it myself. I summoned my reserves and radiated disdain. Snorri would of course assert, and frequently did, that I'd never let go of my royal superiority – though his turn of phrase would run something along the lines of 'still got the sceptre up your arse' – but he'd yet to see me in full flow.

'Prince Jalan Kendeth of Red March, scion of the Red Queen, heir deximal to Vermillion and all its domains.' I paused to let the 'prince' sink in. 'I'm travelling north and have detoured from the Roma Road to pay a courtesy call on King Olidan. In addition to the normal pleasantries I will be offering to bear back to the Red Queen any diplomatic correspondence subsequent to the recent visit of my brother, Prince Martus.' For once in my life I had cause to be thankful that Martus and I looked so alike.

'Welcome to the Tall Castle, your highness.' The man, a sturdy fellow with steel-grey hair escaping his helm, took a step toward me. He ran his beady black eyes over my attire and peered pointedly behind me as if looking for my retinue.

'I'm travelling in haste. This man here is my personal guard. We've rooms down in the Old Town.' I left hanging the suggestion that more retainers might be occupying those rooms.

'Of course, Prince—' He frowned. 'Jalan?'

'Yes. Jalan. Now tell Olidan I'm here and be quick about it.'

That got his attention. There aren't many who'd lose King Olidan his title when face to face with his guards. Even fewer who would want an audience with the king under false pretences. By all accounts King Olidan was not the nicest of men.

'I'll send a messenger immediately, your majesty. Perhaps you would like to wait in my chamber in the gatehouse. I can have a man stable your … horses.'

I considered waiting in the shade of the wall. It promised to be a nice night, but if he kept us waiting too long we'd be standing on our dignity to the amusement of gawkers. 'Lead on,' I said. It's always better to sit on your dignity in private than to stand on it in public.

We followed on beneath the gates to a small door in the thickness of the wall. The stairs behind led upward. The Captain of the Triple Gate had himself a garret above the entranceway, tucked behind the fearsome winding gear and the recesses in which the three portcullises rested when not keeping people out. It proved clean and boasted a table and chairs. I doubted many foreign princes had been entertained there but probably rather few arrived unannounced and all but unaccompanied.

Snorri squeezed his knees in under the table. 'A beer wouldn't go amiss.'

The gate captain raised a brow at that and looked to me. I nodded. Not that I was going to touch the stuff. I'd sworn off it for good that morning. 'I'll see what I can do,' he said, and went out the door. We heard him bellowing in the stairwell a moment later.

'Seems to be going all right.' Snorri reached out for the hunk of bread at the table's centre and started filling his beard with crumbs.

285

'Hmmm.' He had no worries. The risk would all come my way. I had to trust that Olidan would know I wasn't important enough to rank as a hostage and that even a man as cold and ruthless as the King of Ancrath was reputed to be would think twice before earning my grandmother's displeasure. Grandmother was my best chance. There were plenty of stories about how she had made Red March feared among its neighbours and some of them, whilst hard to believe, were the sort that give a man nightmares. In any event, I judged the risk of Ancrath's court worth the chance that I might be released from the chains that bound me to Snorri and set free to scuttle away south once more.

The beer arrived with a jug and two pewter tankards. I watched Snorri savour his while my stomach attempted various feats of acrobatics. Despite the Norseman's easy way I could see the impatience banked behind his gaze. He ached to be back on the road, riding for the coast with all haste, and I could only delay him in Ancrath so long.

The captain returned an hour or so later to say that we were to be given quarters in the keep and most likely summoned to court on the afternoon of the next day. Better than I'd hoped.

We trailed down the narrow steps once more to the entrance where the captain gave us into the care of a velvet-clad pageboy and we finally emerged from the gate tunnel and went on into the Tall Castle.

You could tell at once that the keep was Builder-work: it was ugly, angular, and resilient. The Thousand Suns had scorched the earth all across the Broken Empire. In many places the soil had burned to the bedrock and the bedrock had melted into glass. But the Tall Castle had survived. The fact the Ancraths made their home here said a lot about their character and intentions.

The curtain wall set about the compound and the various outbuildings – barracks, a smithy, stables and the like – were all three or four centuries old but the keep, that was stone poured a thousand years ago. I recall from my lessons that the Builders seldom held on to buildings long. They threw them up then tore them down as if they were no more than tents. But for things not intended to last they did a damn good job of it.

The pageboy led us on toward the keep under the watchful eyes of various guards at station, men patrolling on the walls, and passing knights. It was Snorri who drew their attention of course: not the blasted prince of Red March deigning to grace their mean halls, but some freakishly large Norseman with ten acres of slope to his name. Something about the braids in his hair, or the arctic flash of his eyes, or perhaps the bloody great axe across his back, is apt to make any castle-dweller think for a moment that their defences have been breached.

The keep stood in clear ground with courtyards marked out for training at horse and arms. It made an alarming contrast with the palace at Vermillion and I suspect Grandmother would have swapped in a heartbeat. This was a place built for war, not built to look like it. A castle that had withstood sieges, and fallen to at least one of them, for if Snorri's tales were to be believed, the Ancraths weren't the first to reclaim the place after the tribes of men spread back into the poisoned lands.

'Nice castle.' Snorri gazed up at the Tall Castle while we waited for the great door of iron-banded oak before us to be opened.

The castle was tall. I couldn't complain about that. Though it looked unfinished or more likely broken off. The thing didn't taper or show any concession to height at all as a tower might these days. It simply launched itself straight up at the heavens and gave the impression that before the Thousand Suns had cut short its ambition nothing shy of hitting the clouds would stop it.

'I've seen better,' I lied.

The door swung open and one of Olidan's table-knights, in gleaming half-plate, offered me a bow.

'Prince Jalan, an honour to meet you. I am Sir Gerrant of Treen.' As he straightened I took a half-step back. They'd obviously noted Snorri's stature and decided to put forward their biggest man to receive us. Sir Gerrant stood near as tall and broad with it, a handsome face divided by an ugly scar. He spread his arm out to the side, inviting us in. The smile on his scar-split lips looked genuine enough. 'I'll show you to your rooms. You come too, Stann.' He glanced back at the page. 'Prince Jalan will need someone to fetch and carry for him.'

Sir Gerrant led us up a wide flight of steps and along several corridors. The architecture had an alien quality to it, as if those who made it a thousand years before were not men. Everywhere I saw the signs of more recent work, of efforts made to construct a more human habitation. Floors had been removed, rooms broadened and heightened, curves introduced with carved timber supports, though nothing the Builders made needed any reinforcement.

'I had the honour of meeting Prince Martus during his mission the summer before last.' Sir Gerrant opened another set of doors and held them for us. 'Your family resemblance is remarkable.'

I bit back a sharp reply and grimaced. It's true my brothers both share something of my looks – which came from Father's side of the family, the gold in our hair at least – the height from Grandmother and the handsome from Mother, our father being a short and unprepossessing fellow who would look as suited to being an office clerk as he does to wearing the cardinal's hat. Martus, though, was shaped with a blunt hand. Darin a touch better. The artist had perfected the design by the time he got to me.

We passed through one hall where ladies watched us from a high gallery. I rather suspected Sir Gerrant had been induced to parade us for their inspection. I played the game and affected not to notice. Snorri of course stared up openly, grinning. I heard giggles and one of their number stage-whispered, 'Not another vagabond prince?'

My room, where we finally arrived, was well-appointed and, whilst not quite as grand as a visiting prince might expect, a hundred times better than any accommodation I'd seen since hastily exiting Lisa DeVeer's bedroom what seemed like a lifetime before.

'I'll show your man here to a servant's chamber, or Stann here can do it later,' Sir Gerrant said.

'Take him away,' I said. 'And don't let any of your men mess with him. He's not house-trained and he'll end up breaking them.' I shooed Snorri back into the corridor with fluttering motions of my fingers. He made no reply, only grinned infuriatingly and set off after Gerrant.

I slumped down in an upholstered chair. The first comfortable seat I'd sat in for an age. 'Boots.' I lifted a leg and the page came over to start tugging off the first of them. That's something I'd really missed on the road. Being bone idle. Father was too cheap to staff the hall properly but when we had important visitors he would import a decent number of servants. The ideal level is where if you drop something there's a maid on hand to scoop it up almost before it hits the floor, and if you've an itch that might otherwise require a twist or a stretch, you have only to mention it before indentured fingernails have scratched it for you.

The boot came free with a jerk and the child staggered away, then returned for the next. 'And then you can bring me some fruit. Apples and some pears. Conquence pears mind, not those yellow Maran ones: all mush they are.'

'Yes, sir.' The second boot came free and he took both off to wait beside the door. Hopefully someone would give them a good polish before the morrow, or better still replace them with a nicer pair. The boy opened the door and stepped out. 'I'll get the fruit.'

'Wait a moment.' I leaned forward in my chair, wiggling my toes. 'Stann, ain't it?' It occurred to me the scamp might prove useful.

'Yes, sir.'

'Fruit, and some bread. And find out where this lost prince everyone's celebrating has got to. What's his name anyway?'

'Jorg, sir. Prince Jorg.' And he was off without waiting for a dismissal, or even shutting the door behind him.

'Jorg, eh?' It struck me as odd now that I thought about it. Last night none of the Brothers had so much as mentioned this lost prince, gathered anew to his father's bosom. The whole of Crath City had seemed wrapped in the celebration of the prodigal's return and somehow we had found the only tavern in sight of the Tall Castle where nobody wanted to talk about it. Most odd.

A shadow at the doorway caught my attention and I

let go my musings. 'Yes?' Had young Stann been running *from* rather than running *to*? The man in the doorway didn't look very frightening, but he must have been approaching along the corridor when Stann broke and ran...

The fellow before me would have been the most unremarkable of men, giving even my dear father some competition in the 'ordinary' stakes, if not for the fact that every inch of his exposed skin, which amounted to hands, neck and head, was tattooed with foreign scrawl. The letters even crawled up across his face, crowding his cheeks and forehead with dense calligraphy.

An uncomfortable silence built in the aftermath of his arrival and certainly at home I would have been tempted to damn his eyes and demand that he speak up or get out, possibly encouraging him to one or the other with the aid of whatever was close enough at hand to throw. I'd spent too long on the road though, where any given peasant might stab me for looking at his sister wrong, and my old instincts had rusted up.

'Yes?' Even though it was his place to explain, not mine to ask.

'My name is Sageous. I advise the king on more ... unusual matters.'

'Hallelujah!' Perhaps not the thing to say to someone with such heathen looks, but in the joy of discovering a man who might undo my curse I was prepared to over-look shortcomings such as being of distinctly foreign origin and failing to worship the right deity. Snorri shared those faults after all, and despite my misgivings had proved to have several redeeming features.

'People are not always so pleased to see me, Prince Jalan.' A small smile on his lips.

'Ah, but not everyone needs a miracle.' I got to my feet and advanced on the man, pleased to find I towered over him. I guessed him to be about forty and from my vantage point I could read what was written on the top of his head. Or at least I could if I knew the script. I guessed the writing to be from somewhere east and maybe south too. A long way east and south. A place where the writing looked like spiders mating. I'd seen the like before in my mother's chambers. Sageous tilted his head to meet my gaze and I forgot all about his inconvenient script, lack of stature, even the spice-stink of him that had just reached my nostrils. All of a sudden those unremarkable eyes of his became everything that mattered. Twin pools of contemplation, calm, brown, ordinary...

'Prince Jalan?'

I shook my head to find the damnable little man snapping his fingers in front of my face. If I hadn't wanted something from him I'd have kicked his arse all the way to the Triple Gate. Well, if he hadn't been a sorcerer as well. Not people to rub the wrong way. Rubbed the right way though ... as with Aladdin's lamp, I might get my wish. At least I knew now that he wasn't a charlatan with the mirrors and the smoke and the quick hands.

'Prince Jal—'

'I'm fine. Came over dizzy for a second. Come in. Sit. I need to ask you about something.' I pinched the bridge of my nose and blinked a few times to refocus as I walked a less-than-straight path back to my chair. 'Sit.' I waved at another seat.

Sageous took an elegant ladder-back but stood behind it rather than following my bidding. Tan fingers ran over wood so dark as to be almost black, investigating each polished and gleaming curve as if seeking meaning. 'You're a puzzle, Prince Jalan.'

I bit back on my opinion and resisted damning him for his impudence.

'A puzzle of two pieces.' The heathen watched me with those placid eyes of his. He released the chair and ran his fingers over his forehead, brows, cheekbones, cheeks. Everywhere his fingertips touched it seemed that for a heartbeat the tattooed script grew darker, like fissures through his flesh into some inner blackness. He cocked his head, then looked back toward the corridor. 'And the second piece is close by.'

'I would have expected no less of someone a king such as Olidan seeks counsel from.' I flashed my best grin, the one that says 'amiable bluff hero with the common touch'. 'The truth is I got caught up in some foul spell along with the Norseman I've brought with me. We're bound together by the magics. If we get too far apart bad things happen to us. And all I want to do is have someone unbind us so we can go our separate ways again. The man who could do that would find me a very generous prince indeed!'

Sageous looked far less surprised than I had expected. Almost as if he'd heard the story already. 'I can help you, Prince Jalan.'

'Oh, thank God. I mean, thank any god. You don't know how hard it's been, yoked to that brute. I thought I was going to have to trek all the way to the fjords with him. Cold does not agree with me at all. My sinus—'

Sageous raised a hand and cut off my babbling. Unconscionable that he should interrupt a prince but it's true that the relief of it all had over-loosened my tongue.

'There is, as in many things, an easy way and a hard way.'

'The easy way sounds easiest,' I said, leaning forward for the heathen spoke very soft.

'Kill the other man.'

'Kill Snorri?' I jolted back, surprised. 'But I thought if he—'

'On what grounds did you think this, Prince Jalan? A sensible man may fear certain possibilities but don't let fear turn possibility into certainty. If either of you dies the curse will die with you and the other may carry on unencumbered.'

295

'Oh.' It did seem silly that I had been so sure of what would happen. 'But I can't kill Snorri.' I didn't want him dead. 'I mean, it would be very difficult. You've not met him. When you do you'll understand.'

Sageous shrugged, the slightest raising of shoulders. 'You are in King Olidan's castle. If he commanded the man dead then the man would die. I doubt he would refuse a prince's request for the life of a commoner. Especially a man from the ice and snow, given to the worship of primitive gods.'

My early enthusiasm escaped me in a long sigh. 'Tell me the difficult way...'

18

I woke in a cold sweat, the bed warm around me. For a moment I wondered which tavern I was in. I even thought for one instant that Emma might be lying beside me, but my questing fingers found only linen sheets. Fine linen. The castle. I remembered and sat up, blind night on every side.

Nightmares had been chasing me, one into the next, and my heart still pounded from the exercise, but I couldn't recall any details. Nothing came to me save the memory of something dreadful stalking me through dark places, so close I felt its breath on my neck, felt it clutching, snagging my shirt...

'Castle, Jal: you're in a castle.' My voice rang thin as if I were in some vast and empty space.

The candle I'd left burning must have blown out – not even a scent of it remained. I'd tinder and flint, but they were in a saddlebag wherever Ron had been stabled.

'You're too big a boy to be scared of the dark.' The

fear in my voice convinced me I was better off keeping silent. I listened for any sound other than my own breathing, but none reached me.

I threw myself down into the pillow, pulled the sheets about me, and to distract myself from night terrors I concentrated on my last exchange with Sageous.

'The difficult way?' he had asked, as if surprised I would consider it. 'The difficult way would be to complete the spell's work for it. Each enchantment is an act of will that strives toward completion. The desires of the most powerful, when spoken, when enunciated along the paths that their art has graven within the fabric of what is, become like living things. The spell will twist and turn, it will change, consider, conspire until it achieves the aim that formed it.

'The spell is incomplete because the target remains. Destroy that target and the enchantment, this curse that bends you to its own ends, will fade away.'

I had thought of the eyes behind that mask.

'Kill Snorri, you say?' The easy way did sound easier.

The eyes that had glittered behind the slits in that porcelain work of masquerade, those same eyes had watched me through my nightmares. My skin crawled with the possibility of that scrutiny even now. The linen sheets I held were a child's protection, and even steel armour would offer no salvation against this horror. Kill Snorri?

'A simple matter that I can arrange for you, my prince.' Everything the heathen said sounded reasonable.

'No, truly, I can't. He's become something of a f—' I bit that off. 'Something of a trusted retainer.'

Sageous had shaken his head, lines of text blurring before my eyes. 'This is a madness you have fallen into, my prince. The barbarian has taken you prisoner – a hostage to his own fortunes – and drags you into terrible danger. A wise man, Lord Stoccolm, wrote of this many centuries ago. By degrees the prisoner comes to see his captor as a friend. You have fallen into his dream, Prince Jalan. Time to wake up.'

And lying there in the silent dark of that room, with nothing but two handfuls of sheets for protection from the conviction that the nameless horror from Vermillion stood watching at the foot of my bed, I did try to wake. I ground my teeth and tried either to sleep or to wake – but only the memory of Sageous's voice offered any escape.

'You merely need ask King Olidan for his protection – I will carry the message – and come morning this Norseman will occupy a pauper's grave down by the river. You will wake a free man, ready to return to the life you were snatched from. Free to take up your old ways as if nothing had happened.'

I had to admit it had sounded very tempting. It still did. But my tongue kept refusing the words. Perhaps that too was part of this Stoccolm's disease. 'But he's … well, a loyal retainer.' And of course, whilst I may be a liar and a cheat and a coward, I will never, ever, let down a loyal retainer. Unless of course it requires honesty, fair play, or bravery to avoid doing so – or an act that in some other manner mildly inconveniences me. 'I see your point … still, there must be another way. Can't you do something? A man with your skills?'

Again the shake of the head, so slow and slight that you could almost believe the sorrow. 'Not without great risk, my prince, to myself and to you.' He turned those mild eyes on me and I felt the draw of them immediately, as if at any moment he could pull me in to drown. 'There is a third way. The blood of the person who placed the curse on you.'

'Oh, I couldn't—' The thought of that old witch unmanned me almost as much as the creature at the opera did. 'The Silent Sister is too cunning and Grandmother dotes on her.'

Sageous nodded as if expecting this. 'She has a twin. One whom fate may place in your path. The blood of the twin will accomplish the same goal. It will quench the spell's fire.'

'A twin?' It was hard to imagine two such monsters. The blind-eye woman had always seemed so singular.

'She is named Skilfar.'

'God damn it all!' I'd heard of Skilfar. And anyone you've heard of is trouble. That's bankable wisdom, that is. The Wicked Witch of the North – I'm sure I'd heard

Grandmother call her that, smiling as if she'd said something clever. 'Damn it all.' Killing Snorri would be hard. I'd been happy to spend his life in the blood pits against the possibility of coin. But now I knew him and it put a different shine on things. In fact it soured the whole business of the pits. All the men there had lives, and I wasn't sure I'd ever be able to enjoy the sport again knowing that. Life has ways of getting under your skin, spoiling your fun with too much information. Youth is truly the happiest time where we roll in the bliss of ignorance.

'Your old life, my prince. Returned to you.'

My old life, the pleasures of the flesh, and of the gaming table, and sometimes the first on the second. It had been shallow and balanced on Maeres's knife-edge, but sometimes shallow is more than enough. You can drown in deep. 'I'll sleep on it,' I had said.

Except that I couldn't sleep. Instead I lay in the cold sweat that fear had wrapped me in and stared at the night. Snorri's death, the monster's destruction, the blood of the Silent Sister or her northern twin. None of them easy. Each hard in its separate way.

'Ask the king for the Norseman's head,' Sageous had told me. 'It's the easiest way.' *Aren't you good at easy?* That's what the writing seemed to say – offered up on his palms. *Aren't you good at leaving?*

If I were good at leaving I would know where the blasted door was. I normally kept good tabs on such things, plotted my escape routes, got the lie of the land.

But when the heathen left the room a great weariness wrapped itself around me and I fell into the bed like a stone into the deepest pool.

'Kill the Norseman.' It sounded more reasonable each time he said it. After all, it would save Snorri the discovery that his family were dead. All he had before him was a long trip to the worst news in the world. Didn't he greet battle like an old friend, eager to meet his end? '*Kill the Norseman.*' I couldn't tell if I'd said it or Sageous.

I had sat in the softness of the great chair, facing the heathen, listening to his truths. Had sat? Was sitting? I sat opposite him now as he stood behind the ladder-back chair, fingers running over its rungs as if they were a harp on which a melody could be played. 'So you'll ask for his head.' Not a question. Those mild eyes fatherly now. A father and friend. Though lord knows, not *my* father: he always seemed embarrassed by the whole business of father and son.

Yes. Sageous was right. I started to say the words. 'I'll ask for his—'

The point of a sword emerged from Sageous's narrow chest, and not your common or garden sword either but one as brilliant as the dawn, bright as steel drawn from the white heat of the furnace. Sageous looked down at the point, astonished, and it advanced until a foot of gleaming blade stood from his chest.

'What?' Blood ran from the corners of his mouth.

302

'This is not your place, heathen.' Wings unfurled behind the man as if they were his own. White wings. White like summer clouds, eagle-feathered, broad enough to bear a man skyward.

'How?' Sageous gargled blood now, spilling it down his chin with the word.

The sword withdrew and a head unbowed, rising above the heathen, a face as proud and inhuman as those wrought in marble upon statues of Greek gods or Roman emperors. 'He is of the light.' And in a flash the blade took the heathen's head, shearing through his neck as a scythe takes grass.

'Wake up.' Not a voice from the angel that loomed above Sageous's corpse. A voice that came from outside the castle, huger than sound should be, loud enough to break stone. 'Wake.'

It made no sense. 'What—'

'Wake up.'

I blinked. Blinked again. Opened my eyes. Instead of blackness, post-dawn grey. I sat up, sheets still clinging to my sweat-soaked limbs. Behind the pale ghosts of lace curtains the sky lightening in the east.

'Baraqel?'

'A lowly dream-smith thinking he could sully one of the light-sworn!' Baraqel sounded smug. Then in a more serious tone, 'I see a hand behind him, though. With a more deadly touch ... blue fingered. The L—'

'T-that was you? But, you're so ... well ... such a

303

pain.' I slid from the bed, each part of me aching as if I'd spent the night wrestling a Barbary ape. The room lay bare, the angel confined to my head again.

'I speak in the voice you give me, Jalan. I'm limited by your imagination, shaped by your conceits. Each of your failings diminishes me, and they are many. I—'

The last burning edge of the sun broke the horizon, turning a whole forest to gold. And the silence was golden. Baraqel had had his moment. I returned to the comfortable chair, pulling on my trews, but found I didn't want to sit in it. I looked at the ladder-back and imagined Sageous there as he'd been in my dream, head severed and just starting to drop. He wanted me to have Snorri killed. His arguments had seemed sound enough, but although I lost more money at the card table than I won, I'd spent enough time there to know when I was being played.

By the time I'd washed and dressed the day had entered stage east, cocks crowed, people with jobs to do bustled about them, and below the Tall Castle Crath City shook itself awake. A timid tapping turned me from my contemplation at the window.

'What?'

'It's S-Stann, your majesty.' A pause. 'Did you need a dresser or should I—'

'Go get my Viking and bring him here. We'll take breakfast where they serve the best stuff.'

He scampered away, the sounds of his retreat fading. I sat on the bed and pulled out my locket. A patchwork thing now, each gem I'd sold leaving an empty socket to stare at me in blind accusation. It seemed fitting. Justice is blind. Love is blind. Another gem would buy me back to Vermillion in the comfort of a fine carriage. One more would buy wine and company at every stop. Two more sockets to watch my passage, to watch me leave a friend in a pauper's grave and return to the shallows. I wondered if Baraqel saw my soul when he looked at me. Did it look like this? Bartered away, a little each day, buying a coward's path through the margins of life?

'Still,' I told myself. 'Better a long ignoble life of shallow pleasures than a short stab at heroism, ending with a short stab. And just because one man plays another doesn't always mean that it's not the right direction for both of them.' I thought of the cold North, and the horror-laden stories Snorri told of it, and shivered.

'Jal!' Snorri filled the doorway and his grin filled his face. 'You look worse after a night alone in silk sheets than after a night at the Angel wrestling with your friend who likes to bite.' Behind him Stann hovered in the corridor, trying to find a way past.

I stood up. 'Come on. We'll let the boy find us some breakfast.'

The two of us trailed Stann, matching his jog with an easy stride. 'Food can be brought to your rooms, my lords.' He said it over his shoulder, catching his breath.

'I like to mingle,' I said. 'And I'm a royal highness to you boy. He's a … hauldr. The correct address for one of that station is "oi you".'

'Yes, your royal highness.'

'Better.'

Another corridor, another turn, and we came through an arch into a sizeable hall boasting three long tables. Men ate at two of the tables, guests by the look of them, or figures of some rank within the castle. None of them royalty but not common folk. Stann indicated the unoccupied table. 'Your royal highness.' He eyed Snorri up, biting his lip, hopping from one foot to the other in his indecision, doubting now that the Norseman's rank warranted a place at any of the tables.

'Snorri will eat with me,' I said. 'Special dispensation.'

Stann breathed a sigh of relief and showed us to our chairs.

'I'll have eggs, scrambled with a pinch of salt, a pinch of black pepper, and then a fish. Kipper, mackerel, something smoked. The Viking will probably have a pig, lightly killed.'

'Bacon.' Snorri nodded. 'And bread. The blacker the better. And beer.'

The boy ran off, repeating his orders as fast as he could.

Snorri leaned back in his chair and yawned mightily.

'How did you sleep?' I asked.

He grinned and gave me an appraising look. 'I had strange dreams.'

306

'How strange?'

'I dream of Loki's daughter each night. If a dream makes Aslaug's appearances seem ordinary then you can imagine it to be very strange.'

'Try me.'

'A small man covered in scribble spent the night trying to convince me to kill you this morning. At least most of the night … until Aslaug ate him.'

'Ah.'

We sat in silence for a minute, until a serving man arrived with two flagons of small beer and a loaf of bread.

'So?' I asked, more than a little tense. A long knife lay between us, next to the bread.

'I decided against it.' Snorri reached out and broke the loaf in half.

'Good.' I relaxed with a sigh.

'Better to wait until we're out of the castle then do it.' He chomped down on the bread to hide his grin. 'And you? How'd you sleep?'

'About the same,' I said, but Snorri had lost interest, his gaze drawn to the doorway.

I turned to see a young woman approaching: tall, slender but not weak, not a conventional beauty but she had something about her that filled me with unconventional thoughts. I watched her advance with sure steps. High cheekbones, expressive lips, dark red curls frothing down around her shoulders. I stood, ready with my bow. Snorri kept his seat.

'My lady.' I held her gaze. Extraordinary eyes, green but giving back more light than they took in. 'Prince Jalan Kendeth at your service.' I waved a hand at the table. 'My man Snorri.' Her dress was a simple thing but made with a care and understated quality that said she came from money.

'Katherine ap Scorron.' She looked from me to Snorri, back again. Her accent confirmed Teuton origins. 'My sister, Sareth, would like the pleasure of your company for a light lunch.'

A grin spread across my face. 'I'd be delighted, Katherine.'

'Well and good then.' She ran an eye over the length of me. 'I wish you a good stay and safe travels onward then, prince.' And she turned with a swish of skirts, making for the corridor. Nothing in her tone or pale face had suggested she thought my company might be a pleasure for her sister. In fact a redness around her eyes made me wonder if she had been crying.

I leaned down to Snorri. 'I sense sisterly conflict! Big sister got to dine with the prince and little sister's pretty nose is out of joint about it.' My instincts in these matters are seldom wrong. The dynamics of sisterly rivalry are well known to me. Snorri frowned – a touch of the green-eyed monster himself, no doubt. 'Don't wait up for me!' And I made to follow the girl.

A big hand caught at my wrist, snatched back at the sharp crackle between us. Enough to stop me, though. 'I don't think that was an invitation of that sort.'

'Nonsense. A highborn lady doesn't deliver messages. She would have sent a page. There's more than one message here!' I could forgive the barbarian for his ignorance of court subtleties.

Katherine reached the doorway. It's true that her retreat lacked the swaying come-on one sees in places like the Falling Angel. I found it tempting even so. 'Trust me. I know castle life. This is my game.' And I hurried after her.

'But her arm—' Snorri called after me. Something about an armband.

I had to smirk at the thought of a hut-born Norseman trying to instruct me in the ways of castle women. She'd come without chaperone or champion, bolder than brass, taking a good look at all the prince on offer.

'Katherine.' I caught her in the corridor, yards from the hall. 'Don't run away now.' Lowering my voice into a seductive growl. I took hold of her backside in my cupped hand through the layers of taffeta. Smooth and firm.

She turned more swiftly than I thought possible in such a garment and— Well the next eternity or so I spent in a blind white place full of pain.

I've always felt that the placement of a man's testicles is an eloquent argument against intelligent design. The fact that a slight young woman can with a well-placed knee reduce the hero of the Aral Pass to a helpless creature too full of agony to do anything but roll on the floor hoping to squeeze the occasional breath past his pain – well that's just poor planning on God's part. Surely?

'Jal?' A shadow against the white agony. 'Jal?'

'Go. Away.' Past clenched teeth. 'And. Let. Me. Die.'

'It's just, you're blocking the corridor, Jal. I'd pick you up, but … you know. Stann, get a guardsman to help you haul the prince back to his room, will you?'

Some dim awareness of motion penetrated my misery. I knew my heels were dragging over stone floors, and somewhere behind them Snorri was trailing along, engaging in cheerful banter with the people towing me.

'A misunderstanding, I expect.' And he chuckled. Chuckled! It's in the code – when one man is wounded so ignominiously, all men must wince and show sympathy, not chuckle. 'They probably do things differently down south…'

'Losing my touch.' I managed to gasp the words.

'I think you probably touched too much, knowing you, Jal! Didn't you see the black armband? The girl's in mourning!' Another chuckle. 'Might have given him a proper beating if she hadn't been! She's got spirit, that one. Saw it the moment she arrived. Norse blood probably.'

I just groaned and let them haul me to my chamber.

'Damned if I'm going to see the sister. She'll be a monster.' They lifted me onto my bed.

'Gently, lads,' Snorri said. 'Gently!' Though he still sounded far too good humoured about the whole thing.

'Damnable Scorron bitch. Ahh!' Another wave of pain shut me off. 'Countries have gone to war for less!'

'Technically you *are* at war, aren't you?' The chair creaked as Snorri lowered himself into it. 'I mean those men you heroed over at this Aral Pass, they were Scorrons weren't they?'

He had me there. 'I wish I'd killed fifty more of them!'

'Anyway, the sister's even prettier.'

'How the hell would you know?' I tried to roll over and gave up.

'Saw them both on a balcony yesterday.'

'Yes?' I managed to roll. It didn't help. 'Well she can go hang.' I gave him the dirtiest look that would fit through my squint.

Snorri shrugged and bit into the pear he'd stolen off my side table. 'Dangerous way to talk about the queen if you ask me.' All through a full mouth.

'Queen?' I rolled back to face the wall. 'Ah shit.'

19

I hobbled behind Stann as he led the way to Queen Sareth's personal chambers. I wondered that the meeting had been arranged for her rooms but didn't doubt that her virtue would be well guarded.

It struck me as peculiar that our path led through the underbelly of the castle, down steps and into a long corridor where kitchen stores lay stacked ceiling-high in stockrooms right and left, but I *had* told Stann to lead me by the shortest route owing to the delicacy with which I needed to walk. We ascended by a narrow stair, surely a servants' passage for the delivery of meals to the royal quarters.

'The queen asks that you be discreet if questioned about any visits,' Stann said, holding the lantern high in a long windowless passage.

'Do you know what discreet means, boy?'

'No, sir.'

I harrumphed at that, not certain whether he was displaying ignorance or discretion.

Stann tapped at a narrow door, a key turned in a heavy lock and we entered. It took a moment to realize that the queen herself had unlocked the door. I thought at first it must be a lady-in-waiting but when she turned back to watch me emerge there could be no mistaking her. A lady-in-waiting would never have worn so fine a gown, and Sareth shared too many of Katherine's looks to be anyone but her sister. I judged her to be in the midst of her twenties, a touch shorter than her sister, her face softer and more classically beautiful: full lips, waves of deepest red hair. She had green eyes too but without the peculiar inner-light of her sister's.

The other thing to notice about Queen Sareth, a fact that no gown short of a pavilion would be able to disguise, was that she had either recently swallowed a piglet, or she was quite pregnant.

'You may show Prince Jalan to his chair and pour his wine, Stann, then scuttle off.' She made a shooing action with her hands.

The lad plumped a cushion for me in a large chair acceptably far from the queen's, which is to say in the opposite corner. In truth a properly acceptable distance would be one that put me out in the corridor for no queen should be alone with a strange man in their private chambers, especially if that strange man is me.

I walked carefully to the chair, moved the cushion and lowered myself on to it.

'Are you well, Prince Jalan?' A look of genuine concern furrowed the smoothness of her brow.

'Ah, just…' I settled. 'Just an old war wound, my queen. It plays up from time to time. Especially if I've been too long without a good fight.'

Beside me Stann pressed his lips tight together and filled the silver goblet on the service table from a tall ewer of wine. His job done, he retreated through the servant door and the patter of his feet diminished into the distance. It occurred to me that if I were found here, unattended, then my life might well depend upon whatever story the queen decided to tell. It seemed unlikely that she would admit to extending an invitation and I'm sure her vicious younger sister would paint an unflattering picture of my earlier advances if the whole matter were brought before Olidan. I resolved to extricate myself from the situation at the first opportunity.

'And how are you enjoying Ancrath, Prince Jalan?' Sareth's accent kept more of the Teuton edge than her sister's and recalled to mind the cries of the Scorron patrolmen who had tried to ride me down in the Aral Pass. It did little to calm my nerves.

'It's a lovely country,' I said. 'And Crath City is very impressive. Celebrations were in full swing when we arrived.'

She frowned at that, pursing her lips. Evidently, I'd struck a sour note. Pregnant or not, she was very pretty. 'Scorron is a more beautiful land, and the Eisenschloss a finer fortress.' She didn't seem aware that we men of Red March counted the Scorrons as our mortal enemies. No matter – I've long been a proponent of love not war, though they often make close bedfellows. 'But you are right, Prince Jalan, Ancrath has much to recommend it.'

'Indeed. I fear though, my queen, that I'm somewhat at a loss here. I think perhaps it would be more seemly if we discussed these matters this afternoon at court? Your beauty is talked of far and wide and people might mistake my intentions if it were known that…' Normally I would be happy to cuckold any man foolish enough to leave a woman like Sareth wanting more … but Olidan Ancrath? No. And besides, her pregnancy and my present invalid status both helped to lessen my interest in the opportunity.

Sareth's face crumpled in dismay, her bottom lip wobbled and, hefting herself from her chair, she hastened across to kneel beside mine. 'Forgive me, Prince Jalan!' She took my dark and callused hands in her slim white ones. 'It's just— just— we've all had such a shock what with the arrival of this dreadful boy.'

'Boy?' I'd had very little sleep for two nights now and none of this was making sense.

'Jorg, Olidan's son.'

'Ah, the lost prince,' I said, enjoying her hands around mine.

'Better he had stayed lost.' And I glimpsed some steel behind her tear-stained prettiness.

Suddenly even my sleep-deprived mind couldn't refuse to see the problem any longer. This returned prince couldn't be Sareth's son, she wasn't old enough for that... A second wife then, busy producing what she had thought would be an heir of her own?

'Ah.' I leaned forward, my glance falling to her belly. 'I can see his return might be a problem for you.' Her face contorted in misery again. 'There, there, don't cry, my queen.' And I pawed her a bit, the bluff hero comforting a damsel in distress, and perhaps running his hands through that wonderful hair.

'Why couldn't the boy stay lost and wandering?' She turned those wet-lashed eyes on me.

'Boy, you say?' I'd thought the prince a grown man for some reason. 'Just how old is—'

'A child! A week ago he was thirteen and forgotten. Past all care. Now he's reached majority and...' Another flood of tears, her face buried against my shoulder. 'Oh, the trouble he's caused. The chaos in the throne room.'

'It's a difficult age.' I nodded wisely and drew her closer. It's an instinct. I can't help it. She smelled gorgeous, of lilac and honeysuckle, and pregnancy hadn't just filled her womb – her bodice overflowed with nature's gifts too.

'In my homeland they call you the Devil of the Aral,' she said. 'The Red Prince.'

'They do?' I tried the words again, removing the surprise from my voice. 'They do.'

A nod against my shoulder. 'Sir Karlan survived the battle in which you fought, and escaped to the North. At court he told us how you battled without fear – like a madman, striking down man after man. Sir Gort among them. Sir Gort was the son of my father's cousin. A warrior of some renown.'

'Well…' I guessed some tales grew in the telling and that too much fear might sometimes look like no fear at all. Either way, the queen had given me a gift and it was beholden to me to milk it. 'My people *do* call me the hero of the pass. I supposed it's fitting that the Scorrons call me the devil. I will wear the name with pride.'

'A hero.' Sareth sniffed, wiped at her eyes, one slim hand on my chest. 'You could help.' Soft words, almost a whisper, and close enough to my ear to make me shiver deliciously.

'Of course, of course, dear lady.' I caught myself before I promised too much. 'How?'

'He's a bully, this Jorg. He needs putting in his place. Of course he's too highborn for just anyone to deliver the lessons he deserves. But a prince could challenge him. He'd have to accept a challenge from a prince.'

'Well…' I breathed in her scent and covered the hand on my chest with my own. Visions of chasing those damnable bucket-boys through the back corridors of the opera house floated before me. I'd kicked a few backsides that day! A ragged thirteen year-old princeling, returned cap-in-hand after a month starving by the waysides

317

before hunger defeated his pride and he came home to Daddy … I could see myself delivering a sharp lesson to such a lad. Especially if it won favour with his lovely stepmother.

Sareth nuzzled closer, lips very near to my neck, her over-full breasts squashing against me. 'Say you will, my prince.'

'But Olidan…'

'He's an old man, and cold. He barely sees me now he's done his duty.' Her lips touched my throat, hand sliding to my stomach. 'Say you'll help me, Jalan.'

'Of course, lady.' I closed my eyes, surrendering to her ministrations. Kicking an arrogant little boy-prince around the court would be fun, and by the time I came to tell the tale in Vermillion Prince Jorg would be older and my audience would forget that he'd been a child when I taught him his lesson.

'I don't mind if you hurt him.' She walked her hand two-fingered across my shirt, scratching at the buttons, playful.

'Accidents do happen,' I murmured.

That proved somewhat prophetic as the words inspired Sareth to explore rather more robustly and her hand plunged down into my trousers.

As any man wounded in the line of duty can tell you, a knee to the groin takes a while to recover from, and it may be several days before a prince's crown jewels are ready for inspection once more. Sareth's over-hasty 'cupping' re-ignited the earlier agonies and I must admit that my cry of pain could be described as somewhat high-pitched. Possibly even … girly. Which would explain why the queen's door guard took it upon themselves to crash in through her bolted door to rescue their charge from whatever fiend assaulted her.

Fear can be an excellent anaesthetic. Certainly the sudden appearance of two mean-faced men in Ancrath livery with bare steel in their hands gets rid of ball-ache double quick. A catapult could have ejected me from that chair no faster and I was clattering down the servant stair before you could say 'adultery', door slamming behind me.

I reached my room, panting and still in panic. Snorri had abandoned the chair I'd placed him in and now lay sprawled on the bed. 'That was quick.' He raised his head.

'We should probably leave,' I said, realizing as I looked about for my belongings that I didn't actually have any.

'Why?' Snorri swung his legs over the side of the bed and sat up, the structure creaking alarmingly beneath him.

'Uh…' I leaned back out into the corridor, looking for the approach of guardsmen. 'I may have…'

'Not the queen?' Snorri stood and I became acutely aware once more of just how much he towered over me. 'Who saw you?' Anger in his voice now.

'Two guards.'

'Her guards?'

'Yes.'

'She'll buy them off. It will all be buried.'

'I'm just not wanting to get buried with it.'

'It'll be fine.' I could see him thinking about that meeting with King Olidan, about all the lines I had sold him regarding knowing his enemy and getting the curse taken off us.

'You think?'

'Yes.' He nodded. 'Idiot.'

'We could leave anyway. I mean. I spoke to the king's magician last night and he wasn't that helpful—'

'Hah!' Snorri sat down again with a thump. 'That old dream-witch! We'll have to look elsewhere for help, Jal. His power's broken. The boy smashed Sageous's totem a couple of days back. Some kind of glass tree. Jorg pushed it over in the throne room. Pieces of it everywhere!'

'Where— where do you get all this stuff?'

'I talk to people, Jal. While the queen's sticking her tongue in your ear I'm busy listening instead. Prince Jorg undid Sageous's power, and boldly. There must be some other sorcerer or wise woman who can help us. Sageous can't be the only one in the whole country. We need King Olidan to advise us if we want this curse taken off.'

'Ah…'

'Ah?'

'I made a promise to rough up this boy-prince for Sareth. I'm hoping that won't sour things with King Olidan. If he dotes on the child it could cause problems.'

'Why?' Snorri looked up at me, spreading his broad hands. 'Why would you do that?' His axe lay by the bed and I toed it underneath, out of sight, just in case.

'You did see her, the queen?' I asked. 'How could I say no?'

Snorri shook his head. 'I've never seen a man who understands so little about women and yet is so led about by them.'

'So, this boy. Will it cause problems if I knock him around a bit?' I asked. 'Since you seem to know all there is to know about the Ancraths.'

'Well. The father doesn't love the son. I know that much,' Snorri said.

'That's a relief.' I relaxed enough to sink into the chair.

'And I know you're a brave man, Jal, and a hero from the war...'

'Yes...'

'But I wouldn't be so sure about knocking this Prince Jorg around. You did see him at the Angel the other night?'

'The Angel? What are you talking about?'

'The Falling Angel. I know you had other things on your mind, but you might have noticed the place was packed with his band. The Brothers.'

'What?' The chair contrived to trap me in its clutches as I tried to stand again.

'The prince was there, you know? In the corner with Sir Makin.'

'Oh God.' I remembered his eyes.

'And banging Sally in the room next to yours, I hear. Nice girl. From Totten just south of the Lure.'

'Dear God.' I'd thought Makin's young companion to be eighteen at the least. He couldn't have been less than six foot.

'And of course you know what prompted him to take another trip so soon after his return to the Tall Castle?'

'Remind me.' I would have thought making a mortal enemy of a dream-witch would be enough to get most men planning a long journey.

'He killed the king's champion, the Captain of the Guard, Sir Galen. That's who Sareth's sister was in mourning for.'

'You're going to tell me it wasn't by poisoning his mead?'

'Single combat.'

'We're leaving.' I called it from the corridor.

20

Nobody had orders to stop a visiting prince taking a ride around the city before his appointment at court. We collected Ron and Sleipnir and clattered down into Crath City. And kept on going. Riding proved a misery and I shifted constantly in my saddle, seeking more comfortable positions and cursing all Scorrons, their damned women most of all.

'Both of them had their eyes too close together too... I never liked ginger hair in any case, and I'm sure that younger one had—'

'She had something about her, that Katherine,' Snorri interrupted. 'I could imagine her going places – doing great things. She had the look.'

'If you liked her so much you should have made your move.' Pain made me goad him, seeking distraction. 'Perhaps she was looking for a bit of rough.'

Snorri shrugged, rolling in his saddle as we followed the Roma Road. 'She's a child yet. And I'm a married man.'

'She was seventeen if she was a day. And I thought you Vikings operated under ship-rules?'

'Ship-rules?' Snorri raised a brow. Crath City was nothing more than a stain in the air behind us now.

'If you get there by ship there are no rules,' I said.

'Ha.' He narrowed his eyes a touch. 'We're men as any other. Some good. Some bad. Most in between.'

I blew through my lips. 'How old are you anyway, Snorri?'

'Thirty. I think.'

'Thirty! When I'm thirty I want to still be having fun.'

Again the shrug, a small smile. Snorri didn't take offence at much. Which was a good thing all told. 'Where we're going living to thirty is hard work.'

'Is there anything good about the North? Anything at all? Any single thing that I can't better find somewhere warm?'

'Snow.'

'Snow's not good. It's just cold water gone wrong.'

'Mountains. The mountains are beautiful.'

'Mountains are inconvenient lumps of rock that get in people's way. Besides if it's mountains I want I have the Aups on my doorstep.'

We clomped along in silence for a minute. The traffic on the Roma Road had thinned but on its long straight sections you could still see carts and horsemen, even travellers afoot, stretching off into the distance.

'My family,' he said.

324

And though I laid no claim to wisdom I was wise enough to say nothing to that.

The summer that had welcomed us belatedly in Ancrath wore thin as we progressed north. At the town of Hoff, amid fields ripe for harvest and on a cold day with more of autumn in it than any other season, Snorri led us east from the Roma Road.

'We could take ship from a Conaught port,' I said.

'Men of the true North are not loved in Conaught,' Snorri replied. 'We have visited too often.' He urged Sleipnir onto the unkempt and rutted track that pointed east toward the mountains of northern Gelleth.

'And the Thurtans will be better?'

'Well, the Thurtans will be bad too,' he admitted. 'But in Maladon a warmer welcome awaits.'

'Fewer visits?'

'There we stayed. We'll take ship in Maladon. I have cousins there.'

'We'd better, because I'm not going any further east.' East of Maladon was Osheim, and nobody went to Osheim. Osheim was where the Builders built the Wheel, and every fairytale that ever launched a nightmare starts 'Once upon a time, not far from the Wheel of Osheim'.

Snorri nodded, solemn. 'Maladon. We'll take ship in Maladon.'

The mountains thrust us up through autumn and into winter. Those were bad days, despite warm clothing and good provisions bought in Hoff. I'd paid the coin out with more than the usual measure of begrudging, knowing that the pieces of silver could have been paving my way back to the heat of Vermillion.

Amid the high places of Gelleth I came to miss the small taste of luxury our night in the Tall Castle had afforded us. Even the stinking cots of the Falling Angel would have been heaven compared to bedding among rocks in the teeth of a gale halfway up some nameless mountain. I suggested to Snorri that we take the longer but less arduous path via the Castle Red. Merl Gellethar, the duke who kept that seat, was Grandmother's nephew and would have some family duty to help us on our way.

'No.'

'Why the hell not?'

'It's too long a detour.' Snorri muttered the words, ill tempered – an unusual thing for him.

'That's not the reason.' He always grew cross when lying.

'No.'

I waited.

'Aslaug cautioned against it,' he growled.

'Aslaug? Isn't Loki the Father of Lies? And she's his daughter…' I paused for him to deny it. 'So that would make her … a lie?'

'I believe her this time,' he said.

'Hmmm.' I didn't like the sound of that. When your

sole travelling companion is a seven foot maniac with an axe it can be unsettling to hear that he's starting to believe the devil that whispers in his ear when the sun sets. Even so, I didn't argue the point. Baraqel had told me the same thing that morning. Perhaps when an angel whispered to me at sunrise I should start believing what he said.

I dreamed of Sageous that night, smiling a calm smile to himself as he watched the board across which I was pushed, from black square to white, white to black, dark to light... Snorri beside me, matching my moves, and all about us, shadowed pieces, orchestrated to some complex design. A grey hand pushed its pawns forward – I felt the Silent Sister's touch and stepped forward, black to white. Behind her loomed another, more huge, deepest crimson, the Red Queen playing the longest game. A dead black hand reached across the board, high above it a larger hand, midnight blue, guiding. I could almost see the strings. Together the Lady Blue and the Dead King advanced a knight and without warning the unborn stood before me, only a plain porcelain mask to preserve my sanity from its horror. I woke screaming and waited for dawn without sleeping.

In the Thurtans we kept to ourselves, avoiding inns and towns, sleeping in hedges, drinking from the rivers, of which there are too many, dividing the country into innumerable strips.

On the border between East and West Thurtan there lies a great forest known as Gowfaugh, a vast expanse of pine, dark and threatening evil.

'We could just take the road,' I said.

'Better to cross the border without notice.' Snorri eyed the forest margins. 'Thurtan guards are like as not to give us a month inside one of their cells and take any valuables as payment for the privilege.'

I looked back along the trail we'd taken down from the hills, a faint line across a dour moorland. The Gowfaugh had nothing inviting about it but the threat behind worried me more. I felt it daily, nipping at our heels. I had been expecting trouble since we left Crath City, and not from King Olidan worried that I'd sullied his queen's honour. The Dead King had moved twice to stop us and the third time could be the charm.

'Forward, Jal, that's the place to keep your attention. You southerners are always looking back.'

'That's because we're no fools,' I said. 'You've forgotten the unborn at the circus? Edris and his hired men, and what they became when you killed them?'

'Someone is seeding our path to stop us, but they're not chasing us.'

'But the thing in Vermillion – it escaped, Sageous said we would meet it, he—'

'He told me the same thing.' Snorri nodded. 'You don't want to believe much that man says, but I think he's right. It did escape. I suspect the creature you saw in the opera house was an unborn, one grown old in its power, the target of the Silent Sister's spell. Probably an important lieutenant to the Dead King. A captain of his armies maybe.'

'But it's not following us?' It was following us. I knew it.

'Did you not listen to the dream-witch, Jal?'

'He said a lot of things … Mostly about killing you – and how I could go home if I did.'

'The curse, the Silent Sister's spell? Why's it still on us?'

That did ring a bell. 'Because the unborn wasn't destroyed. The enchantment is an act of will. It needs to complete its purpose.' I crossed my arms, pleased with myself.

'That's right. And we're heading north and the spell is giving us no problems.'

'Yes.' I frowned. This was going somewhere bad.

'The unborn isn't chasing us, Jal. We're chasing it. The thing's gone north.'

'Hell.' I tried to calm myself. 'But … but, come on, what are the odds? We're headed for the same place?'

'The Silent Sister sees the future.' Snorri touched a finger to his eye. 'Her magic is aimed toward tomorrow. The spell sought out a way to reach the unborn – it followed the path that would see it carried by someone, some somebodies, who would end up in the same place as its target.'

'Hell.' I hadn't any more to say this time.

'Yup.'

We skirted the Gowfaugh until we found a trail, too wide for a deer path, too narrow for a woodsman's track. On reflection, as we pushed our way along it, leading the horses and trying to avoid getting a branch in the eye, the Gowfaugh wasn't the kind of forest you'd hope to find deer in. Or woodsmen.

'Forests.' Snorri rubbed at three parallel scratches on his bicep and shook his head. 'I'll be glad to be free of this one.'

'Woods where a man can hunt stag and boar, that's what we have in Red March, with proper trees, not all this pine, with charcoal burners, timber-cutters, the occasional bear or wolf. But in the North...' I waved at the close-packed trunks, branches interlaced so a man would have to cut his path every yard of the way. 'Dead places. Just trees and trees and more trees. Listen! Not even a bird.'

Snorri shouldered his way ahead. 'Jal – this one point I'll cede you. The south has better forests.'

We crumped along, following convoluted paths, footsteps muffled by the thick blanket of old dry needles. It didn't take long to become lost. Even the sun offered few clues as to direction, its light coming diffuse from louring clouds.

'I do *not* want to spend a night in here.' The darkness would be utter.

'Eventually we'll find a stream and follow it out.' Snorri snapped a branch from his path. Needles fell with a faint patter. 'Shouldn't take long. These are the Thurtans. You can't take three steps without finding yourself ankle-deep in a river.'

I made no reply but followed him. It sounded like sense but the Gowfaugh lay tinder-dry and I imagined the woven roots drinking up any stream before it penetrated half a mile.

The forest seemed to press closer on every side. The slow lives of trees overwhelming all else, insensate and implacable. The light started to fail early and we pressed on through a forest twilight, though far above us the sun still scraped across the treetops.

'I'd swap a gold coin for a clearing.' I would have paid that much for room to stretch my arms. Ron and Sleipnir followed behind, heads down, brushed on both sides, miserable in the way that only horses can be.

Somewhere the sun had started to sink. The temperature dropped with it, and in the half-light we struggled against unyielding walls of dead branches in the airless gloom. The noise when it came was startling, shattering the arboreal silence through which we had laboured so long.

'Deer?' More in hope than belief. Something big and less subtle than a deer, snapping branches as it moved.

'More than one.' Snorri nodded to the other side.

The sound of dry wood breaking grew louder from that direction too.

Soon they were flanking us on both sides. Pale somethings. Tall somethings.

'They had to wait until it got dark.' I spat out dry needles and drew my sword with difficulty. I'd have no hope of swinging it.

Snorri stopped and turned. In the gloom I couldn't see his eyes, but something in the stillness of the man told me they would be black, without feature or soul.

'They would have been wiser to come in the light.' His mouth moved but it didn't sound like him.

All of a sudden I wasn't sure whether the path might not be the least safe place for me in the whole of Gowfaugh. One of the creatures flanking us drew momentarily closer and I saw a flash of pale arms, a man's legs but naked and whitish-green. A glimpse of a white face, gums and teeth exposed in a snarl, a glittering eye fixed for a heartbeat on mine, betraying an awful hunger.

'Dead men!' I may have shrieked it.

'Almost.' And Snorri swung his axe in a great loop, shearing off branches in scores. I would have bet against even a blade of razor-honed Builder-steel carving through like that. Again, another huge loop. I lunged away, stopped only by Ron's blunt head, blocking the path we'd forged. Snorri sang now, a wordless song, or perhaps a language lay behind it, but not of men, and he carved a space, ever more wide, until he strode from one side to hack deeper and then four paces to the other, five paces, six. The stumps of trees, some thicker than my arm, studded the space, poking up knee-high through drifts of fallen timber. In the clearing, despite open sky above, twilight-blue and cradling the evening star, it was darker than the forest. And the darkness trailed his axe.

'Wh— what?' Snorri came to a halt, panting. The twilight had taken on a new quality. The sun had set. Aslaug confined once more to whatever hell she inhabited. 'He looked down at his weapon. 'It's not a wood-axe! Gods damn it!'

I stepped closer, smartish, worried that corpse-white arms might reach for me from the darker shadows.

'Make a light, Jal. Quick.'

So with Snorri standing over me and the horses nervous, wedged along the trail, I fumbled in my pack, whilst all around us branches broke and pale men moved between the trees.

'Come out. I'll bet you cut easier than wood,' Snorri called to them, though I detected an edge of fear in his voice – something I'd never heard before. I think the forest unnerved him more than the enemy within it. I found tinder and then flint, managing to drop both in the darkness, finding them again with trembling fingers. The scent of pine-sap grew around us, strong and sickly, almost overpowering.

I struck spark to tinder as Snorri swung at the first

of the men to rush from the trees. Branches snapped on all sides, more of them pushing through. An ill-advised glance upward showed them lean and naked, pale greenish-white ghosts in the dimness. The passage of Snorri's axe carved a great furrow through the creature from left hip to right nipple, slicing through gut, ribs, sternum and lungs. Evidently the axe retained some edge despite being used to cut timber. Still the pine-man came on, the stink of sap overwhelming as the stuff oozed from his bloodless wound. At the last he tripped on a stump, crashed down and became snarled in a mess of loose entrails and stray branches. By then Snorri had plenty of other problems to worry about.

Success! Spark became glow became smoke became flame. A month earlier it would have taken me half an hour to get the same result. Crouched close to the ground and with Snorri swinging and grunting above me, and the scream of terrified horses, I managed to transfer the fire to one of the pitch torches I'd bought back in Crath City, offered there for exploring the extensive municipal catacombs.

'Burn it!' A pale, twitching limb landed beside my foot.

'What?'

'Burn it!' Another grunt and a head dropped close by. A pine-man leapt onto Snorri's back.

'Burn what?' I shouted.

'Everything.' He fell backward, impaling his passenger on several stumps.

'That's madness!' We'd burn up too.

Snorri's move, whilst genius in the short term, left me exposed, and at least four pine-men were pulling free of the trees to enter the clearing, more behind them. The look in their eyes frightened me more than the fire. I shoved the pitch brand into the mass of broken branches before me.

Flames rose up almost immediately. The pine-men took two or three more steps before halting, each with their face to the fire. Behind me Snorri tore free of his opponent and rose with a groan. 'Follow the horses!'

Already the flames were spreading, a fierce crackling building as needles popped in the heat and the fire raced along desiccated branches, quickened by pine-men's blood. Terrified out of whatever wits horses possess Sleipnir and Ron bolted, stampeding across the small clearing Snorri had carved, scattering both pine-men and fire. I managed to follow Snorri's example and roll clear, very nearly impaling myself on a couple of inch-thick stumps.

The two horses punched their own passage through the trees. I hoped they'd avoid being blinded, but it seemed a damn sight better than being barbecued. Snorri gave chase and I stumbled along in their wake. Behind me the fire roared like a living thing and the pine-men answered it with thin cries of their own agony.

335

For a brief while we left the fire behind us, plunging unseeing along the horses' path. As my breath grew short I paused for a moment, and glancing back, saw the whole forest lit from within by an orange glow, countless trunks and branches in black silhouette. 'Run!' I shouted uselessly, thereafter saving my breath to better follow my own order.

The inferno leapt through the trees with spectacular speed. It jumped between treetops faster than it moved on the ground, and several times we found ourselves beneath a roof of flame whilst the beast roared behind us. Trees exploded within moments of the inferno wrapping them. Literally blown apart, great swirls of orange embers rising above them. The flame rushed through the needled branches like a wind, consuming everything. A burning hand pressed against my back, driving me to greater exertions. Ron's path split from Sleipnir's: I chose the one to the left. A hundred yards on I saw my horse through the trees to the side, snared on something, hook-briar most like, screaming. It takes a lot to snare a horse, and Ron was a strong one, fuelled with terror of the flame. But he hung there and I raced on, cursing. At least the fire put a quick end to him. The gelding would have been molten fat and charring bones before he knew the fire-storm had him.

I saw Snorri up ahead, fire-lit. Sleipnir's strength failing her, both of them toiling up a steep slope.

'Run.' A gasp, little louder than my rasping breath.

We made the ridge before the flames, save those dancing high above us in the treetops. 'Hel be praised.' Snorri leaned against a trunk, gasping. The slope ran away from us, just as steep on the way down as it was on the rise, trees thinning yard by yard and where the ground grew level, stretching out before us, mile upon mile of moonlit grassland.

21

A man can drown in the grass seas of Thurtan. In the swaying green, wind-rippled, with twenty miles and more of cold bog and saw-grass on every side, it can seem that you've been set adrift in an ocean without end.

The fire at our back at least provided a reference point, an idea of distance and measure. These are things easily lost in the grass. As we walked Snorri had told me the men of the pines had haunted forests like Gowfaugh for generations. The stories differed on the source of the original evil but now they perpetuated themselves, letting out the blood of their victims and replacing it with the sap of the oldest trees. The creatures kept some measure of intelligence but if they served any master other than their own hunger it wasn't spoken of. It seemed hard to credit though that the Dead King hadn't steered them into our path.

"No more forests," I said.

Snorri wiped the soot from his eyes and nodded.

We trekked a mile, another mile, and collapsed on the

side of a gentle rise, looking back to watch the smoke and flame swirl above the burning forest. It seemed inconceivable that such an inferno, lofting embers into the heavens and scorching the clouds themselves, could have started with the tiny spark struck from my flint and nursed by my breath. Still, perhaps that's all lives are, all the world is, a collision of vast conflagrations, each sparked from nothing. It might be said that the whole course of my own adventure sprang from a die that should have rolled a five or a two, landing instead with a single snake eye pointing at me, a pitiless eye watching me plunge further into Maeres Allus's debt.

'That,' I said, 'was close.'

'Yes.' Snorri sat knees to chest, watching the fire. He pulled a stick loose, tangled in his hair.

'We can't go on like this. The next time we won't be so lucky.' He had to see sense. Two men couldn't carry on against such opposition. I'd gambled on long odds before – not my life, but my fortune – but never on so hopeless a bet as Snorri offered. Without prize or purpose.

'I would have given Karl such a pyre.' Snorri waved a hand at the burning horizon. 'I built his beside the Wodinswood from deadfall. The trees were too heavy with the winter's snow for the fire to spread, but I would have burned them all.

'He should have had a ship, my Karl. A longship. I would have laid him before the mast with my father's

339

axe and such armour as would serve him in Valhalla. But there was no time and I couldn't leave him for the dead to find and use. Better wolves have him than that.'

'He told you about a key?' I said. Snorri had spoken of it back in the ruins of Compere but fallen silent. Perhaps now, with mile upon mile of blazing forest burning as Compere had burned, he would speak again. His eldest boy broke bones to escape his shackles and his last words to Snorri had been of a key.

And in the darkness of the grassland, with Gowfaugh burning red behind us, Snorri told me a story.

'My father told me the tale of Olaaf Rikeson and his march to the Bitter Ice. I heard it by the hearth many times. Father would spin it out on the deepest nights of winter when the ice on the Uulisk made sharp complaint against the cold.

'It takes more than a warrior or a general to lead ten thousand men into the Bitter Ice. Ten thousand who were not Viking would die before they reached the true ice. Ten thousand who knew enough to survive would know enough not to go. There is nothing there for men. Even the Inowen keep to the shore and the sea ice. Whale, seal and fish is all that will sustain men in such places.

'It might be that no jarl ever had more longboats at his command than Olaaf Rikeson, or had brought more treasure across the North Sea, won with axe and fire from weaker men. Even so it took more than his word to gather ten thousand from the bleak shores of the fjords where a hundred men were counted an army, and to march them into the Bitter Ice.

'Olaaf Rikeson had a vision. He had the gods at his side. The wise echoed what he said. The rune stones spoke for him. And more than this. He had a key. Even now the völvas argue over how he came to own it, but in the tale Snorri's father told, Loki had given it to Olaaf after he burned the cathedral of the White Christ at York and slaughtered twice a hundred monks there. What Olaaf had to promise in return was never told.

'The fact that the god's gift had been a key had always disappointed Snorri, but then Loki was the god of disappointment, among other things, things such as lies and trickery. Snorri would have preferred a battle ram. A warrior destroys the door – he doesn't unlock it. But his father told him that Olaaf's key was a talisman. It opened any lock, any door, and more than that – it opened men's hearts.

'The oldest legends have it that Olaaf marched to open the gates of Niflheim and beard the frost giants in their lair, to shame the gods and their false Ragnarok of many suns, and to bring about the true end of all things in a last battle. Snorri's father never denied the tale but spoke of how one thing might hide another, like a feint in combat. Men, he said, were more often moved by more basic wants – hunger, greed, and lust. Stories grew from seed and spread like weeds. Perhaps the gods touched Rikeson, or perhaps a bloody-handed reaver took a few hundred men north to raid the Inowen and from his failure sprang a song that bards wove into a saga and placed among the treasured memories of the North. Whatever truth there was, years have stolen it from us.'

Snorri left his son's pyre, the last logs still blazing, the snow on all sides retreating to expose the black earth of the Wodinswood. Behind him embers swirled skyward amid dark smoke. He trekked the hills of the hinterland, leaving the Uulisk far behind, tracking Sven Broke-Oar and the men of the Drowned Isles across the boulderfields of Törn where vicious winds shape the rocks themselves. Above Törn the Jarlson Uplands, and beyond those, the Bitter Ice.

What he would do when he reached his enemy Snorri had no idea, other than to die well. Grief and guilt and rage consumed him. Perhaps any of these on its own would have destroyed him, but in conflict, each with the next, they achieved a balance within him and he carried on.

The pace the raiders set was fierce and Snorri couldn't think it one that Freja or Egil, with just ten years to his name, could match. In grim visions he saw them dead, marching with the tireless corpses that had come ashore at Eight Quays. But Karl had been alive: they had shackled prisoners – it made no sense to be taking them inland but the necromancers had wanted live prisoners, that much was clear.

Only night stopped him. The light fled early, still new to the world after the winter darkness that had held the ice for months. Without sight a man can't follow a trail. All he'll find in the dark is a broken leg for the hinterlands are treacherous, the rocky ground ice-clad and fissured.

The night had lasted forever, a misery of cold, haunted by visions of the slaughter at Eight Quays. Of Karl, broken and dying by the Wodinswood, of Emy… Her screaming had followed Snorri into the wilderness and the wind spoke it all through the long wait for dawn.

And when the light came snow came also, falling heavy from leaden skies though Snorri had thought it too cold for snow. He'd roared at it. Lofted his axe at the clouds and threatened every god he could name. But still the snow fell, careless, dropping into his open mouth as he shouted, filling his eyes.

Snorri carried on without a trail to follow, lost in the trackless white. What else was there for him? He took the direction his quarry had taken and struck out into the empty wastes.

He found the dead man hours later. One of the Islanders who had been dead on the deck of his ship as it sailed the North Sea bound for the mouth of the Uulisk. No less dead now and no less hungry. The man struggled uselessly, bound chest-deep in a drift whose soft snow had accepted his dead flesh then locked about it as his efforts to escape compressed the walls of his prison into something hard as rock. He reached for Snorri, his fingers black with the freezing blood locked inside. A sword blow had opened his face from eye to chin, exposing a jawbone wrapped in freeze-dried muscle, shattered teeth, frost-darkened and bloodless flesh. The remaining eye fixed Snorri with inhuman intensity.

'You should be solid.' He had found men dead in the snow before: their limbs froze hard as ice. He stared a moment longer. 'You're no part of what is right,' Snorri told it. 'This is Hel.' He lifted his axe, knuckles white on the haft. 'But you didn't come from there, and this won't send you to the river of swords.'

The dead man only watched him, straining at the snow, tearing at it, without the wit to dig.

'Even the frost giants would want no part of you.' Snorri struck the man's head from his shoulders and watched it roll away, spattering the clean snow with rotten blood, sluggish and half-frozen. The air held a strange chemical scent, like lamp-oil, but different.

Snorri wiped Hel's blades in the snow until all trace of the creature had gone, then walked on, leaving the body still twitching in the drift.

By the time a man reaches the Bitter Ice he will have seen nothing but a world in shades of white for day upon day. He will have walked upon ice sheets and seen no tree or blade of grass, no rock or stone, heard no sound but that of his own loneliness and the mockery of the wind. He will believe there is in all the world no place more cruel, no place less suited to the business of living. And then he will see the Bitter Ice.

In places the Bitter Ice may be gained by snow-clad slopes as one might scale a mountain. In other places the ice-shelf towers in a series of vast cliff faces, some frost-white, some glacial blue and offering clear depths. When the midnight sun shines on such faces it reaches in and hints of shapes are revealed as if the ice has swallowed and held great ocean whales, and leviathans that dwarf even these, all trapped for eternity beneath a mile and more of glacier. For the Bitter Ice is just that, one huge glacier, spread across a continent, always advancing or retreating at a pace that makes men's lives seem brief as mayflies.

Snorri couldn't believe the Broke-Oar would allow himself to be led up onto the high ice, whatever madness might infect the Islanders with their dead men. Greed drove Sven Broke-Oar, he would accept risk, but never suicidal risk. Armed with this assessment of the man, Snorri trekked along the margins of the ice cliffs, low on food, as numb with the cold as he had been with the ghouls' poisons.

When Snorri first saw the black spot he thought it part of dying, his vision failing as the wilderness claimed him. But the spot persisted, kept its place, grew as he staggered on. And in time it became the Black Fort.

'Black Fort?' I asked.

'An ancient stronghold built at the furthest reach of the Bitter Ice. Miles from it now. Built in days when that land was green.'

'And what— Who holds it? Was your wife there?'

'Not tonight, Jal. I can't speak of it. Not tonight.'

Snorri turned his face to the blaze in the west. He sat, lit with the fire-glow, and I saw the memories take him, back to the Wodinswood once again, where he had burned his son.

22

Maladon is Norse-land. Crossing from East Thurtan you see it almost immediately. In the use of the land, the monuments, rough-hewn works of stone, carrying a power and a beauty not seen in the road-side chapels of the Thurtans. Many of the houses are roofed with turf and the roof beams sport curving prows to remember the longboats that bore their ancestors to these shores. Perhaps some are even those same timbers, taken from ships beached on once-hostile shores.

'These are Vikings then?' I asked on passing our first Maladon peasants at work gathering in their harvest.

'*Fit-firar*. Land men. Good stock, brave, but the sea spat them out. A true Viking knows the oceans like a lover.'

'Says the man who has ridden a thousand miles rather than go by ship.'

Snorri harrumphed at that. I didn't mention that now he wasn't even riding but walking. Although technically both the horses were mine since I paid for them, I felt

I was riding Sleipnir on sufferance and that any mention of it might get me turfed off, or at the very least mocked for being such a footsore southerner.

The mare bore deep scratches all along her neck, chest and shoulders from our escape the night before. I'd spent much of the morning digging out splinters and cleaning the wounds. Both her eyes were scratched and thick with rheum. I did what I could with them but thought she might lose the left in time. Later I dug a good number of splinters from my own arms and two particularly painful ones from under my fingernails. I may not be much of a man but I count myself an excellent horseman, and a horseman takes care of his mount before himself. I'm not given to praying, but I said a prayer for Ron out on the grass and I'm not ashamed to say so.

In the distance the sky held an ominous yellow cast. 'Some city?' I asked. Crath City stained the skies with the smoke of ten thousand chimneys, and that had been in summer, just cook-fires and industry. I hadn't thought the North held such cities though.

'The Heimrift.'

'Oh.'

'You don't know what that is, do you?'

'I'll have you know I was educated by the finest scholars, including Harram Lodt, the famed geographer who made the world map that hangs in the pope's own library.'

'Do you?'

'No.'

'It's a set of volcanoes.'

'Fire mountains.' I was pretty certain that's what a volcano was.

'Yes.'

'Finest scholars. Very clever men.'

A mile or two along the track we passed a hammer-stone, a crude representation of Thor's hammer hacked from a piece of rock about five foot high and set by the road. Snorri seemed more interested in the pebbles lying around it. He bent to investigate and I had to rein Sleipnir in or leave him crouched by the verge. Pride kept me there, waiting in the middle of the track rather than go back to see what the hauldr had found.

'Interesting rocks?' I asked when he finally deigned to join me.

'Rune-stones. Wise men and völvas leave them. It's a kind of message system.'

'And you can read it?'

'No.' Snorri admitted it with a grin. 'But these ones were pretty clear.'

'And?'

'And our friendly dream-witch seems to have been right. The stones say Skilfar is at her Maladon seat. It's been many years since that one came south.'

'If she's the Silent Sister's twin we should stay well away. She's nobody we should have dealings with.'

'Even if her blood could break this curse?' He reached up for me with his palm open and I shrunk back.

'You don't believe that?' I said. Sageous had no reason to tell the truth and some men's tongues are burned by truths in any case. They tend to leave mine a little sore, I've found.

'Believe she's the twin … and her blood might help us. Believe she's not the twin and your reasons for fearing her go away. Both ways mean we should see her. Even if every word Sageous spoke was false Skilfar is a völva of vast renown. I know of none more famed. If she can't break this curse then no one can. And even if she can't break the spell she will know about the necromancers and their doings at the Bitter Ice.' Snorri ran a finger along the blade of his axe. 'Charging in didn't serve me so well last time. Knowledge is power they say, and I may need a better edge than this.'

I spat into the road. 'Damn your barbarian logic.' It was all the counter-argument I could muster.

'So it's settled then. We'll go.' Snorri smiled and walked on up the track.

I nudged Sleipnir after him. 'Surely if she's so all-powerful she won't just see the likes of anyone.'

'We're not just anyone, Jal,' Snorri called over his shoulder. 'I'm a hauldr of the Uuliskind. You and I bear unusual magics, and Sleipnir is possibly the descendent of a horse of legend.' Ten more paces and then, 'And you're a prince of somewhere.'

Damned if I ever wanted to see another witch long as I lived – I hadn't even wanted to see the first one – but options were running short if I didn't want to find myself on a boat sailing heathen seas in search of an unborn captain of the Dead King's army.

I drew level with the Norseman. 'So how do we find her?'

'That's the easy part,' Snorri said. 'We catch a train.'

What a train might be I had no idea but I wasn't going to let the Viking taunt me with my ignorance again, so I followed without complaint.

We passed a few farmsteads, locals carting the harvest to be sold and stored against the winter. All of them remarked us, Snorri in particular, and whilst it still irked that a commoner, and Norseman at that, upstaged a full-blooded prince of Red March, it was pleasing to see he was as much a rarity in his stature in the North as in the South. Part of me had secretly worried that all men might be built along Snorri's lines up among the fjords and I might find myself a dwarf amidst giants.

Some among the fit-firar tried to speak to Snorri in the old tongue of the North, but he answered them in Empire tongue with good humour, thanking them for their courtesy. Each person we encountered told the same story about Skilfar. The völva had arrived without warning a month earlier and none had seen her save those foolhardy enough to seek her out. Snorri asked for the nearest station and armed with directions we abandoned the road north and headed out across open country.

The station turned out to be nothing more than a broad and grassy ditch in the ground, overhung on one side by some kind of stone lip. We reached it under grey skies and a chill drizzle.

'She lives in a ditch?' I'd heard of trolls living under bridges and witches in caves...

'Now we follow the tracks,' Snorri said, and headed off along the side of the ditch, bound north and east.

In time the ditch became shallow, then invisible, but we carried on through moor and meadow, finding the line again, now as a ridge, raised a yard above the surrounding terrain. Not until we reached the uplands did I first get an impression of what a fearsome creature the train must have been to leave such tracks. Where a man might go around, or weave a path of least resistance up a slope, the train had just ploughed on. We walked in one place along a rock-walled ravine thirty yards deep where the train had scored its path through the bedrock.

Finally the land rose in a series of more substantial hills and still the train had kept its course. Ahead of us a circular hole waited, punched into the hillside, ten yards in diameter and blacker than sin. The rain strength- ened, trickling down my neck and carrying its own cold and peculiar misery with it.

'Yeah ... I'm not going in there, Snorri.' Sir George

might have followed his dragon into the cave but damned if I was hunting train down in the bowels of the earth.

'Ha!' Snorri punched me on the shoulder as if I'd made a joke. It really hurt, and I reminded myself not to make any actual jokes with him in arms' reach.

'Seriously. I'll wait here. You let me know how it went when you come back.'

'There are no trains, Jal. They're long gone. Not so much as a bone left behind.' He looked back across the rough country behind us. 'You can stay here alone though if you like while I go in to see Skilfar.' He pursed his lips.

Something in the word 'alone', spoken in empty country, made me change my mind. Suddenly I didn't want to be left standing out in the rain. Besides, I needed to hear what this witch had to say about the curse, rather than whatever Snorri might remember of her words or choose to share. So together we went in, Snorri taking the lead and me guiding Sleipnir behind.

Within a hundred yards the circle of light to our rear did little but offer a reminder that once upon a time we could see.

'I've still got two torches.' I reached for my pack.

'Better to keep them,' Snorri said. 'There's only one way to go.'

Horrors stalked us in the dark, of course. Well, they stalked me. I imagined the pale men from the forest padding behind me on quiet feet, or waiting silent to either side as we marched past.

We walked for miles. Snorri trailed a stick along the wall so he wouldn't lose contact with it, and I followed the sound of scraping. Sleipnir clip-clopped along behind. In places the roof dripped or slime hung in long ropes. Every five hundred yards or so a shaft led up, no thicker than a man and offering a pale glimpse of sky. Strange plants clustered around these openings, reaching for the light with many-fingered leaves. In other places partial collapses saw us clambering up mounds of loose rubble, Sleipnir's hooves dislodging small avalanches of broken rock. In one section some huge piece of Builder-rock blocked all but a narrow gap to one side and we had to edge through. Snorri allowed that I lit the torch for that transit but had me quench it in a standing pool thereafter. I didn't argue – both torches would most likely have been burned out along the path we'd taken so far, and what the light revealed looked boring enough, with no monsters on show, not even a discarded skull or shattered bone.

When stiff arms enfolded me without warning I screamed loud enough to collapse the roof and went down swinging wildly. My fist made contact with something hard and the pain only amplified my distress. A hollow clattering went up on all sides.

'Jal!'

'Getoff! Get the fuck off!'

'Jal!' Snorri, louder this time, tense but calm enough.

'Oh you fucker!' Something hard jabbed me in the eye as my assailant fell away, clattering.

'Now would be the time for that torch, Jal.'

Silence, except for my panting and the nervous stamp of Sleipnir's hooves.

'Fuckers!' I got my knife in hand and slashed the air a couple of times for good measure.

'Torch.'

'I've got— It's somewhere.' A minute or two of fumbling straps and digging through my pack and I'd set flame to tinder. The torch took the fire and spread its glow. 'Christ Jesu!'

Ahead of us pale figures filled the tunnel, rank upon rank upon rank of them. Statues all of them, men and women, most of regular height, all naked and without genitalia. On every side of me lay toppled examples, my most recent foe reaching for the ceiling with a straight arm.

'Hemrod's army,' Snorri said.

'What?' Some of the statues had eyes painted into their sockets, some hair, also painted, but most were bald, eyeless, many lacking definition, some to the degree that their fingers were fused, faces blank. Many struck oddly nonchalant poses, looking more like idle nobility than marching warriors. There was space to walk between each rank and somehow Snorri had ended up doing so, leaving me to crash into the first line.

355

'Hemrod,' Snorri said.

'Hemroids to you. I've never heard of him.' I took hold of the outstretched arm before me and pulled the figure to its feet. The thing had almost no weight to it. Whatever it had been fashioned from was far lighter than wood. I tapped it. 'Hollow?'

'These are Builder things. Statues I guess. Hemrod held sway in this region before the empire grew across his lands. When they buried him down here they set an army of these plasteek warriors to guard him and to serve him in the life beyond. Perhaps they wait for Ragnarok with him in Valhalla.'

'Pah.' I stood and dusted myself down. 'I'd want better soldiers. Look: I felled seven of them while fighting blind.'

Snorri nodded. 'Though to be fair you did have a screaming girl to help you.' He glanced back down the tunnel. 'I wonder where she ran off to.'

'Eat dung, Norseman.' I started off between the rows.

'Someone must keep standing them up, you know.' Snorri spoke from behind me.

I paused and swapped the torch from one hand to the other. My arm hurt from holding it overhead and dribbles of hot pitch kept escaping to burn my fingers.

'Why?'

'It stands to reason. They've stood here five hundred

years and more. You can't be the first to fetch up against one.'

'I mean why bother?'

'Magic.' Snorri puffed a breath through his lips. 'It's an old charm, a defence. They say old magic runs deepest. Skilfar makes her home here for a reason when she comes south.'

'Well *I* ain't going back to stand them up again.' I lifted the torch higher. 'Some kind of chamber up ahead...'

As we drew closer I saw that the space might better be called a cavern – not for the nature of it – men had built this – but for the size of the place. Cavernous would be the word to use. The blackness within swallowed the light of my torch. A rust-covered floor stretched away and Builder statues filled the portion of the chamber I could see, all pointing outward from some hidden centre. To either side, tunnel mouths opened, statues marching away into the darkness. If the spacing held constant I guessed maybe eight or ten tunnels met here. Truly it must once have been a den of trains, coiling about each other like great serpents.

Snorri nudged me on and I advanced with caution between the ranks. Some prurient part of me that is always on duty noted that the vast majority of the statues here were of women, all in the same kinds of stiff and awkward poses, my torchlight flickering across hundreds if not thousands of ancient but perky plasteek breasts.

'Getting colder.' Snorri at my shoulder.

'Yes.' I stopped, handed him the torch and circled around a nude plasteek woman to stand behind him. 'After you. She's your Wicked Witch of the North after all.' Somehow the 'wicked witch' part contrived to echo about the chamber, taking a damnably long time to die away.

Snorri shrugged and went ahead. 'Leave the horse.'

The radial aisles of statues created a steady narrowing as we approached the centre and soon Sleipnir would be knocking them over left and right. I let go her reins. 'Stay.' She blinked one gunked-up eye at me, the other glued tight with secretions, and lowered her head.

The temperature fell by the yard now and frost glittered on plasteek arms to every side. I hugged myself and let my breath plume before me.

In the middle of the chamber a circular platform rose in four steps and in the centre of that in an ice-clad chair sat Skilfar: tall, angular, white skin stretched tight across sharp bones, draped in the skins of several arctic foxes and with a white mist running from her limbs as if they might be cold enough to shatter steel. Eyes like frozen sea-water fixed upon Snorri's torch and out it went, the firelight replaced instead by a star-glow that rose from the frost-wrapped limbs of her ancient guardians.

'Visitors.' She rolled her neck and ice crunched.

'Hail Skilfar.' Snorri bowed. Behind him I wondered

just what it was this witch did sitting here in the dark when she didn't have us to talk to.

'Warrior.' She inclined her head. 'Prince.' Cold eyes found me again. 'Two of you, bound by the Sister, how droll. She does enjoy her little jokes.'

Little jokes? Anger rose, elbowing aside a measure of my sensible fear. 'Your sister, madam?' I wondered how cold her blood was.

'She would tell you she was everybody's sister. If she ever spoke.' Skilfar rose from her chair, the freezing air flowing from her skin like milk, pouring to the floor. 'A stench of ill-dreaming hangs around you both.' She wrinkled her nose. 'Whose taint is this? It was not well done.'

'Are you twin to the Silent Sister?' Snorri, through gritted teeth, his axe moving.

'She has a twin, certainly.' Skilfar advanced to the front of the platform, just yards from us. My face ached with the cold. 'You don't want to strike me, Snorri Snagason.' She pointed one long white finger at his axe, the blades now level with his shoulder.

'No,' he agreed, but his body remained coiled for the blow.

I found myself advancing, sword raised, though I'd no recollection of drawing it or desire to get any closer than I was. Everything held a dreamlike quality. My eyes filled with visions of the witch dying on the blade before me.

Skilfar wafted the air toward her face, inhaling deeply

through a sharp nose. 'Sageous has touched your minds. You particularly, prince. But crude work. He normally has a more subtle hand.'

'Do it!' The words burst from me. 'Do it now, Snorri!' I clapped a hand to my mouth before I could damn myself further.

Two bounds had him on the step below Skilfar, his axe high above her, the huge muscles of his arms ready to haul it down through her narrow body. And yet he held the blow.

'Ask the right question, child.' Skilfar glanced away from Snorri, meeting my gaze across the sea of statues. 'Better that you shrug Sageous off for yourself. Safer than if I do it.'

'I—' I remembered Sageous's mild eyes, his suggestions that had turned into truths as I'd considered them. 'Who— who is the Sister's twin?'

'Pah.' Skilfar snorted out a breath which wrapped white and serpentine around her thin torso. 'I thought she would choose better.' She extended a hand toward me, clawed, talons of ice springing from her nails.

'Wait!' A shout. For some reason I saw my locket. Whole, its gems in place. 'I— Who— Garyus! Who is Garyus?'

'Better.' The hand relaxed. Still no smile though. 'Garyus is the Sister's brother.'

I saw him, my great-uncle, twisted and ancient in his tower room, the locket in his hand. 'I had a twin,' he had told me once. 'They broke us apart. But we didn't break evenly.'

On the step below Skilfar Snorri lowered his axe, blinking as if shaking off the dregs of sleep.

'And his blood could break this curse?' The question billowed white before me.

'His sister's spell would be broken.' Skilfar nodded.

'How else can it be broken?' I asked.

'You know the ways.'

'Can't you do it?' I tried a hopeful smile but my frozen face wouldn't cooperate.

'I don't wish to.' Skilfar returned to her chair. 'The unborn have no place among us. The Dead King plays a dangerous game. I would see his ambition broken. Many hidden hands are turned against him. Perhaps every hand but that of the Lady Blue, and her game is more dangerous still. So no, Prince Jalan, you carry the Silent Sister's purpose and the magics with which she sought to destroy the greatest of the Dead King's servants. I've no interest in taking it from you. The Dead King needs his claws trimmed. His strength is like a forest fire.' I wondered at her choice of words. 'But like such conflagrations it will burn itself out, and the forest will prevail. Unless of course it burns the very bedrock itself. Destroy the unborn: that will complete the spell's purpose and it will fade from you. There are no other choices for you, Prince Jalan, and when there are no choices all men are equally brave.'

361

'How?' I asked, without really wanting to know. 'Destroy the unborn? How?'

'How do the living ever defeat the dead?' She smiled a small cold smile. 'With every beat of your heart, every hot drop of your blood. The truth of the Sister's spell is hidden from me, but carry it where it leads you and pray it proves sufficient. These are the ends you serve.'

Snorri came down the steps, dropping from one to the next, and stood at my side. 'I have my own ends, Skilfar. Men do not serve the völvas.' He covered the blades of his axe with the leather protectors he had stripped off a minute before.

'Everything serves everything else, Snorri ver Snagason.' No heat in the witch's voice. If anything it felt colder than ever.

To distract the pair of them from further disagreements I raised my voice in a question. 'Pray it proves sufficient? Praying's all well and good but I never set much faith by it. The Silent Sister had to take her enemies unaware. She had to paint her runes and slowly draw her net around them. Even then the unborn escaped when I broke just one rune ... so say we do find some way to release this spell ... how can it defeat even one unborn, let alone several?'

Skilfar raised her brows a fraction as if wondering herself. 'They say some wines improve with age when bottled.'

'Wine?' I glanced up at Snorri to see if he understood.

362

'These magics couldn't be carried by just any two men,' Skilfar said. 'Magic requires the right receptacles. Something about this spell, about you two, just fits together. You're her blood, Prince Jalan, and Snorri has something to him, something that suits him to this task. Pray or don't pray, but the only hope you have is that the spell strengthens within you, because of who and what you are, because of your journey, and that when the time comes it will be stronger rather than weaker than it was.'

'I'm not going north as a witch's lapdog,' Snorri growled. 'I'm bound there on my own purpose and I'll—'

'Why is she silent?' I elbowed the Norseman to shut him up, offering the question up to distract them both from the quarrel brewing on his lips. "Why does the Sister never speak?"

'It's the price she pays for knowing the future.' Skilfar looked away from Snorri. 'She may not speak of it. She says nothing so that the bargain will remain unbroken by any accident or slip of tongue.'

I pursed my lips, nodding with interest. 'Well. That's … that sounds reasonable. In any event, we really must be going.' I reached out and tugged at Snorri's belt. 'She's not going to help us,' I hissed.

Snorri though, obstinate as ever would not be pulled away, 'We met a man named Taproot. He also spoke of hidden hands. A grey one behind us, a black one blocking our path.'

'Yes, yes.' Skilfar waved the question away. The Sister set you on your path, the Dead King seeks to stop you. A reasonable ambition considering you've been sent to stop him gathering an army of dead men from the ice.'

'No one sent us!' Snorri said, louder than is advisable in front of an ice-witch. 'I escaped! I'm bound north to save my—'

'Yes, yes, your family. If you say so.' Skilfar met his gaze and it was Snorri who looked aside. 'Men who've made choices always feel they own their destiny. Few ever think to ask who shaped and offered up those choices. Who dangles the carrot they think they've chosen to follow.'

Now that Snorri mentioned Taproot's whitterings and Skilfar lent them a measure of importance with her interpretation I remembered something else he'd said.

'A blue hand behind the black, a red behind the grey.' The words tripped off my tongue.

Those eyes turned my way and I felt the winter settle cold upon me. 'Elias Taproot said that?'

'Uh … yes.'

'Well now, that man has been paying closer attention than I gave him credit for.' She steepled white fingers beneath the angularity of her chin. 'The Red and the Blue. There you have the battle of our age, Prince Jalan. Lady Blue and the Red Queen. Your grandmother wants an emperor, prince. Did you know that? She wants to make the Broken Empire whole again … seal all the

364

cracks, seen and unseen. She wants an emperor because such a man … well, he could turn the wheel back. She wants this and the Lady Blue does not.'

'And you, völva?' Snorri asked. 'What wheel?' I would have asked.

'Ah. Both courses require a terrible price be paid, and both are fraught with risk.'

'And there's no third way?'

Skilfar shook her head. 'I have cast the runes until they broke from falling. I see nothing but the red and the blue.'

Snorri shrugged. 'Emperor or no emperor, it makes no difference to me. My wife and son, Freja and Egil, that's what calls me to the ice. I'll see Sven Broke-Oar die and have my justice. Can you tell me if he still bides at the Black Fort?'

'Still fixed upon your carrot, Snorri ver Snagason? Look past it. Look ahead. When the Uuliskind sail do they navigate by staring at the water beneath their prow? You should ask why it might be that he is there at all. Do they dig beneath the ice just for more corpses? And if not, what else do they seek and to what purpose?'

Something like a growl, but worse, rose in Snorri's throat. 'The Broke-Oar—'

'Let's go!' I yanked harder at Snorri's belt before his temper buried both of us.

Snorri hunched his massive shoulders and made a stiff bow. 'Gods keep you, Skilfar.'

I let him pass and made my own much deeper bow. Social standing is one thing but I always feel a scary hell-born witch deserves as much bowing and scraping as it takes to avoid being made into a toad. 'My thanks, ma'am. I'll take my leave and pray your army keeps you safe.' With an instinctive sideways glance at a particularly well-formed young plasteek woman, I turned to go.

'Step carefully on the ice.' Skilfar called after us as if she had an audience. 'Two heroes, one led willy-nilly by his cock, the other northward by his heart. Neither bringing their brain into any decision of import. Let us not judge them harshly, my soldiers, for nothing is truly deep, nothing holds consequence. It's from the shallows that emotions born of simple wanting arise to steer us as they have always steered man, steered the Builders, steered the gods themselves, toward true Ragnarok, an end to all things. A peace.' She couldn't resist a commentary. I guess it's hard for even the wisest not to show off that they are wise.

Her words followed us from the chamber. I halted a short way into the tunnel to relight my torch. 'Ragnarok. Is that all the North ever thinks about? Is that what you want, Snorri? Some great battle and the world ruined and dead?' I couldn't blame him if he did. Not with what had befallen him this past year, but I would be disturbed to know he had always lusted after such an end, even on the night before the black ships came to Eight Quays.

366

The light kindling on my torch caught him in mid shrug. 'Do you want the paradise your priests paint for you on cathedral ceilings?'

'Good point.'

We left without further theological discussion. When my brand started to gutter and flare I lit the last of our torches from the old, tired of being slapped in the face by slime ropes, tripped by stray plasteek legs, soaking my feet in cold pools and stubbing my toe on blocks fallen from the ceiling. Also the possibility of ghosts disturbed me. For all my bravado in the witch's chamber the long night of the tunnels had shattered my nerves. Her guardians looked more ominous by the minute: in the dancing shadows their limbs seemed to move. At the corner of my eye I kept seeing motion but when I swung round their ranks remained unbroken.

I've never been one for wandering in the dark. It seemed though that our light couldn't last the journey. I held the torch high and prayed that before it failed we'd see a circle of daylight far ahead.

'Come on. Come on.' Muttered in short breaths as we walked. The plasteek soldiers had been left far behind, but for all I knew they stalked us just beyond the range of the torch's illumination. 'Come on.'

Somehow the torch kept going.

'Thank God!' I pointed up ahead to the long-awaited spot of daytime. 'I didn't think it would last.'

'Jal.' Snorri tapped my shoulder. I looked round, my

gaze following his to my hand, raised above my head. 'Holy sh—' The torch was a blackened stump, no longer even smoking. The fingers gripping it were, however, another matter, glowing fiercely with an inner light. At least they were until Snorri drew them to my attention. At that point they blinked out, plunging us into darkness, and I did what any sensible man would. I ran hell for leather for the outside.

A storm waited for us.

23

The port of Den Hagen sits where the River Oout washes into the Karlswater, that stretch of brine the Norse call the Devouring Sea. A collection of fine homes huddle on the rising slopes to the east, well, fine for the North where every building crouches low, granite-built to withstand the weather that sweeps in from the frozen wastes. Log cabins, round houses, inns, ale-halls, and fish-markets reach down to huge warehouses that fringe the docks like receiving mouths. Greater ships sit at anchor in the quiet waters of the bay; other vessels crowd the quays, masts rising in a profusion of spars and rigging. Seagulls circle overhead, ever mournful, and men fill the air with their own cries, voices raised to call out prices, summon fresh hands to load or unload, issue challenge, share jokes, curse or praise the many gods of Asgard, or to bring the followers of Christ to the small and salt-rimed church at the water's edge.

'What a hole.' The stink of old fish reached me even

on the cliff tops where the coast road snaked in from the west.

Snorri, walking ahead of me, growled but said nothing. I leaned forward and patted Sleipnir's neck. 'Time for us to part soon, old one-eye.'

I would miss the horse. I've never liked walking. If God had meant man to walk he wouldn't have given us horses. Wonderful animals. I think of them as the word 'escape', covered in hair and with a leg at each corner.

We wound down into Den Hagen, the road lined with shacks that looked as though the first winds of winter would clear them from the slopes. On a high corner overlooking the sea seven troll-stones watched the waves. They looked like stones to me, but Snorri claimed to see a troll in each of them. He pulled open his weather-jacket and jerked up the layers of his shirts to reveal a fearsome scar across the hard-packed muscles of his stomach. 'Troll.' With a finger he implied a series of additional scars from hip to shoulder. 'I was lucky.'

In a world where dead men walked, unborn rose from fresh graves, and the people of the pines haunted forests, I could hardly dispute his claim.

On the final stretch of the road we passed three or four hammer-stones set on the verges to honour the thunder-god. Snorri checked for rune-stones around each, but found only a stray black pebble, river-smoothed and wide enough to cover his palm, bearing a single rune. Perhaps local children made off with the rest.

'Thuriaz.' He let it fall.

'Hmmm?'

'Thorns.' He shrugged. 'It means nothing.'

The town boasted no wall and nobody save a handful of sorry-looking merchants watched the entrance – not that there was an entrance, just an increase in the crowding of houses. After weeks of rough living and hard travelling even a place such as Den Hagen has its appeal. Every piece of clothing on me still held its measure of rain from the storm that had lashed us for two days across the moorland fastness surrounding Skilfar's seat. A man could have slaked his thirst on what he could squeeze from my trews. He'd have to be damnable dry to risk it though.

'We could pop in there and see if the ale tastes any better here?' I pointed to a tavern just ahead, barrels placed in the street before it for men to rest their tankards on, a painted wooden swordfish hanging above the door.

'Maladon beer is fine.' Snorri walked on past the entrance.

'It would be if they forgot to salt it.' Foul stuff, but sometimes foul will do. I'd asked for wine back in the town of Goaten and they'd looked at me as if I'd asked them to roast a small child for my meal.

'Come on.' Snorri turned toward the sea, waving away a man trying to sell him dried fish. 'We'll check the harbour first.' A tension had built in him as we approached the coast and when we first saw the sea from a high ridge he had sunk to his knees and muttered heathen prayers. Since the troll-stones he'd been walking with such purpose I had to nudge Sleipnir along to keep up.

Several boats were tied at mooring points along the dock front, among them one that required neither loading nor unloading.

'A longboat,' I said, spotting at last the classic lines that Snorri must have recognized from the coast road. I slipped from Sleipnir's back as Snorri strode toward the vessel, breaking into a run over the last fifty yards. Even a land-lubber like myself could see the ship had been through rough times, the mast broken some yards short of its proper height, the sail ragged.

Without slowing Snorri reached the harbour's edge and dropped from sight, presumably onto the unseen deck of the longboat. Cries and shouts went up. I prepared myself for the sight of carnage.

Making a slow advance and peering over the side, with the caution of a man not wanting a spear in the forehead, I expected to be met with a boat full of blood and body parts. Instead Snorri stood amid the rowing benches grinning like a loon with six or seven pale and hairy men crowding around him, exchanging welcome punches. And all of them trying to talk at once in some godforsaken language that sounded like it needed to be retched up from the depths of a man's belly.

'Jal!' He glanced up and waved. 'Get down here!'

I debated the matter but there seemed no escape. I slung Sleipnir's reins over one of the ship lines and went off to find a means of descent that didn't involve breaking both ankles on arrival.

Disentangling myself from a rickety ladder of salty rope and rotting planks, I turned to find myself an object of study for eight Vikings. The most immediate thing to strike me was not the traditional Norse 'fist of welcome' but the fact that most of them were identical.

'Quins now is it?' I counted them off.

Snorri slung an arm about two of the five, white-blonde types with ice-chip eyes and beards far more close-cut than the usual 'big-enough-to-lose-a-baby-in' style of the North. 'Sore point, Jal. These are Jarl Torsteff's octuplets. Atta sits at Odin's table now, in Valhalla, with Sex and Sjau.' He cast me a stern look and I kept my face a mask. 'These are Ein, Tveir, Thrir, Fjórir, and Fimm.'

My guess was that I'd just had a lesson in counting to eight in Norse, and simultaneously a look at the meagre state of Jarl Torsteff's imagination. I decided to call them the quins in any event. Less morbid.

'Also Tuttugu.' Snorri reached out to pummel the shoulder of a short fat man. A ginger beard fluffed out from both sides of the man's head with great enthusiasm but failed to quite meet across his chins. Older this one, mid-thirties, a decade over the quins. 'And Arne

Dead-Eye, our greatest shot!' This last the oldest of them, tall, thin, melancholy, bad teeth, balding, grey in the black of his beard. If I'd seen him bent over weeds in a field I'd have thought him a common peasant.

'Ah,' I said, hoping we wouldn't have to mix blood or spit in each other's hands. 'Delighted to make your acquaintance.'

Seven Vikings looked at me as if I might be some kind of hitherto unseen fish they'd just landed. 'Run into trouble?' I pointed at the broken mast, but unless the thirty or so additional men required to fill the rowing benches were up at the Swordfish enjoying tankards of salt-beer then the trouble had entailed much more than a shortening of the mast and some ripped sailcloth.

'Drowned Isles trouble!' A quin, possibly Ein.

'We don't have a settlement on Umbra any more.' This another quin, directed at Snorri.

'Call them the Dead Isles now.' Tuttugu, jowls wobbling as he shook his head.

'Necromancers chased us onto our ships. Storms chased us south.' Arne Dead-Eye, looking at the calluses on his hand.

'Got wrecked on Brit. Took months to repair. And the locals?' A quin spat over the side and a remarkably long way out to sea.

'Been hopping along the coast ever since, trying to get home.' Arne shook his head. 'Dodging Normardy's navy, patrol boats off Arrow, Conaught pirates… And Aegir hates us. Sent storm after storm to beat us back.'

'I was expecting sea serpents next, a leviathan why not?' Tuttugu rolled his eyes. 'But we're here. Friendly waters. Few more repairs and we can cross the Karlswater!' He slapped a random quin across the shoulders.

'You don't know?' I asked.

Snorri's brow furrowed and he moved to the side of the boat, leaning out to stare north across the open water.

'Know what?' From many mouths, all eyes on me.

I realized my mistake. Don't board a man's ship bearing bad news. You're likely to leave again swiftly and by the wet side.

'We know there's no word of the Undoreth in Den Hagen.' One of the quins, Ein with the scar at the corner of his eye. 'No longships docking. Tales come from the Hardanger ports of raids along the Uulisk, but no detail. We've been here four days and that's all we've discovered. You know more?'

'Snorri's the one to tell it,' I said. 'My stories are all from him and I'd not trust myself to remember them right.' And that turned all those pointed stares Snorri's way.

He stood, towering above us all, grim, a hand on his axe. 'It's a thing that must be told where we can toast the dead, brothers.' And he walked to the harbour wall, climbing quickly up a series of jutting stones that I'd missed on my way down.

* * *

Snorri led us to a dockside tavern where the drinking tables would afford a view of the longship. I didn't judge it worth stealing, but perhaps he was wise not put that to the test. After all, a place like Den Hagen would make anyone frantic to leave after a short while, so there might have been men there desperate enough to sail off in any untended vessel, even a leaking tub like the one that brought the Norsemen to harbour.

I walked along at the rear of the group with Tuttugu. 'I thought longships would be, you know, longer.'

'It's a snekkja.'

'Oh.'

'The smallest type.' Tuttugu managed a grin at my ignorance, though his mind must have been on what Snorri would tell. 'Twenty benches. Skei carry twice as many. Ours is called *Ikea*, after the dragon, you know?'

'Yes.' I didn't, but lying is easier than listening to explanations. I wasn't even that interested in their boat, but it looked as though I might be trusting myself to it, and sooner than I wanted to. Twice the size of their snekkja still didn't sound like a big ship – but the strength of the North had always been in swift boats, and many of them. I had to pray that with all that prac-tice the damn things were at least seaworthy.

We drew up stools around a long bench, several locals wisely deciding to relocate to other tables. Snorri called for ale and sat at the head of the table, looking out across the length of it at the snekkja's sails flapping above the harbour wall. The sky behind them held a complex mix of dark and moody clouds, some trailing rain, but all lit by the slanting rays of the afternoon sun.

'Valhalla!' Snorri swiped the first foaming tankard off the tray as the serving women brought them out.

'Valhalla!' A pounding of the table.

'A warrior fears the battle he missed. More than any fight he can make his own, he fears the fight that's gone, that ended without him, that no feat of arms can change.' Snorri had their attention. He paused to drink deep and long. 'I didn't fight at Einhaur, but I heard the tale of it from Sven Broke-Oar if any straight word can come from his crooked tongue.'

The crew of the *Ikea* exchanged glances at that, muttering amongst themselves. The tone of the snatches I caught made it clear they shared a low opinion of the Broke-Oar.

'The battle at Eight Quays I fought in. A massacre more than a battle. My survival shames me every day.' He drank again, and told the story.

The sun dropped, shadows stretched, the world went by, but unnoticed. Snorri held us under the spell of his voice and I listened, sipping my ale without tasting it, even though I had heard it all before. All of it until he reached the Black Fort.

When Snorri first saw the black spot he thought it part of dying, his vision failing as the wilderness claimed him.

But the spot persisted, kept its place, grew as he staggered on. And in time it became the Black Fort.

Built of huge blocks carved from the ancient basalt fields beneath the snows, the Black Fort sat in squat defiance of the Bitter Ice, dwarfed by the vast and rising cliffs of the ice sheet just five miles to the north. In all the long years of the fort's existence the ice had advanced, retreated, advanced again, but never quite reached those black walls, as if the fort stood as man's final guardian against the dominion of the frost giants.

Strengthened by the sight, Snorri journeyed closer, drawing his sealskin cloak all about him, white with snow. An east wind picked up, scouring across the ice, picking up fine dry snow and driving it in eddies and streams. Snorri leaned into the teeth of the gale, the last scraps of warmth stolen away from him, each step threatening to end in a huddle from which there would be no rising.

When the fort's bulk blocked the wind Snorri almost toppled, as if his support had been snatched away. He hadn't seen that he was so close, or truly believed that he would ever reach his goal. Nobody watched from the battlements. Each narrow window stood shuttered and snow-clad. No guard waited on duty at the great gates. Numb of hand and brain Snorri stood, uncertain. He had carried no plan with him, just the desire to finish what had started in Eight Quays and what should have ended there. He had outlived two children. He had no desire to outlive Egil or Freja, only to battle to save them.

Feeble as he was, Snorri knew that he would only grow weaker waiting in the snow. He could no more scale the walls of the fort than he could climb the cliffs of the Bitter Ice. He took Hel in both hands and with his father's axe he beat upon the doors of the Black Fort.

After an age a shutter high above broke open, scattering ice and snow upon Snorri's head. By the time he looked up the shutters had closed once more. He pounded the door again, knowing his mind clouded with the slowness and stupidity that cold brings, but unable to think of an alternative.

'You!' A voice from on high. 'Who are you?'

Snorri looked up and there in wolf furs, leaning out for a better look, Sven Broke-Oar, face unreadable in the red-gold swirl of his hair.

'Snorri...' For a moment Snorri couldn't summon his full name to numb lips.

'Snorri ver Snagason?' the Broke-Oar boomed in amazement. 'You vanished! Fled the battle, men said. Oh, this is most fine. I'll be down to open the doors myself. Wait there. Don't run away again.'

So Snorri stood, white hands tight around his axe, trying to let his anger warm him. But the cold had wrapped around his bones, sapping strength, sapping will, and even memory. Cold has its own taste. It tastes of a bitten tongue. It coils around you, a living thing, a beast that means to kill you, not with wrath, not with tooth nor claw, but with the mercy of surrender, with the kindness of letting you go gentle into the long night after such a burden of pain and misery.

The scraping of the doors shook him from his reverie. He startled backward. The grunting of men at labour as the two great slabs of timber juddered back over icy stone. If they had simply left him waiting he might never have moved again.

Ten yards back, beyond the thickness of the walls, standing in the open courtyard Sven Broke-Oar waited, axe in one gloved hand, his small iron buckler across the other.

'I could have finished you with a spear from the walls, or let the snows have you, but the champion of the Iron Fields deserves a better end than that now.'

Snorri wanted to say that a man concerned with honour, or with the rights and wrongs of how a warrior dies, should have come to Eight Quays in the daylight, sounding his horn across the fjord. He wanted to say a lot of things. He wanted to talk of Emy and of Karl, but ice had sealed his lips and whatever strength remained he would use to kill the man before him.

'Come then.' The Broke-Oar beckoned him in. 'You've come this far. It would be a shame for fear to keep you from the last few paces of the journey.'

Snorri made a shambling run, his feet too frozen for speed. Sven Broke-Oar's laugh – that was the last thing he remembered before the club struck the back of his head. The men who had drawn open the doors simply waited behind them and brought him down once he'd passed by.

A blazing heat woke him. Heat in his arms, stretched above him. Heat in his extremities, as if they burned. Heat across his face. And pain. Pain everywhere.

'Wh—'

The breath that broke from him plumed the air. Fragments of ice still clung to his beard, water dripping to his chest. Neither so hot as it felt then, nor so cold as it had been.

Raising his head brought the wound at the back of his skull against the rough stone wall and half an oath burst from his cracked lips. The hall before him housed a dozen men, crowded before a small fire in a cavernous hearth around the far end of a long stone table. Broke-Oar's men, Red Vikings from the Hardanger, even less at home so close to the Bitter Ice than the Undoreth who kept to the Uulisk shores.

Snorri roared at his captors, bellowed his rage, uttered dire curses, shouted until his throat grew raw and his voice weak. They ignored him, sparing hardly a glance, and at last sense prevailed over his anger. No hope remained to him but he realized what a pathetic figure he cut, tied there on the wall and issuing threats. He had had his chance to act. Twice. He had failed both times.

The Broke-Oar entered the hall from a doorway close by the fire and warmed his hands there, exchanging

381

words with his men before walking the length of the table to inspect his prisoner.

'Well that was foolish.' He rubbed his chin between thumb and forefinger. Even close up his age proved elusive. Forty? Fifty? Scarred, weathered, raw-boned, huger even than Snorri, his mane of red-gold hair still thick, crow's feet at the corner of each dark eye, a shrewdness in his gaze as he weighed his man.

Snorri made no reply. He *had* been foolish.

'I expected more from a man trailing so many mead-hall tales.'

'Where is my wife? My son?' Snorri made no threats. The Broke-Oar would laugh at them.

'Tell me why you ran. Snorri ver Snagason has been shown to be stupid and I'm not greatly surprised. Though I expected more. But a coward?'

'Your creatures' poison brought me down. I fell and snow covered me. Where is my son?' He couldn't speak of Freja before these men.

'Ah.' Broke-Oar glanced back at his men, all of them listening. There could be scant entertainment in the Black Fort. Even the coals they burned must have been hauled in by sled at great effort. 'Well he's safe enough, as long as you carry on being no threat.'

'I didn't tell you his name.' Snorri tugged at his ropes.

The Broke-Oar merely raised a brow. 'You think the son of the great Snorri ver Snagason hasn't been telling anyone who'll listen how his father will storm our gates with an army to rescue him? Apparently you'll take all our heads with an axe and roll them across the fjord.'

'Why do you have them?' Snorri met the man's gaze. His pain helped distract him from thoughts of Egil's trust in a failed father.

'Ah well.' Sven Broke-Oar pulled over a chair and sat with his axe across his knees. 'Out at sea a man's a small thing, his ship not much bigger, and we go where the weather wills. We run before the storm. We rise and fall with the waves. Skinny fisherman off the Afrique coast, big Viking with a hundred kills to his name out on the Devouring Sea, it's all the same – we're driven by the wind.

'Here's the thing, Snorri ver Snagason. The wind has changed. It blows from the Isles now and there's a new god making the weather. Not a good god, not a clean one, but that's not ours to change. We're at sea and we bow our heads to our tasks and hope to stay afloat.

'The Dead King holds the Isles now. He broke Jarl Torsteff's strength there, and that of the Iron Jarl, of the Red Jarls of Hardanger. All driven back to their ports.

'Now he comes for us, with dead men, our dead among them, and monsters from beyond death.'

'You should fight them!' Snorri found himself straining, useless against the ropes' strength.

'How is that working out for you, Snorri?' A hardness around his eyes, something bitter and difficult to read. 'Fight the sea and you drown.' He hefted the axe on his lap, finding comfort in its weight. 'The Dead King is persuasive. If I brought this wife and son of yours here, to this room, held a hot iron to their faces … you might find me persuasive, no?'

'Vikings don't make war on children.' Snorri knew defeat. Better to have let the ice claim him than come here to fail his family.

'The Undoreth leave orphans and widows untouched when they raid?' A snort of derision at that from the men around the hearth. 'Snorri Red-Axe has adopted the sons and daughters of the many men he's sent on their final voyage?'

Snorri had no answers. 'Why are they here? Why take captives? Why here?'

The Broke-Oar only shook his head, looking older now, closer to fifty than to forty. 'You'll sleep better not knowing.'

'The dreams I've had.' Snorri raised his head at the end of the tavern table. Aslaug looked out at us from his eyes, now beads of jet glimmering and bloody with the last light of the setting sun. You could imagine them watching from the web and believe for a moment the tale of Loki, the god of lies, cleaving to a jötnar beauty with nothing but a spider's shadow to betray her true

384

nature. 'Such dreams.' That gaze fell cold upon me. 'Hard to imagine them darker still.'

I felt Baraqel move beneath my skin, and half-expected that glow to start, ready for light to fracture through the scars I still bore from the Gowfaugh, for radiance to bleed from beneath my nails. Across the length of the table that crackling force we knew from brief contacts began to build. I knew it now for the energy between Aslaug and Baraqel, between avatars of darkness and light, ready for war.

I wanted to ask why, to echo Snorri's demand of the Broke-Oar: why? I wanted to know how he came to be sold and to what end. Most of all though, I wanted Aslaug to look away, and so I lowered my gaze and held my peace. The others around the table saw or sensed the strangeness that had come over their countryman and kept silent also – though perhaps their quiet held a touch of mourning in it for the Undoreth.

'Einhaur was sacked too?' A quin, breaking the moment.

'Before they came to Eight Quays?' Another.

'What of Dark Falls?' Tuttugu.

'It must be all of them.' Arne Dead-Eye kept his gaze on the table. 'Or we would have heard the tale a dozen times by now.'

Every man at the table, save Snorri, took their ale and drank until they had no more.

'The enemy is there, past the Black Fort,' Snorri said.

The night pooled around him, darker than it should be while the sun still sunk in the west, not yet swallowed by the sea. 'We will go there. Kill everyone. Raze their works. Show them a horror darker than death.'

The northmen lowered their tankards, watching Snorri with uneasy fascination. I looked out to sea once more, west, along the coast to where the burning rim of the sun still beaded the horizon with red jewels. Fewer, fewer, gone.

'I said, Undoreth, we will paint the snows with Hardanger blood!' Snorri surged to his feet, freed by the sunset, eyes clear, the table scraping back across the stones. 'We will take back what we love and show these Red Vikings how to bleed.' He raised his axe above his head. 'We are of the Undoreth, The Children of the Hammer. The blood of Odin runs in our veins. Storm-born we!'

And where Aslaug left the Northmen unmoved with her dark threats Snorri ver Snagason had them on their feet in a moment, roaring their defiance at the evening sky, pounding the table until the wood splintered and the tankards leapt.

'More ale!' Snorri sat at last, thumping the table one more time. 'We drink for the dead.'

'Will you come with us, Prince Jalan?' Tuttugu asked, taking a tall flagon from the server, the head of foam as white as the quins'. 'Snorri says they call you a hero in your homeland, and your foes named you "Devil".'

'Duty compels me to see Snorri to his homeland.' I nodded. When a course of action is forced upon you it's best to accept it with grace and milk it for whatever you can get, right up to the moment the first opportunity to weasel out of the deal presents itself. 'We'll see what these Hardanger scavengers make of a man of the Red March.' Hopefully I'd find a way for it not to be a corpse.

'What makes us think we'll fare any better with nine than Snorri did with one?' Arne Dead-Eye wiped ale foam from his moustache, his voice morose rather than fearful. 'The Broke-Oar had enough men to lay waste to Einhaur and every village along the Uulisk.'

'Fair question.' Snorri, reached out to point at Arne. 'First understand that there were very few men at the Black Fort and it's not a place that could ever be garrisoned to its capacity. Every meal eaten there must be hauled across the ice. Every log or sack of coal must be carried there. And what is there to defend against? Slaves labouring beneath the Bitter Ice, digging tunnels in search of a myth?

'Second, we will go better prepared, not dressed in what could be scavenged from ruins in the moment. We will go with clear heads, the murder in our hearts locked away until it is needed.

'Third and finally. What else are we to do? We are the last of the free Undoreth. Anything that survives of our people is there, on the ice, in the hands of other men.' He paused and set his broad hands upon the table, staring at the spread of his fingers. 'My wife. My son. All my life. Each good thing I have done.' Something twitched at his mouth and became a snarl as he stood, voice growing toward a roar once more.

'So I'm not offering you victory, or a return to your old lives, or the promise that we will build again. Just pain, and blood, and red axes, and the chance to make war upon our enemies together, this last time. What do you say?'

And of course the maniacs roared their approval, and I banged my fist half-heartedly against the table and wondered how I could get the hell out of this mess. If Sageous hadn't been lying, or wrong, then perhaps if Snorri fell in the assault and I lurked near the back I could run off once the spell had broken. Of course with nine men there aren't exactly a lot of ranks to hide behind, and this Black Fort sounded inconveniently far from any safe haven that a man might run to.

I decided the best policy for the now would be to drink myself insensible and hope the morrow had better to offer.

'The most important message here,' I said into a gap where the Norsemen were all momentarily silenced by their tankards. 'Is not to act too hastily. Planning is the key. Strategy. Equipment. All those things that Snorri missed out on the first time in his impatience.'

The longer we delayed the more chance there was

that this curse might wear off or some opportunity for escape would happen along. The important thing was for the *Ikea* not to sail before I'd exhausted all opportunities for me not to be onboard when it did. With a shrug I drained my ale and signalled for another.

24

Some hangovers are so horrific that it seems the whole world rocks and sways around you, the very walls creaking with the motion. Others are relatively mild and it just turns out that in your drunkenness a collection of Vikings have thrown you onto a heap of coiled ropes in their longship and set to sea.

'Oh, you bastards.' I cracked open an eye to see a broad sail flapping overhead and gulls wheeling far above me beneath a mackerel sky.

I sat up, threw up, stood up, tripped up, threw up, crawled to the side of the boat, vomited copiously, crawled to the other side and groaned at the thin dark line on the horizon, the only hint at the world I knew and might never see again.

'Not a sailor then?' Arne Dead-Eye, watching me from a bench, his oar locked before him, a pipe in his hand.

'Vikings smoke?' It just looked wrong, as if his beard might catch light.

'This one does. You don't get handed a book of rules, you know.'

'I suppose not.' I wiped my mouth and hung there on the boat's side. The quins were doing complicated things with sail and rope. Tuttugu watched the waves from the prow and Snorri held the tiller at the stern. After a while I felt strong enough to lurch over and collapse on the bench beside Arne. Thankfully the wind carried his smoke the other way or we would have had a chance to see whether any of last week's meals might reappear if I tried really hard.

'What other rules in this handbook that you don't get have you broken?' I needed distraction from the heave and swell. We appeared to be weathering some kind of storm, despite the clearing skies and moderate winds.

'Well.' Arne puffed on his pipe. 'I'm not really one for the mead-hall and the singing of all those songs. I'd rather be out on the ice doing a spot of fishing.'

'You'd think a man of your talents would want to be stalking prey that he could bring down with a shot rather than hook out of the water through a small hole in the ice.' I'd placed a fair measure of my hope for survival in Arne Dead-Eye. The great thing about a man who is deadly with a bow is that not much gets close enough to trouble him. Those are the sort of men I like to stand next to in a battle if events conspire to keep me from galloping off into the distance. 'Hell! Where's my damn horse?'

'Bits of it are probably all over the lower slopes of Den Hagen.' Arne mimed chewing. 'Stew, sausages, horse-bacon, roast horse, tongue soup, liver with onions, fried horse, mwah. All good.'

'What? I—' My stomach had the last word of that sentence. A long word full of vowels and spoken mostly over the side at the rolling sea.

'Snorri took her up to the stockyard this morning and sold her,' Arne called at my back. 'Got more for the saddle than the mare.'

'Hell.' I wiped more drool from my chin before the wind had a chance to decorate the rest of me with it. Back on the bench I rested a moment, head in hands. It seemed we were coming full circle. This nightmare had started with me being bundled into a boat full of Viking and now here we were again. A bigger boat, more water, more Vikings, and the same number of horses.

'Dead-Eye, heh?' I hoped to cheer myself with the idea Arne might keep me safe. 'How'd you earn *that* title?'

Arne puffed out a cloud of vile smoke, which was quickly stripped away by the wind. 'There's two ways to hit a small target that's a long way off. Skill or luck. Now I'm not a bad shot – I'm not saying that. Better'n average for sure. Especially now with all the practice I get. It's "Let the Dead-Eye take the shot", "Give Arne the bow". But that day at Jarl Torsteff's wedding celebrations...' Arne shrugged. 'Had men from all over come to take part in the contests. Axe-throwing. Rock-lifting. Wrestling. All that. Archery, well, it's never been our strong point, but there were plenty willing. The jarl set up this coin, far too far out, and nobody could hit the damn thing. It was getting dark before they let me have a go. Took it down first try. Never heard the last of it. And that's how it is in this world, boy. Start a tale, just a little tale that should fade and die – take your eye off it for just a moment and when you turn back it's grown big enough to grab you up in its teeth and shake you. That's how it is. All our lives are tales. Some spread, and grow in the telling. Others are just told between us and the gods, muttered back and forth behind our days, but those tales grow too and shake us just as fierce.'

I groaned and lay back across the bench, trying to find some angle that brought it past the halfway mark on the line dividing 'torture device' and 'bed'. I would have just lain down between the benches but each lunge of the boat brought foul-smelling bilge water sloshing along the aisle in miniature imitation of the vast waves on which we tossed.

'Wake me when the storm's passed.'

'Storm?' A shadow fell across me.

'You're going to tell me that it's always like this, aren't you?' I squinted up at the figure, dark against the bright sky, sunlight fracturing around him to sting my eyes. A tall man, annoyingly athletic. One of the quins.

393

'Oh no.' He sat on the bench opposite, his good cheer like acid on my hangover. 'It's rarely as good as this.'

'Urrrg.' Actual words seemed insufficient to express my feelings on the matter. I wondered if Skilfar had seen that I was destined to fill a longship with vomit and drown in the resulting mess.

'Snorri says you're good with wounds.' He started tugging up his sleeve without invitation. 'I'm Fjórir, by the way – we can be hard to tell apart.'

'Jesus!' I winced as Fjórir unwrapped the soiled linen from around his forearm. The jagged tear went right down into the meat of him, with every shade from black to puce on show in the puffy flesh to either side. The stink of it told the story. When a man's wound starts to smell wrong you know they're on a slow walk to the cemetery. Perhaps losing the arm might save him – I didn't really know. Beyond adjusting the odds when betting on pit fights my experience didn't really concern such things. True, there had been similar unpleasantness on the Scorron borders, but I'd successfully discarded those memories. Or at least I had until a whiff Norseman's putrid arm brought them all back in a flood. At least this time I made it to the side before retching into the dark swell of the waves. I spent a long time hanging there, holding a loud but wordless conversation with the sea.

Fjórir was still sitting where I left him when I came

back empty-stomached and trembling. The whole boat continued to threaten capsize at each surge of the waves but nobody else seemed concerned.

'That's ... That's a hell of a cut you've got there,' I said.

Ripped it on a loose spear in a storm off the Thurtans.' Fjórir nodded. 'Nasty though. Gives me no peace.'

'I'm sorry.' And I was. I liked the quins. They were that sort. And soon they'd be quads.

'Snorri says you're good with wounds.' Fjórir returned to his theme. He seemed unaccountably cheerful about the whole business, though I wouldn't bet on him lasting the week.

'Well I'm not.' I peered at the mess with morbid fascination. 'You seem less worried about it than I am.'

'The gods are taking us in order. Youngest first.' Again that grin. 'Atta fell to ghouls in Ullaswater. Then a dead man pulled Sjau into the bog at Fenmire. Sex took an arrow from a Conaught bowman. So Fimm's next, not me.'

And all of a sudden I found myself scared as hell. Snorri I understood. I didn't share his passions or bravery, but I could feel them as greater or lesser versions of my own emotions or thinking. The man before me looked like one of us on the outside, but inside? The gods had put the Torsteff octuplets together differently from other men. Or at least this one. Perhaps the parts he was missing were present two-fold in one of his brothers. Or maybe when the eight started dying each death left the survivors more broken. Fjórir still had the amiability, the immediate sense of dependability, but I couldn't know what else might be missing behind that too-easy grin and those wide, ice-blue eyes.

'I don't know why Snorri said that – I'm no doctor. I don't even—'

'He said you'd try to weasel out of it. He said for you to do what you did in the mountains.' Fjórir held his arm out for me, no hint of trepidation on his face.

'Go on!' Snorri shouted from the back of the boat. 'Do it, Jal!'

Pressing my lips tight against revulsion I extended a hand without enthusiasm, holding it several inches above the injury. Almost immediately a warmth built in my palm. I snatched the hand back. My plan of faking it seemed unlikely to succeed now – the reaction had been far stronger and more immediate than with Meegan's wound back in the Aups.

'The last person I did this to Snorri threw off a cliff a moment later.'

'No cliffs at sea. That felt good. Do it again.' Fjórir had no guile in his eyes, like a child.

'Ah hell.' I stuck my hand back out, as close to the rotting flesh as I could without risk of being slimed. Within seconds I could see the glow from my hand, as if it were a white handprint through that blustery northern day into the desert blaze of the Indus. My bones buzzed with whatever ran through them and the heat built. The wind grew icy around me, the weakness from my vomiting became enfeeblement to the point that even holding my hand up was a labour of Hercules. And suddenly I wasn't holding anything up. The boat revolved around me and I pitched into darkness.

A bucket of cold and salty water hauled me back into the waking world.

'Jal? Jal?'

'Is he going to be all right?'

A reply in their heathen tongue.

'…soft these southerners…'

'…bury at sea—'

More nonsense words in northern gibberish.

Another bucket. 'Jal? Talk to me.'

'If I do will you stop pouring seawater over me?' I kept my eyes shut. All I wanted to do was lie very still. Even moving my lips seemed too much effort.

'Thank the gods.' Snorri paused. I heard a heavy bucket being put down.

They left me alone to dry after that. I sprawled on the bench until a particularly big wave rolled me off. Then I lay against the hull. Occasionally I called on Jesu. It didn't help much.

The light was failing by the time I found the strength to haul myself up and sit on the spot where I'd fallen from. Fjórir brought me over some dry fish and cornmeal cake but I couldn't do much more than glance at it. My stomach still rolled with each wave and made no promise to keep anything I gave it.

'My arm's better!' Fjórir held it out by way of proof. The wound still looked ugly but free of infection now, and healing. 'My thanks, Jal.'

'Don't mention it.' A weak murmur. I guessed he really was invulnerable until poor Fimm took his place in line. Hopefully he'd pay me back by putting his invulnerable self between me and harm's way.

The sun set and Snorri spent that time in the *Ikea*'s prow, staring north, his black eyes no doubt hunting the Norsheim coast. My strength made no return: if anything I grew weaker as the night fell. I tried some dry bread and water, donated them to the sea, and dropped into a dreamless slumber.

Dreamless at least until I started dreaming of angels.

I stood in the pre-dawn, on the hills just beyond Vermillion's farmlands, looking down at the Seleen snaking westward toward the distant sea. Baraqel stood above me, on the hilltop, statued against the sky, unmoving until the rays of the rising sun lit his shoulders.

'Hear me, Jalan Kendeth, son of—'

'I know who I'm son of.'

The angel had far more gravitas about him now than he had in his early visits. As if he spoke more with his own voice than the one I'd fashioned for him back when he was nine parts imagination.

'The time will soon come when you will need to remember where you sprang from. You sail into the land of sagas – a place where heroes are needed, and made. You will need your courage.'

'I don't think remembering my father will help there. The good cardinal would turn and run if a goat blocked his path. It wouldn't have to be a big one either.'

'It's in the nature of children to see past the strengths of their parents. Time to grow up, Jalan Kendeth.' He lifted his face to me, golden-eyed, glowing with the dawn.

'And what's so great about being brave? Skilfar had the right of it. We're all running around each according to our nature, some cunning, some honest, some sly, some brave – but what of it?'

Baraqel flexed his wings. 'Your grandmother spoke to her sister of you. "Has he the mettle? Has he the courage required?" An "idle, shallow boy, full of bluster but ringing hollow," she called you, Jalan. "A mind blunted by sloth, blinkered by a dry wit," she said, "but whet it and that mind could take an edge. Had we but world enough and time what we might make of the child … but we have neither world nor time. Our cause is narrowing to a point not so many miles distant, a second not so many years hence and in that spot, in that moment, will come a test on which the world will turn." These are the words she drew you with.'

'I'd be surprised if she knew which one I was. And I'm sharp enough when I need to be. Bravery is just a different kind of broken. The quins are missing whatever it is a man needs in order to feel fear. Snorri's scared of being a coward. There's a wyrm like that in their heathen stories, Oroborus, eating its own tail. Scared of being a coward, is that what bravery is? Am I brave because I don't fear being afraid? You're of the light: the light reveals. Shine a bright enough light on any kind of bravery and isn't it just a more complex form of cowardice?'

I stood a moment, the heels of my palms pressed to my forehead, hunting the words.

'Humanity can be divided into madmen and cowards. My personal tragedy is in being born into a world where sanity is held to be a character flaw.' I ran out of words under his gaze.

'Cleverness builds ever more elaborate structures of self-justification,' he said, judgment spilling from his mouth. 'But in the end you know what is and what is not right. All men do, though they may spend their years trying to bury that knowing, burying it beneath words, hatreds, lusts, sorrow, or any of the other bricks from which they build their lives. You know what is right, Jalan. When the time comes you'll know. But knowing is never enough.'

They told me I spent the best part of a week insensible. Sleeping twenty-two hours in twenty-four, half-waking to let Tuttugu spoon warm gruel down my throat – some of it down the inside, some down the outside. A quin had to hold each arm when nature called me on infrequent trips to the side, or I'd have pitched in and not have been seen again. We crossed the open sea then followed the Norsheim coast day upon day, heading north.

'Wake up.' The angel's only instruction this sunrise.

I opened my eyes. Grey dawn, flapping sailcloth, the cry of gulls. Baraqel silenced. The angel spoke true. I always know what is right. I just don't do it. 'Are we nearly there yet?' I felt better. Almost good.

'Not far.' Tuttugu sitting close by. Others moved about the longship in the dimness.

'Oh.' From behind closed eyelids I tried to imagine terra firma, hoping to stave off a pre-breakfast vomit.

'Snorri says you're good with wounds,' Tuttugu said.

'Christ. This voyage is going to kill me.' I tried to sit and fell off the bench, still weak. 'I thought it would be the undead horrors and mad axe-men out on the ice. But no. I'm going to die at sea.'

'Probably for the best.' Tuttugu offered a hand to help me up. 'Good clean death.'

I almost took his hand then snatched mine back. 'Oh no. Not falling for that one.' It wouldn't be long before I couldn't beat a leper out of my way without curing the bastard. 'You don't look injured.'

Tuttugu buried his fingers in the ginger bush of his beard and scratched furiously, muttering something.

'What?' I asked.

'Brothel rash,' he said.

'Whore pox?' That at least made me smile. 'Ha!'

'Snorri said—'

'I ain't laying on hands down there! I'm a prince of Red March for God's sake! Not some travelling apothecary-cum-faith-healer!'

The fat man's face fell.

'Look,' I said, knowing I'd need all the friends I could make once we hit dry land. 'I might not know much about wounds, but whore pox I know far more about than any man ever should. Do you have mustard seed aboard?'

'We might.' Tuttugu furrowed his brow.

'Rock salt? Some black treacle, tanners' acid, turpentine, string, two needles, very sharp ones, and some ginger … well, that's optional, but it helps.'

A slow shake of the head.

'Ah, well, we'll pick it up in port. I can cook it up to an old family recipe. Apply as a topical paste to the affected regions and you'll be a new man within six days. Seven tops.'

Tuttugu grinned, which was good, and gave me the Norse punch of friendship, which hurt a lot more than the traditional manly shoulder punch down south, and that was that. At least until he frowned and asked, 'And the needles?'

'Well, when I said "apply" what I really meant was

"smear on a needle and jab in". You'll need more than one as the mixture corrodes them.'

'Oh.' Little remained of Tuttugu's grin. 'And the string's to hang myself with?'

'To tie the bag on... Look, I'll explain the gory details when you've got the stuff.'

'Land ho!' One of the quins from the prow, providing a welcome distraction.

My nightmare at sea was all but done.

25

Mist shrouded Norsheim, offering me only glimpses of wet black cliffs and menacing reefs of rock as we closed the last mile or so to reach the shore. We came in past other Norse vessels plying their trade. Fatter bodied boats in the main, trailing nets or laden with cargo, but all with northern lines to their construction. We saw other longships too, most of the dozen or so at anchor, one heading out to open sea, red sails already too small to make out the device set upon them.

Coming in closer still we saw the port of Trond rising from a shoreline of black stone to crowd the lower slopes of mountains that stepped wet-footed from the sea. I had thought Den Hagen looked dour and uninviting but compared to Trond the port of Den Hagen was a paradise, practically open-legged with welcome. The Northmen built their homes of slate and heavy timber, turf-roofed, windows mere slits to defy the slim fingers of the wind that already had filched most of my warmth. Rain started to fall, lacing the wind and stinging like ice where it hit my cheeks.

'And this is summer? How can you tell?'

'Glorious summer!' Snorri spread his arms beside me.

'You can tell because in the winter there are no midges,' said Arne behind me. 'Also the snow is six foot deep.'

'And you could walk to the port from here,' Snorri said.

'I didn't even know the sea could freeze…' I went to the side to consider the matter and leaned out between two of the shields the men had fixed there in preparation for our arrival. 'At least it would stop it bobbing about all the time.'

We rowed in the last quarter mile, sail down. I say 'we'. I provided moral support.

'How is it the Broke-Oar got his name?' I asked, seeing them all bending to their task.

'The first time he went to row a longship.' Quin Ein.

'He must have been fourteen, or fifteen.' Quin Tveir, probably.

'Hauled on the oar so hard he broke it.' Quin Thrir, possibly.

'Didn't know his own strength, even then.' Fjórir, his arm still scarred.

'Never seen anyone pull an oar that hard.' Fimm, by process of elimination.

'Is he stronger than you, Snorri?' I found the thought unsettling.

Snorri pulled back on his oar, keeping rhythm with

the others. 'Who can say?' Another stroke. 'The Broke-Oar doesn't know his own strength.' Another stroke. 'But I know mine.' And the look he gave me, all ice and fire, made me very glad not to be his enemy.

At the dockside I was pleasantly surprised to find the North wasn't all hairy men in animal skins. There were also hairy women in animal skins. And, to be fair, also some townsfolk in cloaks woven from wool, with tweed or linen jackets, trews cross-bound from ankle to thigh as is the fashion in the Thurtans.

We disembarked and I staggered at the unfamiliar feeling of something solid and unmoving beneath my feet. I could have kissed it, but didn't. Instead I followed on, burdened by my pack, now adorned with tightly bundled winter gear, more to be added soon. Snorri knew the port well and led us up toward a tavern that he held a good opinion of.

Trond, unlike many of the smaller towns and villages along the coast and fjords, wasn't the fiefdom of some jarl, dominated by his mead-hall and with every arrival noted, taxed, and subject to his approval. Trade ruled in Trond. The port's external security balanced upon a number of well-financed alliances, and its internal security depended on a militia paid in Empire coin by the collective of merchant lords who governed the place. As such it presented an ideal landing spot and place to resupply. Snorri planned to travel overland to the Uulisk, a journey of two days or so across mountainous terrain. To limp up the fjord on a badly undermanned snekkja would lose the only advantages a small band possesses, namely agility, speed, and surprise. It sounded a sensible plan given that we were determined foolishly to head into trouble, and Snorri even credited me with helping to formulate it during my more lucid moments on the long voyage, though I had no memory of it.

As we'd pulled into harbour I'd made out stormclouds louring across the ranges to the north, lightning deep inside them as if Thor himself were present. Somewhere out there beyond those peaks Sven Broke-Oar waited for us in the Black Fort, and beyond him the Bitter Ice with its frozen dead, necromancers, and the unborn. My chances to escape had all but slipped away and our long journey was at last closing on what would likely prove to be a short sharp end.

The tavern of Snorri's choosing bore three rusting axes, stapled to the wall high above the doorway. The Norsemen installed me at a table then ordered most of a pig to be roasted and brought out along with copious ale, maintaining that both were excellent cures for a man in weakened health.

The rest of the clientele were a rough lot but none of them appeared to be looking for trouble. You develop an instinct for such things if you frequent as many low dives as I have. Additionally the fact that I had eight

Undoreth warriors in my corner would not have gone unnoticed.

'We'll meet up here come nightfall.' Snorri sniffed the air with a certain longing. The smell of roasting dominated over all the usual tavern stink of smoke and sweat and ale. And with a sigh he led his men off into the town, Tuttugu armed with my pox recipe. I assumed that Jarl Torsteff's men must have escaped with at least some of the proceeds of their looting on the Drowned Isles because for once Snorri hadn't asked me for funds, and he had plenty he needed to buy – warm gear and provisions for nine not the least of it. I patted for my locket, just to be sure.

A lean southerner walked in as the last of my Vikings departed, wrapped in a motley cape, dulled by age, and with a mandolin under his arm. He settled by the fire-place, raising an arm for beer. Another man opened the street door, half-lowered his hood, thought better of it then left. Not a music lover, perhaps, or finding the place too packed. Something about him struck me as familiar but my meal arrived and my stomach demanded my full attention.

'There you go, my lovely.' A perky, fair-haired tavern-girl set down my roast pork, a heel of bread, a steaming jug of gravy, and a tankard of ale. 'Enjoy.' I watched her leave and started to feel twenty-two again rather than ninety-two. Good food, ale and a floor beneath me that had the manners to stay where it was put …

the world had started looking up. All I needed was a plausible excuse for staying in Trond until the nastiness up north had been dealt with and I could look upon this whole sorry affair as a vacation gone tragically astray.

I noticed a blonde woman watching me from beside her companion, young and really quite striking once you looked past the homespun and dirt. Another pretty young thing, white-blonde and pale, slanted glances my way from beside an older man. None of them dressed like professional company, even accounting for the summer chill. It seemed as though taking your sister or daughter to the tavern might just be the done thing in Trond. Another woman walked in through the street door, this one solid and dour, and pushed a path to the bar to order black ale. I chewed over that one with my meat. Things appeared to run very differently in the North. Still, I had no objections. I might complain about Cousin Serah and my grandmother's plan to circumvent the rightful chain of succession, but in general I found the women with the most freedom to act were by far the most fun to be around. After all it's hard for the old Jalan charm to get to work if there's a chaperone or inconvenient brother like Alain DeVeer in the way.

I sat for a moment, letting the conversations flow across me. Many of the locals spoke in the Empire Tongue. Arne told me it was common enough in the larger port towns. In the villages along the fjords a man could go for weeks without hearing a word not spoken in the old speech.

Across the room the troubadour began to pick at his mandolin, scattering a few notes over the crowd. I wiped pork-fat from my mouth and swigged my ale. The older blonde kept watching me and I gave her the Jalan smile, the one the hero of Aral Pass offers to the masses. The man beside her seemed to have no interest in our exchange, a slightly-built fellow with a drooping moustache and twitchy eye. Still, any peasant can stick a knife in you so I curbed my instinct to barge over there and introduce myself. Instead I decided to put my goods on show and let the bees come to the honey.

'Do you know "The Red March"?' I called across to the mandolin player. Most bards do and he looked well-travelled in any case.

By way of answer, fingers flickered across strings and the first few bars rolled out. I stood, bowed to the various ladies, and crossed to the fireplace. 'Prince Jalan of Red March at your service one and all. A guest to your shores and pleased to be here among such fierce warriors and fair maids.' I nodded to my new friend and he started to play. I've got a decent baritone and the princes of Red March are trained in all the arts: we declaim poetry, we dance, we sing. Mostly we're trained in the arts of war, but wordcraft and painting are not neglected. Add to this that "The Red March" is a rousing military chorus that forgives a singer's weaknesses and encourages others

410

to join in and you have the ideal icebreaker. Even the frozen seas of the North couldn't withstand my charm! I hoisted my tankard and gave full voice with the troubadour filling in the gaps with his own mellow tones.

I'll say this for Norsemen, they like to sing. Before I'd finished either my ale or song almost everyone under that roof was roaring out "The Red March", ignorance of the words proving no obstacle. Better still, my delicious blonde had detached herself from Droopy Moustache to stand at my side, showing herself during her approach to have been blessed in all the right places by the gods of Asgard. The pretty pale waif had also ditched her father to keep me company on the other side.

'So you're a prince?' As the din of the last verse subsided. The blonde beauty, more attractive by the moment, leaned in. 'I'm Astrid.'

'I'm Edda.' The pale girl, hair flowing like milk, very fine-featured. 'Who was that warrior with you? You know, the big one.'

I did my best to keep the irritation from my face. 'You don't want to worry about him, Edda. He's tall, yes, but women report that he's very unsatisfactory in the furs. Used all his growing getting too high off the ground and didn't save enough for the important things. It's a sad story. His mother and father … well, brother and sister—'

'No?' Her lips made a circle.

411

'Yes.' I shook my head sadly. 'And you know how it goes with those sorts of children. They never grow up properly. I do my best to look out for him.'

'So generous of you,' Astrid purred, steering my attention away from sweet Edda.

'My dear lady, it's the moral duty of nobility to—'

Someone crashed in through the street door, cutting me off. 'A brandy if you please!'

A commotion as the crowd parted. A young man, a touch taller than me, a touch older, walked forward grasping the wrist of his right hand, blood dripping on the floor.

'Oh my—What happened?' Edda clutched her hands below her breasts.

'Just a dog.' The fellow was golden-haired, not white-blonde like her, and handsome with it. 'The baby's fine though.'

'Baby?' Astrid, coming over all motherly.

The man reached the bar and a hairy warrior signalled he'd get the drink for him. 'Snatched him from his mother's arms,' the man said. Someone passed him a cloth and he started wrapping it around his hand.

'Oh let me help!' And Edda fled my side, Astrid in hot pursuit.

'Well I chased it. The cur didn't want to give up his prize. We disagreed and I got the baby, and this.' He held up his bandaged hand.

'Isn't that marvellous, Prince Jalan?' Edda glanced

back over her shoulder at me. She looked even more tempting at a distance.

'Marvellous.' I managed a mutter.

'Prince?' The fellow bowed. 'Delighted to meet you.'

Now I'm a good-looking fellow. No doubts about that. Good thick hair, honest smile, face in order, but this interloper could have stepped from some frieze of the sagas, chiselled to perfection. I hated him with a rare and instant passion.

'And you are?' I aimed for a level of disdain with enough edge to cut but not to make me look bad whilst doing it.

'Hakon of Maladon. Duke Alaric is my uncle. Perhaps you know him? My longships are the green-sailed ones in the harbour.' He knocked back the brandy. 'Ah a mandolin!' He spied the troubadour. 'May I?'

Hakon took the instrument, strumming with his injured hand, and immediately music began to flow like liquid gold. 'I'm better on the harp, but I've tried these a few times.'

'Oh, would you sing for us?' Astrid, pressing her gifts against him.

And that was that. I slunk back to my table while Golden Boy held the tavern spellbound with a gloriously rich tenor, running through all their favourite songs. I chewed my lukewarm roast and found it hard to swallow, my ale sour rather than salt. I glowered through narrowed eyes as Hakon stood bracketed by Edda, Astrid and various other wenches drawn from the shadows by his cheap show.

At last I could take it no longer and got up to go out back for a piss. A final resentful glance at Hakon saw him disentangling from Astrid to follow me out. I pretended not to notice. Once in the blustery yard rather than making immediately for the latrine I waited, leaving the door ajar and listening for his approach.

The wind had picked up something fierce and put me in mind to play a trick I'd used a time or two back in Red March. On hearing him take the handle I gave the door a hearty kick, slamming it shut. A meaty thud and an oath rewarded me. I counted to three and hauled the door open.

'Hell! Are you all right, man?' He was on his backside clutching his face. 'The wind must have caught the door. Terrible thing.'

'…be ok.' Both hands still clasped over his nose, the injured one atop the good.

I crouched beside him. 'Best have a look.' And pulled back his bad hand. Immediately that familiar warmth built, and with it came an idea both despicable and delicious in equal parts. I gripped his bitten hand tight. The day went dim around me.

'Ow! What the—' Hakon pulled away.

'You're fine.' I hauled him to his feet. Fortunately he helped, because I could barely lift myself.

'But what—'

'You're just a bit dazed.' I steered him back into the tavern room. 'You got hit by a door.'

Astrid and Edda converged on Golden Boy and I stepped away, letting them at their prey. As I left I tugged the loose end of the bloodstained cloth about his hand and pulled it away with me.

'What—' Hakon lifted his uncovered hand.

'How many babies did you save?' I said it quiet enough over my shoulder as I returned to my table, but too loud to miss.

'There's no bite there!' Astrid exclaimed.

'Not even a scratch.' Edda stepped back as if Hakon's lies might be contagious.

'But I—' Hakon stared at his hand, holding it up even higher, turning it this way and that in astonishment.

'He can pay for his own damn brandy!' The warrior at the bar.

'A cheap trick.' The thickset woman, slamming down her tankard of ale.

'He's no kin of Alaric!' Anger starting to colour the complaints.

'I doubt he's spoke a true word since he came in.'

'Liar!'

'Thief!'

'Wife-beater!' That last one was me.

The crowd folded about poor Hakon, their shouts drowning him out, punches flying. Somehow he made it through them, half-running through the street door, half-thrown. He sprawled in the mud, slipped, fell, scrambled up and was gone, the door slamming behind him.

I leaned back in my chair and took the last chunk of pork off my knife. It tasted sweet. I can't say I was entirely proud about using the healing gift of angels to screw over the better man just for being more handsome, taller, and more talented than me, but then again I couldn't bring myself to feel too bad about it either. I looked out over the crowd and wondered which of the girls to reel back in.

'You, boy.' A stout ginger-haired man blocked my view of Astrid.

'I'm—'

'I don't care who you are, you're in my seat.' The fellow had the kind of aggressive red face that makes you want to slap it, his bulk girded in thick leathers set with black iron studs, knife and hatchet at his hips.

I stood up – not without effort, for healing Hakon's bite wound had taken a lot out of me. I towered over the man, which is always unfortunate if you want an excuse to duck out of a fight. In any event, standing was a necessary part of the process since I intended to vacate the chair rather than get cut into chunks over the issue. I puffed out my cheeks even so and blustered a piece – you can't let the weakness show or you're dead.

'Men of my standing don't cross the seas to brawl in taverns. Damned if I care which chair I'm in.' The weight of my sword tugged at me and I wished Snorri hadn't forced the thing on me. It's always easier to back out of such confrontations if you can claim to have left your sharp iron at home.

'Dirty bastard, aren't you?' The Norseman looked up at me with a sneer. 'I hope you've not left any of that stain on my chair?' He frowned in pantomime. 'Or doesn't that stain come off however you scrub?'

To be fair we were probably equally dirty, with his grime smeared over skin so fish-belly white you could see the veins snaking blue paths underneath, and mine the proud olive hue that a man of Red March retains however long it's been since he saw the sun, darkened still further with Mother's heritage from the Indus.

'Your chair.' I stepped aside, indicating the free seat. My whole attention focused on the man, every muscle I owned ready for action.

The tavern held quiet now, anticipating violence and waiting for the show. Sometimes such things can't be avoided – unless you're a true professional. Most, for example, wouldn't think to just run like hell.

'It *is* dirty!' The Viking pointed to the chair, as filthy as any other in the place. 'Suppose you get down there and clean it. Right now.' More men pressed through the street door, not that he needed the back-up.

'I'm sure a cleaner chair can be found for you.' I puffed up, pretending I thought he was joking and hoping the size of me would intimidate the man.

Just as cowards often have an instinct for trouble,

many bullies have a nose for fear. Some small clue hidden in the way I carried myself told him I wouldn't be a problem. 'I said, you do it, foreigner.' He raised a fist to menace me.

Snorri loomed behind the man, caught his wrist, broke it and tossed him into the corner. 'We've no time for games, Jal. There's three boatloads of Maladon sailors headed up here – something about Lord Hakon being set upon … anyway, we don't want to get caught up in it.'

And with that he bundled me through the room, Arne, Tuttugu, and the quins in tow, and out of the back door.

'We'll make camp in the hills,' he said, hefting open a gate in the wall of the enclosed yard.

And like that my dreams of a warm bed and warmer company blew away in a cold wind.

26

I trailed along at the back of the party, bent double under my pack. It felt as though Snorri had decided it was important we each took several large rocks with us to the Bitter Ice. Tuttugu laboured along beside me, short of breath and walking awkwardly.

'You "applied" the paste then?'

He nodded, striding on with the gait of a man who didn't make it to the dung-hole in time. 'It really stings.'

'That'll be the mustard seed.' On reflection it had probably been fennel seed the recipe called for, but I decided not to mention it now.

I shifted my pack to what turned out to be a less comfortable position. 'So, Tuttugu, looking forward to wetting your axe in the blood of your enemies?' I needed some insight into the Viking mindset. My only escape route lay through understanding what made these men tick.

'Honestly?' Tuttugu glanced ahead at the others, the first pair of quins some twenty yards further up the slope.

'Let's try honesty first and move on to lies if it proves too upsetting.'

'Honestly … I'd much rather be back in Trond with a big plate of liver and onions. I could settle there, do a spot of fishing, find a wife.'

'And the axe-wetting?'

'Scares me shitless. The only thing that stops me running away in battle is knowing everyone else is faster than me and I'd get cut down from behind. The best chance lies in facing the enemy head on. If the gods had given me longer legs … well, I'd be gone.'

'Hmmm.' I shifted the pack to the least comfortable position so far. The thing was already making my lungs ache. 'So why are you trekking up this mountain?'

Tuttugu shrugged. 'I'm not brave like you. But I've got nothing else. These are my people. I can't leave them. And if the Undoreth really have all been slaughtered… someone has to pay. Even if I don't want to be the one to make them – someone has to pay.'

Toiling across the mountainside gave fresh impetus to the finding of reasons not to go. With gritted teeth I put in the effort needed to catch up to Snorri at the head of our trek.

'This Broke-Oar of yours. He's a war leader, important among his people?'

'He has a reputation. His over-clan is the Hardassa.' Snorri nodded. 'Many followers, but he doesn't rule in

Hardanger. He's feared more than loved. He has a way about him. When he focuses on a man many find it hard to resist him, they're swept along with his energy, but when he turns away often that man will remember reasons to hate him again.'

'Even so.' I paused to recover my breath. 'Even so. He's not going to spend year after year sitting in this little fort in an icy wasteland? Not a man like that? You can't expect to find him where you left him?'

'We weren't just buying furs in Trond, Jal.' Snorri glanced back at the stragglers. Well, straggler. Tuttugu. 'There's no other place in the North like Trond for finding out what's going on. Tales come in on the ships. Sven Broke-Oar has been raiding up and down the coast. The Waylander and Crassis clans in Otins Fjord, the Ice Jarls in Myänar Fjord, and the Hørost on the Grey Coast. All of them have been hit, and hard. Many captives, many slaughtered. And last reports have him entering the Uulisk. There's nothing there for him except the trek to the fort. He's set to winter there. Ice locks up all the high North in the long night. Everyone draws in, holds fast, waits for spring. The Broke-Oar reckons himself secure at the Black Fort. We'll teach him a different lesson.'

I had no answer to that, other than that I was a worse teacher of lessons than I was a pupil, and I was a terrible pupil.

*   *   *

421

We trudged on, mile after mile, up unforgiving slopes of bedrock shelving skyward from the sea and angled toward daunting heights. Weariness took me into dark places. I grumbled about the weight of my pack until I hadn't even the energy for that. Several times I thought about ditching my sword just to be free of the weight. At last I fell into a kind of reverie, plodding on whilst replaying the highlights of my afternoon, Astrid and Edda's highlights in particular. All of a sudden it hit me. The man who had stepped in, lowered his hood a fraction, then ducked out ... a band of raven-dark hair, greying to the sides.

'Edris!' I stopped in my tracks. 'Snorri! That fucker Edris Dean was there. In town!'

Up ahead Snorri turned, raising a hand to stop the quins. 'I saw him too,' he called back. 'With a dozen men of the Hardanger. Another reason we left in a hurry. The Red Vikings are a significant force in Trond.'

They waited until Tuttugu and I caught up. 'We'll camp here,' Snorri said. 'And keep a watch for anyone following up the slopes.'

Sleeping on mountains is a miserable business but I have to admit that it's less miserable in a thick fur-lined sleep-sack with a canvas and leather awning to divert the worst of the wind around you. Snorri and the others had spent their money well and we had an untroubled night.

Come morning we broke fast on black bread, cold

chicken, apples and other perishables from Trond. Before long we'd be back on hardtack and dried meat but for the now we ate like kings. At least like impoverished kings who happen to be stuck on a mountainside.

'Why the hell is Edris in Trond?' I asked the question I'd been too bone-tired to voice the previous evening.

'The thing we're chasing – being dragged after – it seeded its trail with trouble for us.' Snorri chewed off another piece of bread, attacking it like meat on the bone. 'The Dead King lies behind all this, and he collects men, living ones as well as the dead. The right kind of man he'll draw to him. Men like the Broke-Oar and this Edris.'

'Edris will be chasing us now?' I hoped not. The man scared me, and more than trouble did in general. Something about him gnawed at me. Whatever quality ran through individuals like Maeres Allus, Edris had his measure of it too. An understated menace – the kind you know that when it *does* speak will be worse than any threat or posture from men capable only of common cruelty.

'Trying to get ahead of us, most like.' Snorri swallowed and stood, stretching until his bones creaked. 'He'll aim for the Black Fort, or maybe the mining at the Ice first. If they're warned we don't stand much chance.'

We didn't stand a chance in any event. I kept that opinion to myself. Perhaps if Edris *did* warn them the others would see it was hopeless and abandon the effort.

423

'All right, but...' I got up too, lugging my pack up onto my shoulder. 'Explain to me again why a horror from Red March runs a thousand miles and more to some godforsaken hole in the ice?'

'I don't know it all, Jal. Sageous told me some of it, though that may be lies. Skilfar had more to say—'

'What? When?' I didn't remember any of that.

'She didn't speak to you?' Snorri raised his brows.

'Of course she did. You heard her. Some nonsense about my Great-uncle Garyus and being led by my cock. Dreadful old crone, mad as a brush.'

'I meant ... without words.' He frowned. 'She spoke in my head, the whole time.'

'Hmmm.' I wondered how much faith to place in words spoken in Snorri ver Snagason's head. It seemed quite crowded in there and who knew how many voices Aslaug might use? Or perhaps Baraqel might be responsible for Skilfar's words not reaching me – though whether he would be acting in my best interests with such selective deafness I didn't know. 'Remind me.'

'The unborn are hard to summon. Very hard. Only a few come through, where the conditions are right, where the timing, the place, the circumstances all align.'

'Well anyone knows *that*!' All new to me.

'And so they are scattered.'

'Yes.'

'But what the Dead King has ordered in the Bitter Ice, the work his minions are accomplishing there ... is drawing the unborn, from all corners of the earth. To one place. Perhaps when your friend at the opera found himself targeted and escaped he abandoned whatever mission called him there and ran for the gathering in the North. Or maybe he was always bound there after whatever business drew him into Vermillion.'

'Ah.' Oh hell. 'But your wife is in the Black Fort, right? And the unborn are beneath the Bitter Ice? Yes? So we never have to meet them … right?'

Snorri didn't answer immediately, only started walking.

'Yes?' At his back.

'We're taking the Black Fort.'

I tried to remember Snorri's tale from the tavern in Den Hagen. The Broke-Oar had told him his son was safe. That's all he said. He'd also talked Snorri into getting clubbed around the back of the head. All about me the Norsemen were hefting packs, moving on. Already I could feel the faintest tug as the curse binding me to their leader began to stretch out across the slope. 'Crap on it.' And I followed in his footsteps.

The True North is much as Snorri described it from experience and much as I described it from ignorance. All of it appears to be sloping up to start with, though later it slopes both up and down as if in a great hurry to get somewhere. The air is thin, cold, and full of winged insects that want to suck your blood. Drawing your breath through your teeth helps strain the buggers out and keep your lungs clear. Also they die away as you gain height.

Much of the place is bare rock. As soon as you gain any altitude it's bare rock covered with last winter's snow. From the heights you can see mountains, mountains, and more mountains, with lakes and pine forests huddling in the dents between them. I took Tuttugu's advice early on and bound about my boots the rabbit furs and seal-skin over-guards from my pack. With this and my feet in thick woollen socks the snows didn't freeze my toes. It would only get worse as we headed north though, into the Jarlson Uplands where the wind off the interior came armed with knives.

We paused in the lee of one high ridge whilst Snorri and Arne discussed our route.

'Ein, is it?' The scar by his eye gave it away.

'Yes.' The quin with the longest life expectancy flashed me a smile.

'How is it that Snorri's in charge here?' I asked. 'You're Jarl Torsteff's heir aren't you?' I didn't plan to undermine Snorri's authority, unless it turned out Ein could order him to give up his quest – which seemed unlikely what-ever the chain of command should be – but as a prince it did strike me as odd that a man whose only birthright was a few acres of sloping rockfields should be ordering the North's aristocracy about.

'Actually I have seven older brothers. Two sets of triplets and a singleton, Agar, Father's heir. It might be that they're all dead now, I suppose.' He pursed his lips at that, as if seeing how the idea tasted. 'But Snorri is a champion of the Undoreth. There are songs about his deeds in battle. If Einhaur and my father's halls are burned – then my authority stands on nothing but ash. Better to let a man who truly knows war to lead us on our last raid.'

I nodded. If we were bound to our course then Snorri was the man to take us to the bitter end. Even so, I didn't like the concept of a man's rank being something that could so easily be set aside. It might be true for a jarl's son here amid the snows, but in the warmth of Red March a prince would be a prince no matter what came. I took a measure of comfort in that, and in the fact that dawn had long since passed so Baraqel couldn't sour my mood with his own judgment on the matter of princes.

Toward evening of that second day we reached a great work and wonder of the Builders, high among the peaks. A huge dam wall had been constructed, spanning a valley, taller than any tower, thick enough at the top for four wagons to drive along it side by side, and wider still at the bottom. A vast lake must once have been held behind it, though to what purpose I couldn't say.

'Wait!' I needed a rest and the ruins provided the perfect excuse.

Snorri came back along the slope, frowning, but he

allowed that we might stop for a few minutes whilst I satisfied my aristocratic curiosity. I satisfied it from a sitting position, letting my gaze roam along the valley sides. Enormous stone pipes ran out through the bedrock beneath the dam, obviously to control the flow of water, but why I couldn't guess. The whole place was built on the scale of the mountains, each structure huge enough to make ants of men. Even the pipes would accommodate several elephants walking side by side, with headroom for riders. In such a place you could believe the Norse stories of frost giants who shaped the world and cared nothing for humanity.

I sat on my pack beside Tuttugu, staring out across the valley, both of us munching on apples he'd dug from his pack, wizened but still sweet with the taste of summer.

'So every Viking name seems to mean something … "Snorri" means "attack", "Arne" is "eagle", the quins came out numbered…' I broke off to let Tuttugu supply the explanation of his own, something heroic probably. If they applied names with any accuracy 'Tuttugu' would mean 'timid fatty' and 'Jalan' would mean 'runs away screaming'.

'Twenty,' he said.

'What?'

'Twenty.'

I glanced toward the huddle of quins. 'Good God! Your poor mother!'

Tuttugu grinned at that. 'No, it's not my birth

name, just what people call me. There was a contest at Jarl Torsteff's feast after the victory over Hoddof of Iron Tors, and I won.'

'A contest?' I frowned, trying to puzzle how Tuttugu won anything.

'An eating contest.' He patted his belly.

'You ate twenty…' I tried to think of something a person might reasonably eat twenty of. Eggs?'

'Close.' He rubbed his chins, short fingers buried in ginger fuzz. 'Chickens.'

It took four days rather than the promised two before we looked down upon the sparkling length of the Uulisk from a high ridge, endless miles of mountain trekking to our rear. Snorri pointed out a dark spot along the shoreline.

'Einhaur.' I could tell nothing of its fate from our remove, save there were no fishing boats at its quays.

'Look.' Arne pointed out along the fjord, further seaward. A longship, tiny from where we stood, a child's toy out on the flat waters of the Uulisk. Near the prow a red dot … a painted eye?

'Edris and his Hardanger friends, I'm guessing,' Snorri said. 'Best press on.'

27

The trek to the Black Fort proved much as Snorri had
described it. Only a lot worse. Although Edris might
have followed us, or have been ahead in the race to the
fort, in such a huge and empty expanse it's impossible
to think of yourself as chased or chasing. You are either
alone, or not alone. We were alone, and our enemy
pressed us on every side. The wind and the cold of the
Uplands are things that must be experienced: words will
not tame them into something that can be given over.
We left behind trees, then bushes, then even the hardiest
of grasses until the world was nothing but rock and
snow. The snow patches joined each to the next to
become unbroken. The days grew shorter with frightening speed and each morning Baraqel would no longer
harangue me but merely unfold his wings, golden with
the dawn, and bid me be worthy of my line. Snorri
would sit apart from us when the sun fell, plunging from
the sky and drawing the long night behind it. In those
moments, as ice devoured sun, I could see her walk

about him, Aslaug, a lean beauty fashioned from the gloom, her spider-form scurrying in her footsteps, black across the snow.

Each hour became a process of taking a dull future and squeezing it into a dull past through the narrow slot of the moment – a moment, like each other, crowded with pain and exhaustion, and with a cold that crept around you like a lover carrying murder in her heart. I tried to keep myself warm with thoughts of better times, most of them in someone else's bed. Strange to say, and surely a sign of my brain's slow freeze, although I could summon to mind countless moments of coitus, long limbs, smooth curves, waves of hair, the only face that would appear was Lisa DeVeer's, showing – as it always did – part amusement, part exasperation, part affection. In fact, as the cold North sucked the life out of me I found myself remembering times outside her bed more than within it – conversations, the way she ran her fingers through her hair when puzzling, the cleverness of her replies. I blamed it on snow fever.

We camped in the lee of any outcrop we could find and burned charcoal from our packs to put a little warmth into our food. The snows south of the Bitter Ice would thaw occasionally. Maybe two years would pass, maybe five, but eventually a particularly high summer would melt them back to bare rock in all but the deep places, and so the ice we walked on was never thick enough to cover every rise and fold of the land. The

Bitter Ice itself however, that glacial sheet never melted though it might retreat a mile or three over the course of lifetimes. And the land beneath it hadn't seen the sun in centuries, maybe since Christ walked the world. Maybe never.

On the long march through an icy waste no one talks. You keep your mouth closed to seal the heat in your body. You cover your face and watch a white world through the slit that remains. You put one foot before the next and hope that it's a straight line you're plotting – letting the rise and fall of the sun guide your progress. And while you try to force your body along the straightest path, the paths your mind follows become increasingly twisted. Your thoughts wander. Old friends revisit. Old times catch you up once more. You dream. With your eyes open, and with the plod and plod of numb feet to punctuate each minute, you dream.

I dreamed of Great-uncle Garyus, lying broken in his high tower, older than sin and smelling only slightly better. His nurses cleaned him, carried him, fed him, took away a measure of his dignity every day, though he never seemed to lack for more.

Garyus probably would have thanked any god that could give him even a day of walking, even in a place like this. And even at the end of a day of such labour, bone-cold, bone-tired, hunched within my misery, I wouldn't have swapped with him.

My great-uncle had lain there year upon year, placed by age and infirmity on death's doorstep. The Red Queen had told us that there really was a door into death, and it seemed that Garyus had been knocking on it since the day he'd come broken into the world.

In my dreams I returned to that day with the sun slanting in past his shutters, when Garyus had folded my hands around that locket in his own, large knuckled, liver-spotted and tremulous. 'Your mother's likeness,' he had said. 'Keep it safe.' And safe meant secret. I knew that, even at six.

I'd sat and watched that old and broken man. Listened to his stories, laughed at them as children do, sat silent and round-eyed when the tales turned dark. Most of that time I never knew him as my great-uncle. And none of that time did I know him as brother to the Silent Sister – though of course it seemed only right the Sister should be *someone's* sister.

I wondered if Garyus were scared of his twin, the blind-eye woman, his silent sister. Could a person be scared of their twin? Would that be like being scared of yourself? I knew that many men were scared of themselves, frightened that they would let themselves down, that they would run rather than fight, choose the dishonourable path, the easy path rather than the hard. Me, I trusted myself always to do what was right – for Jalan Kendeth. The only times I scared myself were the rare occasions I was tempted to stand and fight, those few times when anger had got the better of me and almost stepped me into danger.

How much did Garyus, there in his tower with his stories and gifts for children, know of his sisters' battles? I looked at those memories now as a puzzle. Was there another way to see them? Like those trick drawings where everything is obvious until someone tells you 'the lump is a dent' and suddenly you see it – what was a bump is now a hollow, pushed in, not standing out – they all are, every rise and hollow reversed, the image has changed, its meaning flipped around, and try as you like you can't see it as before, solid, unambiguous, worthy of your trust.

Did Garyus know his younger sister thought she knew where death's door lay?

'Jal.' A tired voice. 'Jal.'

I thought of Garyus, the Red Queen's brother, eyes aglitter in that narrow bed. Older than her, surely? Had he known her plans? How much of all this had that crippled old man set in motion?

'Jal!'

Shouldn't he have been king? Wouldn't he have been King of the Red March if he weren't broken so?

'JAL!'

'What?' I stumbled, almost fell.

'We're stopping.' Snorri, bowed and tired, the ice wastes making mock of his strength just as it did of all men's strength. He raised a hand, pointing within his glove. I followed his direction. Ahead of us the walls of the Bitter Ice rose without preamble, sheer, beautiful, taller than my imagination.

We ate despite the effort it took, fumbling with dead fingers to make a spark, using the last of our kindling, lighting the charcoal to heat a pot and knowing there would be no heat but what our bodies made from then on.

That night for the longest time I didn't sleep. The skies grew clear overhead and stars dazzled down upon us as the temperature fell away. Each breath hurt, drawing frozen razors of air into my chest. Death seemed both near and inviting. I shivered despite the furs, despite layers and more layers. And when at last dreams took me down I held no surety of ever waking.

In some dead hour past midnight the silence woke me. The unrelenting wind had for once relented, dropping away to nothing. I cracked open an eye and stared into the darkness. The miracle came suddenly and without warning. In one moment the sky lit with shifting veils of light, rolling through the colours, first red, then an eerie green, next a blue I'd not seen before. And always shifting, from one serpentlike form to the next. The silence and the scale of it kept the breath in my chest. The whole sky overwritten, a hundred miles and more of the heavens dancing with glory to some tune that only angels hear.

I know now that it must have been a dream, but in

that moment I believed it with all my heart, and it filled me with wonder and with fear. Nothing before or since has made me feel so small, and yet that great and dancing mystery of light, huger than mountains, played out above an empty wasteland to no audience but me … it made me feel, just for the briefest time … significant.

In the morning Fimm did not rise.

'Now it is my turn.' Fjórir sewed his brother into his sleeping sack with a long bone needle and gut thread.

'Will he rise?' I eyed the sack, half-expecting it to move.

Snorri shook his head, solemn. Behind him Tuttugu rubbed his eyes. Of all of us the quins, now quads, seemed least moved.

'He's frozen,' Snorri said.

'But.' My face felt too solid for frowning. 'But you found a dead man struggling after a day or more in a snowbank.'

'The necromancers inject them with an elixir. Something of oils and salts, the Broke-Oar said. It keeps them from locking solid.' Snorri had told me this before but the cold had frozen my memory.

'This army beneath the ice… Olaaf Rikeson's troops – the Dead King's men – will need to thaw them and treat them in this manner. Unless they have some new magics it doesn't seem possible. The effort involved to drag them frozen to the south, or to bear sufficient fuel north…' I thought of the other part to the tale Snorri had told. The key that would open the frost giants' gates – Loki's gift. The key that would open anything. 'Perhaps all they ever wanted was Rikeson's key. That one thing.' And for some reason that thought worried me more than an army of corpses rising from the ice.

Snorri had aimed west of the fort so that the line of the Bitter Ice could lead us east toward it. If he had steered us wrong then we were walking away from the fort into the ice-bound wastelands of the interior where we would all die without the least inconvenience to anyone. Death seemed certain either way and if turning back alone offered even the slightest hope of survival then I would have been off without delay. Unfortunately, as Tuttugu had discovered in battle, running away is sometimes the least safe option, and whilst dying was the last thing I wanted to do, dying by myself seemed somehow worse.

I staggered on, across the unending whiteness, wondering if the Silent Sister had already watched my suffering when she looked beyond tomorrow. I crunched the ice, feet numb, the wind's keening filling my head. Had she counted out each frozen step or just seen the great white shape of our trek across the snows? How many possibilities had lain strewn across the future for her? And how many of them saw us dead? Foot before foot, too cold for shivering, dying by degrees. Perhaps in some futures the crack that chased me had caught and destroyed me before I even reached Snorri – in others he may have killed me as I ran into him. Did she know for certain that her spell would find a home in us, be carried north to the very edge of the Bitter Ice? Did she know whether her magics would wither inside us or take root and grow into more than they had been? Was she certain, or was she maybe, like her great nephew, a gambler always ready to roll those dice one time too many? I saw her narrow smile in my mind's eye and it did little to warm me. Foot before foot. Endlessly on.

Just as Snorri had described, the Black Fort took me by surprise. The landscape offered no clues, no build-up, no growing promise of journey's end. One moment it was a featureless white wasteland, bounded on one side by the Bitter Ice; the next moment it was the same featureless wasteland, except there *was* a feature, a black dot.

The trek had worn us to our final strength – Fimm it had worn past even that – but we were none of us the shambling, frost-bitten wreck that Snorri had been when he had last stumbled to the gates. We came with at least some measure of fight in us, some final reserve to draw upon. And, as little as I wanted to battle anyone, I knew for sure that without the chance to rest and restock in the shelter offered by the Black Fort I for one would not survive a return journey.

Snorri led us closer. Urging swiftness. He wanted to be inside before the sun set – wanted Aslaug's strength in the fight to come. The terrain offered no cover and we relied only on being white upon a white background to hide us, and also on the hope that nobody would be looking out for us. This latter proved an unfounded hope.

'Wait.' Ein, raising a gloved hand. 'Man in the south tower.'

However well we blended against the snow, with the sun sinking behind us our shadow might yet announce our approach if the man were paying close enough attention.

The Black Fort is a squat, square construction with a crenellated tower at each corner. A central keep, barely taller than the outer walls, sits amid a large courtyard. Snorri believed the keep unmanned and that the small garrison kept to chambers within the thickness of the walls around the main gates.

'The Dead-Eye will shoot him,' Snorri said. 'Then we climb.'

Arne rubbed gloved fingers across his face-guard, the soft hide frozen stiff and hanging with miniature icicles. The wind swirled around us, full of razors. 'It's a long shot.'

'Not for the Dead-Eye!' A quad slapped him on the shoulder.

'And the light's failing.' A shake of the head.

'Easy!' Another quad.

A slump of shoulders. 'I'll get my bow ready,' Arne said. 'Then we move closer.'

It took a damned long time, extracting and

unwrapping the bow, finding the string, waxing that, flexing this, warming fingers, hooking one thing to another. They'd taught me archery back in Vermillion of course. Every prince had to know the art. Rather than us becoming crack shots Grandmother was, apparently, more interested that we know and understand the possibilities and limitations of the weapon so that we could better utilize it en masse upon the battlefield. Even so, we still had to hit the bull's-eye.

If all those long hours of much-resented archery practice had taught me anything it was that wind will make a fool of even the best archer, a swirling, gusty wind especially so.

At last Arne had equipped himself and we crept forward across the snow, crouching low now, as if that might make a difference. The figure in the tower moved several times, facing our way for a heart-stopping moment, but showed no signs of interest.

'Do it here.' Snorri caught Arne's shoulder. I think the Dead-Eye would have closed to fifty yards if they'd let him.

'Odin guide my arrow.' Arne removed a glove and set a shaft to his bow.

On a still day with warm hands and no pressure on the outcome it was a shot I might hope to make four times in five. Arne loosed his shaft and it hissed away, invisible against the sky.

'Miss.' I stated the obvious to break the still moment

that held us all. The shot had gone so wide the man in the tower hadn't even noticed it.

Arne tried again, taking deep breaths to steady himself. Fingers white on the bowstring. He loosed.

'Miss.' I hadn't meant to say anything, the word just spoke itself into the expectant hush.

Arne pulled away his face-guard and gave me a sour look. He ran his tongue over an array of teeth, most brown, one black, one grey, one white, two missing. He took another arrow, one of maybe a dozen remaining, and returned his attention to the tower. Three breaths, hauled in, released slowly, and he took the shot.

To be fair I waited several seconds. It was lucky all three shots had gone high rather than striking the stonework. The man on the tower hadn't so much as flinched. 'Miss,' I said.

'You fucking do it!' Arne shoved the bow at me.

Safe in the knowledge I couldn't do much worse I stripped off a glove and strung an arrow. The wind made an agony of my fingers within moments. Those moments would be all I had before the wind stopped them hurting and made them useless. I lined up on the man, guessed at compensation for the wind and shifted my aim yards to the right. The lack of time helped. It stopped me thinking about what I intended to do. I'm told that I killed men in the Aral Pass but I've no clear memory of it. On the mountain with Snorri a man had pretty much impaled himself on my sword – and I'd apologized to him for the accident before I knew what I was saying. That had all been in hot blood. But here I crouched, arms trembling, blood as cold as it had ever been, ready to punch an arrow through a man's chest, to take his life without warning, without seeing his face. A different matter entirely.

'Miss.' I whispered it as I let fly.

Two heartbeats passed and I was sure I'd done no better than Arne.

'Yes!' The man spun around as if from a sudden impact. 'Yes!' Snorri shouted.

'Shit!' That from Tuttugu as the guardsman remained standing, advanced to the wall, unsteady and clutching his arm, then turned to flee.

'Hel! Shoot him again!' Snorri shouted.

The man had descended by steps to the main wall and was running hell for leather toward the far tower where presumably his companions were housed. Why he wasn't watching from that tower I couldn't tell you.

'We're done.' I gestured at the distant wall. The man could be glimpsed every half second or so as a dark streak through the crenels notched down into the battlements.

Arne snatched his bow back, strung an arrow and loosed it at the sky. 'A pox on all the gods.' He spat and his phlegm froze before it landed.

'Why waste another arrow?' I watched the walls, wondering if they would come out to kill us or leave us to freeze.

The man fell with a thin cry, nailed as he and Arne's arrow arrived together at the third crenel before the tower door, six yards short of his sanctuary.

'Dead-Eye!' A quad punched Arne in the shoulder.

'Dead arm if you're not careful.' But he sounded pleased.

Snorri had already hurried away from us, toward the walls. We gave chase. It seemed to take forever to cross the hundred yard gap. He had out a long coil of rope, knotted for climbing and stored away from the ice for this moment. At one end a grapple hook that looked suspiciously like the anchor from a small fishing boat. He threw it over the wall and it caught first time. Snorri had already reached the top as I made it to the base of the wall. A quad went up next, then Arne, then me, slipping and cursing now the knots were slippery with ice from the others' boots. The body of the man Arne shot plummeted past me as I reached the halfway point. I bit off another complaint and kept my mouth shut after that.

With only Tuttugu yet to climb we pulled our packs up on a rope and then hauled Tuttugu after them. That effort at last got a little warmth into my blood. I helped him to his feet after his rather undignified struggle between the battlements to reach the walkway.

'Thanks.' He grinned, a nervous thing, quick then gone, and unslung his axe from across his back. An unusual weapon, closer to the armour-piercing wedge design favoured down south.

On the gritted ice beneath my feet spatters of the tower guard's blood – shocking colour after what seemed an eternity of white. The droplets captured my gaze. All the talk, all the travel, had come to this moment, these crimson splashes. From abstract to real – too real.

'Are we ready?' Snorri from before the door our man had been running for. The word 'no' fought to get past my lips. 'Good.' Snorri held his axe in a double grip, Arne a broadsword, the brothers each with a double-headed broadaxe, short-handled, a knife in the off-hand. I drew my longsword, last of all of them. Satisfied, Snorri nodded and set his hand to the iron door-handle. The plan did not have to be reiterated. It was, as plans go, a simple one. Kill everyone.

The door opened with a squeal of hinges, shedding ice, and we were through, crowding onto the steps beyond. Snorri closed it behind us and I shut my eyes, taking a moment to enjoy the simple ecstasy of being out of that wind. No winter night of Red March had ever been as cold as it was there in that corridor within the Black Fort, but without the wind it was a paradise compared to the outside. We all took a moment, several moments, stamping a touch of life back into our feet, swinging our arms to recover a little of that lost flexibility.

Snorri led on, down the steps and into a long corridor. We expected to find most of Sven Broke-Oar's men in one spot. It's what men do in cold places. They huddle by the hearth, shoulder to shoulder, for as long as they can stand each other's company. With fuel so hard to come by they would not light many fires.

Although in many places the interior walls were ice-clad it felt hot in the Black Fort. My skin burned with it, life creeping back into my hands and even threatening to invade my fingers.

Arne lit a small lantern, the oil carefully hoarded during our long trip for just this purpose. Perhaps with its warmth Fimm would not have died in the night. The guard had carried no source of light, knowing his path through the dark.

At each door we paused and Snorri tried the handle. None of them were locked, though some were jammed and opening them quietly tested even Snorri's strength. The first two proved empty: long, narrow chambers with no hint of their purpose save a lack of fireplaces that told us they had never been intended for habitation. A third chamber stood stacked high with blocks of the same basalt that formed the walls themselves. Materials for repair. A fourth had been used as a latrine, though not recently: the mounds of frozen dung gave not the slightest scent.

The fifth door yielded after a silent struggle, one loud scrape echoing along the corridor as it gave. We held still, waiting for the challenge, but none came. The horror of my situation had started to settle on me as my body began to recover. I grew warm enough to shiver at about the same time that I grew scared enough to shake.

'Hel,' Snorri drew back from the part-open door, his face thrown into eerie relief by the lantern held beneath it.

'Is it safe?' Tuttugu, unwilling to lower his axe.

Snorri nodded. 'Take a look.' He beckoned me, raising the lantern overhead.

The scene reminded me of Skilfar's lair. Figures, row upon row, so close they leaned one upon the next, unable to fall. Men, shrouded in ice, bearded with frost, caught in every pose from curled in sleep to contorted in agony, but most just head down, captured in that plodding motion I knew so well from the past few days.

'Olaaf Rikeson's men?'

'Must be...' Snorri pulled the door closed.

The next five halls all held frozen corpses, all warriors. Hundreds of them in total. Dead for centuries but ice-locked against the years. I wondered if whatever spirit a necromancer might return to them would be all the darker for those lifetimes spent with the devil.

The quads huddled together and the momentary joy we'd all known at escaping the wind faded swiftly in that grim place, surrounded on all sides by the ancient dead.

The corridor passed two sets of spiral stairs, coiling up and down in their narrow shafts. Snorri passed them by. This section seemed more often used, the walls free of ice, grit on the floor to make for surer footing.

There was no missing or mistaking our target. The air grew warm, thick with the smell of smoke and cooking, something meaty stewing in a pot if I were any judge. My mouth began to water immediately. Just the scent of that hot food had me ready to kill for my supper. The door at the end of the corridor stood taller than the side doors, studded with black iron, muffled sounds emerging.

We looked, one to the other, preparing to organize for an entry. As often happens in life the decision was taken from us. A heavy-set Viking emerged without warning, calling some insult back over his shoulder.

Arne's arm flickered and the hatchet he'd carried so long at his hip now sprouted from the dark red curls of the man's beard. It didn't look quite real. Snorri and the others surged forward without a sound save for boots on stone. The man scrabbled at the hatchet, blood pouring down his neck, and fell beneath them.

I found myself standing with only Tuttugu at my side. He gave an embarrassed grin and jogged off after the others. That left me alone in a corridor with frozen dead men packed into all the rooms to either side. The first battle cry rang out, Snorri's roar of joyous violence as the others barged through the big door behind him. I screwed up whatever courage I could find and set off after Tuttugu, sword at the ready.

The sight beyond the door proved arresting. So arresting that even with all his momentum Tuttugu had come to a dead halt and I ran into his back, sandwiching my blade between us. A score or more Red Vikings had been crowded into the far end of the hall before the large fireplace. Stone tables ran nearly the length of the hall and I could only think this was where Snorri had been brought and hung upon the wall.

The Hardanger men, Red Vikings as they're known, hailed from a tribe darker in colouring than the Undoreth, more red heads among them, more dark-haired men, a tough breed, broad in the chest and blunt-featured. They weren't armoured or armed for war, but Norse warriors are seldom beyond reach of their axes and will always wear a knife or hatchet.

Snorri had leapt onto the table to the left and run its length, taking the head from one man sitting at it, close to the door, and carving a furrow through the face of another sitting on the opposite side, further along, closer to the fire. He'd dropped among the crowd by the hearth, swinging in great red arcs. Hardanger men scattered away into the length of the hall, grabbing their weapons, putting space between themselves and Snorri, only to be engaged by the quads, broadaxes flashing firelight as they ploughed flesh.

A quad went down, a backhand swing by a black-haired Viking burying an axe in his neck. The man was fearsomely fast, tall, lean, muscles like knots in rope along dirt-stained arms. Tuttugu ran forward, screaming as if gripped by the worst kind of terror, and hammered his axe into the black-haired man's chest before he could wrench his own axe from the quad's vertebrae. I saw Hardanger men hurrying along either wall of the hall, weapons drawn. A path that would see them converge on the doorway where I stood. In response I chased after Tuttugu, between the tables. Sometimes advance is the best form of retreat. Inadvertently I kicked the severed head of the first man to die and sent it rolling away toward the melee.

Crimson arcs decorated the far end of the hall. The fire smoked with spattered blood and a hand sizzled there, forearm still attached. Men staggered back from Snorri's blizzard of sharp iron, some with gaping wounds, guts vomiting from slits running groin to shoulder, others screaming, blood jetting from sliced limbs with sufficient pressure to stain the ceiling five yards above us. Others still hurled themselves at Snorri and the Undoreth with deadly intent, axes swinging.

The noise of it, the stink, the colour. The room revolved around me, the din fading in and out, time seeming to slow. Tuttugu hauled his narrow axe from his enemy's sternum. I heard the crack of bone, saw the blood gush, the man fall away, arms reaching, face dark with fury, not understanding that he'd died. A big red-haired man with a two-handed sword rushed at Tuttugu. Behind me three men vaulted the tables, two from the left, one from the right, eager to wet their blades. The door to the left of the great fireplace burst open, disgorging more Vikings, the first with an iron helm, studded all over, a crosspiece noseguard beneath. The man behind him raised a wide round shield, a spike on its central boss. More men crowded behind.

A spear sprung from a quad's chest as he rushed the doorway. The force of it took him backwards, white hair flying. Blood sprayed across me from closer at hand, filling my eyes, filling my mouth with salt and copper. I heard screaming and knew it was mine. The Red Vikings closed on me from both sides and I watched them from behind a crimson veil. My sword flickered out—

'Jal?' Faint beneath the pounding in my ears, the thunder in my chest, the harshness of each drawn breath. 'Jal?'

I could see the flagstones, awash with blood, black points of my fringe hanging before my eyes, dripping.

'Jal?' Snorri's voice.

I was standing. My hand still held my sword. A table to either side. Corpses leaking – some under the tables, some sprawled across them.

'Jal?' Tuttugu, nervous.

'Is he safe?' A twin. Or perhaps just Ein now.

I looked up. Three Undoreth watched me at a safe distance, Snorri glancing toward the doorway through which the reinforcements had come.

'Baresarker!' Ein smacked his fist to his chest.

Snorri spared me a grin. 'I'm starting to understand

the hero and devil of Aral Pass!' His scalskins were ripped wide across his hip exposing an ugly wound. Another deep cut on the muscle mounded around the join of shoulder and neck bled copiously.

My free hand started to shake uncontrollably. I looked around the room. The dead lay strewn. Around the hearth they lay in heaps. Arne sat on the table behind me, deathly pale, his cheek ripped so badly I could see through to the rotten teeth, half of them smashed out of his jawbone. The spreading pool of crimson around him told me that dentistry was the last of his worries. A wound to his thigh had cut the artery deep in the meat of him.

'Jal.' Arne offered me a broken grin, his words blurred by the face wound. He slumped down, almost graceful. 'It was a great shot though, wasn't it … Jal?'

'I—' My voice cracked. 'A great shot, Arne. The best.' But the Dead-Eye was past hearing. Past everything now.

'Snorri ver Snagason!' A roar issuing from the doorway beyond the hearth.

'Sven Broke-Oar!' Snorri shouted in return. He hefted his axe and approached the fire. 'You must have known I'd be back. For my wife, my boy, my vengeance. Why would you even sell me?'

'Oh, I knew.' The Broke-Oar even sounded pleased about it which, now that the strange sense of dissociation was fading, brought all my fears back from whatever

451

corners of my mind the battle-madness had driven them into. 'It was hardly fair to rob you of your fight now, was it? And we of the Hardanger do love our gold. And of course my new masters have expenses. The elixir they need for the dead in these cold climes requires oils from Araby, and those are hard to find. A man must trade good coin for such exotics.'

Even dazed I recognized the taunt. Telling Snorri he had financed this horror with his own flesh and failure. Whatever was said of the Broke-Oar none called him stupid.

Ein, Tuttugu and I went to stand at Snorri's side. Another chamber lay beyond the doorway, most of it out of our line of sight. A Red Viking lay half in one room, half in the other, his head split wide. Ein tugged the spear from his brother – Thrir if the order had held true.

'There's more to it than that, Broke-Oar. You could have killed me and still had nine-tenths and more of your blood gold.' Snorri paused as if struggling to voice his question. 'Where's my wife? My boy? If you've harmed—' He snapped his jaw shut on the words, the muscles in his cheeks working.

Tuttugu hastened to bind Snorri's side with strips from a cloak, Ein holding Snorri back as the warrior made to advance. Snorri relented and let them — the shoulder wound would bleed the strength from him soon if not staunched.

'There's more to it than that,' Snorri repeated.

'It's true, Snorri.' A touch of sadness in the Broke-Oar's voice. Despite his reputation the man sounded … regal, a king declaiming from his throne. Sven Broke-Oar had the voice of a hero and a sage, and he wound it around us like a spell. 'I've fallen. You know it. I know it. I bent in the wind. But Snorri? Snorri ver Snagason still stands tall, pure as autumn snow, as if he stepped from the sagas to save us all. And whatever else I might be, Snorri, I am a Viking first. The sagas must be told, the hero must have his chance to stand against the long winter. Vikings we – born to hold against trolls, frost giants, even the sea. Even the gods themselves.

'Come, Snorri. Let's make an end of this. Just you and me. Let your friends bear witness. I stand ready.'

Snorri started forward.

'No!' I grabbed hold of his arm and heaved back with whatever strength I had left. The curse flared between us, the resulting blast shredding his sleeve and throwing me back across the table, afterimages of ink and sunlight overwriting my vision. The scent of burned air filled my nostrils, a sharp astringency that took me back to that street in Vermillion, running as if all Satan's devils were at my heels, the cobbles cracking open behind me.

'What in Hel?' Snorri spun in my direction.

'I know—' Only a whisper came. I coughed and spoke again. 'I know bastards.'

453

Ein bent and picked up the discarded shield. Tuttugu took another two from a display on the wall.

'These are your last moments, Broke-Oar!' Snorri shouted and, bearing the shields high and low, Tuttugu and Ein stepped toward the doorway.

Crossbow bolts hammered into the shields in the instant Snorri's guardians crossed the archers' line of sight. Snorri unleashed a wordless roar and pushing between his companions launched himself into the next room.

I followed, still a touch dazed. If I'd had my wits about me I would have sat down with Arne and played dead.

Sven Broke-Oar stood at the far side of a chamber smaller than the one we'd come from, dwarfing the three crossbow-men beside him. I won't say he made Snorri look small, but he sure as hell stopped him looking biggest. The man's mother must have slept with trolls. Handsome trolls though. With his great red-gold beard plaited across his chest and his hair flowing free, the Broke-Oar looked every inch a Viking king, down to the gold chasing at the edges of the scarred iron breast-plate he had on. He held a fine axe in one hand, the iron buckler on his other about the size of a dinner plate, smooth and thick.

Ein veered toward the two men on the left; Tuttugu charged the one to the right. Sven Broke-Oar advanced to meet Snorri.

There's not much you can do about an axe swinging your way with a man's strength behind it. Killing the axe's owner before he completes his blow is your best option. With a sword you can impale your foe. But if like your foe you're armed with an axe then 'swing faster and hope' seems to be the best advice on offer. And of course to swing at your man you need to be a certain distance off – exactly the same distance he needs you to be at in order to swing at you.

Snorri had a different solution. He reached out before him, axe extended, running faster than is possible for any man building for a swing. The turn of speed spoiled the Broke-Oar's timing, his cutting edge arriving a split-second too late, the haft of his axe just below the blade hammered into Snorri's raised shoulder, while Snorri's axe smashed into the Broke-Oar's neck, not with the cutting edge but bracketing the man's throat with the horns of the blade.

That should have been an end to it. A narrow piece of metal driven against a throat by a powerful man. Somehow though the Broke-Oar slammed his buckler into the side of Snorri's head and fell back clasping his neck. Both men should have been down, but instead they reeled, unsteady on their feet then came together like bears, grappling.

Ein had killed one of his two opponents and now wrestled the second, both men clutching knives, trying to drive them into each other's faces whilst stopping the other man doing the same. Tuttugu had killed his foe but the Red Viking had loosed his dagger before Tuttugu split his head. I couldn't see how bad the wound was, but the speed with which the blood spilled over the fat man's hands where he clutched his belly said it couldn't be good.

The two giants stood, fingers interlocked, straining one against the other. Purple in the face and spraying crimson with each explosive exhalation, the Broke-Oar forced Snorri down, inch by inch. Muscle heaped, veins bulged fit to burst, both men groaned and laboured for breath. It seemed bones must give – that in a sudden snap the immense forces would shatter limbs – but all that happened was that by degrees, pumping blood past the bindings on shoulder and side, Snorri gave, until with a swift release he was on his knees, the Broke-Oar still pressing down upon him.

Tuttugu took one dripping hand from his belly and bent with agonizing slowness to retrieve his axe. The Broke-Oar, without even seeming to have looked, kicked behind him and broke the Undoreth's knee, sending Tuttugu sprawling with a scream of pain. Snorri tried to surge up and got a leg beneath him but with a roar the Broke-Oar drove him back down.

Ein and the Hardanger man were still rolling on the floor, both cut now. I looked at my sword, already scarlet from tip to pommel. *That's Snorri there*. I had to say it to myself. Companion through innumerable miles, through weeks of hardship, dangers… The Broke-Oar pressed him lower, both men howling animal threats. A sudden twist and Sven Broke-Oar had Snorri's throat in his huge right paw, their other hands still locked, Snorri's unburdened hand trying to tear the fingers from his neck.

The Broke-Oar was exposed. Head bowed. 'Christ, Jalan, just do it!' I had to shout the words at myself. And, reluctant at first, picking up speed, I ran toward them, sword overhead. I'd not wanted to hit the man in the tower, not even with an arrow from a hundred yards off. Sven Broke-Oar I wanted to die, right then, right there, and if it had to be me to do it…

I brought both arms down, scything my blade through the air, and somehow in that instant the Broke-Oar tore his off-hand from Snorri's grasp and interposed his buckler. The shock of it rang through my sword as if I'd hit stone, shaking it from my grip. One swift lunge, pushing Snorri over backward with the hand still locked to his throat, and the giant punched me just below the heart, a combined impact of broad knuckles and the edge of his buckler. The breath left me in a wordless whoosh, ribs snapped, and I fell as if hamstrung.

From the floor I saw the Broke-Oar flick off the buckler and lock his second hand around Snorri's throat. I managed to draw the breath that Snorri couldn't. The air wheezing into me like acid poured into my lungs, ribs grating around their fractures.

Sven Broke-Oar started to shake Snorri, slowly at first, then more fiercely as the younger man's face darkened with the strangulation. 'You should have stayed gone, Snagason. The North has nothing else like me. It takes more than a boy to bring me down.'

I could see the life leaving Snorri, arms falling away limp, and still all I could manage was the next breath. Ein had fallen away from his enemy, both of them lying spent. Tuttugu lay in a spreading pool of his own blood, watching but beyond helping.

'Time to die, Snorri.' And the muscles bunched in the Broke-Oar's forearms, tightening a grip that could snap an oar.

Somewhere, unseen, the sun set.

Snorri lifted his arms. His hands closed on Sven Broke-Oar's wrists and where they touched the Hardanger man's flesh it turned black. A snarl twisted the Broke-Oar's lips as Snorri raised his head and pulled the fingers from his neck. A sudden, vicious downwards yank and both the Broke-Oar's forearms snapped, the bone jutting from crimson gore. A backhanded blow and he fell, sprawling beside Tuttugu.

'You?' Snorri's voice blending with Aslaug's as he stood. 'It's me the North should walk in fear of.' He held the discarded buckler now, nothing but darkness in his eyes.

'Better.' From his place on the ground Sven Broke-Oar managed a laugh. 'Better. You might even stand a chance. Make a ruin of them, Snorri, send them howling back to Hel!'

Snorri knelt beside Sven Broke-Oar, leaning in.

'They put a fear in me, Snorri, gods damn them. Gods damn them all.'

'Where's Freja?' Snorri took Broke-Oar around the neck, pounding his head against the floor. My son? Where is he?' Each question roared into the man's face.

'You know!' Broke-Oar spat out a bloody answer.

'You'll tell me!' Snorri set his thumbs against the Broke-Oar's eyes.

I fainted at that point, just as Snorri started to press and Broke-Oar let out a scream that was half laughter.

Those dark and insensible moments were the only period of comfort I had in that black fort. Washed away too soon by the passage of what could only have been seconds.

'Time to die, Broke-Oar.' Snorri bent low over the fallen giant, hands crimson.

A wet red splutter, then, 'Burn the dead—'

Sven Broke-Oar had time for no more. Snorri crushed his skull with a sharp blow of the heavy buckler.

'Snorri.' I couldn't manage above a whisper, but he looked up, the darkness fading from his eyes, leaving them clear and ice-blue.

'Jal!' Despite his wounds he was at my side in a moment, seizing the hood of my winter coat, deaf to my protests. For one moment I thought he was going to help me, but instead he dragged me across to lie beside Ein.

The Red Viking next to Ein looked dead enough but Snorri took the knife from the man's hand and cut his throat with it just to be sure. 'Alive?' He turned to Ein and slapped him. Ein groaned and opened his eyes. 'Good. What can you do for him, Jal?'

'Me?' I lifted an arm. I don't know why – perhaps to ward off the suggestion – and found that I'd been stabbed, high in the bicep. 'Hell!' Rolling over was an agony but it let me confirm another flash of memory from the red haze of my battle – I'd been cut on the thigh too. 'I'm worse than Ein is.' With the injuries I'd taken without knowing or remembering them it was almost true. But Ein had a stab wound in his chest. One that bubbled and sucked with each breath out and in. The killing kind.

'He's worse, Jal. And you can't heal yourself. We know that.'

'I can't heal anyone without half-dying myself. It'd kill me.' Though dying would at least stop each breath being a torture. My side had been filled with broken glass, I was sure of it.

'The magic is stronger here, Jal, you must feel it trying to break out? I can almost see it glowing in you.' An edge of pleading in his voice. Not for himself, never that, but for the last of his countrymen.

'Jesus! You people will be the death of me.' And I

460

slapped my palm to Ein's stab wound – harder than necessary.

In an instant my hand flared, too bright to look at, and every ache I had became an agony, my ribs something beyond comprehension. I snatched my hand back almost immediately, panting and cursing, blood and drool dripping from my mouth.

'Good. Now Tuttugu!' And I felt myself dragged. I watched through one eye as Ein struggled to sit up, poking at the unbroken but blood-stained skin where the knife had slid beneath his ribs.

Snorri set me beside Tuttugu and we met each other's gaze, both of us too weak for talking. The Viking, who had been pale to start with, now lay as white as frost. Snorri pulled Tuttugu around, moving him without effort despite his girth. He tugged Tuttugu's hand clear of the stomach wound and drew in an involuntary breath.

'It's bad. You've got to heal this, Jal. The rest can wait, but this will sour. The guts are cut inside.'

'I can't do it.' I'd more easily stab a knife through my hand or put a hot coal in my mouth. 'You don't understand…'

'He'll die! I know Arne was too far gone, but this, this is a slow death – you can stop it.' Snorri kept talking. It washed over me. Tuttugu said nothing, only watched me as I watched him, both of us lying on the cold stone floor, too weak to move. I remembered him on the mountainside overlooking Trond, telling me he would

461

run from every battle if only his legs were longer. A kindred soul, almost as deep in his fears as me, but he'd gone to war in the Black Fort even so.

'Shut up,' I told Snorri. And he did.

Ein came to join him, moving with an old man's care.

'I can't do it. I really can't.' I pointed my gaze toward my free hand. The other still clutched my sword for some reason: it was probably glued on by all the gore. 'I can't do it. But no man should go to Valhalla with brothel-rash.' Again, pointing with my gaze.

Finally Ein took the hint. I screwed both eyes shut, gritted my teeth, clenched what could be clenched, and he grabbed my forearm, setting my hand against the rip in Tuttugu's belly.

It made healing Ein seem like a simple thing.

28

I woke before the heat of a fire. My side ached like a bastard but the heat felt wonderful and if I didn't move a single muscle it was almost comfortable.

Gradually other hurts made themselves known. A throbbing pain in my thigh, a stabbing pain in my arm, a generalized wretchedness from all the muscles I could name and many I couldn't.

I opened an eye. 'Where's Snorri?'

They'd laid me out on one of the long tables at the end closest to the hearth. Ein and Tuttugu sat before the fire, Tuttugu binding a splint about his knee, Ein sharpening his axe. Both had cleaned and stitched their wounds, or had the other do it.

'Burning the dead.' Tuttugu pointed toward the far door. 'He's building a pyre on the wall.'

I tried to sit up, and lay back cursing. 'There's not enough wood, surely? Why not leave them to freeze?'

'He found the wood store, and he's been knocking doors off hinges, ripping down shutters.'

'But why?' I asked, not sure I wanted an answer.

'Because of what will be coming from the Bitter Ice,' Ein said. 'He doesn't want the bodies raised against us.' He didn't say that his last three brothers lay among them, but something in his face told it anyway.

'If they're frozen they won't be able to...' I tried to sit again. Sitting is an important precursor to running away.

'Might not freeze in time,' Tuttugu said.

'And Snorri doesn't want anything left to be defiled after...' Ein set his whetstone down and admired his edge in the firelight.

Between them the two men I'd saved had managed to make my blood run cold. That 'in time' and that 'after' were not encouraging. A corpse would freeze solid overnight.

'We're expecting ... trouble ... before morning?' I tried to make it not sound like whining, and failed.

'No "we" about it. It's what Snorri says. He says they're coming.' Tuttugu tightened the bindings about his knee and whimpered in pain.

'How does he know?' I made a third attempt to sit, galvanized by fear, and succeeded, ribs grating.

'Snorri says the dark told him.' Ein set his axe down and looked my way. 'And if he doesn't end this in the dark then you'll have to do it in the light.'

'This—' I eased down from the table and the pain cut me off. 'This is madness. He finds his wife and child, and then we go!' I left off the 'finds them dead or alive' part. 'Broke-Oar is dead – it's done.'

Without waiting to be contradicted, I hobbled off toward the far door. The blood smears, drying to black and deepest scarlet now, showed the way. Where Snorri found the energy to drag approaching thirty corpses out along that corridor and onto the fort wall I didn't know, but I did know that he would have neither the fuel, stamina, nor time to add the frozen dead of Olaaf Rikeson's army to his pyre.

The stairs up to the outer door were slippery with blood, already freezing where it had dripped from one step to the next. Opening the door, I found the night lit with a vast blaze, the wind trailing orange flame out over the battlements. Even with all that heat not twenty yards off the cold bit me immediately, the alien cold of a landscape that held in it nothing for men or for any other living thing.

Snorri stood silhouetted against the inferno. I could see corpses and timbers, some black against the hot glow, others melting into it. Even the wind's strength couldn't keep the scent of roasting flesh from my nostrils. The walkway ran with hot fats, burning even as they spilled down the inner wall.

'It's done then?' I had to raise my voice above the crackle of the fire and the wind's discontent.

'They're coming, Jal. The dead men from the Bitter Ice, the necromancers who herd them, Edris and the

465

rest of the Broke-Oar's following.' He paused. 'The unborn.'

'What the hell are you doing out here then?' I shouted. 'Search for your wife and let's be gone.' I ignored the fact that I could barely walk the length of the corridor and that if his child were here we couldn't march across the Uplands with him. Such truths were too uncomfortable. Besides, the woman and boy were probably dead, and I would rather die trying to cross the ice than facing necromancers and their horrors.

Snorri turned away from the fire, eyes red with smoke. 'Let's go in. I've spoken the words. The flames will carry them to Valhalla.'

'Well, not Broke-Oar and his bastards,' I said.

'Even them.' Snorri glanced back at the blaze, a half-smile twisting his split lip. 'They died in battle, Jal. That's all it takes. When we arm against the jotün and the jotnär at Ragnarok all men with fire in their blood will stand together.'

We walked in side by side, Snorri matching my snail's pace as I hobbled down the stairs, miss-stepping once and uttering every foul word I knew until I reached the bottom. 'We can't stay here, Snorri.'

'It's a fortress. Where better to stay when your enemies march?'

He had me there.

'How long was I out? How much time is left?'

'It's two hours until dawn. They'll be here before that.'

466

'What will we do?' Sven Broke-Oar had been bad enough. I had no desire to wait to see whatever it was that had terrified a monster like him.

'Barricade ourselves in the gatehouse. Wait.'

As much as I liked the idea of defence it didn't sound like Snorri. His very name meant attack. To hold back sounded like an admission of defeat. But the man was all done in. I could see that. I could no more heal his wounds than I could my own. Just walking beside him set the air crackling with uncomfortable energies. Even with a yard between us my skin crawled as if somewhere in the marrow of my bones that crack, the one the Silent Sister's magic had fractured into the world – between worlds – as if that crack were seeking to break out. It wanted to run through me and join its dark twin as it broke from Snorri, to join together and race toward the horizon, splitting and splitting again until the world lay shattered.

The gatehouse held several chambers, the foremost of which offered views down over the gate should a man be motivated to crack open the shutters and lean out. In addition three covered murder-holes would allow the pouring of whatever unpleasant liquid one might wish to flush upon the heads of any standing at the great doors. This close to the Bitter Ice just pouring water onto unwelcome guests would be fatal for most. The room held a fireplace with wood stacked to either side and two copper buckets filled with coal. Tuttugu and Ein set to lighting a fire, both of them moving awkwardly as their injuries had stiffened. Tuttugu had fashioned a crutch from a spear, pieces of furniture, and a wadded cloak, but it was clear he could cover no great distance on it. Our serious fighting force consisted of Snorri and Ein, both much diminished by their injuries. Tuttugu and me together could have been defeated by a single determined twelve-year-old armed with a stick.

The doors and shutters were all of heavy construction, iron bolts oiled and locked in place.

'They'll come over the walls,' I said.

'The dead won't.' Snorri swung his arms to loosen them. He had Sven Broke-Oar's axe now, or rather I suspected he had reclaimed his father's axe from the man.

'Then the Hardanger men will.' Edris would be with them. I couldn't say why he frightened me more than the Vikings, but he did.

'I doubt they have grapples, probably not even rope. But maybe.' Snorri shrugged. 'We can't patrol the walls of this fort with two men. They would just try in three places at once. They'll get in or they won't. Either way they will be cold. We'll keep watch from the gate-house roof and decide what to do when it needs to be done.'

'But it's dark.'

468

'If they come in the night, Jal, they'll carry lights, now won't they? The ones that can climb need to see. I don't know what the dead see, or if they need it to be light, but the dead I saw in Eight Quays were like the dead on the mountain by Chamy-Nix. They won't be scaling walls.'

'And the unborn?'

'Let those come.' He made a sudden lunging strike at the air with his axe.

It fell to Tuttugu and me to keep watch, one taking a turn after the other. It made no sense for either man who could still fight to freeze his arse off on the roof. Tuttugu took the first hour. I could only guess what it cost him to climb the stairs with his shattered knee. I found him huddled in his furs, blue with cold and semi-conscious when I hobbled up the long spiral of steps to relieve him an hour later. Ein had to come up to help his friend down again.

I stood my turn, there in the dark with the wind howling all about and nothing to see but the glow of the bone-fire by the east tower. I'd been warm for only a few hours but already the bitter chill outside came as a shock. I found it hard to imagine we had endured it day after day.

In the dark, making a slow tour of the guard wall, my mind played tricks, voices on the wind, colours in the night, faces from my past come to visit. I imagined the Silent Sister, here on the ice, her tatters flying in the wind as she made her circuit of the Black Fort, painting out her curse across its walls as she went. She should be here, that old woman. She'd brought us to this, somehow, in some way I couldn't quite fathom. It was her fault. I'd called her evil, the blind-eye woman, a witch burning people in their homes. And yet it seemed perhaps that on each occasion it had been an unborn or some other minion of the Dead King that had been her true target. The people had just been in the way. Or bait, perhaps.

As a prince I'd been taught that good opposes evil. I'd been shown the good, shining in chivalric honour, and the evil hunched about its wrongness, crowned with horns. And always I wondered where I fitted into this grand scheme, little Jalan built of petty wants and empty lusts, nothing so grand as evil, nothing closer to good than imitation. And now it seemed that the blind-eye woman of my childhood terrors was in fact a great-aunt of mine. Indeed if Great-uncle Garyus were the true king then surely the Silent Sister, older than my grandmother, was his heir?

I knuckled my eyes through the stiff leather of my faceguard, trying to knead the tiredness from them, perhaps the confusion too. I blinked to clear my blurred vision. Embers from the bone-fire danced on the wind, out against the blackness of the ice plain. Despite the wind, they hung there. Another blink, and another, wouldn't clear them.

'Ah hell.' Through numb lips.

Lanterns.

They were coming.

29

Snorri watched the advance through a crack he'd opened in the shutters. I felt the wind's knife even at my place by the fire.

'They're coming to the front gate.'

'How many?' I asked.

'Two dozen, a few more perhaps.'

I had been expecting an army but it made sense that there were so few. Supporting any significant numbers out here on the edge of survival would be a huge undertaking, and pointless if there were dead men to do the bulk of the labour. But that made me wonder once again about the captives. They had sold the men south. I'd not given it much thought before but surely if they wanted captives for digging in the ice then... It made no sense at all – they would have killed any captives they kept and let them serve the same purpose in death, tireless and requiring no sustenance.

'There are no captives!' I spoke it aloud – not a whisper, not a shout, just a statement.

'About fifty dead ranked behind those ... at least that's all I can see in their lights, but it's a tight-packed group.' Snorri continued his report. 'There may be necromancers and Island men among them – I can't tell.'

'What—' I couldn't find the right words. 'Why—' If there were no captives ... where were Freja and little Egil?

'Men coming to the doors.' Snorri crossed over to the central murder-hole. 'Oil.'

Ein came across with the iron bucket of oil they'd had heating on the fire. Carrying it with padded tongs. Apparently boiling water would freeze and spread as it fell, landing as a dust of ice crystals.

Three muffled thuds from below as someone hammered on the great door. Snorri pulled the cover of the murder-hole clear and Ein poured. When the bucket was empty Snorri replaced the cover, muting the screams.

'What now?' Tuttugu, wide-eyed, recovered enough to be terrified.

'Jal, back to the roof to watch,' Snorri said.

'The steps will kill me if nothing else does.' I shook my head and made what speed I could up the coiled stair.

From the roof I could see what Snorri had described, and nothing more. Perhaps what he saw had been the sum of them. Heart pounding, and shaking with both the cold and with the thought of what the dark might hide, I made a circuit of the guard wall. Nothing. No other light. Nothing to see at all. That worried me, both in general and for some other reason I couldn't quite put my finger on.

For long minutes only the wind howled, the Vikings held their ranks in the lee of the walls, the dead behind them, and nothing moved. A dread grew in me, but it hardly required any extra malign influence for that. There were dead things out there, wanting us to share their state: only a madman wouldn't be quaking.

With only the lights to watch I watched the lights. I wondered how I could ever have fooled myself they were just embers from the bone-fire blown out across the ice-field. The mind spends half its time in self-deception it seems. Or maybe I'm deceiving myself… I watched the lights a moment longer, then slapped my brow. It's not often that people actually do slap their brow when a sudden realization illuminates their skull from the inside, especially without an audience. But I did it. And then I ran down the icy stairs, two and three at a time, swearing at the pain with each impact.

'What? What is it? What did you see?' All three of them together as I hunched over my hurt, clutching my ribs, fighting to draw breath.

'Give him some room.' Snorri, stepping back.

'I—' The cut on my leg had broken past the stitches Ein had set there while I slept, blood running down my thigh.

'What did you see?' Tuttugu, white-faced.

'Nothing.' I gasped it out and drew a breath.

'What?' Three blank looks.

'Nothing,' I said. 'Just the Hardanger men's lanterns.' Another moment of incomprehension.

'There's no fire on the wall.' I pointed in the rough direction of Snorri's great pyre.

'It can't have gone out,' Ein said. 'It'll still be hot this time tomorrow.'

'Yes.' I nodded. When I came down to report the visitors from the Bitter Ice the bone-fire had been ten yards of orange embers with flames licking over them when the wind gusted.

'I'll go check.' Ein took up a lantern from the mantel-piece and went to the heavy door that connected back to the corridor and halls beyond. A pounding from down below stopped him in his tracks. It sounded more like a battering ram than the crash of shield on wood that we'd heard before.

'Tuttugu! Oil!' And Snorri hauled the cover from the murder-hole. He stared down, brow furrowing. 'There's nothing th—'

BOOM!

The sound of the impact drowned him out.

'Hel! It's coming from the inside!' Snorri whipped round toward Ein who stood at the doorway with his back toward it.

'I'll find out—' Ein bit his sentence short and staggered forward, accompanied by a splintering thud. Something sharp and thick and gore-coated now jutted from beneath his sternum. A moment later the door came off its hinges and the horror beyond shook the door and Ein's corpse from the appendage it had impaled them both with.

'Jesus!' A shriek. Something hot ran down my leg. I'd like to say it was blood. The thing blocked the corridor, a rolling mass of melted and blackened flesh, bones embedded, here a cloven helmet, there a skull, still smouldering – the stinking remnants of the bone-fire, quenched and animated into something more like a corrupt and giant slug than any man.

Snorri leapt past me, roaring and hacking. Chunks of steaming flesh flew across the room. The stench of the thing put me on my knees vomiting. Most of my puke went down the murder-hole but there was nobody to receive the torrent. Snorri's roaring continued for quite a while, punctuated by the booms from below.

At about the time I finally raised my head Snorri paused in his assault. The nightmare had sagged in the doorway, spilling a yard or so into the room, overflowing part of the door and covering Ein's legs to the hip. Apart from where Snorri sunk his axe into it once more, for good measure, it didn't seem to have any motion left in it.

'It's done.' Tuttugu from beside the fire, nervous, almost hopping on his one good leg.

Tuttugu had barely shut his mouth when Ein's head snapped up from the floor. The eyes he fixed me with were eyes I last saw on a mountain in Rhone and held the same undead hunger. Lips twitched but whatever the thing that was Ein had been about to say was cut off, with his head, by way of Snorri's descending axe.

'Sorry, brother.' He snatched the severed head up by the hair and threw it into the blazing hearth.

'This isn't all of it,' I said. There had been much more in the bone-fire than the mass before us.

By way of confirmation the doors below splintered open: in truth the restraints on the locking bar must have broken rather than the doors. Two men could have opened the gates from inside without much problem, but the insensate monster the necromancers had raised lacked the required dexterity or intelligence. Instead it had battered the locking bar free and now, spent like its smaller counterpart up above, it collapsed through the opening it had made.

'What now?' I needed somewhere to run.

'We run,' said Snorri.

'Oh thank God!' Although I couldn't do more than hobble with my shattered ribs. I paused a moment and looked at him. It seemed his final admission of defeat, Snorri running from the fight. 'Where to?'

Already he'd pulled open the second door, the one leading to the chambers within the walls' thickness on the left of the gatehouse, opposite those where we'd battled the Broke-Oar.

'There's a strong-room in the keep. Iron doors. Many locks. We need to hold out for morning.' He hurried through into the freezing corridor beyond, breath steaming around him.

'Why?' I hollered after him, trying to keep up. I was all for running and hiding, but I hoped there was a better reason than delaying the inevitable. Behind me Tuttugu's crutch clacked against the flagstones as he swung along with what speed he could muster.

'Why?' With almost no breath as I caught up a hundred yards on.

Snorri, waiting at the head of a flight of stairs, looked past me to the light of Tuttugu's swinging lantern. 'Hurry!'

'Why?' I almost reached to catch hold of him.

'Because we can't win. Not in the dark. Maybe in the morning such magics, such creatures … maybe they won't be so strong. Maybe not. Either way, we'll die in the daylight.' He paused. 'I don't care about Aslaug's gifts. I don't like what she's tried to turn me into.' A grin. 'Let's go to Valhalla with the sun on our faces.'

Snorri paused for me to answer. All I had to say was

I didn't think the sun would find us in a strong-room buried in the middle of the keep, but I kept those words behind my teeth. He grinned again, tentative this time, turned and set off down the stairs. I followed, cursing that I had yet more icy steps to contend with, though fat Tuttugu and his broken knee would have a still harder time of it behind me.

Ice had sealed the door to the courtyard. Snorri broke it open and waited for us, the wind howling outside.

'How will we even get in?' I panted the question.

'I took keys off Sven Broke-Oar.' Snorri patted his jacket. 'I've been over there already. Opened it all up… I had to search…' He hooded his lantern so no glimmer of it showed. Tuttugu did the same when he arrived puffing at the bottom of the stairs.

We stepped out into the courtyard. I could see nothing but a scattering of lights around the great doors as the Red Vikings came through. No doubt they'd be checking on their companions and stores first. Without food and fuel they faced a bleak future. Fort or no fort the Bitter Ice would kill them all.

'Come.' Snorri led off.

'Wait!' I literally couldn't see him. We could be separated and lose each other in the dark. The dawn was much less than an hour away but the sky held no hint of it.

Tuttugu hobbled between us and set a hand on Snorri's shoulder. 'Take a hold, Jal.'

I held onto Tuttugu, and in a blind convoy we set out, crunching over the ice and snow, across the expanse of courtyard.

The Red Vikings might be busying themselves securing their old holdings but I worried more about those who had brought them here. The night felt haunted – the wind speaking with a new voice, more chill and more deadly than before, though I hadn't thought it possible. We pressed on, and with each step I expected some hand to be laid upon *my* shoulder, pulling me back.

Sometimes our worst fears aren't realized – though in my experience it's only to make room for the fears our imagination was insufficient to house. In any event we reached the keep and Snorri set a great iron key into the lock of the sub-door that sat within a greater portal large enough to admit wagons. With effort he turned the key – I thought to find the lock too frozen but again my fears were unfounded, the lock had after all been built in the cold by people who understood the winter.

Snorri led the way inside. He closed the door, locked it, unhooded his lantern. We stood for a moment, the three of us, looking at each other's pale, blood-spattered faces, our breath pluming before us. 'Come.' Snorri pressed on, threading through various empty chambers, more doors, more stairs – less icy here deep within the building. We hurried through deserted halls, shadows swinging all around us with the sway of our two lanterns. Our bubble of tentative illumination sailed through a consuming darkness. Our footsteps echoed in those cold and empty places and it seemed we made an awful clatter. I pushed the phrase 'loud enough to wake the dead' to the back of my mind. Side passages yawned at us as we passed, dark with threat. Onward, through a tall archway into a long hall, an iron door standing ajar at the end of it.

'There.' Snorri gestured with his axe. 'That's our stronghold.'

Salvation! In the worst of times even temporary salvation feels like a blessing. I glanced back at the archway, convinced some grave horror would step from the shadows at any moment and tear after us. 'Hurry!'

Snorri jogged across and, with a squeal of hinges, pulled the door wide for us to pass through. Beyond it lay a narrow corridor set with a series of thick iron doors. It was as well that Snorri had unlocked them on his previous visit or we'd be fumbling with keys while the shadows reached for our backs. When he pulled the first one closed behind us the sound of him locking it was a special kind of music to my ears. My whole body slumped as that awful tension eased.

I wondered where Freja and Egil might be and hoped it was somewhere secure. I didn't mention it though in case Snorri decided to go out searching for them again. If they'd lasted this long they'd last a little longer, I told myself. In my mind's eye I pictured them, clothing their names in Snorri's descriptions, Freja capable, determined ... she wouldn't give up hope, not in him, not while her son lived. I saw the boy too, scrawny, freckled, inquisitive. I saw him smile – the easy grin his father had – and scamper off about some mischief among the huts of Eight Quays. I couldn't picture them here, couldn't imagine what this place might have made of them.

I leaned back against the wall for a moment, closing my eyes and trying to convince myself that the grave-scent hanging in the air was imagination. Perhaps it was, or perhaps the pursuit had been as close as I feared, but either way the locking of that door was a good thing. A very good thing indeed. Snorri shot home heavy bolts, top and bottom. Better still.

'Keep moving.' He waved me on, careful not to touch me: the air crackled and spat if we got too close and my skin glowed so bright I could almost light the way. Four doors stood between the hall and the strong-room. Snorri locked all four behind us, bolting them too in case the enemy held additional copies of the keys.

With the last door sealed behind us we collapsed upon the sacks heaped around the walls. The lanterns revealed a small cubic room without windows or any exit but the one we entered by.

'What's in the sacks?' Tuttugu asked, patting one that protruded from beneath him.

'Black corn, wheat flour, some salt.' Snorri gestured at two barrels in the opposite corner. 'Crushed ice, and in the other one, whiskey.'

482

'We could survive a month on this,' I said, trying to imagine it.

'Daylight. That's all we're waiting for. In the morning we attack.' Snorri looked grim.

As much as I wanted to argue it made sense. No relief would come, no reinforcements were inbound. Either they would break in eventually, or we would starve in our own filth. Even so, I knew when it came to leaving, to actually putting ourselves in the hands of the unborn, they would have to drag me. I'd rather slit my wrists and be done with it.

'What's out there, Snorri?' I lay back and watched the shadows dance on the ceiling. 'Did Aslaug tell you that? Did she say what she'd seen in the darkness?'

'Unborn. Maybe a dozen of them. And the worst of them, the Unborn Captain. The Dead King's hand in the North. All digging out troops for whatever war he's planning. The troops are just a bonus. What they're really after is Rikeson's key. Not that Rikeson fashioned it. Aslaug says he tricked Loki out of it. Or Loki let it seem that way but really it was Loki who tricked Olaaf Rikeson into taking it.'

Tuttugu stretched out his leg, sniffing and pulling his furs about him. He wrinkled his nose, disapproving of the air.

'Baraqel doesn't tell me anything useful. I guess all the best secrets are told at night.' I didn't pay too close a heed to Aslaug's talk of Loki. It seemed the voices that the light and the dark used to speak to us were ones we'd given them, taken from our expectations. Only natural then that explanations should come to Snorri wrapped in heathen tales, whilst I got the true version, spoken by an angel such as one might see in the stained glass at the cathedral in Vermillion.

Vermillion! God how I wanted to be back there. I remembered that day, the day I left the city – that crazy chaotic whirl of a day – and before I had even broken my fast on that morning the Red Queen had been bending our ears, all of us grandchildren, and at the last when I was desperate to be off about my own plans, hadn't Grandmother been talking of tasks, of quests, of hunting for … a key?

'Smells like something crawled in here and died.' Tuttugu interrupted my thoughts. He sniffed again, casting a suspicious glance my way.

I shushed him with a waved hand. The pieces were coming together in my mind. The Red Queen's story about a door into death, an actual door. Who would ever want to open such a door?

'The Dead King—'

'Jal—' Tuttugu tried to cut across me.

'I'm *thinking*!' But death's door couldn't ever be opened – the lock had no… 'Loki's key can open anything!'

'Jal!' Snorri surging to his feet. 'Get down!'

An empty sack fell across my shoulders as I threw

myself forward, forgetting how much it would hurt. I heard grain shifting and spilling. The grave stink intensified into something almost physical.

'No!' Tuttugu, screamed and threw himself at whatever had risen behind me, axe raised. I hit the ground and my world lit with the agony of the impact against my broken ribs. A meaty thud and through slitted eyes I caught a glimpse of Tuttugu flying back across the room. He hit the wall with the kind of crunch that meant he wouldn't be getting up again.

I rolled over and the unborn towered above me, uncoiling long and scabrous limbs, shedding the full sacks and empty sacking that it had hidden beneath. A freshly-skinned face peered down at me, the top of that wet and hairless scalp nearly scraping the ceiling. The eyes held the same feral hunger as those that had haunted me for all this long and wild flight from Red March, but they weren't the same eyes that had set me running on the night of the opera what seemed a lifetime ago. These terrified, but held little of that awful knowing.

I lurched aside and tried to crawl for the door as a hand made of dripping flesh and too many bones reached down for me.

'Jal!' Snorri leapt in. Snorri would always leap in. He hacked at the arm, sweeping it aside. The unborn clawed at him with its other hand, sickle talons shredding through many layers to the skin and muscle beneath.

I almost made it to the door. What I would have done there if I had reached it I can't say. Scrabbled at the cold iron in desperation, most likely. The unborn saved me from those broken fingernails by spearing a long and unclean finger through my side and dragging me back. I fought every inch of the way, kicking and screaming. Mostly screaming.

Snorri charged again, soaked with his own blood, and the unborn caught him about the waist, raising him off the ground, talons sinking deep.

'Die, you bastard!' A howl as his eyes darkened. And with the last of his strength Snorri ver Snagason swung his father's axe, hauling the heavy weapon through the air in a sideways swing, turning in the unborn's grip, driving its talons deeper still but adding momentum to his blow. The blade cut through lantern light, trailing streaks of darkness. It sheared into the unborn's head, splitting that unholy skull, and with a roar Snorri yanked the axe clear, splattering grey filth as he cracked the monster wide.

The unborn's convulsions threw us both clear, scattering grain, salt, pieces of torn sack while it thrashed and diminished. I lay with blood pouring in a river from the dark hole the creature had put through me. Snorri found his feet again, though barely, swaying as he dragged his axe back toward the foe.

By the time the Norseman made it across the room

all that remained amid a welter of old bones and shed skin, curled and blackened, was a small red thing. It looked almost like a baby. And, falling to his knees before it, Snorri bent double and wept as though his heart had broken.

30

'We're fucked up.' I raised my hand to wipe the blood from my mouth. The arm felt like someone else's, almost too heavy to move. Too much blood to wipe. I must have bitten my tongue.

'We are.' Snorri lay back, the sacks around him stained crimson. His leg looked uncomfortable, folded awkwardly beneath him, but if it bothered him he lacked the strength to move it. It bothered me, seeing him like that, without fight in him. Snorri never gave up. He never would, not with his wife and child so close. I looked at him again, sprawled, bleeding, defeated. And then I knew.

'Tell me.' I lay on sacks every bit as bloody as those beneath him. We would both bleed to death soon enough. I wanted to know if this had ever been a rescue mission – if his wife and child could ever have been saved. 'Tell it all.'

Snorri spat blood and opened his hand to let his axe drop. 'The Broke-Oar told me, back in the hall, he would have told me back when he had me captive. He told me not to ask, that day when they caught me – and he scared me out of it… I hadn't the courage to ask. He said I shouldn't ask or he would tell. And I didn't, and he kept his silence.' Snorri drew a great slow breath, his cheekbone had been shattered, pieces of bone showed through the skin. 'But in the hall with Aslaug filling me and his eyes put out, I asked him again … and this time he answered.' Snorri drew a shuddering breath and my face grew numb, my cheekbones tingling, eyes hot and full. 'Egil and the other children they gave to the necromancers. The lives of children can be fed to unborn and to the lichkin – horrors just as bad.' Another breath, hitched in. 'The women were killed and their corpses raised then used to mine the ice. Only Freja and a handful of others were spared.'

'Why?' Maybe I didn't want to know after all. My life was pooling crimson on the floor around me. Bright memories called to me, lazy days, sweet moments. Better to spend what time remained with them instead. But Snorri needed to tell me, and I needed to let him.

Dying wasn't as bad as I had imagined. I'd spent so long afraid, endured so many deaths in my imagination, but here I lay, close to the end, almost at peace. It hurt, yes, but I had a friend close by and a certain calmness enfolded me. 'Why?' I asked it again.

'I didn't tell you.' Snorri gasped at some sudden pain. 'I couldn't. It wasn't a lie. I just couldn't say the words … too big … if you—'

'I understand.' And I did. Some truths you can't speak. Some truths come barbed, each word would tear you inside out if you forced them from your lips.

'She— Freja, my wife.' A breath hitched in. 'Freja was pregnant. She carried our child. That's why they kept her. To make unborn. She died when they cut the baby from her belly.' A breath burst from him in a crimson spray, hurt escaping in the short wet gasps we men make to keep from crying like children.

'Pregnant?' All this time and he hadn't spoken of it. Our long journey a hopeless race against that baby's fate. A tear rolled down my cheek, hot and slow, cooling as it met the frigid air.

'I just killed my son.' Snorri closed his eyes.

I rolled my head and saw once more the foetus curled amid the ruin of the body the unborn had built – the core of it, the potential, misused and ill-spent by some horror that had never lived.

'Your son...' I didn't ask how he could know. Perhaps that bond between them had let the unborn know his mind, had led it to wait for us in this room. I didn't ask anything – I hadn't the words. Instead I spoke the smallest one – the one I should have used more in my short and foolish life.

'Sorry.'

We lay a long moment without speaking. Life leaked away from me, drop by drop. I felt I should miss it more.

A squealing noise broke the silence.

'What in hell?' I lifted my head a fraction. It sounded like—

'Hinges!' Snorri raised up, slowly, supporting himself on his elbows.

'But you locked that door.' The squeal of iron on iron set my teeth on edge. 'Bolted it too.'

'Yes.'

Another squealing sound. Louder this time, closer.

'How is that possible?' Some energy returning to my voice now. A whining edge too, I'll admit. 'Why aren't they having to break them down?'

'They have the key.' Snorri reached for his axe, groaning.

'But you bolted all the doors! I saw you.'

Another shriek, the noise of old iron scraped across stone as the third door surrendered. Only one remained – the door I had my horrified gaze fixed upon.

'The key. Rikeson's key. Loki's key. The key that opens all doors.' Snorri managed to sit, deathly pale, a tremor in his limbs. 'It's the Unborn Captain. They must have found the key under the ice.'

Moments remained to us. I heard a dry scratching beyond the door and rust bloomed across the ancient black iron. It felt suddenly colder in that room, and more sad, as if a weight of sorrow had settled across my shoulders. More than I could bear.

'Jal – it has been an honour,' Snorri held his hand out toward me. 'I'm proud to have known you.' He brushed his palm over the blade of his father's axe, slicing it open. 'Bleed with me, brother.'

'Ah, hell.' The bolts shot back on the last door with loud retorts. 'I always knew you'd try this Viking shit on me.' The door started to judder open, inch by inch, pushing sacks aside. 'Likewise, Hauldr Snagason.' I slit my palm on my sword blade, wincing at the deep sting of it, and held my hand out toward Snorri, cupping the blood.

The door jerked open the last half of its swing and there in the dying light of our lanterns the Unborn Captain waited, hunched within the confines of the corridor, a parody of flesh, drawn out into malformations of every kind, a plague of bones jutting out around a face that spoke only of awful needs.

Somewhere out beyond the walls of the Black Fort the sun pushed its brilliant edge above the ice horizon and broke the long night.

The air between Snorri and me spat and sparked as our hands shaped to grasp the other. My arm filled with light so fierce I couldn't look at it. Snorri's became jet, a hole in the world that ate all illumination and returned nothing.

The unborn launched itself forward.

We clasped hands.

The world fractured.

Night interlaced day.

Pretty much everything exploded.

★   ★   ★

The Silent Sister's magic left us and pursued its prey. Detonations rang out throughout the keep, out into the dawn-dark courtyard, and off beyond the walls. The Unborn Captain had lasted less than a heartbeat. The twin cracks had run through him, dark had crossed light, and small pieces of him had ricocheted about the corridor as the cracks raced on.

The force of the blast set us both on our backs and blew us apart. I lacked the strength to disagree and lay where the explosion had dumped me.

The crack that had raced away from us began in the floor at the spot where we had clasped hands, the spot where our blood had mixed and spilled. The free end of it began to spread, slow this one, fracturing stone with a sound like breaking ice, the bright fissure woven with the dark one.

'Christ!' I blasphemed. May as well die with a final sin on my lips.

The crack veered toward me, blindingly bright, blindingly dark. I blinked at it and behind my eyes an echo of Baraqel stood, wings folded. 'It's in your hands now, Jalan Kendeth.'

I cursed him to be gone and let me die.

'It's in your hands.' Quieter now, the image more faint.

Snorri struggled to get to his feet, using his axe for support. Somehow the big bastard was actually doing it – too dumb to know when to quit. Still, it didn't do for a prince of Red March to be outdone by a northern hauldr. I rolled, cursing, set the point of my sword into the gap between flagstones, and tried to heave myself up. It was too hard. Somewhere in the back of my mind Grandmother loomed, tall, regal, scary as hell in her scarlets. *Get up!* And, roaring with the effort and the pain, I did.

A step back and my shoulders were to the wall, the crack a yard from me, sacks splitting as it fractured the stone beneath, corn kernels leaping into the air and turning inside out with curious popping sounds.

When there's nowhere to run you sometimes have to resort to extreme measures. Baraqel had kept talking about my line. The Red Queen's image dominated my imagination in that moment, commanding, fearless, but over her shoulders I saw Garyus and the Silent Sister, and before her, my father. I've taken his name in vain time enough, called him a coward, a drunk, a hollow priest, but I knew deep down what had broken him and that he had stood his ground when my mother needed him and not surrendered to his demons until she was past saving.

I stepped toward the fracture, that crack between worlds, knelt before it on one knee, reached out.

'This is mine – I made it and the enchantment from which it spread started with my line, an unbroken chain of blood joins me to the one that set the spell.' And I reached out with my hand and with whatever else lay in the core of me and I pinched it shut.

All along its length the fissure flared, darkened, flared again, and shrank back upon itself until only a foot of it remained, bright and dark, leading out from the point where I pinched it between finger and thumb.

The fracture flexed and groaned, miniature breaks spreading up from where I held it, out across the back of my hand, the pain excruciating.

'I can't hold it, Snorri.' I was already dying but my great-aunt's spell seemed ready to make that happen immediately rather than an hour hence.

He had to crawl, heaving himself over the sacks, the thick muscles in his arms trembling with the effort, black blood spilling from his mouth. But he made it. His gaze met mine as he reached to close the other end.

'Will it die with us? Will this be an end to it?'

I nodded, and he closed finger and thumb on the other end.

31

The crackle of logs, burning in a hearth. I relaxed. In my dream it had been the fires of hell waiting to feed on my sin. I lay for long minutes just enjoying the warmth, seeing only the play of light and shadow through closed eyes.

'Run!' I jerked into a sitting position as I remembered the strong-room, the unborn, the doors opening.

'What the hell?' I looked down at the furs that had slid from me, at the smooth skin where I'd been skewered through, no doubt puncturing several of the squidgy, vital organs that men are packed with. I pressed the region, and apart from a little tenderness, nothing. Running my hands over myself, patting and pinching, I found no injury worse than the odd bruise.

I looked around. A hall in the Black Fort, Tuttugu walking toward me with a slight limp.

'You're dead!' I cast about for my sword. 'I saw you hit that wall!'

Tuttugu grinned and grabbed his belly. 'Padding!'

Then, more serious, 'I would have died if I hadn't been healed. You would too.'

'The unborn?' Snorri had said there were a dozen or more. The spit dried from my mouth and spread hands were all I could manage to frame the question.

'Any of them that weren't destroyed have fled. Necromancers, Red Vikings, corpse-men … all gone.' Tuttugu said. 'How are you feeling?' He seemed a touch apprehensive.

'Fine. Good. Better than good.' Fingers pressed to where my thigh had been cut produced no twinge at all. 'How is that possible?'

'You're not feeling … evil … then?' Tuttugu pressed his lips into a line, his face a mask.

'Um, no … not especially.' I looked around for Snorri but saw nothing apart from heaps of furs and some supplies tight-bound into bails. 'How did this happen?' I couldn't heal myself.

'Snorri did it,' Tuttugu sounded grim. 'He said a valkyrie—'

'An angel?'

'He said valkyrie. He said the valkyrie helped him. There was more but he couldn't speak much at the end. He said … but there are no male valkyrie… I think the valkyrie was a god…'

'Baraqel? Did he say Baraqel?'

Tuttugu nodded.

'At the end?' My stomach became a cold knot. I

recalled how much any healing had taken from me. 'Is he—'

'Dead?' Tuttugu limped to the heaped furs. 'No. But he should be.' He pulled a wolfskin aside and there lay Snorri, pale but breathing. He looked to be asleep rather than unconscious. The broken bones in his face had been repositioned and the skin sewn over them. 'I've done what I can. We can only wait now.'

'How long have I been sleeping?' It seemed important, even with our enemies fled.

'All day, Jal. It's nearly sunset.'

'But if Snorri … Baraqel you said? And healing … So he's light-sworn now.' I looked again where my wounds should be. 'Then the one who's dark-sworn is…'

Tuttugu nodded.

'Ah.'

I lay back. It would be a long journey back to Vermillion, and if we didn't beat the arrival of winter then the Black Fort would be our home until spring. I'd make it though, and I'd take whatever still remained of my newfound courage and stand before the Red Queen's throne and demand she get her damned sister to take this spell out of us.

All that of course depended on no one being able to talk me out of it between now and then.

Somewhere the sun was setting. I closed my eyes and waited to see just how persuasive Aslaug would be.

★   ★   ★

Six weeks later and the first deep snows of winter came, falling from leaden skies, driven by a cruel wind.

'Bring me another ale will you, Tuttugu, there's a good chap!'

Tuttugu gave a complacent shrug, pushed his roast chicken to one side and went to fill a tankard at the barrel.

Outside, the streets of Trond lay clogged with snow. I didn't care. I snuggled back deeper into the fur of what must have been a white bear every bit as big as the one Snorri vaulted in the Blood Holes. Very cosy. Nobody came or went without good cause, and the Three Axes tavern saw little trade – which was probably the reason the owner had sold me the whole place, lock, stock, and no small number of barrels, for just two of the diamonds pried from Mother's locket.

It was good to have so many fears lifted from me, so many cares shed, to be safe and warm in the grip of winter. The only worries to trouble me now in the long nights were little ones, or at least far away. The problem of Maeres Allus seemed small compared to the problem of how to get home. In fact the only thing to steal my sleep, at least the only non-invited thing, was the thought that though the Unborn Captain had frightened me to the point at which my heart forgot to beat, and though his gaze was a terrible thing, those weren't the eyes that had watched me through the slit of that porcelain mask back in the opera so very many miles and months ago.

That stare had been worse still and haunted me even now.

Life is good.

Today Astrid has to be about her work in town, but I have the lovely Edda to warm me up instead. Snorri says it will end in tears and has taken to giving me disgusted looks as if I should have learned something by now. My own opinion is that if I keep juggling then all the balls will stay in the air (even Hedwig, a beauty I've my eye on and daughter to Jarl Sorren) and my comeuppance will never come down, however richly deserved. Aslaug agrees. She is, it must be said, far more agreeable than Baraqel ever was. I'm amazed Snorri took against her so.

Yes, I should grow up, and yes, I will, but there's time for that tomorrow. Today is for living.

So here we are, snug in the Three Axes with nothing to do but do nothing. Winter has us locked in, safe from the outside world, trapped in our own little inside world. Ironic when our prize was a key that can open anything, and here we are locked in, kept in Trond until the spring unlocks the ice and sets us free.

For a time back there in that awful fort, with Baraqel nagging at me and my rotten little existence coming rapidly to a sharp point, I did start to wonder if I could have made a better job of the business of living. I started to see my old life of wine, song, and as many women as would have me as something shallow. Tawdry even. On the trek across the ice and in that long dark night within the Black Fort I will confess to wishing for my time over, to promising I would treat everyone better, set aside ugly prejudice. I resolved to seek out Lisa DeVeer, vow fidelity, throw myself on her mercy, to be the man my age demanded, not the child it allowed. And the horror of it all was that I really meant it!

It didn't take Aslaug long to talk me down. All I truly needed was someone to let me know I'd been fine as I was, slap me on the back and tell me that the world was waiting for me out there, and to go and get it!

As for Snorri, he's gloomier than ever now that Baraqel lectures him each dawn. You'd think with his family lost and his vengeance exacted he would move on. Tuttugu has. He goes out ice-fishing with the locals now that the harbour has frozen over. Even has himself a girl in town, so he says. Snorri though, he broods on the past. He'll sit there on the porch when it's cold enough to freeze waves in place, wrapped up, axe across his lap, staring at that key.

Now I like keys by and large, but that thing, that piece of obsidian – that I don't like. You look at it and it makes you think. Too much thinking isn't good for anyone. Especially for a man like Snorri ver Snagason who's apt to act upon his thoughts. He sits there staring at it and I can tell the ideas that are spinning in his head – I didn't need Aslaug to tell me that. He has a key that

501

will open any door. He has a dead family. And somewhere out there is a door that leads into death, a door
that swings both ways, a door that shouldn't ever be
opened, a door that couldn't ever be opened.

Until now.